THE WRANGLER

William R. Vaughn

WILLIAM VAUGHN, REDMOND, WASHINGTON

Published by William Vaughn
16212 NE 113th Ct.
Redmond, Washington 98052 USA
http://TheOwlWrangler.com
http://facebook.com/owlwrangler
http://WilliamVaughn.Blogspot.com
@VaughnWilliam

First Print Edition Published May 2011
Illustrated Print Edition Published September 2011
Updated edition published October 2013

Also available in Kindle™
ISBN: 9781492339397
Library of Congress Control Number: 2011918118

The Owl Wrangler V9.4.docx October, 2013
10 9 8 7 6 5 4

❧The Author❧

William Vaughn is an award-winning author, dad, and granddad who has written over a dozen books and many dozens of magazine articles over the last forty years. He's also an avid nature photographer capturing nature's beauty all over the world. This is the first book in the author's full-length fiction series *The Seldith Chronicles*.

❧ Acknowledgements ❧

I want to thank a host of people who have encouraged the development of this book. These include my wife Marilyn and countless people trapped next to me on long airline trips who showed (or at least feigned) genuine interest in the project. I would also like to thank Nan Schweiger, my initial editor who worked well beyond the call of duty. I also want to thank Pam Binder who fanned the embers of my passion for fiction writing. Her characterization of The Owl Wrangler as "…another Watership Down…" kept me writing and polishing. I would also like to thank early draft readers including Rita Sanders, Peggy Vaughn, and Patt and Ryan Beise. I also received some excellent suggestions from a couple of 10-year-old reviewers, Cameron Allen-Shipman and Will Brooks. I would also like to thank Mary Jo Carpenter as well as Rachele (from choir) for their reviews.

I also treasure the patient efforts put in by my daughter "Fred" (Christina) whose encouragement, professional and insightful edits made this project worth all of the work. I would also like to thank my daughter "George" (Victoria) whose children (my granddaughters Mary and Katie), provided considerable inspiration.

❧ Cover Art and Illustrations ❧

The book's cover is a digital composite of a snowy owl photographed by the world-famous nature photographer David G. Hemmings (used with permission) and a landscape photograph taken by the author in the mountains above Skagway, Alaska.

The illustrations were hand-drawn by Sarah Livingston, artist extraordinaire from the United Kingdom.

http://www.pawprints.me.uk/.

❧ The Series ❧

The Owl Wrangler is the first book in the series *The Seldith Chronicles*. Books two, *Guardian of the Sacred Seven* and three, *Quest for the Truth* are currently available on in print and eBook formats from Amazon, CreateSpace, and Kindle.

❧ Dedication ❧

For my daughters Victoria and Christina of whom I could not be more proud and for Ink and Mink who took turns keeping my lap warm.

Stone Valley and Surrounding Area

Gollsaer Awaits his Fate

One—The Hunter and the Hunted

ollsaer pulled his trembling legs up tighter against his body trying to stave off the cold. Swaddled amongst the cradling roots of an aging red cedar, the tiny forest elf, no taller than a mushroom, had no choice but to quietly endure. He knew that his life depended on remaining hidden and still—and intensely alert.

Downing the last of his flask only briefly steadied his hand as he tightened the thin cloak covering his head. Its gossamer fabric was meant to magically disguise his presence, not keep him from freezing to death. But Gollsaer was not afraid of succumbing to the cold—it was his prey that made his bones shiver.

His mind drifted to a cozy room warmed by a metal stove and the final embraces of his family. He remembered how he had said farewell to each sad face, as he always did when he went out to hunt. A sigh later, his eyes began to droop.

Wake up! I've got to stay awake, he screamed to himself.

But at long last, his wait was over. The creeping dark had finally drained the soft evening shadows into the black pools of night's uncertainty. *It's time,* he told himself. *Let's get this over with.* He knew from experience that this was when the forest owls began hunting for the weak, the witless, or the distracted.

Gollsaer slowly unfolded his body and got to his feet. His weatherworn face, now cast with a weary resolve, was framed by healed-over wounds suffered on the previous hunts that nearly took his life. He knew if it hadn't been for his wife's heal-ing touch he would have perished long ago.

His elongated ears tipped and twisted as they strained to catch every ripple of sound that floated on the air like snow-flakes. A familiar rush of air on feathers told Gollsaer, the Seldith clan's Owl Wrangler, his prey was nearby. Another cold chill challenged his resolve. His fingers tightened into a fist.

High above, a large Snowy Owl circled his sentry post on the edge of a grassy meadow. Extending its feathery feet tipped with razor-sharp talons, the bird landed on a branch as quietly as a dry leaf falling to the forest floor. The owl's large yellow eyes quickly found its next victim.

Ratcheting up his resolve, Gollsaer pushed a short length of rope into his tunic pocket and dropped his pack and sword at the base of the tree. As his camouflaging cloak covered the rucksack, its shimmering colors morphed into the soft colors and rough texture of the forest floor. While the tiny elf hated giving up his only means of defense, he recalled what his pre-decessor had taught him. *'You cannot harm that which bears you aloft lest it thrust your soul against the rocks.'* He hoped that his son Hisbil had learned this lesson. It would be his duty to take over the job if he failed. *But he's too young. He's not ready,* Gollsaer said to himself.

The Owl Wrangler re-scanned the treetops, now starkly sil-houetted against the darkening sky—like a forest scene cut from black paper. He saw nothing. Pushing his leathery hand inside his tunic, his fingers touched the rounded tip of a small stick. *It's there.* He was ready.

Taking a deep breath, Gollsaer strode out into the meadow, no longer caring if he was seen or heard. "Come and get me," he taunted. He knew that he would make an easy target in the shallow sea of rippling grass ahead of him. As he walked, he pulled out the rope and tied a loop knot in the end before making a few sudden movements to better lure his quarry. He knew the owl, an equally experienced hunter, would be patiently waiting for just the right moment.

As if on cue, the owl unfurled and then tucked its wings, and dropped from the branch, diving nearly silently toward its prey.

Gollsaer's pointed ears heard every rustle of the wind in the owl's feathers. *He's diving on me*, he said to himself. Steeling his courage, he began to sprint through the grass toward cover on the opposite end of the clearing; just as the owl would expect. He ran as if he was fleeing for his life—because he was.

Leveling off, the owl's wingtips splashed dew off the high grass as it twisted and turned to track its fleeing prey's every movement. With Gollsaer just ahead, the bird extended its talons to snatch up its prey mid-flight but at the last possible instant, Gollsaer leapt up and grabbed the owl's legs behind its talons. Quickly looping the rope around its feathery leg he tied a quick knot. With a great flap of its wings, the startled owl carried the tiny Seldith aloft still holding on for dear life.

Gollsaer knew it was far too soon to declare victory—the battle had just begun. Nevertheless, he shouted up against the wind, "I have another surprise for you!" Reaching into his tunic now billowing in the wind, the tiny elf searched his pockets—calmly at first, but then frantically.

"It's not there!" he screamed. But no one but the owl could hear him.

The hunter, now prey, looked down and caught a glimpse of his short stick tumbling end over end into the dark. It was over in a heartbeat.

Two—The Owl Wrangler's Son

*I*n a remote forested valley bounded by steep, rocky cliffs, lacy threads of smoke drifted up from a chimney pipe poking out of a dwelling sheltered under the roots of an ancient Douglas fir. If you stood silently, you might have heard the boughs above you creak as the spring breeze tossed fir cones across a nearby meadow, but you would not have heard, seen or smelled anything to betray the presence of a community of forest elves cleverly camouflaging their tiny homes and the nearby honeycomb of caves and underground tunnels.

These secretive creatures, only a head taller than a large mushroom, live, learn, work, love, and hate in these tiny dwellings. Over time, human men, 'umans' have been called them many things, but for millennia they have called themselves *Seldith*.

Hisbil, the Owl Wrangler's son, found it hard to get comfortable on his classroom's backside-polished bench. Bright for a an elf that had survived seventeen winters, perhaps too bright for the tedious lessons he was forced to endure, Hisbil sometimes used his intelligence and insight to his advantage—as often as not, it got him in trouble with his parents, his teachers and the village elders. Hisbil's kind face had his mother Rachele's nose and her smallish, pointed ears. His cheeks were beginning to fill in with a dusting of fur, which he had begun to groom like some of the older sems. Like any son, Hisbil enjoyed spending time with his father Gollsaer when he was at home or invited to go along on his hunting trips. It didn't help that Gollsaer had been away awakening owls far more often and had rarely invited Hisbil along—this made his days especially long.

Because the community was so small, everyone knew everyone. Hisbil had a few friends but far fewer close friends. Since his father's mysterious disappearance, everyone in the village seemed unsure how to deal with the ugly rumors, so most left him to his grief. As a result, Hisbil spent more afternoons with his secret horde of books, maps and drawings, doing chores around the house or talking with Alred, the old wizard—anything to pass the time, anything to get his mind off of his father's fate.

The classroom was setup in a small cavern behind the stony walls of the valley. Its long wooden tables were divided by a wide aisle that segregated students by social class—Hisbil's and the other poorer northenders on one side and the more affluent southenders on the other. "So they won't distract one another..." the new *Council of Truth* explained.

Being a rare sunny day in late winter, the classroom was sparsely populated with restless elflings from about five to eighteen winters old, the youngest at the front and those about to graduate in the back. Hisbil ached to escape this musty dungeon and enjoy the sunshine—if there was any left. He propped his face on a bipod of pointed elbows, but nothing could keep his eyelids open—they started to flutter again as he dreamt of hunting with his father. *Perhaps he's come home,* Hisbil thought.

"Hisbil, sit up and pay attention," Professor Nadeel snapped as she lumbered like a great duck toward Hisbil. She tried to regain his attention with a long wooden pointer that she swooshed through the stale air like a broadsword. Hisbil lethargically found a posture more pleasing to the aging nesem. The rest of the class began to titter.

"Now, where were we?" she said to Hisbil, who was convinced the professor had a PhD in evil looks. She was using her fairly severe 'you-had-better-stay-awake' scowl on him.

"We were discussing Seldith history as recorded in the *Books of Truth*," a youngster chimed in from a bench near the middle of the classroom. As the professor shuffled back toward the front of the room, the yenesem looked back and stuck out her tongue at Hisbil. He ignored her and stifled the urge to throw something.

"Yes, of course. Thank you, Yenesem Anasta; perhaps if your brother Yesem Hisbil paid better attention…," the professor chided as she returned to the front of the room and continued her seemingly interminable lecture, which echoed off the stone walls of the cave.

"So, Yenesem Kassie, how *did* our ancestors arrive in this world?" Professor Nadeel asked after she noticed another student had passed her a note.

"Excuse me?" Kassie said, looking up from the scrap of paper that had captured her attention. She was a pretty thing, with long hair that cascaded down her back in waves. Her place was in the row just ahead of Hisbil but on the southenders' side of the classroom. Looking a bit flushed, she rose slowly, put her hands behind her back, balled up the paper, and began to recite the answer in a monotone.

"It's not clear how the Seldith came here. Some say we have always lived in these forests and have simply escaped notice. As you have told us *countless* times, any record of our arrival on this planet has been lost to history and the unavoidable decay of…"

"That will *do*, Yenesem Kassie," said the professor, cutting her off. "Someone else needs to pay closer attention," she said sharply as she held out her hand and motioned for Kassie to give her the note. Kassie begrudgingly went to the front of the classroom, handed over the note but not before tearing off a piece. The professor glanced at the note and tucked it in her apron pocket, but not before contorting her face into a classic frown.

A moment later, a broad smile crossed Professor Nadeel's face. Hisbil spun around when he realized that his teacher had been distracted by something toward the back of the classroom. It was not Gollsaer.

As the others turned, a fog of whispers and shuffling rustled the silence. Raising her hand to regain control, Professor Nadeel chirped, "Class, we have a special guest today. He's going to tell you youngsters a story that can save your life. Please welcome His Honor Sem Alred." She began to clap. Hisbil and some of the students joined in, but a few of the older southenders just turned to whisper amongst themselves.

Hisbil recognized Alred at once. As the clan wizard and a senior member of the governing Council of Truth, Sem Alred had seen more and done more than most—at least that's what he told anyone who would listen. Quite some time ago, Alred took Hisbil under his wing, inviting him over to his cottage where he spent many long afternoons listening to his stories and discussing the goings on in the village—especially when his father was out hunting.

Slowly making his way to the front of the room, Alred favored one leg with the aid of an experienced cane made from gnarly oak polished smooth with wear. The jagged scars on his face gave silent testament to his encounters with predators and as he tells it, evil wizards and enchanted beasts. Around his neck he wore a brass chain festooned with medals that signified his senior rank on the Council—it seemed an onerous, heavy burden that pulled his wide neck down like an ox's yoke. His face and head were covered with disheveled gray fur somewhat longer, and his long coat a bit more tattered than most of the other elders.

As Alred passed Hisbil, he briefly leaned in to whisper. "I need to talk with you. Come over directly after class." Hisbil nodded. As the old sem got comfortable on the classroom's tall punishment stool, he pulled down his sleeves hiding several dark bands, like artfully tattooed bracelets on his arms.

"What's he want to talk to you about?" the yesem next to Hisbil whispered.

"*The Sacred Seven Books of Truth*; he wants me to go out and retrieve the lost volumes," Hisbil said, whispering the most preposterous thing he could think of.

"Really?" the yesem said, his eyes widening.

"Right," Hisbil said sarcastically. In fact, Hisbil had a pretty good idea of what was on Alred's mind: when was he going to take up his father's job—his herditas of Owl Wrangler?

"Thank you, Professor," Alred said as he began in a voice roughened by living close to the earth. "I've been tasked to re-tell the story of Ruthet." Despite the muffled groans from the back of the room, Alred began to spin the age-old yarn of a yenesem that fell in harm's way when she wandered too far away from the village and was captured by a uman child.

Hisbil had heard this story countless times, but each time, it seemed to be told with subtly different facts, names, and places—often to fit the current circumstances or the agenda of the storyteller. Like Alred, Hisbil had a penchant for memorizing and reciting stories. As Alred retold the timeworn story, Hisbil's mind wandered back to his last trip with his Gollsaer— when they visited the dairy farm near the uman town three days walk to the northeast.

Hisbil returned from his daydream just as Alred finished the story. "This incident also meant that our settlement would have to relocate—and quickly—the uman child might still be able to convince her parents that there was more than youthful fantasy to the story of the tiny creature she found in the woods and tucked into her pocket like a lost toy. She herself might return looking for Ruthet, her lost 'dolly.'"

"Are there any questions?" Alred asked, as Professor Nadeel reappeared with a tray of tea and cookies. Alred sipped tea as a yesem in the second row got to his feet, not daring to look the old wizard in the eye.

"Your Honor, is that why we…we had to move here?" he said with a tremor in his voice.

"I'm afraid so," Alred answered. "Actually, as your parents know, we had been forced to move many times before settling here over ten winters ago—before you were born. It wasn't until we were offered the *benevolence* of Lord Lensmacher that we had the luxury of building a permanent village here in his valley" he said with a sneer. An ugly scowl returned to Professor Nadeel's face. In her lectures, she had made it clear that she appreciated *everything* the uman Lord Lensmacher had done for the Seldith and would hear no disparaging remarks about him or the new Council's policies.

Alred smiled at the yesem and stepped down from the stool to reassure him with a gentle pat on the cheek.

"Will we have to move again?" asked another yenesem in a tiny voice as she rose to her feet in the third row.

"Perhaps. Lord Lensmacher has threatened to let the loggers cut all of the trees around us and let the farmers plant the hills with vineyards unless we pay his taxes."

"Will he *really* send dragons to devour the maze like my papa says?" another yenesem on the northenders side of the classroom whimpered, nearly in tears.

"No, not really," the old Sem said in a calm voice. "While he has not a single dragons, they do say he owns a herd of goats that could devour the briar wall in no time."

A few more of the youngsters at the front of the classroom began to weep quietly—and some not so quietly. Facing the class, professor Nadeel stepped in front of Alred with an alarmed look on her face, now split nearly in two with a deep frown.

"I…I'm sure that these stories about Lord Lensmacher have been exaggerated—and you know, *anything* that isn't recorded in the *Books of Truth,* can't be true," she assured the class. "Nothing of this sort has been accepted as The Truth by the Council, Sem Alred and you know it."

At that, Alred returned the professor's angry glare with his own look of disdain as he slammed his cup down, nearly breaking the saucer. Moving toward the door, he grumbled out loud, "I won't be doing *this* again…and that's *also* not in *The Books.*" He looked right at Hisbil and mouthed that he wanted to talk to him right after class. Hisbil nodded.

A silence came over the room, and Professor Nadeel finally said, "Thank you, Your *Honor*" to his back as he slammed the classroom door behind him. Professor Nadeel clapped her hands in an attempt to restore order. "Read the first twenty pages of Chapter 2770 for tomorrow. Class dismissed."

Hisbil sprang back to life as the students around him stuffed their rucksacks with their books and as they pushed toward the door like sheep exiting a stock pen.

A yesem several rows in front of Hisbil, on the southenders' side, looked up to his older brother "Do you think Lord Lens…Lemmaker will send goats to debower the wall?"

"Of course not, silly," the brother replied. "Father says that's just talk—meant to scare us into moving again. None of it's been accepted by the Council; and until it is, it can't be true. It even says so in *The Fox*."

Hisbil just shook his head. *Mush-brained ignoramus.* He had witnessed first-hand far more than any of these youngsters, many of whom had grown up sheltered within the protective walls of the briar maze and the sheer walls of Stone Valley. Alred had told him stories of how the Seldith had changed in since the conservative "truth or exile" radicals like Sem Neychen had taken over the "new" Council and their newspaper *"The Final Opinion Examiner"* had become their mouthpiece. All too often, he had heard the "If it's not in *The Books*, it can't be true" intolerant ignorance spouted in unison by southenders and northenders alike.

As Hisbil moved toward the door, Professor Nadeel look up from her desk and announced, "Yenesem Kassie? I need to see you." Hanging back just inside the door and fumbling with his rucksack, Hisbil pretended to study the large hand-carved placard that had been hung over the door.

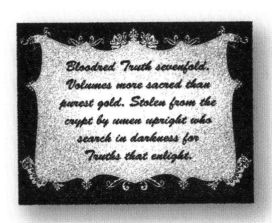

Anasta came up to Hisbil and asked, "Are you going home? I want to go over to Herbeverly's house to see her new…"

"I think you had better go home and finish your chores," Hisbil interrupted. "Mom might let you go once you have finished the sweeping and put away your laundry," he said, but did not move any closer to the door. "Run along now."

"But I promised!" Anasta said in a voice a bit too loud for the small classroom. She looked up to Hisbil with her soft, round eyes.

"Scoot," Hisbil said, gently encouraging her out the door. "And thanks for saving my hide."

Anasta smiled and disappeared out into the corridor.

Hisbil's attention was still focused on the unfolding events in the front of the classroom. Kassie put her books down and walked to the front of the classroom with the glee of a condemned prisoner walking to the gallows.

"Yes, Professor Nadeel?" she said looking down at the top of the professor's head as she read the confiscated note. She was clucking again—as she tended to do when she did not approve of something.

The professor's head snapped up. In a piercing voice that echoed down the tunnels she said, "Yesem Hisbil, you don't need to eavesdrop—go on home. Don't you have a special reading assignment from *The Fox* to finish?" She waved her arms as if she was shooing sugar ants out of her kitchen.

"Yes, Professor," Hisbil replied sullenly as he gently herded the last few students ahead of him out the door and almost closed it behind him. He walked down the hall a few steps but remained within earshot of the professor's conversation with Kassie.

"You're still here?" Hisbil said to Anasta who was also trying to listen.

"I want to…," Anasta began.

"Okay, okay, go to Herbeverly's; just get home before mom starts looking for you," Hisbil said. Anasta dashed down the hall to catch up with her clutch of friends waiting for her. They went off toward the daylight—all taking at once.

"I don't think you need get involved with *those* yesems," Hisbil heard the professor hiss.

"Yesems like *who?*" Kassie demanded defiantly. Hisbil moved a bit closer to the door.

"Like 'whom' she corrected, "Like Yesem Hisbil, for one—you know he's from the *wrong* side of the commons, and he has not accepted his father's herditas. I also don't expect your parents would approve. Do I need to tell them what this note says?"

"Go ahead and *tell* my mother. She knows all about Hisbil. I've been his friend, his good friend for as long as I can remember. If you're worried about his herditas, he just hasn't made up his mind yet, and his father might still return. Anyway, we're not breaking any *truths*."

The words "good friend" echoed off the walls of Hisbil's mind over and over. He has always liked Kassie and they had spent some casual time together but almost always with other friends. He now saw her in a new light, especially since she had been one of the only ones to be soothingly sensitive to his concerns for his father the last couple of weeks. *She's a good friend.*

Now straining again to hear, Hisbil could just barely hear Professor Nadeel retort in a cool, even tone, "I'll have to pass this on to the school elders. I'm sure they will have a stern word with your father."

With this response, Hisbil could not stand it any longer. He leaned closer to look through the crack in the doorjamb. Kassie was standing with her eyes fixed on the professor like a cobra about to strike. But all at once, her countenance changed and softened. Hisbil could hear Kassie as clearly as if she was whispering in his ear. "I *lost* my father. He's been gone for a long time." Her voice was strangely piercing. "You won't need to make any more trouble for me or my mother—do you?" she said, casually tossing her hair.

Professor Nadeel did not answer at once, but said meekly, "Of course, my dear. There is no need to worry your mother.

Consider the matter dropped…." Her eyes stared blankly into Kassie's eyes.

Kassie tossed her hair again and said, "You can go now, my dear Kassie, and here is your note," her eyes still fixed on the professor's.

"You can go now, my dear Kassie," the professor echoed quietly as she handed Kassie the note.

Kassie took the note, scooped up her books, and stomped toward the door, rattling the floorboards as she went. Hisbil quickly moved across the tunnel into the shadows. He watched from the darkness as Kassie passed. *How did she get away with that?*

Kassie paused a few steps past where Hisbil was hiding in the shadows—close enough to smell the jasmine in her hair. A moment later she moved down the hall and outside with an almost giddy cadence in her step. Her joy was contagious.

Hisbil started down the tunnel to follow her outside. *There's something about* Kassie…*something special.*

As Hisbil walked toward the daylight, the door to the Temple of Truth opened on the opposite side of the tunnel—just wide enough for Hisbil to see inside. This ornately decorated room held *The Books of Truth* entrusted to the village Council by the Grand Council and the Arbiters of Truth, few had seen inside.

Hisbil caught sight of the back of His Honor Dubjay framed in the Temple doorway immersed in a hushed conversation with someone Hisbil didn't recognize. The short and stocky stranger was very well dressed, festooned with gold jewelry, and crowned with a hat that covered his forehead. While speaking too softly for Hisbil to hear, the two seemed to be in nodding agreement about something as they wrapped up their discussion with a warm handshake and backslaps.

Lining the left wall of the room, Hisbil was able to see the row of floor-to-ceiling bookcases that held *The Books of Truth* bound in red leather. In the center of the room, several Council ministers festooned with their badges of office were seated at polished wooden tables with several of the large red volumes open before them. While it was hard to hear their conversation, they seemed to be discussing the nuance of one of the passages, while another took notes using light from a multi-wicked candle. Hisbil suddenly realized that *The Books* were written right here—the "truth" was being created in this room—a room that was never illuminated by the truth of direct sunlight. Over in the corner, a couple of Council ministers seemed to be discussing changes to a large diagram of what appeared to be a new room in the cave—one he had never seen. He only saw the words "Final Escape" written in large letters across the bottom.

On the far side of the chamber, a niche had been carved into the stone wall, protected by heavy metal doors and an elaborate lock—it was empty. Here is where *The Sacred Seven Books of Truth* would reside if they were ever found.

When Dubjay caught sight of Hisbil, he hurriedly closed the heavy door with a thud.

Hisbil wasted no time getting away from the darkness that permeated the tunnels and into the afternoon daylight and fresh air. He would have to ask Alred about what he had seen.

Three—Anasta's Herditas

*L*ooking forward to basking in the warm rays of the early afternoon sun, Anasta quickly waded through the crowd with her friends in tow. Her sweet smile bloomed as they scanned the commons for their schoolmates. The commons was teaming with Seldith of all ages—parents collecting their offspring and the usual snack and trinket vendors hawking their wares from small wheeled carts. Anasta didn't really relish going home—not right away. There were chores to do, but these could wait, at least for a while. But something was tugging on the strings of her mind, pulling her toward home.

In the surrounding trees, an immense flock of blackbirds and starlings noisily passed the time but showed little interest in the Seldith below. But when an unfriendly bird approached, they made it clear that this valley was out of bounds. As a result, the Seldith enjoyed a welcome respite from predators from above.

"Are you coming over to Nancia's? She's heard something juicy about Professor *Nadeeel*," asked Sue, one of Anasta's closer friends.

"Uh, sure," Anasta said distractedly. She welcomed the excuse to delay the confrontation she needed to have with her mother and walked alongside the other yenesems a while before stopping mid-stride.

"Sue, I just remembered. I need to go home first. I'll catch up with you at Nancia's. Okay?"

"Oh, okay," Sue said, quickly turning away and rejoining the gaggle of yenesems walking arm-in-arm. "I'll fill you in later," Sue said over her shoulder.

Anasta was already thinking about what she would say to her mother and didn't look back. Like her mother and Hisbil, she was heartbroken that her father had not returned and what his disappearance had done to her mother. Anasta had wrapped herself in the velvet blankets of her friends for comfort; they never spoke of Gollsaer, the Council, or the troubles in the village. Like so many others, so many lived in their own sheltered universe—blocking out all news of the real world that seemed to be crumbling around them like a paper-mache dollhouse in a rainstorm.

As she lifted the latch of the front door, Anasta could hear her mother's chair creak as she began to stand. "It's me, Mom," she said.

"Did you have a good day at school?" Rachele said, sitting back down in her chair and returning her attention to the pile of mending on her lap.

"It was okay," Anasta began. "I came straight home 'cause I wanted to talk to you about something."

Rachele did not respond at first, her mind focused on one of her husband's socks—the one she had mended and re-mended more than a dozen times since he had left.

"Mother?" Anasta said again.

"Yes, dear," she said looking up. "Is that yesem Hesjason bothering you again? I'm going to talk to Professor..."

"No, no...Hesjason doesn't bother me since I socked him in the stomach last week. But that's not what I want to talk to you about."

"Oh, dear. You shouldn't go around hitting..."

"Mom, I want to know about my herditas," she blurted. There was a long silence, as Rachele's eyes focused on her mending.

"Mom, I know you're worried about father, but I want to help," Anasta said kneeling beside the chair and placing her hands over her mother's. "I *know* I can help. You're too weak and sad now to help those that come to the door for healing. The village knows it. They have started to use the crows to fly their sick down to Flat Rock Landing."

"No." Rachele said. "You're too young. I won't hear of it. And, just yesterday, I cured a yenesem with a bad cold. I'm completely over it already."

"Mom, that was Nancia's sister. She wasn't really sick; they were just trying to make you feel useful again."

"Nonsense. She was sick and I cured her," Rachele snapped.

"*The Books of Truth* say that yenesems of seven winters should begin their apprenticeship in their parent's herditas. I was seven three winters ago. It's time—it's way past time."

"Don't quote *The Books* to me, young yenesem."

"Mom. I *can* help," Anasta pleaded. "If you teach me, I can take on some of the less serious cases so you can rest and get well. It's what I *want* to do. It's what I am *destined* to do. It's what…"

"I don't *want* you to be a healer. Look at what misery it's brought on me," Rachele sobbed, looking up from her chair with tears now trickling down her cheeks.

"I know. I know," Anasta said. "But it's the way. It's the Seldith way," She said softly. "Please teach me. I already know about the embrace and the herb soup—I watched you heal many times; I've even helped. And someday, I might need to use the skill to help Hisbil—if he's going to be the…"

"Don't say it," Rachele said in a clear, firm voice.

Anasta put her arm around her mother's shoulders. A moment later the look on her Rachele's face was noticeably brighter. In the same moment, Anasta felt a deep longing unlike any she had felt before. Without really knowing it, Anasta had just taken on her mother's pain.

Anasta sat curled up in her mother's lap for some time that afternoon. They talked of many things, including the herditas that one wanted and the other did not. It was not long before the burden Anasta had lifted from her mother had dissolved into the warmth they both felt as they shared a cup of tea—with a few chosen herbs and mushrooms Rachele had added for "flavor".

"Yes, you might need to heal Hisbil someday, but I hope that day never comes, or at least not for some time," Rachele said as she shooed her daughter out the door to rejoin her friends.

Anasta found herself on the stoop feeling better, but she knew she was no closer to taking on her mother's role as healer. *She can't protect me forever...* she thought as she made her way back toward Nancia's home at the far end of the commons.

Four—Alred's Ultimatum

*H*isbil was about to cross the wide, grassy commons to his house when a familiar voice beckoned from behind him.

"Hisbil, I need to talk to you."

He turned to see Alred standing in the shadows between the ironsmith and the Crow Air office. "I'll come back after I drop off my books," he said, turning back toward his home.

"Now. We need to talk *now*. Come on," Alred said, using an insistent and unmistakably serious tone.

Perhaps, he has heard about my father, Hisbil thought as he turned and followed Alred down past the shops and toward his cottage that faced out on the commons almost directly across from his own.

Alred said not another word until he had opened the front door of his simple one-room cottage and stood to one side waving his arm to encourage Hisbil to go inside. The door, like all Seldith doors, was round and thick with a fist-sized hole in the middle—these doors served as wagon wheels when the Seldith were forced to make a hasty escape.

"Come in and sit down," Alred said solemnly.

Hisbil's heart sank. Alred *had* heard about his father; he must want to break the news to him in private. Hisbil crossed the small room and found the chair he had used so many times before. While the room was lit only with the failing sunshine from a small window that faced out on the commons, Hisbil had no trouble navigating the clutter of books, papers, strange implements, and other random detritus that filled the room. "No need to worry your mother about what we discuss today," Alred counseled.

"Yes, I know. You told me before. Mom probably thinks I'm with my friends."

Alred made his way over to his own armchair by way of the small stove, which he poked a bit to encourage the fire. He removed his chain of office and hung it on a peg. Turning, he looked Hisbil in the eye.

"Hisbil, I…"

"He's dead. My father is dead. I…I know it."

"No, we haven't heard anything," Alred replied.

"Then, why have you brought me here?" Hisbil asked, fighting off images of his father being torn to pieces by an owl.

"It's been over two weeks since he left, so it's time for you to decide."

"Decide? Don't tell me that *you* want me to take up his herditas! I'm *not* ready—even my father said so. We have only gone on a dozen or so practice hunts where I *watched*. I know the words to the spells, but I don't…I've never…I'm not…"

They were interrupted by a loud knock on the door. Alred raised his hand, but before he could speak, the door opened, and His Honor Dubjay walked in as if entering the home of one of his servants. Dressed and groomed elegantly, the well-fed Seldith proudly wore the yellow-metal chain and medallion of the Council. As he came in, Hisbil quickly rose from his chair and stepped back into the shadows, not sure what to make of this intrusion.

"*Your Honor*—come right in. What calls you to descend to the north end? Is there another widow's house to foreclose?" Alred said with a sneer.

"No, I…there are no widows in arrears, with the possible exception of the Owl Wrangler's widow."

"My father's not dead," Hisbil said emphatically as he stepped out of the shadows and boldly stared down the imperious intruder.

"Of course not, but…," Dubjay said a bit startled, taking a step back.

"But what?" Alred said. "Why don't you just toddle on back to Neychen and the Council and tell them I will deal with this as I said I would."

"Well!" Dubjay said in a huff. "It has been two weeks today, and *The Books* say…"

"As well I know," Alred said abruptly.

"Perhaps, you don't remember that Lord Lensmacher has just informed the Council that we must double the owl quota until the deficit is made up," Dubjay said.

"I was there. I know what his toady said," Alred countered angrily. "You, on the other hand, had better make sure no one sees you when you leave. They don't really take very kindly to you and your cronies on this side of the commons." Alred put his hand on the balding councilman's shoulder and turned him back toward the open door. "And give my regards to Emperor." In a moment, he had slammed the heavy round door on Dubjay's rump as the councilman was 'encouraged' across the threshold.

After Alred bolted the door, closed the shutters and lit a stubby candle, both of them settled back into their chairs. "Perhaps now we won't be disturbed…"

"They want me to take on the Owl Wrangler's herditas, don't they?" Hisbil said.

"Yes. I'm afraid they do. We both know there's no one else that is as capable."

"Capable? As I told you before, I've never cast the spell, at least not for real. How does that make me capable?" Hisbil said, transfixed by the glimmering embers seen through the cracks in the stove.

"At least you know the words. No one else even knows them; they aren't in *The Books*, at least, not in the volumes we still have."

"What do you mean? Don't you have all...?"

"No, as you know, while the Council archives more than fifty volumes of *The Books of Truth* here in the caves, but only *The Sacred Seven Books of Truth* has the awakening spell. As you should know, these were stolen some time ago—well before my time. The ordinary volumes of *The Books* only contain the *established* 'truths' as agreed upon by the Council. They're just diaries, but *The Sacred Seven* contain nearly all of our most powerful and most dangerous spells and potions—including the awakening spell your father uses on the owls.

Hisbil recalled how Alred had talked about what the diaries contain and how each clan records what it learns and passes on to other clans all over the world, but no-one talks about the secrets recorded and now lost in *The Sacred Seven Books of Truth*.

"Yes, yes, that's been drilled into us from our first days at school." Hisbil said.

"So you should know that since *The Sacred Seven* were taken, the Seldith were only able to cast the spells we still knew, the few spells passed on by word of mouth—from father to son and from mother to daughter. They could not be written as..."

"It's against *The Truth*," Hisbil interrupted. "Yes, I know that much. My father made that very clear. I'm not even supposed to tell you or my mother."

"And you shouldn't. The spell should only be passed to your son or to the Seldith that takes up the herditas if you do not or cannot..."

"Like after I get torn to pieces by an owl!" Hisbil said.

"If you cannot continue, then, yes, someone must carry on the herditas."

"But I'm not ready. Anyway, my father might still come back," Hisbil protested again. "I know it's been a long time, but he still might come back." Hisbil's eyes were now on Alred's, which mirrored his concern.

"No...I don't think he will...," Alred said as he reached out to put his hand on Hisbil's shoulder. "He's never been gone this long so you need to brace yourself for that reality and make your decision. I can hold off the Council for a few more suns, but by the new moon, they'll insist that you either take up the herditas or accept exile. I know this is hard—it's very hard—but I think you can do it.

"Surely you know how the awakening spell works—your father must have told you. Do you at least know its history?" Alred asked.

"No, not really. Father never told me much beyond how to pronounce the words and how to leap up on the owl's legs without getting skewered. He did tell me that the spells have something to do with an ancient curse."

"Yes, but you need to know more than the basic facts, and while I don't know the words of the spell I can teach you what you need to know so hopefully you can better control it and understand what it does. I've done some research on the spell—even before Gollsaer took over the herditas. There are scattered references in the archived *Books of Truth* that we have here in Stone Valley."

After a long-winded story, Hisbil learned that the spell reversed an ancient curse that prevented creatures of all kinds from understanding one another.

"But Gollsaer said that the awakening spell *reverses* the curse."

"Yes, well, after many ages—nay millennia—of research and experimentation, Seldith wizards finally discovered a set of counter-spells to awaken themselves and all Seldith clans to the ancient Common language. We have spoken and understood this tongue ever since.

"But umans can't speak our Common language. How is it that we can understand them?" Hisbil asked pouring himself another cup of tea. "I've heard stories about umans and how they interrogate and torture their Seldith captives."

"We're not sure. I expect we interact with umans through ways we don't fully understand," Alred said as he refilled Hisbil's tea. "I certainly hope you never have to find out."

Hisbil took a deep breath as a chill ran up his back as he imagined an encounter with a uman. "Why do the awakened do what we ask? Why don't the owls just eat us anyway?" Hisbil asked trying to change the subject.

"Some do...some *few* do. But the herditas training helps the awakener understand how to negotiate with and calm the awakened beast long enough for the spell to take full effect. After that, they usually feel an obligation to the awakener, much like a newborn bonds with a parent. The awakener is often called 'ontwaker' by the awakened as a sign of this fellowship. But this obligation can wane if the awakened feels abused."

"But why owls?" Hisbil asked. "I can see awakening bees, as they can share their honeycombs, and crows to carry us long distances and moles that help us dig tunnels, but owls?"

Alred looked down at the cup of tea he was cradling in his hands. "That's a good question," he began. "Not long after we made our first encampment here in Stone Valley, we were approached by a reprobate exile called Emperor. He said that he knew the uman that owned the land all around Stone Valley, and he promised to negotiate with him to secure our safety. The Council assumed he simply wanted to get back into good graces with the clan; so after a long, bitter debate, they agreed. Not long afterwards, Emperor contacted the uman land owners, Lord and Lady Lensmacher, and negotiated an arrangement. According to Emperor, it seems that Lady Lensmacher was quite fond of the Seldith and wanted to create a haven for us."

"An arrangement?" Hisbil asked. "Why wasn't anyone told of this?"

"Yes, we were to be protected here in Stone Valley in exchange for awakened owls. It seems Lord Lensmacher was training owls to deliver messages and small parcels for some wizards in another land. We're not sure of the details—we were simply required to deliver one owl a fortnight to his castle. The details were kept secret because the Council was afraid of what the village would think of dealing with an exile and a uman."

"But my father was awakening eight or ten every new moon. Why so many?"

"Yes, something changed," Alred said shaking his head. "Two springs ago, we had heard nothing from Lord Lensmacher for quite some time. We assumed he had lost interest in the owls or had just moved away. However, Lensmacher eventually reappeared—but he was different. Something had happened to his wife, and he was bitter and broken. It wasn't long before he raised the owl quota again and again on one pretext or another. We had no choice but to try to deliver more owls or face having to pack up and move—or worse."

"So we're trapped. Stuck between having to move back out into the uncertainty of the forest or pay the Lord's owl tax."

"Yes. I'm afraid that's it. And unfortunately you're stuck in the middle. Everyone has grown so spoiled with our permanent settlement that no one wants to even consider moving again."

"My father never said anything about this," Hisbil said, staring into the hypnotic light of the flickering candle.

I should have, Alred said to himself.

"He should have," Alred said looking into Hisbil's eyes.

"I saw something today," Hisbil said after a long pause.

"Oh? Have you been snooping through the library again?"

"I saw a large diagram of a cave excavation. I didn't know there was more working being done in the caves."

"They didn't want anyone to know. It's nothing you need to be concerned about. Let's have some tea and try to figure out what to do."

Hisbil spent much of the afternoon discussing the history of the awakening spell and trying to understand the herditas that everyone except his mother seemed to want him to take on—for life. And now, as Hisbil walked back home, he kept thinking, *I'm not ready…I'm not ready…I'm not…*

Five—The Vision

*I*t was early the next morning when Kassie asked, "What should we do about Hisbil?" as she put the breakfast dishes away. Her mother Casandra was pulling up the bed quilt and straightening the linens. She did not answer.

"He's very troubled." Kassie continued, "Yesterday in class I could feel him worrying himself sick. We really need to do something, or at least *I* do."

"It's best that we not interfere," Cassandra said softly. "If he or his mother wants help, they can come to me, but I can't help unless asked. As I've told you before, I haven't seen that his father met his end or any other visions that make sense."

As the last dish was put away, Kassie turned and loaded her rucksack with a few wrapped pieces of cheese, dried mushrooms, a chunk of bread, a metal canteen of water, and a rolled blanket. She hadn't told her mother about the vision of Gollsaer's whereabouts that had come to her as she passed Hisbil hiding in the shadows outside the classroom. As with most of her visions, it was as if she could walk into a painting that had come to life. In her vision, Kassie had seen a towering fir tree with the bark worn down close to the ground; a sword lay on the ground nearby. Her vision rising above the treetops, she could see that the tree was at the edge of a quiet glen some distance away, somewhere she had never been. She did not know what it meant, but she was confident that these clues would lead her and Hisbil to learn Gollsaer's fate.

Kassie wished that her mother had taught her more about her own herditas so she could understand the visions and what they meant. She had visions many times before but all too often, she found herself embroiled in other people's affairs because she had misinterpreted what she had seen, or had simply revealed a truth that was better left hidden. She also knew that it would be best to conceal her own thoughts and intentions in regard to Hisbil as her mother shared her gift of insight but was far more adept at its use. For now, it would be best if her mother did not know where she was going, especially this time.

"So, what are you and Hisbil planning?" her mother asked. Kassie was already flooding her mind with an imaginary trip to Windrush, the cliffside park at the north end of the valley where families went to enjoy their offspring—a place her mother would certainly approve.

"To Windrush—we're going to have a picnic and sit out in the sun. We might even go to the puppet show later."

"That's just fine, dear. Just make sure you stay inside the thorn maze and keep your eyes…"

"Yes, *Mother*," Kassie interrupted. "I know how to be safe. You know I can sense danger from a great distance—long before anyone else."

"Perhaps, you think you can, but when you're distracted or your mind is wandering, you…"

"Of *course*, Mother," Kassie said as she darted out the door before her mother could finish lecture number 24. *I'll bet she already knows where we're going…*

Kassie put the rucksack down on the covered porch that extended across the front of their house and plopped down into one of the large, white rocking chairs. Being a prosperous southender, Kassie's father had been able to find an ideal location when their Seldith clan had first discovered this valley. Hisbil's father had even done some of the carpentry work after her father was lost. She and Hisbil had spent the summer trying to help, but mostly got in the way.

Kassie didn't want to think of her father, his loss was too painful to recall so she purposely began to think of Hisbil. *Perhaps, if I can help him.* Almost immediately, she could visualize Hisbil as he sat at a round table trying to concentrate on a book. Reaching out, she put her hand on the vision's shoulder; she so desperately wanted to free Hisbil from grief; a pain that she knew all too well.

"Go look for your father", she leaned in and whispered with her face next to Hisbil's ear. "You can find him if you just look hard enough." Almost immediately, she envisioned Hisbil rising from the table and quickly leaving his home and coming toward her end of the village. She smiled as she realized how very little suggestion it took to pull him out of his thoughts and making up his mind for him.

Kassie went inside and quietly retrieved her father's sword, belt and scabbard; she could see that Hisbil was not bringing a blade. She donned her *amiculum obscurum*, her cloak of invisibility, which hung just inside the door on a peg, but kept the hood down which prevented the cloak from making her disappear into the surrounding shapes and colors. She wanted Hisbil to see her—which was a challenge lately as he had been so distracted of late. Before Hisbil came into view, she could envision him crossing the commons and begin walking down the hill. Looking up from the porch, she could see Hisbil draw closer and the determined look on his face. *I hope I'm doing the right thing. I'm not sure he's ready for the whole truth.*

Six—Mourning and Exploring

*H*isbil's one-room home was small, compared to the other dwellings on the north end of the Seldith village. Made of leaves, fir cones and bark, it could easily be missed by someone passing by. Like most other Seldith homes, it had a round door about shoulder-high with the axle hole fitted with a decorative wooden handle. As a reminder of their nomadic roots, the doors served as cart wheels when the need arose.

At one time, Hisbil's father was an accomplished, perhaps magical carpenter. But since Lord Lensmacher's quota had increased, Gollsaer had not had time to practice these talents, so he had been unable to keep the house, furniture and fixtures in good repair. Hisbil did what he could, but he had not inherited his father's carpentry skills.

Warmed by a small metal stove, a tattered chair padded with robin-chick down carried Rachele, Hisbil's mother's imprint. She had spent many nights waiting in this chair, listening, and all too often, quietly weeping prayers for the return of her second husband. Her first husband had also been an Owl Wrangler who failed to return, so she knew all too well the uncertainty the future held for her and her family.

Along the back wall of the room was an alcove Gollsaer had skillfully carved into the tree root where Rachele and her daughter slept between simple down quilts. Hisbil's bed was carved into the tree root next to the door. It was where his father and mother had once slept. The bed had always been his when his father was away, as it was Hisbil's job to fend off anything trying to breach the door.

It was halfway through the morning when Hisbil realized that he must go out and look for his father—suddenly convinced he could find him or at least learn his fate. He jumped up from the table where he had been pretending to do homework. "I'm going out," he suddenly announced, pulling on his coat and grabbing his *amiculum obscurum* cloak as he darted out the door.

"Be back before dark!" he could hear his mother plead as her son pulled the door closed behind him with a thump.

The crisp, spring morning had grown into a warm, sunny day as Hisbil crossed the commons that separated the homes in the north end of the village from those in the south. The commons was peppered with sems and nesems, their children and pets enjoying the rare sunshine, seemingly oblivious of his grief and concern for his father. But Hisbil didn't miss the sideways looks and furtive whispers as he passed by.

"Why doesn't he take up his father's *herditas*?" Hisbil heard them whisper loud enough for him to hear. "Doesn't he know His Lordship will make us move if he doesn't?" Hisbil was all too aware of what the village wanted. They wanted *security*, even though it might mean loss of yet another life—probably his. And just how long would Lord Lensmacher leave them in peace before levying yet another demand? He resisted the temptation to turn and shout: *He's not dead. He'll be back any day!* Perhaps it was because he didn't really believe it himself. Hisbil pushed through a small throng of yesems playing with a tame ant on a leash and headed toward the briar patch where he and his father had said their last good-bye. *I know I can find him if I search hard enough...*

As Hisbil pulled his full-length camouflage cloak up over his head and much of his face, its color and texture morphed to match the shifting colors and textures of the foliage around him so that he seemed to disappear from sight. If they didn't see him, they wouldn't bother gossiping about him as he passed.

He was almost to the briar wall when he heard a familiar voice from behind. "You'll need this." Hisbil turned to see Kassie standing by her house. She was holding out a short sword, belt, and scabbard. "You'll never get through the under-brush without a good blade," she said, walking toward where she had last seen Hisbil's footprints.

Hisbil stopped for a moment and realized she was right. He had not planned this ad hoc expedition very well. If he was go-ing to find his father, he would need a blade of some kind—for any number of contingencies.

"Thanks," Hisbil said as he pulled the cloak off his head and walked a bit closer. The cloak changed to a mottled green as Hisbil came into full view. As he reached out for the blade and scabbard, his hand touched Kassie's. She was close enough that he could smell a haunting tinge of jasmine, and his mind mean-dered to better, happier days.

"You're going to look for your father, aren't you?"

Hisbil took a moment to answer. "Yes. I can't just sit and wait any longer. It's been…"

"Over two weeks. Yes, I know. We all…the whole vil-lage…knows," Kassie interrupted softly. "Can I come?" she said as the blade and belted scabbard changed hands.

"No, of course not," he said as he strapped on the scabbard under his cloak and withdrew the short blade to inspect its edge.

"Why not?" she said, gazing up into his eyes and stepping a bit closer. *Don't you need all the help you can get to locate your father?* she seemed to say. He could see her mouth move, but the words seemed jumbled. *You want to take me with you.*

Hisbil thought back to the last time he had seen his father alive—the moment before he turned away into the briar maze.

He was reminded of his own pleading request to join him, much like Kassie's.

"Yes," Hisbil said, *I can use all the help I can get.* "You can come. But you can't tell your mother," he admonished.

"I wouldn't think of it," she said with a sly smile. Kassie raced a few steps back to her porch only to return a moment later with a small rucksack. A blanket was rolled and tied over the top.

"What's all this?" Hisbil asked.

"Oh, I figured we would need a bit to eat and a blanket for…our picnic."

Hisbil's eyes rolled as he turned toward the thicket. A moment later, he realized that the blanket was probably intended to help carry back his father's remains.

"Okay, give me that," Hisbil said, reaching for the rucksack as Kassie slung it over her shoulder.

"I don't think so. I can carry my share. You just worry about getting us through the briars."

"Sure, why not…you're the one that'll be sorry for bringing all that stuff."

Hisbil drew the sword, and as he cut one of the woody tendrils that barred the opening, he softly whispered, "*Ostium Abierto,*" so Kassie could not hear. The blackberry tendrils parted like a curtain, and a number of narrow paths appeared before them—a few steps ahead, some turned to the left and another to the right. Hisbil and Kassie pulled their cloaks up over their heads, and they disappeared into the briar maze. Hisbil had to concentrate to remember the right combination of turns at each divide in the maze. He only had to backtrack once when his mind wandered, but Kassie said not a word, following close behind.

Once they had arrived on the other side of the maze, Hisbil raised the sword again, and while touching the vines, he whispered "*Ostium Cerrado.*" At this command, the vines regrew tiny, twisting tendrils that quickly closed off the gap like water rushing in to fill a vessel.

Hisbil turned back to see if Kassie was impressed at this skill. She smiled and again said nothing but he heard a soft voice: *Turn east…*"

Hisbil turned east and headed up the indistinct trail. He realized this was a fool's errand and that he had brought along one of the few people outside his family that he really cared about—and he was now putting her in danger.

"Can you tell me how you did that?" Kassie asked, walking a few paces behind Hisbil.

"I could. But then I would be banished. I'm not sure it would do you any good anyway. Only Owl Wranglers and a few others on the Council can open the briar maze," he said seriously.

"Oh," Kassie said, "Like Alred?" She shoved her way past Hisbil. "I see. So you don't trust me," she snipped and pushing past Hisbil, moved off down the trail ahead of him.

Hisbil did not bother to reply. He was old enough to know not to respond to that tone of voice—especially from a female. He continued working his way down the faint trail a few paces behind Kassie. For some reason, she seemed to be making all of the turns his father would have made. It was not long before the pair came to the clearing in the center of a long wooded valley.

Ahead of them, they could see a grove of tall fir, cedar, and other evergreens, salted with a stand of birch and peppered with oaks and maples growing in the clear spaces where the uman loggers had harvested the firs long ago.

"Which way should we go?" Kassie pondered aloud but knew that the meadow was *northwest from here—to their left.* She stopped at a point in the trail where it branched northwest and north.

Hisbil kept watching the nearby grassy meadow to the right, as he thought he had seen movement near the tree line. He motioned to the left, not looking at Kassie. "That way, he always took me up the side of the meadow at the tree line to avoid crossing out in the open." Before he finished speaking, Kassie had started up the left fork and Hisbil followed.

"Have you read *The Books*?" she asked over her shoulder after walking some distance in silence.

"Not many have," he replied, but his attention was again focused on the sky and nearby forest. He feared that they should not be this far out in daylight. To make matters worse, the path did not seem familiar to Hisbil, and he saw no sign of his father's passing this way. *Where is she taking me?*

"But have *you*?" she said, stepping over a branch.

"Yes...yes, I have—at least the parts the elders and teachers let us read. Are you sure we should go this way?"

"Do you believe everything that's written?" she said, continuing up the trail, picking her way between the intertwined vines and tendrils of a large marionberry bush, the promise of its fruit hanging down in a blanket of tiny white flowers. *We're on the right trail.*

"Certainly," he said, knowing that it would be heresy to say otherwise.

"I don't," Kassie said flatly as she stopped in a small clearing, turning toward Hisbil.

Hisbil paused a few steps away, and their eyes met, but she was not smiling. She turned and kept walking.

"You don't?" he said after he caught up with her. It was as if he were seeing her for the first time. In the midafternoon sunshine, she seemed truly beautiful—as beautiful as any yenesem he had ever seen. At once, her face was angelic, covered with soft tan fur, and her hair was long and flowing, falling in ribboned cascades down her shoulders. Her eyes were as none he had ever seen—he longed to look into them again, and deeply.

"No, there are some stories that I simply don't think are true—they just can't be," she said still looking at his face as he stepped closer.

"That's dangerous talk. What makes you think the stories aren't true? You know that anything that gets inscribed in *The Books* is endlessly discussed, verified and reverified. The writings *must* be true."

"I've seen…I've been…I just don't…," she said.

Hisbil could tell she was struggling to be honest with him. Hisbil said nothing at first.

"Neither do I," he said, walking a bit closer and kicking at a fir cone.

Kassie stood still but looked down at the glistening maple leaves caking the forest floor. A gentle smile came over his face. It's as if she knew how he felt inside.

This same ground had been covered with snow only weeks before, but sprigs of grass and miniature snowdrops were struggling to poke out their tiny porcelain white-capped shoots. She knelt down and held a bloom to her face to appreciate the delicate aroma.

"Some things that *The Books* says are just not possible, and some things that I know are true are said to be wrong or evil…," she said as she got back on her feet.

"…but they aren't," Hisbil said, finishing her sentence. "And some important things that have happened—happened to *me*—are not recorded."

"Yes, I know," she said and paused. "How could *everything*, every truth be recorded?" she said, looking up at Hisbil.

Hisbil scanned the treetops again for movement, but his inexperience hid the large bird circling high above. "They can't be," he said. "Some things are better left unrecorded."

"Like this?" she said, putting her hands on his shoulders and standing on her toes to give Hisbil a fleeting kiss. Hisbil had not been kissed before—at least not by anyone besides his mother and aunt Herlynn whose breath smelled of blackberry wine. It was a unique feeling unlike any he had felt before. Someone actually cared about him. It made him feel wanted and loved in a special way, a feeling that had been somehow missing in his life. And with it, he suddenly understood how much he wanted to protect Kassie and how much danger he had put her in.

"We need to keep moving," he said abruptly, pulling away as the tips of his ears started to burn.

"Of course," she whispered, turning back up the trail and kicking over the flower.

A moment later, Hisbil started after Kassie and caught up with her almost immediately, touching her arm. Kassie stopped and turned up her face streaked with tears. Hisbil pulled her to him and tenderly kissed her tears away. He felt the warmth of her hand in his. He again smelled the sweet scent of jasmine in her hair and he kissed her again. Her arms wrapped around him, and he could feel her warm body pressed against his.

"Yes, there are some things that should not be recorded....," he breathed.

"I want you to have this," Kassie said as she pulled the silken scarf out of her hair and began to tuck it into his tunic's breast pocket. It carried the same smell of jasmine that clouded his reason and made Hisbil want to kiss her again.

Hisbil pushed the scarf deep in his tunic's breast pocket, leaving only a small tail exposed. "I'll keep it here next to my heart...but we do need to..."

"Yes. We need to finish what we came out here to do. I understand," she said.

They continued their search through the forest as the shadows grew longer. They were both too distracted with each other to notice the white-headed bald eagle perched on a branch high above, watching their every move.

"Shouldn't we get back before dark?" Kassie asked.

"*You* should. I can't go back until I find *something*, even if it takes all night," Hisbil said.

"Then I'll stay too. I don't want to go back alone—it's too dangerous—you've got the sword."

"No, you should head back now so you'll be back well before dark."

Kassie walked back a few steps and asked, "Are you sure I can't stay with you?" Her hair tousled in the breeze, and the fragrance nearly overcame Hisbil. *You need me to help you find Gollsaer.*

His mind clouded briefly, and he heard himself say, "Sure...sure, you can stay."

"Then we had better keep moving and keep looking for trail signs," she said bounding off like a rabbit being chased by a fox.

What just happened? Hisbil again found himself trying to keep up with Kassie as she dashed off into the forest.

Over the next hour, Kassie led Hisbil through many parts of the forest Hisbil had never travelled. Somehow, she seemed to find subtle signs that led them deeper into the darkest parts of the forest—the canopy filtering the bright sunshine into a quilt of random spots of light that danced over the forest floor.

Before long, Hisbil lost sight of Kassie as she raced ahead. He dared not call out to her, so he stopped to listen but heard nothing but the wind pulling over the tops of the trees as like the towering masts of sailing ships catching a stiffening breeze. Then he heard it—a twig snapped. There *was* something back there—a dozen paces behind him. *Did it hear us talking? Dumb, dumb, stupid.* Pulling his camouflage cloak even higher, Hisbil lay flat on the ground and tucked himself under a large fallen branch. It was coming closer. He froze as it came up to his hiding place and paused.

"Why are you laying down there?" Kassie said. "And you need to tuck your feet in under the cloak if you don't want a raccoon to nibble them off."

"I thought you were up *ahead*," Hisbil said, getting to his feet.

"I was. But the trail led me in a circle, so I came back here," she said as she brushed off his cloak and wiped the mud off his face with her sleeve.

"Great. So we're lost?"

"No, there is a clearing up ahead and…," Kassie's chin dropped to her chest.

"And what?"

"And I found this," Kassie said as she handed Hisbil a short stick.

Hisbil recognized it immediately. "It's his wand—it's my father's wand." Over the last ten winters, growing up at his father's knee, Hisbil had wielded it to conquer imaginary beasts on countless occasions.

"Where did you find it? Show me," Hisbil demanded.

"Ahead, about fifty paces—in the clearing."

Hisbil didn't hesitate a moment. As Kassie guided him, they soon approached a wide meadow. When Hisbil reached the tree line, he paused as if he had hit an invisible but impenetrable wall. His father had told him many times that it would be exceedingly foolhardy to cross out into the open. He could tell Kassie had already run out into the meadow—she had trampled down the brown grass in a straight line to the center of the grassy clearing; almost as if she knew where to look.

"Look! Look over there—on the other side of the meadow," she said.

"What is it?"

"Do you see that tree? It looks as if something has scraped off some of the bark near the ground. Let's go look," Kassie said as she again started to across the clearing, making a beeline for the tree at the opposite side.

Hisbil grabbed her arm and held her back. He had seen this tree before.

"Wait a minute. You were lucky the last time you went out into the meadow. Your trail through the grass is a dead giveaway; a blind moose could see where you've been."

Kassie turned back toward Hisbil and looked up at him. He dropped her arm. Looking up into his eyes, she said softly, "We'll be fine." *I think we should just cross over.*

Hisbil had trouble concentrating. *She's doing it again.*

"No. No, I won't let you…trick me with your mind games. Not this time, it's just too dangerous."

"I see," Kassie said with a thin smile. "So you care enough about me to protect me from myself?" Her eyes were still locked on his.

Hisbil thought for a moment and blushed. "Let's just skirt the meadow and get to the tree. It will be safer for both of us." He turned and began to find his way around the tree line. Kassie did not hesitate to follow, and follow she did, this time a pace behind.

Before they reached the tree, Hisbil spotted something on the ground, and he ran the rest of the way. By the time Kassie caught up, he was holding his father's cloak, scabbarded sword, and rucksack.

"Are those his?" she whispered.

Hisbil did not answer at first. His knees seemed to melt, unable to support his weight. He crumbled to the ground clutching the last remains of his father to his breast—burying his face in his father's cloak. He could smell his pipe tobacco and his sweet sweat. *He's gone. He's really gone.*

Kassie stood over him and placed her hand on his bowed head. She began to weep.

"Hisbil, this does *not* mean your father is…," Kassie said through her tears.

"Dead? Eaten alive? Torn in a thousand pieces and strewn over this very meadow? Swallowed whole?"

"No…I…I just don't know. I can't see…," she began. "We need to go home. It's getting late," she said as she wiped away her tears. "We need to tell your mother and sister…and the elders what we have found. At least we know *something*…"

Hisbil was powerless to resist her suggestion. He rose as if in a trance, folded his father's cloak. Kassie gently packed it into Gollsaer's rucksack along with the wand.

"I'll take that," he said as Kassie closed up the rucksack. He picked up his father's belt and sword and slung them all over his shoulder. With Hisbil dutifully following, Kassie led him by the hand around the edge of the clearing and back toward the village. Trying as hard as he could, Hisbil could not get the image of his father's horrible death out of his mind. Kassie could only weep.

Sometime later, they were back at the main trail. By this time, they were walking side by side. "How did you find the wand?" Hisbil asked.

"Don't you know?" Kassie said in a whisper.

"Know what? That you are good at finding lost wands?"

"My herditas…my gift…at least part of it, is the ability to find the lost and the things they have lost. I can help them find the way back. I inherited this from my father."

"I know where I am, and I know my way back," Hisbil said sharply, dropping her hand as his pride took a body blow.

"Yes, of course. You know these forests as well as your...as well as Gollsaer, but you're lost in other ways. You feel a duty, an obligation to protect your family and the village, and me..."

"Don't you think I know that?" Hisbil interrupted.

"Yes," she said, stopping and turning toward Hisbil—he could feel her warm breath on his face.

"Yes," she said softly in a breathy whisper. "I feel that you need someone. Someone you can talk to. Someone who won't judge you, just listen. Perhaps you need someone to help you decide what you need to do." *Hisbil let me help you.*

"There's no deciding, no choosing, no choices," Hisbil said firmly. She reached out for his hand again.

Feeling suddenly uncomfortable, Hisbil stepped around Kassie and walked up the trail another couple of steps. "I *have* to take up my father's herditas—it's my duty," he said. "What else can I do? What else *could* I do?"

How can I be close to anyone if I don't have long to live? Hisbil told himself.

As if Kassie had heard him say this aloud, another tear dropped down her cheek. "You can find *another* way to contribute—your *true* herditas," she said a bit louder as she closed the distance between them again.

"Never. I would never—I could never...," Hisbil said, raising his voice a bit. "My father has *always* been an Owl Wrangler—and those that came before him. He told me. He said it was my challenge, my destiny, my...fate to work, live, and die as an Owl Wrangler."

"No," she said firmly. "It isn't. Your father hasn't...Gollsaer isn't..."

"What do you mean?" Hisbil interrupted.

Kassie flushed, and after a moment said, "You'll have to ask Alred or your mother. It's not my place to tell you." She turned and began to run down the trail back toward the village.

"I'll talk to you about this again but only after you ask them about your *real* father," she said over her shoulder.

Hisbil took a moment to gather his thoughts. *My real father?* When he looked up, Hisbil realized that Kassie had dashed far ahead and was already out of sight. He ran down the trail following Kassie's small footprints in the wet leaves and muddy puddles still dancing from her passing. *What did she mean?* he kept asking himself over and over again as he tried to catch up but he weight of the backpack and two swords held him back. *What was she going to tell me?*

While still an hour away from the briar maze, he felt it. A slow, rhythmic vibration shook the ground as if someone was pounding the earth with a great club. Hisbil pulled his cloak up over his head, crouched down, and froze just as something eclipsed the sun. A dark shadow passed over him, a shadow larger than any bird. He moved as quietly as he could and hid under a rocky ledge. *Did it see me?* Then he heard Kassie scream—she was not that far away.

Stay hidden until the threat has passed. Keep your wits about you. Don't let your curiosity get the better of you, his father's words screamed to him. But the next time the shadow blotted out the sun, he looked out from his hiding place—it was a giant, dressed in long trousers and heavy boots, standing half again as tall as the blackberry maze. He saw no sign of Kassie.

A uman! Hisbil had never seen one up close before, but recalled the stories and warnings about their cruelty and callous nature. It seemed to be looking for something along the trail. A moment later, it stooped down—reaching toward Hisbil. He pulled back under the overhanging rock as far as he could. The giant hand moved past his hiding place and picked up something from beside the path several dozen paces ahead. Hisbil watched as the uman inspected and shoved what could have been Kassie's rucksack into his cavernous pocket. The uman then passed over Hisbil again and thudded off to the northeast.

I've got to follow it! Hisbil thought, trying not to panic. But what can I do against a giant? I've got to get back to the village and get some help. No, I need to follow it. What would I do if I caught up? It would capture me for sure. No, I need to go back, and fast. Perhaps *Kassie* wasn't captured.

Hisbil threw caution to the wind and began a mindless race for the briar maze wishing under his breath that the uman had frightened away any predatory birds that might have seen him running up the trail. Along the way, he found no sign of Kassie—but he prayed over and over that she would be waiting for him somewhere along the trail.

Before long, Hisbil reached the outer wall of the briar maze. Kassie was still nowhere to be seen. He took a chance and called out to her louder than he should have. "Kassie! Kassie, come out this minute!" Hisbil scanned the darkening sky and the nearby meadow for signs of movement or the sound of an approaching menace. He saw and heard nothing. Kassie was nowhere to be found.

Hisbil's stomach felt as if he had swallowed a stone. He struggled to catch his breath as he tried to get the briar maze to part. After several failed attempts, he finally said the spell correctly, and the briars parted—albeit haltingly. It took some time to work his way through—turning left twice in a row instead of using the correct turning sequence. Once he was past the maze and managed to close the thorn wall behind him, he fell to his knees exhausted with worry and grief.

"Where have you been?" a familiar voice above him asked. Hisbil looked up to see Anasta.

"You went through the maze! You're in such big trouble. I'm going to tell Mom," she said defiantly.

Hisbil immediately found the strength to get to his feet. Grabbing his sister by the shoulders, he said, "Tell her nothing. *Nothing!* If you know what's good for you, you'll just go straight home." Hisbil's face made it clear to his sister that she had best not betray him. Not this time. "I'll be home soon. Just go home and say nothing. *Promise* me."

"Uh…okay," she said with a look of fear on her face. "I *promise.*"

"Now, *get!*" Hisbil commanded. Anasta darted away toward the commons and home. Hisbil made a beeline for Kassie's door and began to knock frantically. A few moments later, a middle-aged nesem came to the door wearing a broad smile and an apron with the badges of a dozen meals decorating the front like a new-age painting.

"Well, hello, Hisbil! What brings you to my door? You look exhausted. What have you two been up to?" she said, raising an eyebrow but still smiling. She looked outside the door to see if anyone else was around.

"Nesem Casandra, I…Kassie…uman…," Hisbil stammered.

"Yes, perhaps you should come in," Kassie's mom said in a way that her daughter had used when she wanted to gently co-erce Hisbil. The smile had left her face. "And you can just call me Casandra—you're almost a sem now and don't have to follow all of the old formalities." *Just relax and tell me what happened…*

"Thank you, Nesem…er, Casandra," Hisbil said as he stepped inside the cottage. "Something…something terrible might have happened—happened to Kassie," he said frantically. "Kassie—have you seen her? Did she come home?" Hisbil said, still hoping she had somehow gotten through the briar maze.

"Why, no—no, I haven't. I thought she was with you. Weren't you going on a picnic?"

"Yes…no, we went through the maze, but…but not for a picnic. I wanted to go look for my father, and she…"

"She wanted to help," Casandra's tone had deepened with concern, and her frown had deepened in her brow. "I told her that she was still too young to use her gift without guidance. Did she get lost? What happened to her?"

"She, she helped me…she helped me find my father's wand and cloak and his sword." Hisbil held up the sword still draped over his shoulder. "We were on our way back and got separated." Hisbil could hardly breathe, and his voice began to shake. "It's my fault. I shouldn't have let her go. We *have* to go find her, before they get too far." Hisbil could see how worried she was—her face had turned quite stern.

"They? Who are *they?*" Casandra demanded as she crossed the room toward Hisbil.

"I think she was taken."

"Taken? Taken by an owl? An eagle? My baby! What have you let happen…"

"She ran off ahead of me," Hisbil interrupted. "I told her to be more careful. She was very convincing and wouldn't listen…but it wasn't a bird—it was worse." Hisbil looked at his muddy boots and then straight into Casandra's eyes. His stomach tightened, and he felt more helpless than ever.

"Worse than what? What took her? Tell me!" Hisbil stepped back as Casandra charged him—his back hit the wall, jarring loose a picture as she came close enough that Hisbil could smell the honeysuckle in her hair. His mind began to swirl as he recalled the time he had just spent with Kassie. The memories streamed out of his mind like juice being squeezed out of a piece of ripe fruit.

"I see," Casandra said. "She was taken by a giant—a uman, from what I can see."

"Ah...yes. How did you know?" Hisbil asked, looking Casandra in the eye—they were Kassie's eyes.

"I just know you're telling the truth at least as *you* know it. You're right. I need to start looking for her *now*—before the uman gets too far away.

Casandra stepped away and began to dart around the room, grabbing a warm sweater. "My cloak, she's taken my cloak...I'll need to find Japheth's." Darting off to an adjoining room she called out "Go get me a crow—and quickly!" she said, returning with a rucksack. "Give me Japheth's sword."

Hisbil unbuckled the sword and handed it over. He stood in the doorway, frozen in uncertainty. "Go!—and *hurry*! I need to collect a few more things. *Go!*" she commanded with a resounding authority that Hisbil could not resist.

Hisbil turned and bolted through the open door. He ran down the center of the village, past a dozen shoppers and kids playing in the commons. Turning down an alley and up another narrow path, he came to a small shop. Above the door swung a wooden sign: *"Crow Air—Anywhere, Anytime."* Underneath was *"Sem* Weiger, *Owner"* all but obscured with mud. Hisbil began to pound on the door. He knocked again—even louder. A few sems walking nearby looked up but quickly went about their business.

When there was no answer, Hisbil pushed down hard on the latch and opened the door. "Is anyone there? Hello?" he said loudly as he stuck his head inside. His only response was the dry creak of the door as it gave way to Hisbil's shoulder.

The small, unlit room held the remains of a small shop with a paper-strewn counter and posters of exotic places on the walls salted with the smell of mold and stale food. *No one has been here in a while* Hisbil said to himself as he remembered that Weiger, who had managed the business, had been banished almost six moons ago. And then he saw the handwritten sign:

'All flights cancelled by order of the Council—Emergency requests are to be submitted in triplicate to the Minister of Travel. No exceptions.'

I have no time to fill out forms. As Alred has told me on many occasions, it's easier to get forgiveness than permission.

Hisbil managed to push open the rear door with his shoulder. To his surprise (and theirs), he found a couple of rather large, unkempt crows pecking at the final remains of a uman's poppy-seed muffin.

"Hello, birds," Hisbil said as the birds looked up a bit startled, but they did not try to fly away. He recognized the crows. Weiger had paid Gollsaer a handsome fee for them; in happier days it kept Hisbil's family fed and in good graces with the village for some time.

"Hello, young ontwaker," the larger of the two crows cawed, tipping his neck as a salute. "And what can we do for you?" His speech was a bit hard to understand as was common for awakened creatures, but Hisbil was accustomed to these strange animal dialects.

"Do you have some work for us?" the smaller crow mumbled with his mouth half-filled with a chunk of muffin. "It's been awhile since we've done anything but ferry the boss to..."

"Yim," the large crow interrupted, throwing an evil look at the smaller crow and stepping in front of him and flapping his wings. "You were saying, ontwaker?"

"I...Nesem Casandra needs you to help her find her daughter, Kassie," Hisbil explained as he quickly walked up to the bigger of the two crows who seemed to be in charge.

"Yes. I need you to fly Nesem Casandra wherever she needs to go. You need to get me back over there *quickly*."

"Did you get the boss to say it's okay?" Yim, the smaller crow asked.

"Keep your beak buttoned, Yim," the larger crow chided. "This is Hisbil, son of Gollsaer. You're lucky he doesn't turn you into a squirrel or something more evil." Turning to Hisbil, "You'll have to excuse Yim— he gets rude when he's bored."

"That's fine. What do they caw you?" Hisbil asked trying to use the crow dialect.

"I go by Yeremy, young sem. And my young cohort here is Yimminy. I just call him "Yim" for short. Where do you need me to take the passenger?" Yeremy said, hopping a bit as he stretched his wings in a less than subtle attempt to keep Yim from speaking.

"I don't know for sure—somewhere off to the northeast. She should be able to guide you. We need to get over to Nesem Casandra's house as quickly as we can."

"Oh, over toward the castle?" Yim said almost to himself. "Cawww, you get to do all of the fun stuff," Yim pouted as he turned back toward the muffin carcass.

"We might have work for you later, Yim,"

Finding the crow tack nearby, Hisbil saddled and mounted Yeremy, albeit with a bit of difficulty. He had done this a few times before, but always under his father's watchful eye. After some adjustments, he lay almost flat on the bird's back, holding onto the harness and hooking his feet in the woven-rope stirrups.

"You ready?" Yeremy cawed, looking over his shoulder.

"As ready as I'll ever be," Hisbil said. He never liked flying, so he closed his eyes and gripped the harness until his knuckles turned white. The crow took a hop or two and was airborne with several flaps of his wings. He soared south into the wind, up over the village, and then back toward the blackberry wall. Before Hisbil could open his eyes, the crow had arrived in the front yard of Casandra's house. She was there still packing supplies into her rucksack.

"Good. That didn't take long," Casandra said, looking up at the rather large, black bird now pacing in anticipation in front of her house. "The civil serpent that took over Crow Air has always been such a pain about paperwork. I'm surprised you were able to find anyone in the old office."

"Uh, sure, I'm glad I could help," Hisbil said, not wanting to tell Casandra that he had cut through a lot of red tape and an uncomfortable conversation by ignoring the Council order. As he stepped away from the prancing crow, Yeremy gave him a wink—but did not say anything.

"This is Yeremy. He's at your disposal. Are you *sure* I shouldn't go along? There was another crow there. I could..."

"You can hand me Japheth's sword. And no, you had best get home. I'll be fine. I'll start by heading northeast. Hopefully, the uman's not far, and easy to spot from the air."

"Are you sure?" Hisbil said again as he handed Casandra the short sword and scabbard.

"Don't worry, I'll find Kassie and bring her home. If I need help, I'll send the crow back with instructions." Casandra buckled Japheth's short sword in place under her cloak.

"And Hisbil, you did the right thing. I'll find her. And yes, you still need to talk to Alred," she said, looking through her eyebrows as she made her final preparations.

Yeremy was strangely silent through all of these preparations and did not seem anxious to leave, but Casandra knew it was time to go as the sky was dissolving into a deep blue in the east and crimson in the west.

"Let's go!" Casandra said firmly. The bird took a few short leaps and flapped hard to climb over the blackberry maze—he barely cleared the top thorny branches.

As he watched them fly out of sight into the forest, Hisbil thought, *I still have one more important stop to make.* He hadn't noticed that they were headed off to the southeast.

Emperor at the Shutz Norte bar

Seven—The Exile

*W*eiger stood and pulled down his wide-brimmed hat to better hide the top of his face. He tucked his slingshot into his belt— it was his only defense against the beasties that would have him for breakfast, lunch, or dinner. Dusting himself off, he continued following a faint trail several days walk north and west of Stone Valley. As Seldith go, Weiger was in his late twenties, ruggedly lean and handsome, although several days of grime and unkempt fur obscured his usually neat appearance. He wore a dark calf-length coat over long, coarsely woven fabric trousers now frayed and smudged with mud and detritus.

As he picked his way through the undergrowth, memories of how he got into this mean state kept him from focusing on his surroundings. Weiger, like so many others, had become a victim of the "new" Council of Truth who banished and forcibly expelled those who would not accept *their* interpretation of *The Truth*. But it might have been something else. Perhaps he had gotten too close to discovering what had happened to his first love Herangelica or some other closely guarded secret— like what was going on deep in the caves.

The last straw came when Weiger suggested that the honorable Council ministers might reduce their copious girth and profits by sharing their own abundance with some of the wandering waifs and homeless that came to the village seeking food, safety, shelter and employment.

At that final insult, charges were woven out of thin air and Weiger soon found himself on trial. When the blitz trial was over, sentence was pronounced and Councilman Neychen's allies nodded their heads like so many marionettes. They stood by grinning as Weiger was strapped into the branding chair.

Well before dawn, Weiger had a hot iron pressed against his forehead that permanently marked him as an exile with a capital "E". As he was being forcibly ejected from Stone Valley, Weiger was 'encouraged' by more than one of the Council of Truth to live with "his own kind". With the iron still glowing and his back striped with welts, he was forced to use the narrow exile's path up the steep cavern wall that led from the underground Council chambers and into lifelong exile with only the clothes on his back. Weiger vowed to never forget that day or His *Honor* Neychen.

Weiger spent the first fortnight of his exile simply trying to survive on his own in the wild and trying to find another Seldith community that would take him in. Everyone knew he could not live for long on his own but the scar on his forehead told others that he could not be trusted. As a result he could not get accepted by the *civilized* encampments. His final alternative was Shutz Norte, a seedy encampment less than two days' walk from Stone Valley.

This dreary jumble of tattered leaf shacks and sagging moss tents overgrown with mold and lichen was home for many other branded exiles. While Weiger was not welcome in Shutz Norte with open arms, he was at least tolerated and able to find shelter and a degree of safety. He had learned from past visits that the predators inside the rough encampment were more treacherous and dangerous than those out in the forest.

About midday Weiger dragged himself into the outskirts of the settlement—tired, thirsty and starving. As he pushed open the swinging doors of the Shutz Norte Hotel, his stomach tightened. He dreaded this dive, but it was the only place in around to get a relatively safe-to-eat meal. After two days living off of berries and mushrooms, he was ready to eat almost anything. It wasn't much of a 'hotel'. The once stick-and-leaf shack had evolved into a gritty bar, a brothel and hangout where one might encounter the entire population of Shutz Norte if you stuck around long enough. Sure, it had rooms where you could sleep, but when you're as tall as a pinecone, bedbugs can be a serious issue—and as often as not, on the menu.

"Get over here, Weiger," a growling voice beckoned from a dark corner as Weiger's silhouette blocked out the midafternoon sun. Weiger ignored the voice and made a bee-line toward the crude wooden bar pushing past a large, unkempt sem that smelled of sweat unsuccessfully masked with cheap dandelion cologne. He stepped over the body of a derelict that had spent his last pouch trying to beat the odds at a game of Gatenenhuizen. Another noisy round was playing out behind him as the next victim tried to beat the house at its own game.

"Black Thunder," Weiger croaked to the stocky sem with his broad back turned to him at the other end of the crude bar. Weiger propped his frame on the boards until the bartender returned with a filthy tankard half-full of purple liquid.

"Thanks, Larry," he said reaching for the mug, "you still chargin' extra for a clean mug?" Larry did not take his dirty, weather-beaten hand off the top. Weiger nodded, reached into an inside pocket, and dropped a thumb-sized packet on the bar amidst the puddles left from other customers long since gone. The bartender snatched it up before it had settled into the wet ooze, and stuck his stubby pinky finger inside. He extracted a few grains of the white substance and gingerly touched it to his tongue.

"It's pure," Weiger said, his voice still rattling like a wood rasp drawn against dry oak.

Larry nodded. "Ya gotta be careful dees days. Just yestiday, some crud tried ta pawn off a packet of sea-sand—hardly any salt at all. He turned out to be a filthy faerie. We tore off his wings and tossed what was left in the mine hole."

"Well, that's just salt, pure salt," Weiger said after taking a long pull on the contents of the mug. "That should be good for some food and a couple more drinks—and none of that bug meat you pass off as bear-caught salmon." He realized that even the low-life maggots here in Shutz Norte had their limits. *Faeries. Now there's a hated breed.*

"Sorry 'bout dat. Times ah tough evreweh," Larry said as he pushed the packet of salt into his pocket. "Hey, Emperor wants da see youse." He cocked his head toward the dark corner of the room where a small gaggle of unkempt sems were huddled around a table littered with half-full mugs, wooden plates and the shredded remains of their meal.

Weiger didn't look past his own mug. "I'm not in the mood for any new friends." A moment later, a bony finger tapped a bruise on his right shoulder.

"He wants you should speak wid 'im—*now!*" the gnarly voice said. The large, brutish sem continued his insistent tapping. This smelly lump of flesh didn't smell any better than the sem he had pushed aside coming in the door. No, wait—it was the same clod.

Weiger still didn't turn around but got a firm grip on his mug and whirled around, aiming the mug at the creature's protruding jaw. His swing was stopped mid swing by a cast-iron arm attached to a crushing hand. Weiger's assailant was about to part his skull with Weiger's own mug when a smoother, but none-theless firm, voice snapped out of the darkness. It froze his assailant's arm in place, the mug dripping purple liquor on the floor.

"Hey *cretin*! Just ask the gentleman nicely. Can you do that simple thing, you great oaf?" The beast's handler slowly walked across the room and into the light. Weiger's rescuer pulled down the brim of his hat to shade his eyes from the light until he stood with his back to the door.

"I apologize for the crudeness of my little messenger. I don't think we have formally met; permit me to introduce myself. They call me..."

"I know who you are, Emperor. That's why I ignored you when I came in. I don't want any of your kind of trouble." Weiger had heard of Emperor. He basically ran the settlement—his way. This stocky sem was noticeably shorter than his minions, but seemed far smarter, more refined, and far more dangerous. In contrast to the toadies that seemed to orbit around him like so many black flies, he was clean, well dressed, and decorated with the spoils of his conquests: rings and gold braided neck cords and the finest woven cloth for his garments. Littered around the room, a small cadre of armed thugs and an untold number of allies were never far away. He certainly seemed out of place in this bar, like a polished steel dagger among crude clubs and stone axes. Weiger knew that Emperor, who was rarely seen in public, was a deadly shark in these waters.

"Tut, tut, my good sem—let us not be too hasty and get off on the wrong foot," Emperor pushed his henchman away, directing him back to the dark corner as if he was a puppy that had just piddled on the floor. The oaf shuffled to his corner but looked over his shoulder as he retreated, giving Weiger an uneasy feeling as if they still had a score to settle.

"You had better make this worth my while, Emperor."

"Ah, certainly, certainly. There, let me purchase you another refreshment and perhaps a good repast. You look like you're a bit bedraggled from your adventures out among the forest creatures." Emperor nodded to Larry who shuffled off behind the bar to a little window in the wall.

"Make up a special," Larry half-shouted through the hole, "…and make it snappy!" He turned back to the bar. "It'll be jus' a minute, Yur Wrshup."

"Bring it to my table when it's done. Come, come sit with me, my friend. I know you'll be more comfortable."

"No, I don't think so. If you want to talk to me, it'll be here, well away from your warty toadies."

Emperor was halfway across the room when assailed by this latest insolent rebuff of his hospitality. He paused but remained in the shadows. "Perhaps you can meet me halfway. Would that be too much of an imposition?" His voice was more strained, but no less slimy.

Weiger realized he could only push the Emperor so far. "Sure," he said as he pulled up a chair at a table half-way between the bar and Emperor's 'throne'. He swept off the table with his sleeve, and sat down as Emperor pulled up another chair, staying in the shadows. Weiger looked up to see his henchmen moving to join Emperor from across the room. Seeing the expression on Weiger's face, Emperor raised his hand, and the underlings shuffled and scuttled back to their corners like so many roaches.

"So, how is it that you know me?" Weiger asked.

"I have contacts, many contacts. Even some fairly close associates in Stone Valley. They said you might be especially useful in my endeavor so they sent you my way."

"You got me banished from Stone Valley—and *branded?*" Weiger said, putting his hands on the arms of the chair and beginning to stand.

"No, no. Of *course* not. That was not my doing. Those sems on the Council are rather overzealous. I regret that they felt compelled to treat you in that shabby manner." Emperor put his hand on Weiger's arm and encouraged him to sit back down. "They were only to *suggest* that you to venture out on your own..."

"So what brings you out of your cave...," Weiger interrupted, *you mole-faced pile of filth?*

"Well, I have a proposition for you. Have you heard of the stolen volumes of *The Books of Truth*?" Emperor began in a whisper. *"The Sacred Seven?"*

"Most sems above the age of six hear about *The Sacred Seven* in school. But I'll bet a cake of salt they're a myth cooked up by the elders. Aren't they supposed to contain all of the really evil spells and dirty laundry?"

"Oh, no," Emperor retorted, "...they are very real, and very close. And, yes, they are rumored to contain certain impure, but interesting and useful, elements. Perhaps even a tidbit or two that would embarrass the Council."

"They're here in Shutz Norte?" Weiger said with some interest.

"Hardly. I have information that makes me think that they could possibly be in the uman village to the east or very near there."

"So, why don't you send your henchmen to go get them?" Weiger taunted. "Why don't you go yourself?"

"As you can see, my bodyguards and associates do not have sufficient intellectual capacity to dress and bathe themselves, much less be entrusted with the challenging task of fetching a priceless treasure."

"And you think you can trust me...and why *me* and not some other newcomer?"

"You know the area to the east very well. Your crow flights have taken you over the uman town many times. And…"

"And?" Weiger asked.

"And I have something you want more than treasure…," Emperor offered.

"What's that? Neychen's eyes in a sack?"

"Hardly. I offer *Redemption*."

"You can undo an exile? Now, that's hard to believe," Weiger said, rubbing his forehead.

"This is entirely within my power. I work with many of the members of the esteemed Council of Truth in Stone Valley and some of their wives and… quite frequently I might add."

"So all I have to do is get you these sacred heirlooms, a veritable treasure, and I get to return to a village that threw me out to fend off the predators. Not much of a deal."

"Of course, I can offer you far more than restoration to your former status; I'm prepared to give you twenty-five measures of salt—pure salt—and a like amount of sugar to *sweeten* the deal."

Immediately, Weiger's imagination began to venture into the world that this much wealth would bring. As he dreamt of living in palatial luxury surrounded by unlimited food and his own underlings and a life of leisure, the bartender laid a meal in front of him, the likes of which he had never seen before. Every delicacy he could ever imagine was sitting on the plate heaped to overflowing.

"Emperor, you *really* know how to tempt a sem."

"This is *nothing*, nothing, my friend—a mere pittance. With that much salt and sugar, you could create and run your own refuge."

"It's…it's *very* tempting," Weiger said, still staring at the food. He had picked up a piece of poached salmon, but his hand shook as he stared at Emperor's empty, expressionless eyes.

"Eat. Eat! Enjoy yourself. The feast is on me—whether or not you accept my offer."

Weiger didn't hesitate a second. He spent the next half-hour inhaling plate after plate of food and several tankards of spirits while Emperor explained how and where he would find the seven missing volumes of the *Books of Truth,* and what he should do with them once they were secured.

Before the blackberry wine and ale had taken their toll on his already clouding mind, Weiger realized that he had struck gold. Once he had *The Sacred Seven* in his possession, he could renegotiate any deal he made with Emperor and perhaps even buy his way back from exile and hire an army to help find Herangelica. And then he heard it, or he thought he did. His head snapped around toward a voice that came out of the shadows from the other side of the bar. Did some yesem say his name? He did not hear it again, but he did see one of the working yesems being taken away. He did not get a good look at her.

"Do you need some warm comfort? That can be arranged," Emperor said with a leer.

"Who was that? The one they were taking into the back?"

"Oh, just a new yesem that was misbehaving. More ale?"

Weiger nodded and struggled to concentrate. Yea, he thought. Right, they're going to welcome me with open arms—right up until the time they see my banishment brand. Then again, with the kind of power I could wield with the sacred books of secrets, I could set up my own settlement, far away from these cretins and bigots. As he emptied another tankard of ale, his mind reeled with the revenge he could inflict on those who had branded him and thrown him to the wolves.

But then something deep inside reminded him that before his exile, he was a decent law-abiding, tax-paying Seldith. He was respected and honest and had devoted his life to helping others. But the Council had stolen all of that. Bringing down the Council would indeed be satisfying retribution.

When he could hold no more, Weiger pushed the nearly empty plates away, leaned back in his chair, and realized he was in no position to say no. "Churrr," he slurred. "I'll go gettem, old pal." Suddenly, his head did not seem to want to stay on his shoulders, and he fell backwards onto the floor with a great thud.

৵৵৵

Weiger woke up a night and a day later. He was not sure where he was, but as his mind came back into focus, he found himself far away from Shutz Norte alongside the road leading to the uman village to the northeast. He had no idea how he ended up there but he was just as hungry and thirsty as the moment he walked into Shutz Norte. To make matters worse, besides the fact he could feel every bone in his body, he was not sure his head was correctly attached to his neck.

Now what have I stepped into?

Eight—The Obligation

*T*he unusually warm afternoon was all but spent. In Stone Valley, the Seldith still lingering in the village shops prepared to tuck away their stalls and shutter their windows. Small carts laden with unsold goods were pushed along the trodden path that formed the perimeter of the broad grassy commons. Others swept up odd bits of trash or collected stray children to be washed, fed, and bedded, while others finished up their latest idle gossip about a story they had read in the *FOX*.

Hisbil tried to move quickly through this clutter into the north part of the settlement where Alred had chosen to build his home—he never understood why a respected member of the Council would choose to live on the north side, his side, of the village. While some recognized Hisbil with a nod or a brief greeting as he quickly passed by, Hisbil kept his eyes down, making no effort to be polite. He was on a mission.

Before long, Hisbil reached Alred's cottage, which was in sight across the commons from his own home. As to be expected, Alred's home showed no light from within. Hisbil knocked quietly on the door and heard movement from within. After considerable shuffling and clinking of metal on wood, Alred appeared at the door—opening it only a crack as if he was expecting someone unsavory or another unwelcome visit from one of the Council ministers.

"Hisbil? What brings you, young sem? It's getting late… Oh, yes…come in," he said, opening the door just wide enough to admit Hisbil as if he just remembered that he was expecting him. Alred closed the door behind Hisbil, latched it, and lit the stubby candle.

"Your Honor…," Hisbil began at once. "I need to talk with you…about something serious." Hisbil's voice was impatient but firm.

"I expect you do. Did you find your father's body?" Alred said as he settled into a chair at the round table in the center of the tiny room.

"What makes you think he was *killed?*" Hisbil said, steadying himself on the table.

"You've been out looking for him and you've apparently found something. You're wearing his sword, your boots are muddy and unless I'm mistaken, that's his wand sticking out of the top of his rucksack. He would not have given those up without a fight," Alred said, offering Hisbil a chair. "Put those things down by the door."

"Yes. I…Kassie and I found these in the forest several hours' walk from here." His voice shook a bit as he again pondered Kassie's peril. He was not sure if he should reveal her fate—not until he found out what Kassie meant about his father.

Alred busily puttered with the stove—stoking the fire and adding another small, split log and starting tea. "I'm not surprised. So Kassie led you to them? Apparently, she's ready to be graduated to nesem." Turning back to Hisbil, he asked sternly, "So, what is this *serious* matter?"

"My father. Kassie all but said that I did not need to take up his herditas."

"Would you care for some tea, Hisbil, or perhaps something stronger? You're old enough now and I expect you could use a bit of stiffening," the elder said with a little wink, apparently ignoring Hisbil's question. He reached up on a cupboard shelf and poured a slug of dark liquid into his mug.

"No...no, I'm fine. Please, I just need to know more about my family—about my father," Hisbil said as he approached the edge of his courage.

"Your father?" Alred said in a calm voice.

"Yes, my father—and his father before him."

"Heroes...all heroes," the old sem's voice trailed off as he took a long sip from his mug and set it down on the table. His wise, tired eyes met Hisbil's as he pulled up a chair across from him.

Hisbil gulped and asked again. "Why would Kassie...Kassie say that I didn't *have* to take up Gollsaer's herditas?"

Alred said nothing at first but took another long sip from his mug. "Yes, I think you're old enough to understand and accept the truth," he said after a thoughtful pause. "Long before you were born, the Owl Wrangler herditas was fulfilled by Sem Hissamuel who took on the obligation from *his* father as his father had done before him. Some time after Hissamuel had begun awakening owls, he married your mother Rachele, but not long afterwards, Hissamuel was mortally injured. Over many days, Rachele tried many times to heal his terrible wounds. As she embraced him, her empathy drew the injury out of his body and into her own—even when it caused her great pain and spiraled her deep into the darkness, closer and closer to the edge of death. She would have died in his arms if her friends had not pulled them apart before it was too late. Hissamuel succumbed to his wounds the next afternoon—your mother was never really the same.

Unfortunately, Rachele had borne no children to take up Hissamuel's family obligation or hers. It was a dark time, and the village desperately needed someone to accept the Owl Wrangler herditas. Making matters worse, Lord Lensmacher had begun bearing down on the Council to deliver more owls. Thankfully, just before Hissamuel died, he passed the awakening spell to me in a sealed envelope so it would not be lost forever."

"So you don't know the spell?" Hisbil asked.

"No. I didn't *want* to know it. I have learned as many spells as I will ever need. And the price I have to pay…"

"What you don't know can't kill you…," Hisbil said sarcastically, but wondered, as he had before, about Alred's herditas. *What kind of spells does he know?*

"Yes, Hisbil, I expect you're right. But to go on…at the time, Gollsaer was a skilled carpenter but yearned for something more *worthy* that would get him out of the confines of the village, so he welcomed the appointment as Owl Wrangler. He formally took on the herditas in perpetuity, and I gave him the envelope containing the awakening spell and instructions on how to use it.

"Never having practiced the task under an experienced Owl Wrangler, it did not go well at first, and he ended up at Rachele's doorstep after almost every hunt. This put your mother and Gollsaer together after nearly every hunt, even though it was very hard on her in so many ways. Over time, they grew very fond of one another and before long, Gollsaer accepted Rachele as his wife. Soon after that, she gave birth to you."

Hisbil was stunned and sat looking at the old sem in disbelief. His stomach began to tighten.

Alred did not speak for a long time—his gaze fixed on the young sem's eyes.

"So, does that mean I'm *not* obligated to be the Owl Wrangler?" Hisbil said at last. "My father did not *inherit* the skill or the spell from his father?"

"It was Gollsaer's *choice*," Alred said sternly.

"But why would Kassie say it was *not* my obligation? What does she know that you're not telling me?"

"Like her mother, she is a gifted seeker but perhaps spoke out of turn," Alred said.

"She didn't tell me anything, not really. She just implied I was *not* obligated and should ask you...or my mother. Please, just tell me the truth. Am I obligated?"

Alred said nothing for a long time, but finally, "No...you're *not* obligated," he said slowly and almost in a whisper. "If you were born a few moons later, it would have been different—you would have inherited your father's herditas by blood, and you would have no choice but banishment if you did not accept it."

"What are you saying? What does a few moons have to do with this?"

Alred paused again, looking into Hisbil's eyes now red with betrayal and confusion. "It's not certain that Gollsaer was your birth father. Hissamuel disappeared four new moons before Gollsaer took over the Owl Wrangler obligation. Some time after the Council declared Hissamuel dead, Gollsaer married Rachele. It seems that your mother was already carrying you at the time—before she even began to help heal your father."

"Gollsaer, my father...was *not* my father?" Hisbil's mind started to tumble again. His whole world was being dumped out on the floor in shards like fall leaves scattering into the wind. The words *Gollsaer was not my father*, echoed in Hisbil's mind again and again—this revelation of the truth scorched every memory of his father like a wildfire racing through the forest. "So Hissamuel is my father?"

"No, I suspect not." Alred said and hesitated, looking into the fire. "...at least, no one seems to think so. Your mother has never said one way or another. It's the reason she has been shunned by some of the more narrow-minded in the village."

Why wouldn't mother tell anyone my father's name? He put his hands over his face to hide his anger and confusion. At once, he stood up. "So, I'm *not* obligated. I don't have to take on the herditas, the obligation that will get me killed, or worse, before I'm eighteen."

"Yes, of course. Most Seldith have a herditas that we're destined to fulfill, but yours is clouded. Your father made a conscious choice to accept this obligation for himself and his progeny. While it was his wish that you take on this herditas, you are not formally required to do so. This *is* written in *The Books of Truth.*"

Alred turned and pulled down a large book from the shelf above his bed. It was as thick as his arm and bound in red leather like the ones he had seen in the Temple of Truth. "Look here," he said as he opened the book to a page marked with a colored ribbon. "It says: '...unless a child's father is pronounced by its father *and* mother, the herditas need not be bound to the child.' Your mother never told anyone the name of your father. Most villagers think it's because she does not want to lose her only son to the herditas that killed her first husband."

"Is that one of the *Books of Truth*?" Hisbil asked in disbelief, trying to take in this revelation. He then realized that Alred had been researching this point of law for good reason.

"No," Alred said looking down. "It's just a copy we use for ...for reference work," he muttered as he put the book back on the shelf—quickly kissing the binding before he slid it carefully back on the shelf.

"So Kassie is right—I can find another calling!" Hisbil said in a voice louder than he had intended. They both listened for a moment—to see if they had attracted unwanted attention.

Alred did not answer immediately but finally he said in a near whisper but firmly so that Hisbil knew he was serious, "Yes, you're of the age where you need to make the same choice your father made. If you choose to formally accept your father's obligation, it means that your offspring will have no choice. It means your acceptance becomes their lifelong obligation—in perpetuity. That too is written in *The Books of Truth*.

"And understand this: the village is just as desperate for someone to take over the obligation *now* as it was when your father accepted the herditas before you were born. If you don't take it on, the clan won't have someone else fit to take on the task. Of those we would consider, you would be the Council's first choice. You've apprenticed under one of the best Owl Wranglers that ever survived, even though he was not born to the task or trained as an apprentice as you have been. He was highly respected and very brave to take on the herditas."

"But I don't *have* to do it. I don't *have* to take on this herditas," Hisbil said with a defiant tone. "I can live a *normal* life and find another calling. Isn't that right?"

"Yes. I'm afraid so," Alred said, his chin dropping.

"Thank you," Hisbil said as he stood and moved toward the door.

"Please think about this carefully," Alred said as he joined Hisbil at the door.

"That's all I can promise," Hisbil said, feeling for the latch on the crossbar.

"And you need to tell Kassie and her mother to come by. I think we need to have a talk about secrets," Alred said sternly as he moved back to pour himself another mug of tea.

"Kassie's gone," Hisbil said looking at his boots.

"Gone?" Alred said, turning around, nearly tipping over the teakettle.

"Yes, I think she was taken by a uman," Hisbil said, looking into Alred's eyes.

"When did this happen?" Alred demanded as he quickly crossed the room. "What has been done to find her? Have you told her mother? Why didn't you say something earlier? Speak up, yesem, speak up!" Alred said, nearly shouting—his questions came down on Hisbil like a summer hailstorm.

"It was…just before sunset. Nesem Casandra has gone looking for her on a crow, and she seemed confident that she could find her," Hisbil said as he backed away from Alred, his back now against the door. "I didn't know what else to do. I didn't think you would tell me about my herditas obligation if I told you before."

"So is she going to send back the crow if she needs help?"

"Yes, that's her plan. Should we go out and help look for her? There's another crow in the paddock," Hisbil offered.

"No, that would just make matters worse. We need to stay here in the village and prepare to leave at a moment's notice if the crow returns; or at first light, if he does not return, we can follow Casandra's trail. Meet me back here before dawn and we'll plan the search."

"I will. I need to get home and tell my mother what I've found."

"Yes, yes. Get home and try to comfort her. But remember, she has been through a lot—far more than you have—so don't tell her about Kassie. Just…just tell her that I will come by tomorrow morning…," Alred's voice trailed off. "Go. Go on," Alred said as he doused the light.

Hisbil pulled up the iron bar that blocked the door, slipped through the opening, and pulled the heavy door closed. He could hear Alred bar the door behind him. The cold evening air helped clear his mind as he crossed the commons to his home.

Gollsaer is not your father… Alred's words echoed again against the walls of his consciousness. He stood outside his own door for a long time thinking about the sacrifice Gollsaer had made—and how he had accepted him as his own son. *"Who is my father?"* Thinking back, he realized that he never once felt unloved or unwanted and that Gollsaer had treated him no differently than his natural daughter, Anasta. He *was* Gollsaer's son. He would want him to take on the herditas. He would want him to be the Owl Wrangler.

Knowing the door would be barred at this time of day, he quietly knocked four times on the door, thoughtlessly tapping the same rhythm his father had so often used. Almost immediately, he heard muffled footsteps quickly approaching the door. In another moment, the door latch clicked and the door opened.

His mother greeted him with a smile that faded slightly when she saw it was not Gollsaer. "I heard you went out with Kassie looking for your father," his mother said, walking back to relight the candle. Hisbil threw an evil scowl at his sister who had not kept her promise. "I…I would have asked Casandra myself, but…I was afraid of what she might find. Not knowing seemed better than learning Gollsaer had deserted us or… Did you find him?" Rachele said looking into Hisbil's eyes.

Hisbil ducked slightly as he crossed the threshold and closed and bolted the door behind him. Her face could not lie; it told Hisbil that she had been crying again. Her deep-brown eyes were red and swollen, and her face was streaked by wet tracks that darkened the soft, graying fur on her face.

"No…," Hisbil said, looking down at his mother as he put his father's rucksack on his bed next to the door. He drew out his father's wand and his *amiculum obscurum*, his cloak of invisibility, from the rucksack. He unfolded the cloak reverently, which he draped over his arms like the limp corpse of a fallen warrior. "But I did find these."

His mother looked up as Anasta crossed the room and stood next to her mother without making a sound. Neither of them could take her eyes off the outer cloak that hid Gollsaer from the terrors outside the thorn wall.

"It's your father's," Rachele said weakly as her knees finally failed to hold her weight—she collapsed into the cushioned chair at her knee. Her face disappeared into her own embrace as she tried to hide her tears and muffle her sobs. The day she had dreaded, the moment they *all* dreaded, had finally arrived.

Hisbil and Anasta stood motionless at first, feeling powerless to help her, but they tried. Hisbil dropped to one knee by her side and put his arm around his mother's shoulders, his face cast in gray iron. This was not the time to talk to his mother about the past or about the herditas. It was a time to be strong. All at once, he realized that he was now the sole protector of the family—at first, his back bent as if a great weight was placed across his shoulders, but as he fully realized his new role, his backbone was now tempered, like steel, with resolve. Anasta turned to the stove and poured hot water into a short mug. She crushed a few brown leaves from a canister on the shelf, dropped them into the mug, and offered it to her mother. Rachele didn't look up.

"Mother?" Hisbil began. "It will be all right. I know how to hunt. I can take..." He did not believe the words that had just left his lips. *I don't want to do this—I don't,* he screamed silently to himself.

"No!" his mother almost shouted as she suddenly looked up into his eyes and grabbed his arms. "You're too young to take on the herditas. You can't. I—I can't lose you too. I've already lost two... You can't take Gollsaer's...your father's place!" Rachele cried as she covered her face again in her arms, her soft blue tunic now stained with her grief.

"I know," Hisbil said. "No one can take his place. I can't even pretend to. But…," Hisbil said with even more determination and authority in his voice, Hisbil could hear Alred say, *Someone must take on the herditas. There is no one else.*

Hisbil stood up slowly, looking at his sister, Anasta, still standing by the chair with the cup of tea. Hisbil could see fear and uncertainty in her eyes clouded with tears and staring at him like a deer frozen in the flash of a sudden lightning storm.

Hisbil's mind swirled as he wondered what would become of them. How could they live? Would they be exiled or evicted because they could not pay their Council taxes? A hundred unanswerable questions raced in circles around his mind—each one made him less certain of his own future. Up to this day, he had convinced himself and his family that his father would return. Each time there was a knock on the door, they expected to see him come across the threshold wearing a grin, carrying a sack of owl down and some toy he had carved for them on his hunt.

At once, Anasta broke down. "What's to become of us? Will the elders exile us? You *have* to hunt! You *have* to take on the herditas!" she said in a frantic whisper. "How can we *eat* if you don't hunt—they won't give us our share of the food if you don't!" Her voice grew louder and louder as her emotions overcame her reason. "Mother, he just *has* to hunt."

Hisbil hugged Anasta and pulled her to his breast, muffling her sobs. It would be hours before any of them said another word. Eventually, each of them returned to the routines they had practiced since Hisbil's and Anasta's father, and Rachele's husband, went into the darkness to hunt another owl.

"Mother," Hisbil finally said. "Alred said he would come by tomorrow morning if you need to talk to someone." Rachele did not answer at first but looked up at her son.

"You've been talking to him?" she finally answered.

"Yes, we've been talking on and off for some time."

"What do you two talk about?"

"Well about…about all kinds of things. He seems very interested in me and our family's welfare. I'm sure he'll make sure the Council does not pester us or try to collect their taxes—at least for a while."

As Hisbil prepared for bed, he wondered why Alred was being so benevolent and had taken Gollsaer's family under his wing. He would have to ask him in the morning, which Hisbil wished would come far sooner.

Nine—Hisbil Faces His Fears

*L*ate that night, Hisbil found him-self exhausted and covered in a cold sweat standing alone at the edge of an all too familiar meadow. On the other side of the gently undulating grass, a large white owl stood astride its latest victim picking meat out of the nearly dead carcass as its prey desperately tried to fight off his attacker. Using its beak and three-inch talons, the bird deftly rendered the flesh away from the prey's fine fur—tossing aside bones and other inedible parts.

It's... it's one of our clan! Hisbil screamed to himself.

On the far side of the meadow, he could see his father's rucksack still resting against the trunk of a tree just where he found it.

"Father!" he screamed. The owl looked up, but quickly went back to work filleting his supper.

"It's not me...," a voice behind him said quietly. Hisbil wheeled around but saw nothing. He turned back to the owl and it was gone, and so was the meadow. In its place, he found himself standing nearly naked on a cold stone floor in a room with walls so tall he could barely see the roof. Near the far end of the immense room, a uman sat at a table as long as the village commons.

A moment later he was snatched up by a giant hand and thrown down on the table, tumbling down near a great dinner plate of what appeared to be grilled mice. The uman was picking his teeth with a tiny sword or was it a hatpin?

"So, you've come to join your little friend?" the giant bellowed as he shoved a large wooden box across the table toward Hisbil. As the giant turned the box, he could now see it was a cage and Kassie lay in the shadows—her hair no longer beautifully braided but matted with briars and knots. She looked up at him.

"Hisbil, you came for me. I… I feared you would…I hoped you would…," Kassie whispered just before she disappeared. Hisbil could hear her screaming in the distance.

"You can save her…and me," the soft voice said again.

"Father? Is that you?" Hisbil said, turning again only to find himself standing in a moonlit bedroom staring into the familiar shadows of his own home.

Avoiding a return to the nightmares, Hisbil felt his way across the room toward the window, resting his elbows on the sill. Staring out into the night, another thought occurred to him: *Perhaps father ran away—just left his cloak, sword, and rucksack for me to find—for me to use as the Owl Wrangler. Perhaps father could no longer face the terror of being snatched into the air by a hungry owl. Who could?* No one had said it to his face, but he could see it in their empty eyes. Some sincerely believed Gollsaer *had* abandoned the Stone Valley clan and his family. *Perhaps he did…we didn't find his body.*

A breath of cool, fresh air drifted through the room between the cracks in the tiny window. Opening the window and pushing open the wooden shutters, he looked out into the commons and up at the misty dots of starlight masked by the sweeping high clouds of a storm blowing in from the southwest. The night air carried the sweet scent of rain and the bite of winter that hung around like an unwelcome guest who does not know when to go home. A quickening wind jostled its way through the forest, pushing and pulling the treetops and gently rocking his home tree to its roots. He fondly remembered being rocked into blessed, peaceful sleep by the wind gently nudging the tree that sheltered their home—a time when his father's noisy breathing was there to comfort them all.

Anasta turned over groaning in her bed, but her breathing soon returned to a slow, steady pace. *She's having trouble sleeping too…* When the wind changed direction, a few of the dry leaves on the roof rattled a bit as they were dusted with the irregular patter of a light squall passing over the village. Thankfully, the canopy of trees over them shielded the homes from the brunt of most storms. For an instant, a blink of white light illuminated the empty commons, sharpening the moonshine shadows. A dozen counts later, a soft boom echoed off the stone cliff towering over the settlement as if a uman had closed a great iron door in a distant castle. A shiver ran up Hisbil's back as he remembered what must have been a dream about the giant's castle.

The rain increased slowly, but suddenly changed into a downpour as the storm marched in on thunderous feet. As Hisbil stared up at the clouds, another jagged bright-white line stitched across the sky—another resounding boom rattled the dishes two heartbeats later. This strike was followed by a few more over the next half hour, but closer, and then increasingly farther away as the storm unloaded its burden on the forests and farmlands to the northeast. *The northeast—where* Kassie *is being held by the giant,* Hisbil thought. *What am I doing waiting here! I need to go find her, to bring her home…*

As the moon jostled its way past the receding clouds, Hisbil felt a warm arm drape over his back and a soothing hand on his shoulder.

"Go back to bed, Hisbil. You need to rest," his mother whispered.

"I can't sleep."

"Yes, you can," she said as Hisbil's mind cleared. He looked down into her soft, brown eyes, her velvet gray fur a ghostly white as the moonlight reflected off her face. In her eyes, all he saw was sorrow. She began to cry softly as she pulled her son to her breast.

"He hasn't abandoned us," she whispered.

Hisbil realized that his mother had taken on his burden of grief and worry; it was her own herditas and curse as a healer.

As the storm played out its closing scene many leagues away, Hisbil's eyes closed as he tried to sleep once again in his father's bed, his mother watching over him from her chair.

Hisbil spent a restless night listening for a knock from Alred with news that the crow had returned or a knock from his father that he knew in his heart would never come. All he heard was the heavy feet of another storm that eventually backed away from the village and faded off to the east.

I've got to find her. Hisbil told himself over and over again. He quietly got dressed and went outside. *I've got to do something...*

Ten—Casandra's Search

*A*s Casandra stared down into the treetops clutching Yeremy's back, she tried to clear her mind of everything around her—except her daughter, Kassie. She knew Kassie was still out there somewhere, frightened and unable to reach out to anyone. *If only I had been able to get her to better understand how to use her gifts,* she thought as the crow flew into the softening dusk.

Ironically, it was far easier for Casandra to find the lost when they weren't close to her heart. When Seldith from the village came to her frantically screaming about a lost child or missing spouse, she had little difficulty visualizing their whereabouts—even if they had passed or were some considerable distance away. If the lost child or husband did not want to be found, it was a bit more difficult, but as she told her clients, "The difficult just takes a lot less time than the impossible."

"She's probably run off into the forest to be alone," Yeremy said over his shoulder.

"What?" Casandra said incredulously.

"Kassie has probably gone to one of the other settlements like River Landing. A lot of the youngsters do that nowadays. I'll take you there."

"Didn't you understand that Kassie was taken by a uman?"

"Are you sure? Wasn't she last seen running away?"

"No, Hisbil and I are certain she was snatched up by a uman, and he was heading off to the northeast—perhaps to the human village."

"I'll just take you to the River Landing settlement. It's not far—just to the southeast. I'm sure she's there."

Casandra was immediately alarmed by the crow's behavior. Clearly, Yeremy had another agenda, but she was totally at his mercy this high over the treetops. "We need to get back on the ground, Yeremy. I think the saddle is slipping. Just put down in that clearing."

"Oh, I can't do that," he cawed. "It's not safe." Yeremy continued to fly to the southeast—in the opposite direction of where Casandra sensed Kassie could be found.

It was now evident that something more drastic would have to be done to get control of the crow. While Casandra was unsure if her mind-influencing skills would work on beings other than Seldith, it was certainly worth a try.

"Yeremy, listen to me," Casandra said shaking her hair in the wind.

"Yes?" the crow cawed.

"Kassie was taken by a uman. You know Kassie was taken by a uman. You want to take me to Kassie. You…"

"Kassie?" Yeremy cawed sleepily as his wings stiffened. Almost immediately, they began to glide. But a moment later, one wing wilted and they began a wide turn to the right that grew sharper as seconds passed. Before long they were spiraling down toward the tops of the trees.

"Yeremy!" Casandra screamed, holding on for dear life. "Wake up!"

Yeremy's wingtip brushed an outstretched fir branch about eighty feet over the forest floor, and they both began to tumble uncontrollably toward the ground. It took every bit of Casandra's courage and strength to hold onto the saddle and harness that bit into Yeremy's neck as well as her bare hands. Thankfully, the shock seemed to bring Yeremy out of his stupor, and he began a wild set of maneuvers to regain control of his flight. At the last instant, he flared his wings and landed (or tumbled) unceremoniously on to the mossy forest floor—Casandra still holding on.

Well, now I know not to try to influence a bird that's carrying you 150 feet over the forest, Casandra chided herself as she untangled herself from the harness and slid off the crow.

"Yeremy? Are you hurt?" she said to the bird who was still a bit dazed. He was shaking his head as if he had a gnat in his ear and began walking in circles flapping his wings.

"Caw! What? What happened? I…I must have blacked out," Yeremy slurred. "Must have been those poppy seeds…"

Casandra was relieved to find Yeremy was still speaking to her. She was a long way from home and had only a rough idea where they were, so it was important to keep Yeremy on good terms—regardless of his agenda. "You must have." she asked. "I think we need to get back in the air if you feel up to it," Casandra said stepping closer to Yeremy, looking him in the eye and giving her hair a toss. "You know Kassie was taken by a uman and we need to find her." Without the breeze of flight blowing away the smell of honeysuckle, her attempt to influence the bird seemed to be working. As before, Yeremy's eyes rolled a bit and he went a bit limp—although still standing, his wings drooped at his sides.

"Yeremy, Hisbil, son of Gollsaer, the Seldith that awakened you has asked you to help me. You need to help me find Kassie. Yeremy, can you hear me?"

"Of course. A uman—he went off toward the castle," he cawed a bit sleepily. "I saw him. He gave me the muffin."

"The castle? Lord Lensmacher's castle?" Casandra said, still standing close enough to the bird to read his thoughts—and control them to some extent.

"Yes, he's…"

"He's what, Yeremy? Tell me," Casandra pressed, trying to get the crow to reveal the reason for trying to keep her from finding Kassie, but the crow was fighting back. Something had taken control of his mind—a force more powerful than she had ever encountered.

"I'm not supposed to tell anyone, but I can take you to the castle. I have been there many times—taken many Seldith there," he cawed.

Try as she could, Casandra could not ferret out the jumbled mess of the crow's thoughts. She saw glimpses of the crow interacting with umans, Seldith, and other birds—owls or eagles perhaps. Not being able to make any sense out of the visions, she was grateful to at least have the bird cooperating with her on the direction of flight. "Okay, I have your harness straightened out; let's go before it gets any darker," she said remounting the crow. "Let's go!" she commanded.

After several labored hops, Yeremy took off again to the southeast. Casandra was alarmed at first but realized that the crow had to take off into the wind. Yeremy soon turned and put the setting sun, now crimson and purple, behind to the left. They were indeed heading northeast.

As the blanket of night began to surround the ground beneath them, Cassandra could soon see tiny spots of light that appeared in the misty distance. It was the uman town and soon she could see it in the dusky light—an imposing stone castle complete with parapets and what appeared to be expansive gardens surrounding it on three sides standing on a sheer cliff. The top of the castle seemed to glitter in the final rays of the sunset as if the roof were made of glass.

Yeremy did not speak at all as he tirelessly winged across the forest, over the farm, and soared up a thermal to the hill, finally circling high over the castle. By the time they arrived, the sun had disappeared behind the horizon and darkness had all but obscured the castle walls.

"Down there. The window of that room about halfway up is open, and there is a light inside. Can you land on the sill?" Yeremy did not answer but tucked a wing and flew down toward the window. Before she realized what had happened, he flew through the open window and deftly landed on a bird perch on a beautifully carved teak desk—almost as if it was a second home.

Casandra's mind was suddenly flooded with images of Kassie as she realized she was looking into the face of a uman sitting at the desk examining something floating in a bottle.

"Oh, hello, Yeremy. Who is that you've brought with you this time?" he said in a calm voice.

Eleven—The Belluas

*I*t was more than an hour before dawn when Hisbil returned home. In his arms, he carried a generous load of firewood brought in from the neat stash concealed near the house. Walking quietly across the small, dimly lit room, he quietly placed the wood box at the base of the stove so as not to wake his sister. As he opened the stove door, the room was briefly flooded with a flickering yellow light.

His mother stood across the room near the window dressed in a long robe that touched the rough leaf-covered floor and partially shielded her bare feet from the lingering spring cold. In the corner, Anasta still lay sleeping, albeit restlessly, covered with a faded and oft-mended quilted comforter that had warmed many generations of Rachele's family—her foot dangled out from under the quilt. She was certainly growing. He remembered how small she used to look in her bed.

Hisbil closed the stove door and the room was dim again, lit only by a single candle placed on the round table in the center of the room. He tugged the quilt down over his sister's foot and sat at the table. A moment later, Anasta pulled up on the quilt and her foot poked out again.

"Do you have to go out again?" Rachele said, standing at the window as she pulled an edge of the curtain to ensure the candlelight didn't escape into the predawn darkness.

"Yes," he replied. "I cut and split enough wood out back for a few days in case it gets colder again."

She has enough to worry about. She doesn't need to fret about Kassie on top of everything else. I need to get packed up in case...

Hisbil pulled his father's rucksack down from a peg above his bed and stuffed it with a chunk of brown bread, dried mushrooms and a bit of greenery wrapped in rough paper. The bag already held the basic tools his father had always carried— a bandage, and a stone flint and a day or two ration of food.

Where's his rope? He always carried a length of rope to...

But Hisbil was surprised to feel something in the inner lining of the rucksack. Carefully searching for an opening, Hisbil discovered a recently sewn patch that concealed the opening to the inner pocket. Inside, he found an old envelope with a broken red-wax seal. On the outside it was addressed in a hand he did not recognize:

"For the eyes of the Owl Wrangler and no other. Hissamuel OW."

What's this? Is this the awakening spell Alred told me about? Did my father leave it here for me to find? Should I read it? After all, if the Council forces me to be the Owl Wrangler, I'll need to know at least as much as Gollsaer knew when he first took up the herditas.

"Where did you find that?" his mother whispered, snatching the envelope away from Hisbil and clutching it to her breast.

"It was in father's rucksack—sewn into the lining. I didn't read it."

"And read it, you shan't. This needs to be resealed and returned to Alred." Rachele took the envelope over to the table, and after a brief search in the mysterious box that every mother keeps, she produced a red stick used for sealing important envelopes. Heating the tip with the candle, she dripped the hot sealing wax on the envelope's flap and gave it back to Hisbil. "Return this to Alred at first light."

"Of course, Mother...I wasn't going to accept...read it," Hisbil said as he quietly continued packing, replacing the envelope into the secret pocket. His mother had not yet questioned why he was loading his father's rucksack with supplies.

Hisbil crossed the room to refill the metal flask with the dark liquid brewed from fermented blackberries and tucked it into a pouch on the side that neatly fit the flask. "Have you seen his sword?" he asked his mother as he tucked in another coil of rope woven from willow bark.

"What do you need it for?" his mother asked, still in a state after having seen the envelope.

"I expect that it needs to be sharpened and repaired. Remember, it was cracked."

As his mother turned away to fetch the sword she had tucked into a corner behind the brooms, Hisbil quickly pushed something else into his rucksack taken from under his mattress. Turning back to take the sword from his mother, Hisbil said, "Sure, I'll keep my eye out for another good piece of steel." He strapped the scabbarded sword to his waist with a broad, woven belt that was a bit too large for him.

Hisbil hated lying to his mother, but she was simply too fragile to accept even the notion that Hisbil would be going out into the wilds again—perhaps to meet the fate of both of her husbands.

An unusual noise broke the otherwise quiet morning and then the starlings exploded. Something was wrong.

"What's that?" Hisbil whispered.

They both froze—not taking a breath as they listened intently but it was impossible to hear anything over the din of the birds. Rachele pulled off her nightcap and tossed it on the bed she shared with Anasta. The look on his mother's face told Hisbil that she was doing all she could to remain still and calm.

"There…there it is again. It's something pretty big and coming this way," Hisbil whispered as he silently pinched out the candle flame.

Rachele moved away from the window and whispered, "Is it… a bellua?"

Probably. "It's probably nothing—just a stray squirrel again."

Hisbil tiptoed across the room to his sister's bed and put his hand over her mouth. Anasta's eyes bolted open, and she began to sit up—but she made no sound. Hisbil pointed to the small door behind the stove, and signaled to keep quiet. She nodded.

Wrapping the comforter around her shoulders, Anasta stood to cuddle with her mother who stood like a statue in the darkness.

In the room's back wall, a small opening had been dug under the roots for just this kind of emergency. Hopefully, it would lead to safety—or at least to a place where they were less exposed to the sharp digging claws and teeth of the bellua or whatever had been able to get inside the blackberry maze.

Perhaps it's a raccoon or just a chipmunk or squirrel Hisbil rationalized, but something told him it wasn't—not this time.

Hisbil's mother pulled on her clothes and motioned to Anasta to do likewise. Hisbil pushed his arm through one strap of the rucksack, but not before taking out one item. He knew it was too dark in the room for his mother or sister to see what he had done.

It's best that they don't know. He shoved the short stick into his cloak and pulled his *amiculum obscurum* up over his head. A second later its magic made Hisbil all but disappear.

 Hisbil was ready.

Twelve—Courage or Caution

*A*red was still awake; he had been awake most of the night listening for the return of the crow with news from Casandra and fighting off his own demons. Unlike most of the other Seldith, he also felt the soft tread and breathing of something outside and the din made by the guard birds would awaken the dead.

Like Hisbil, Alred had doused his lights and stifled his stove. He fastened on his sword belt and pulled his cloak over his head as he carefully stepped out on to the commons.

The old wizard stood with his back to the tree that sheltered his home and provided most of its protection. While there should have been ample moonlight, a layer of fog lay like a soft quilt over the village, so little moonlight crept through. This worked in the Seldith's favor; without moonlight, there would be no shadows to betray their position or movements but it also made the intruder harder to see. If the mist were to thin, Alred and anyone else caught outside might be exposed unexpectedly—especially, if they weren't wearing an *amiculum obscurum;* and Alred wasn't.

At first, Alred stood as still as his aging muscles would allow, but he soon began to creep around the base of the tree until he caught a brief glimpse of the intruder. A grim frown came over his face once he saw that the creature was a large, unpredictable foe and big enough to be deadly—many times over. It was easily a dozen times Alred's weight and stood twice his height. Despite this advantage, he knew that he might be able to kill the beast if he were skillful and (very) lucky, but this would not be an option—not for his clan. It was against The Truth to kill.

About the time Alred had made up his mind to think a bit longer on this problem (as he had a tendency to do), he thought he saw movement again—perhaps something else even further away—beyond the east side of the commons. Alred nervously waited several long minutes before seeing the black beast again, even though he could hear it and feel it through his bare feet—it was still about fifty paces away. It seemed to be trying to find something it had lost as it unhurriedly sniffed the ground in the commons, closing the distance to Alred. Out of the corner of his eye, Alred discerned the outline of *another* bellua just as it looked up. It was staring directly at him. A chill ran up his back, and his long ears tucked back against his head as he realized how much real danger he faced. *Not one but two!*

It did not take long for Alred to decide that perhaps it would be more prudent to return to the relative safety of his escape tunnel like the others. He had faced a beast like this before—but it was long ago. *But two? Two at once?* His legs seemed to get very cold and heavy as if trudging through murky river sand. Alred's strength and courage had abandoned him—what there was left of it.

The beast continued to move in Alred's direction. It must have found the scent trail of its quarry following it back from the forest and had somehow gotten through the briar maze. As he closed the door to his escape tunnel, Alred thought *It's going after Hisbil…I've got to help him… I've got to.*

Thirteen—Escape into Uncertainty

*L*istening intently, Rachele realized that whatever was out there was getting a lot closer. "Get out through the back door," Hisbil whispered to his mother. "Follow the guide cords in the tunnel, but stay inside and well away from the door at the other end. Do it quickly and as quietly as you can." Hisbil's voice sounded like Gollsaer's when he wanted to make sure everyone knew he was serious. It had that low tone of authority—of someone who did not tolerate discussion.

Rachele turned back toward her only son and whispered, "You...you aren't coming?"

Hisbil's answer was clear—he had already slipped out of the front door, not making another sound.

"I can *help*," Anasta whispered.

"Yes, you can help. You can help by keeping yourself safe so Hisbil can deal with the beast," Rachele said, tugging Anasta's sleeve. She could tell that Anasta was acutely aware of the danger that Hisbil was walking toward while they hid, unable to help.

Anasta's eyes grew wide again, but Rachele could tell she was resisting the urge to cry as she pushed open the escape hatch and pulled herself through the narrow opening into the pitch-black tunnel.

Rachele and Anasta moved noiselessly into the tiny, damp coal-black tunnel as they had done many times before. Farther down the tunnels they could barely hear the footsteps of the others who had made the same decision to hide until the danger had passed. Everyone knew better than to light a candle or make a sound that might be heard or seen from above, or further foul the musty air.

Rachele finally stopped and rested on the crude wooden benches erected near the heavy oak door that guarded one end of their tunnel that faced out into the commons. The door was well out of reach of most beast's claws but close enough that she might be able to see out the small hole in the door and breathe a bit of fresh air that it let pass into the tunnel. The filtered moonlight provided a stiff thread of light that softly illuminated Hisbil's terrified but resolute family that sought refuge from the unknown danger outside.

"We'll wait here until Hisbil comes for us," Rachele said in a barely audible whisper. She heard no response. "Anasta?" she whispered a bit louder. Again, she heard no response.

Fourteen—First Encounter

*T*he beast was far enough away that Hisbil figured that he had enough time to gather his thoughts and come up with a plan.

What would father…Gollsaer do?

Before doing *anything* rash, Hisbil wanted to be sure of what he was facing and whether or not it was a threat. What little experience he had taught him that it's usually best to simply let a menace pass by. He remembered how the entire settlement ran to cover when a wayward cotton-tailed rabbit found itself caught behind the briar wall. It nosily thumped between the houses for an hour before Alred encouraged it to find its own way out—no one really knew how he did it, but Alred was fully spent after the ordeal.

Hisbil was not going to let this happen again; but first, he had to make sure of what they were facing. If it was a real threat, he didn't want to let it continue into the valley to maraud and terrorize the village as the elders had described so vividly on every possible occasion.

Hisbil's hastily made plan positioned him between his home and the threat. It's what father would do. If it's a bellua I need to keep it away from home or track it until it's no longer a problem. Just how am I supposed to keep it away? He asked himself. A bellua was no bunny rabbit.

Hisbil untied the hilt of his sword and made sure it was loose in the scabbard, just as he had seen his father do before a hunt.

Hisbil didn't have to wait long to find out what was moving in and out of the shadows. The animal did not move like a rabbit—it was a bit larger and moved on four long legs. He had seen these beasts before, but at a distance—never close enough to hear one breath—it smelled of stale fish while still less than four paces away.

It's a bellua for sure—a big one. Hisbil's heart began to race and the fur on the back of his neck rose accordingly.

The beast was moving slowly through the village lightly sniffing the ground, turning over leaves with its clawed paws and peering under branches as a child would look for a toy lost in its playroom.

Is it looking for us? Hisbil thought, almost talking aloud. Showing considerable stealth, the creature barely made a sound as it placed each foot carefully as if walking on fresh spring ice. It's a wonder they had heard or felt it at all.

While the guard birds had settled down, an eagle screeching high over his head reminded Hisbil that he did not *want* to be out here, that he did not *need* to be here, that this was not *his* herditas, but it was *his* family in danger.

This is how Gollsaer and Hissamuel had…died—facing beasts far larger and more deadly than anything the *Seldith* encountered huddling together, locked safely away in their escape tunnels.

Hisbil now understood, perhaps for the first time, that it was their duty, their herditas to protect others even though it risked their own lives. Only their awakening spell was powerful enough to neutralize a bellua.

This is crazy, I've never done this. What am I doing out here?

Sticking his head out from behind a sapling, Hisbil thought he saw something *else* move in the misty darkness—something smaller. *Is it another sem?* It was standing motionless—its back to a tree on the other side of the commons and almost invisible, obscured by the shadows and... *Alred. It's Alred—perhaps he can help.* But no, the dark figure moved back inside Alred's darkened home and away to safety.

Hisbil was not that surprised, as he didn't really expect anyone, not even the elderly councilman, to join him to face the threat; nowadays, it seemed that few were willing to step up and protect the village—it seemed like it was every Seldith for himself. *Perhaps the stories Alred told us of conquering great beasts were just stories. Perhaps those hiding in their escape tunnels are smarter and wiser. Then again, Gollsaer said there were old sems, and bold sems, but there were few old, bold sems.*

Hisbil accepted that most of the elders weren't that brave, but perhaps choosing their fights let them live long enough to tell their stories to the young, making them seem brave and experienced. For one reason or another, the clan elders always seemed to depend on others, all too often the young, to risk their lives for the *honor* and 'freedom' of the clan.

Before Hisbil had a chance to reconsider, it was too late. The black beast had worked his way toward Hisbil's tree, his home, and his family—he *had* to face it.

I've got to distract it for a while...

Hisbil threw a stone to other side of the commons where it skittered off a boulder. The instant that the bellua turned to investigate, Hisbil darted through the darkness to lie in an indentation where the beast should walk over him if he kept moving toward his house. Hisbil covered his body with leaves to further conceal his hiding place. *The amiculum obscurum should keep it from seeing me, at least I hope it does...unless it saw me move, I should be able to get close enough to use the wand.*

Digging into his cloak, Hisbil felt for his father's wand as he recalled the spell he had heard his father use so many times before. *Derlumen ahsben wakkan, Derlumen ahsben wakkan!*

Slowly and carefully, he felt high and low in the loose garment but found nothing but his own beating heart. He repeated the search as panic started ripping at him. *Where is it?* Hisbil screamed to himself. *It's not here... I...I must have dropped it!* Cold fear swept over him like a winter rain that washed away what little courage he had left.

It must have seen me digging for my wand! Where is it?

Peeking out from under the leaves, Hisbil could see that the beast had moved considerably closer as his trembling fingers finally touched the stick that had worked its way into the inner lining of his cloak.

Thank the stars. He sighed.

His hands wildly untangled the wand from the fabric of his cloak and once it was free, he tried to regain his composure and lay motionless and breath more slowly.

All I need to do is wait. Yea, wait—to conquer the bellua or be eaten alive. As he laid there on his back, he could still hear and feel the beast's footsteps and its breathing, as it guardedly moved step-by-step toward Hisbil's house and hiding place. The beast was following an invisible trail that seemed to lead right to his door. His only strategy was to let the beast get close enough to cast the awakening spell.

Will it work? I've never heard of the spell being used on a bellua.

Reaching across his body, Hisbil slowly pulled out his sword. *Just in case.*

In the next heartbeat, just before the beast started to cross over Hisbil, it paused. *It knows I'm here. It can smell me! Somehow...somehow I have to stop it.* Hisbil wished that it would take just one more step. His wish was granted; the beast took another tentative step forward—still fixated on Hisbil's front door.

Now! As the bellua took another step, Hisbil rose to his feet alongside the beast and pushed the wand into its chest and shouted: *"Derlumen ahsben wakkan,"* with every bit of conviction he could muster.

The sudden attack startled the animal—so much so that it launched itself straight up—as when a kitten sees a dog for the first time. But as the beast left the ground, the wand began to glow. A bright arc reached out from the wand to envelop the startled beast in a green globe of dancing light. The crack of the

Hisbil Awakens the Bellua

arc echoed off the cliff as the commons was bathed in green light as bright as day. The arc retracted into the wand with a loud pop as quickly as it had struck out. At once, Hisbil's hand and forearm tingled and then began to hurt as if he had stuck his arm into an icy stream but he stood his ground.

The startled bellua hit the ground running as it turned to escape the way it had come. It had not taken more than two strides before being jerked back and off its feet, as if tethered by the thin, green harness anchored to the ground at Hisbil's feet. It immediately began to test the limits of its confinement, straining the green tether in all directions except toward Hisbil. Once it realized that it was constrained, it began to emit a guttural growl. Its oval eyes reflected the brightening moonlight as yellow almonds that flashed with anger and fear.

Hisbil had not fully anticipated the bellua's reaction, as belluas were not his father's usual target and he's never seen one awakened. Hisbil stood his ground holding his sword in one hand and the wand in the other, still quite wary of the frightened animal that now circled around the edge of commons as if trapped in an invisible cage.

It looks like a uman's big, black housecat. Hisbil surmised as he watched the beast settle down, which now seemed more confused than frightened. As he had hoped, the animal stopped pacing, looked at Hisbil, and started to speak. While haltingly at first, and using a voice that seemed to be mostly meows, the cat began to speak.

"Who youuu rrr?" she said. "To meeeow youuu have done what?"

Hisbil was relieved. "You are in the Seldith village of Stone Valley," Hisbil explained. "My people call me Hisbil, son of Gollsaer and Rachele. I have awakened you from a curse—this has given you the ability to speak and understand the Common language. I am your *ontwaker*—your awakener." This was the speech he had heard his father give many times after an awakening. Hisbil thought it was only right to use it for his first awakening. He felt exceedingly proud of himself and wore a grin to match.

"A currrse yooou have brokennn?" the cat questioned as she twisted her head to one side and swished her tail (still several times its normal size) but her ears were no longer lying back on her head.

"Yes, a curse, an ancient curse," Hisbil explained.

"Understand I doooo not…," said the cat, apparently trying to fathom what she had been told. Thankfully, the cat was beginning to relax a bit as she grew more comfortable with her new state of mind.

"Call youuu *ontwaker* I should?" queried the cat, apparently satisfied with this brief explanation. "Miiiink they call me. In the human viiiillage I live. In a nice house with a waaaarm fireplace."

"Yes, Mink, Hisbil or ontwaker is fine. I've heard stories about housecats. You're an interesting species." Hisbil replied. *And a dangerous, unpredictable one too.* Hisbil thought, recalling the lessons read to his class from *The Books of Truth.*

"Hisbil!" a voice behind him shouted, "…behind you!"

Fifteen—Another Beast

The voice had come from Anasta. She had crept out past her mother to investigate—unable to resist her intense desire to help. Hiding at the edge of the commons, she watched in amazement as her brother awakened and gained control over this terrifying bellua. In the darkness, she had seen another beast sneaking up on Hisbil from behind and had screamed a warning.

Before Anasta alerted Hisbil, the second beast had not seen Hisbil's sister. It was still focused intently on her brother, and only a few paces away. Anasta's wish had been granted. She had helped her brother, but in the process, she gave away her presence and put herself in danger as the second bellua now fixed its focus on her. Some dormant instinct told her to freeze, so she pulled her *amiculum obscurum* cloak around her head and stood as still as her trembling knees would permit. Unfortunately, it did not seem to be working as the great black beast never took its eyes off of her—or at least where she was last seen. Perhaps it could sense the acrid fear that boiled up in her mouth as she tried to melt into the darkness. Anasta also knew that if she tried to run to safety, she would certainly give away her mother's hiding place. All she could do was remain motionless.

❧❧❧

Hisbil turned at once to see yet another, even larger, black cat moving slowly through the short grass, sizing up Anasta as its prey. He had been foolishly caught off guard as he chatted with his new convert. Hisbil knew that he could not use his wand again—it was too soon. Gollsaer told him that the spell could not be cast again for at *least* twenty-four hours—and often longer.

Hisbil watched as the second cat now began a low crawl toward Anasta—its chest barely off the ground. In a moment, it would be within easy striking range and ready to pounce. As the terrible dream the night before crossed his mind, Hisbil was blessed with an idea. Without turning around, Hisbil called out to Mink.

"Mink! Do you…do you know this beast?" he asked in a firm voice, with only a mild tremor.

"Yeeesss," she said. "myyy sisterrr, Ink she is. There all along she has been," she continued with a purr. "Toogeether we hunt. Game I flush, catch she does, and share we do."

"Can you ask her to leave us alone?" Hisbil said.

Mink said, "Stubborn she is, and hungry. Hers is to keep that other morsel. Not eaten have we since the human in the town caught us he did."

Hisbil's stomach grew tight as he realized that without a wand to tame and constrain the beast, he and Anasta did not have much of a chance. He needed something to get Ink's attention away from Anasta.

Cats, cats. What do I know about cats? What do cats like… Suddenly, Hisbil hatched another idea. "Mink, I know where there is some fresh cream. Doesn't that sound nice?" Hisbil offered.

"Creammm?" Mink answered eagerly, almost purring. Ink's head cocked a bit as she heard her sister talk like a human, but she didn't take her eyes off of Anasta still standing motionless at the west end of the commons.

"It that your favorite food?" Hisbil asked—keeping an eye on Ink. He called out: "Anasta! Stay where you are—I'll come get you!"

Hisbil moved quickly to Mink's side and was on her back in a flash holding on to the harness collar around the cat's neck. He pulled her head around toward Anasta by tugging on the fur behind the cat's ear.

This had better work, Hisbil said almost audibly.

"Denstrgen relezatus!" he shouted as he jabbed the wand into Mink's neck which resulted in a crisp "pop" and a tiny flash of light. The green tether of light had been released.

Hisbil shouted again, "Now, Mink, now! Run for my sister there at the edge of the commons." Something made Mink want to obey. It was as if she had found a new purpose and it all had to do with this small creature the size of a large mouse now straddling her back. She sprang at once and crossed the distance to the edge of the town commons in two leaps.

Ink quickly began to converge on the frozen figure in the short grass. Ink was not going to let Mink beat her to this meal—but she did. For some reason Ink's right leg seemed to be entangled in a ropey vine that held her back for a few precious moments.

As Mink approached Anasta, Hisbil leaned over and grabbed her arm—swinging her up onto Mink's back. "Get us out of here!" Hisbil shouted to Mink as Anasta put her arms around her brother's waist and held on tight. Mink turned and headed toward the northeast side of the narrow valley. With a few jumps and a dozen leaps, she scrambled up the cliff and began to run down the other side. Hisbil held on to the cat's harness as best he could, and Anasta tightened her grip on her brother's middle.

"Thanks," Anasta said in her brother's ear.

"Sure… you saved my life too," Hisbil said.

"Weeelcomeee You are," Mink purred, thinking Anasta was talking to her.

"I only wish you had stayed in the tunnel..."

"I wish you had too... well, yes, if you had stayed put, I might still be in a lot of trouble."

Once Ink had chewed and tugged her way free of her crude tether, she dashed off in pursuit and chased Mink and her riders off into the early morning darkness. She hadn't noticed the old sem with his sword still drawn standing back in the commons with a length of vine rope at his feet.

Sixteen—The Visual Aberration

After waiting for over an hour without another sound from the commons, the inhabitants of Stone Valley, cautiously at first, began to emerge from their hiding places like a raccoon approaches a handout left behind by a hiker long since gone. Those brave (and curious) souls who came out to investigate discovered the signs of a struggle and a scorch mark or two in the damp commons, but no blood—just a small crocheted hat.

"Where did they go?" Alred asked Neychen's wife, Hersarah, whose curiosity had pulled her into the commons. She poked at the ground with her cane and leaned over to pick up the hat.

"I...I don't know. Some fool said that Hisbil rode the beast up the side of the mountain—but that's impossible," Hersarah said with a tone of superiority in her voice. "There are no accounts of *anyone* riding a bellua in *The Books of Truth*, so it simply can't be true," she continued matter-of-factly as she started padding back home.

Alred had seen her come out into the commons as the cats ran away; she must have seen what happened just as he had, but she was too locked into her beliefs to admit it.

Alred just shook his head as he walked back into his house muttering to himself. It *was* a pretty far-fetched story. Imagine, riding a beast. *Impossible? I've seen a lot of strange things in my day, and I have the bands to show for it—a lot stranger than a young sem riding a bellua.*

It was not long before Alred heard a tap on his door. He turned away from the small fire under the pot of water and opened the door to find the eyes of a frightened nesem looking up at him. "Rachele, what..." he said without thinking and motioned her in.

Rachele hesitated at first but crossed the threshold, steadying herself on the jamb as she ducked down and entered the small room lit by a candle and the flickering embers that peeked out of the cracks in the metal stove. Alred quickly closed and bolted the door behind her offering her his own cushioned chair at the round table. Alred had known Rachele for some time—well before she had joined with Gollsaer in marriage. Alred and Rachele had kept a discreet distance since then, but after her first husband, Hissamuel, failed to return, Rachele had learned to depend on Alred for a few odd jobs and help with the Council, and as someone who would listen to her worries when she found herself frightened and alone—like tonight. She had always found comfort in his warm words and comforting embraces on many a dark, cold night.

"Hisbil is young and he can take care of himself," Alred continued as he tried to comfort his longtime friend.

Rachele looked into Alred's eyes and touched his gnarled hand. "Yes, he does have his father's courage...and perhaps his skills but..."

Alred crossed the room, returning to the now-steaming kettle on the stove. Trying to ease her concern for her children, he said, "Would you like a warm cup of Daintree tea? I brought it in from the far south. It's really quite good..." His voice drifted off as he turned to see Rachele with her face in her hands; she was weeping quietly. He put the mug of tea in front of her on the table and tried to console her. Before he could speak again, Rachele looked up with a despairing look on her face.

"It's Anasta—she's gone," Rachele said, sobbing. "When I called out to her in the dark, she didn't answer. She must have gone out to find Hisbil. I was…I was afraid to follow her out into the commons."

"She's with Hisbil. I…," Alred began. He didn't want to relate what he had seen or his role.

"With Hisbil? Where are they?" she cried, looking up into his eyes.

"They're out in the forest. We can arrange a search for them."

"Casandra, can't we get Casandra to help find them?"

"Of course, it's just not safe with belluas still in the area. We'll find them—they couldn't have gone far."

"Do you really think so?" Rachele asked, a flash of hope crossing her face.

"Of course, of course. They should be home by mid-day." While Alred was not so sure they would return, there was no point in worrying Rachele any more than necessary. "You're welcome to stay here with me and enjoy my tea and company until they return. I'll start some biscuits. I still have some honey and blackberry preserves left."

"That would be nice," Rachele said softly. It had been quite some times since she had spent time with someone, other than her husband, alone and at night. Her first visits with Alred had been in the daylight and with the door open—it was not until the loneliness had overcome her that she had lingered after dark with the door closed.

Rachele settled into the soft chair and began to sip the tea. Alred stoked the fire in the small stove and began to gather the ingredients to make biscuits. He pulled down a small dark-glass bottle from the high shelf above the stove, took Rachele's cup, and added a few drops to her tea. Alred smiled warmly as he turned and handed her the cup. They would spend the remaining hours before daylight waiting, listening, and reassuring each other.

Seventeen—The Chase

*M*ink's confusion only deepened as she loped through the forest north of the village. On her back, Hisbil held on to her harness, with Anasta's arms wrapped around him—for a while, her legs flapped behind like a pennant as she struggled to keep from flying off. Sometime later Mink felt her go limp but Hisbil managed to keep her from falling off.

Looking back, Mink could see that Ink was not far behind, and catching up.

"Can you lose her?" Hisbil shouted against the wind.

"Yell, you don't need," Mink replied. "Every breath I hearrr."

Hisbil replied in a whisper next to Mink's ear, "But can you lose her?"

"Of course. A lazy cat she is. More cleverrrr I am," Mink said.

"Well, good. Try to do so before we fall off or you get too tired."

What kind of a pussy does he think I am? Only a bit winded, I am, she deceived herself. "Hold on, you should," she said.

"Creeeam, did you saaay?" Mink said remembering what Hisbil had promised in the courtyard.

"Yes!" he said. "There is a farm to the northeast that has cows that give milk and cream," Hisbil said enthusiastically. "Turn down that path and follow it to the road. It's over the next hill. It's nearly two-day's walk for us but not that far for you."

"That far—I can try...," Mink said again, but she didn't want to disappoint Hisbil. There was something engaging about the little Seldith that she didn't understand, but she felt compelled to do whatever she could for her ontwaker.

"How did you get past the briar wall?" Hisbil asked.

"Human caught us and he did. And dropped us over during the storm. Quite rude."

"Did you know him? Was he your master?"

"Master he was not. Seen our master we have not, for some time. Searching for him we were, near the old castle."

It was just past dawn when the old farm appeared all at once as they rode past the edge of the forest. The seemingly endless expanse of grass and supported a bountiful herd of black and white Holstein dairy cows scattered around the rolling pasture.

"My father told me that these cows provided milk, butter, and cheese for the uman town to the west," Hisbil said. "This is where I got my first taste of milk—from one of those cows."

"Finally," Mink wheezed.

The wheel-rutted road they followed led up to a wide gate that had slots wide enough for Mink and her riders to easily jump through, and Ink followed soon after. To the right was a long post-and-wire fence that stretched off into the distance to the east and west. To the east, the sky began to glow in a deep red—filtered by the clouds from last night's storm. The cows were mostly asleep, lying in ones and twos on the grass.

Eighteen—Sally Jo and Buster

*S*ally Jo, an aging Holstein cow watched Hisbil astride the large black cat coming across the field. She made no effort to help Hisbil find her.

"Sally Jo!" Hisbil called over and over again as Mink took him from cow to cow with Ink following behind. Most of the cows were still lying on the ground asleep, so he wasn't sure they had even heard him—especially given his tiny voice.

Sally Jo just watched as they worked their way toward her through the herd. She had mixed feelings about seeing Hisbil. While she was able to understand human speech since Gollsaer's awakened her, she felt that she might have been better off not knowing the farmer's intentions to sell off the young bulls and unproductive cows.

But before long, Sally Jo had a change of heart. With her calf nestled at her feet, she got to her feet and let out a low "Mooo?" as Hisbil got within earshot.

At this, Sally Jo's calf awakened and started to push its gangly legs under its unsteady body and rise to greet the strangers. Strangely enough, the baby bull looked at the strange foursome and spoke:

"Hello! Are you looking for my mommy? Her name is Sally Jo," It was as if the calf had been speaking since birth.

"My name is Buster. What's yours? What kind of animals are you? We had better speak softly," whispered the calf, peeking around his mother's legs. It was as if he had been waiting a lifetime to speak to someone—anyone.

"You don't want to scare them; they'll all run off and get lost," he babbled on, "...and the farmer will be very cross with us all. Mom, is it okay if I talk to these strangers? You told me to never talk around the farmer, but is this okay?"

"We'll be quiet," said Hisbil as he helped Anasta slide down off the cat while keeping a close eye on Ink who kept her distance studying the situation, perhaps waiting for another opportunity to strike. Anasta seemed exhausted as she wilted into the tall grass. Hisbil also wobbled a bit on his legs after the long, bounding ride. Mink sat down to rest on her haunches, tucked her tail over her feet but also kept one eye on Ink.

Ink edged in closer to the others but remained about five long paces away.

"Is Ink going to cause trouble?" Hisbil asked Mink.

"Hungry she is—as am I," Mink replied.

When Ink started to make a roundabout move toward the dismounted riders, Mink got to her feet, arched her back, and held Ink off with a low warning growl and a long hiss. That kept Ink at bay—at least for the moment.

"Cream, youuu promised? Hungry I am, as is my sisterrrr," she said.

"Hisbil, how long will the spell last?" Anasta asked trying to talk over the young bull that was still rattling on about anything and everything before Sally Jo encouraged him to nurse.

"I don't know. It might not last another minute or it could be permanent. I just don't know."

"You're not much of an Owl Wrangler are you?" Anasta snapped.

"Well, these aren't owls so we had best figure out how to get rid of these cats in any case—and quickly," Hisbil said, ignoring the cheap shot.

"Sally Jo? Do you still remember me? My name is Hisbil," he began, "and this is my sister, Anasta. I came here some time ago with my father, Gollsaer, before your calf Buster was born."

Sally Jo gave off a short "moo" and a friendly nod to acknowledge Hisbil and his sister.

"So apparently you still seem to understand me but can't speak. We expected that might happen," Hisbil said. "May I speak to your calf Buster? He seems to be able to talk well enough for both of you," he quipped with a smile.

"Moo," the cow said, rolling her eyes.

"Yes, he does seem quite the chatterbox," Hisbil said as Sally Jo nodded again and shook her head in embarrassment.

"I guess that's why I can speak," said Buster as he stopped nursing for a moment, her milk running down his chin. "None of the other cows understand me when I speak human talk, but I understand cow talk too. Mom told me not to talk in front of the farmer; it makes him act silly."

It seemed the young calf would never stop talking. Hisbil had some trouble getting a word in edgewise, and he did not want to seem rude or impatient, but he had a couple of hungry carnivores nearby that needed something to eat.

Before Hisbil could interrupt, Sally Jo swished her tail across the calf's face. Buster knew that was a sign to keep his mouth shut. Sally Jo shook her head.

Now that the calf was quiet (at last), Hisbil asked, "Is there a chance we could get some milk or cream for these starving cats?"

The calf did not answer at first but looked up plaintively to his mom with his big brown eyes. His mom nodded, and the calf answered, "The farmer has many cats and always leaves cream out in the barn. It's early, so there might be some left from last night."

That's all Mink needed to hear. Without so much as a "ta-ta" she bounded off toward the barn below the hill looking for breakfast. Ink did not seem to understand any of the conversation but decided to follow Mink. It was a wise decision, as Hisbil had drawn his sword in case she didn't follow.

Nineteen—A Long Way from Home

*D*aylight had broken through the clouds to brighten the eastern sky over the dairy farm with a promisingly warm, red glow. In the southwest, the sun reflected off the slowly billowing anvils of a line of pink and purple clouds. The Hisbil and Anasta did not really take notice of the changing weather or the large bird circling high overhead.

Hisbil knew that they were indeed a long, long way from home, at least two long days' walk, perhaps more. As he stood looking into the tall grass that surrounded them, he was not *exactly* sure how he had gotten here to the farm, then or now—but he had a rough idea.

In frustration, Hisbil asked his sister in a voice he and his father used only when they were cross, "*Why* didn't you stay safe in the tunnel with your mother?"

Anasta could tell that her brother was tired and a bit angry. "I…I just wanted to help you. I hoped it would be okay if I stayed hidden," she said, sheepishly looking up to Hisbil like the calf had looked up to his mother when he knew he was in trouble.

Hisbil did not buy the big-eyed attempt at forgiveness. He knew his little sister too well.

"You *hoped* it would be okay? What made you *think* for a second it would be okay? Have you ever seen what one of these beasts can do? Don't you remember the story of Ruthet? You have heard it a dozen times in class."

"But those are just stories the elders tell us to keep us away from the secrets behind the briar wall. They aren't *really* true," Anasta said, "…are they?"

"Yes, they *are* true—almost all of them—and there are lots of other dangers out here that are worse than a stray bellua. Just yesterday, Kassie was taken by a uman just outside the briar wall. I should be out looking for her instead of…"

Hisbil's voice grew louder as he tried to help make his sister aware of the danger they were facing. Sally Jo began to take notice and started to move away—something Hisbil had not intended. If she could hear him, so could other, more deadly creatures. He lowered his voice as Anasta's eyes and chin dropped. She began to weep—the tears drawing dark tracks in the dust on her face. She finally crumpled and, sitting down on the grass, buried her face in her arms.

"Does mother know where you are?" Hisbil said more quietly. "Did she see you leave?"

"No, she didn't see me leave—it was too dark," Anasta sobbed through her arms. "I don't know if she followed me. I'm…I'm sorry," she said looking up. "I just wanted to see…I wanted to help. I'm almost ten!" she cried.

Hisbil could see that Anasta was sorry. Perhaps she had learned a lesson that might keep her alive a bit longer. He also knew that they had to find shelter, food, fresh water, and a route back before anything *else* happened. While he had his father's rucksack, it carried hardly enough food for one. Hisbil had not expected to be gone more than a few hours, a day at most.

"I have good news and bad news," Hisbil said trying to lift Anasta's spirits. "Which do you want first?"

"I think I better have the good news first," she replied wiping her tears.

"Mink and her sister have gone looking for breakfast and we aren't on the menu."

"So what's the bad news?"

"Mink has gone looking for breakfast so we don't have a ride back home."

"So how are we going to get home?"

"I expect we'll have to walk."

"Walk? How far? The longest walk I've taken is to River Landing and we made it back before dark."

"Come on, get up, Anasta. Wipe your face, kiddo, and let's get out of sight," he said to his sister in a softer tone. "I don't like that we can't see a foot in front of us in this grass."

Hisbil scanned the sky for those that would snatch them from above without a sound. He knew that there were a number of predators that worked open fields like this. He missed the bird making wide lazy circles high over the farm.

Anasta mopped her face with her sleeve and stood up to brush off her clothes; she then pulled the calf-length cloak she wore around her and retied the sash. It was as if she had just finished a dainty afternoon picnic with her friends. Her *amiculum obscurum* cloak reflected shimmering green and tan almost as if it were made of the soft pasture grass.

"Do you have any food?" she said.

"I'm hungry too but we don't have time to eat just yet. Let's get under the cover of the forest while I work out a plan to get us back home."

"Can't we just rest here awhile? I think the calf is kinda fun."

"Come on, Mother will be frantic, and I expect Alred will be searching organizing a search party to look for us. We need to head back toward the road."

"Are you sure?"

"Pretty sure, I think if we head south we can follow it back to the village. Head off that way," Hisbil said pointing with his arm to the southeast.

Anasta nodded and started parting and walking through the tall pasture grass.

Before following his sister, Hisbil turned and said his farewells to the cows. "Goodbye, and thanks for the help, Sally Jo, and you too, Buster. I hope to be back this way someday."

Sally Jo turned her head and nodded and walked off prodding her calf along, swishing her tail along his backside. Buster turned his head briefly and said, "Bye…it was nice talking to you. We have to go to the barn. I hope…" His mom cut him off with another swat from her tail. Buster turned his head and kept walking. "Perhaps I'll get to talk to that cat!" he said to his mother as he quickened his pace to get ahead of her and out of range of her tail.

Hisbil passed his sister and they both started working their way south, but they still couldn't see very far ahead in the tall pasture grass.

"Why don't we go back the way we came?" Anasta asked.

"The cats didn't leave a trail we can follow. Just keep going." Hisbil took his frustration out on the tall grass by hacking a path through it with his sword. A half-hour later they arrived exhausted at a crushed-down area in the grass.

"Great. We're right back where we started."

"How… how did we get back here?" Anasta whined.

"We just walked in a big circle. We need to find another way out of this grass sea. We'll never get out this way."

If I didn't have her with me, I could…, he said to himself as he passed Anasta to take the lead and head out again into the grass.

And then he heard it—or more accurately, he felt it. Something was coming and fairly quickly. Knowing he could not outrun much of anything in this grass, he called out to his sister,

"Down! Get down and cover yourself with the grass!" Anasta just looked at him. An instant later, Hisbil had thrown his body over hers and covered her mouth. "Quiet!" he whispered in her ear.

Anasta struggled at first but Hisbil clutched her even tighter as she tried to get away. He was convinced his sister had a disease Gollsaer had described to him. She, like too many of the young, had the mistaken idea that she was immortal. She believed that bad, terrible, fatal things only happen to others, to other elves in cautionary stories told only to frighten little kids. Hisbil had been cured of the disease when he saw one of his friends carried away by a hawk. He knew that Anasta still had to learn that she was risking her own life and the lives of all around her when she did not do what her elders (or her big brother) told her to do.

"Hello?" A loud, distinctively bovine voice boomed over them. "What are you doing down there in the mud?" the voice continued. "Are you okay?"

Hisbil rolled over to see a big calf nose sniffing at them. It was Buster.

"I was worried about you. I thought you were going into the woods. You haven't walked very far…," he said, clearly glad to have found them.

Hisbil turned over, releasing his mud-encrusted sister. She got to her feet, fussing under her breath. Hisbil expected to hear the worst of the words Anasta had overheard her elders and the other kids in the village use when they got mad, but he didn't. As she grumbled to herself, Hisbil turned to Buster. "Yes, we were trying to get back to the road."

"I can see you walked in a big circle. I'm not allowed to go to the road or near the fence. Does your mom let you go into the road alone…?" Buster babbled.

Buster was on another talking jag. Hisbil realized that the eager (and talkative) calf could help them as he looked back on the path that Buster had taken. "Buster!" he shouted. "Buster, can you help us get to the forest?" Hisbil interrupted.

"Help you? Sure, I can help…I think. How can I help? I can't carry you—you're too far down there, and if you fell off my back…," Buster was rambling away again.

"No, no. We don't want you to carry us," Hisbil interrupted. "If you just make a smooth path with your hooves by trampling down the grass we could follow you. It would be a lot of help."

"Oh…is that all? That's easy. Mom said not to touch the fence though. I…I can't touch the fence—it hurts!" Buster said.

"Oh, that's *silly*. How can a fence hurt you?" Anasta piped up with a superior tone in her voice.

Hisbil turned and gave Anasta a look that made it clear that she was not to say another word. Sometimes, it just took a look.

"Which way?" Buster asked. "I like that way toward the barn. That's where my mom is going. I don't think she knows I'm over here, so perhaps we should go that way."

"No, no…," Hisbil said patiently. "We need to go back to *our* barn—our home. We need to go toward the fence and the road—I think it's over that way, up the hill," he said, pointing with his arm in the direction he believed they should go—in the general direction from which they came by cat-back. Hisbil was also trying to help Buster get over his reluctance to go toward the fence.

"Oh…okay. If you think it's safe. Just follow me," Buster said as he began walking toward the edge of the pasture.

"Just walk slowly and trample the grass," said Hisbil as he followed along about twenty paces behind the calf. "Anasta, just walk ahead of me so I can keep an eye on you."

Buster kept talking nearly nonstop as they walked. He chattered on and on about every aspect of his life on the farm and what he planned to be when he grew up.

"I want to be a farmer someday—and have my own herd of cows," he declared. Hisbil shook his head and motioned to Anasta to squelch the laughter she was bottling up behind her hand.

The trail Buster's shuffling hooves made was not as smooth as a road or a well-worn forest trail, but it made it far easier to get through the tall grass.

"Don't get too close to his heels," Hisbil said. At this latest warning, Anasta turned her head and made a face. Hisbil could tell she was long since tired of being told what to do. To emphasize the point, she got even closer to Buster, and before long was walking along just under his tail as it swished away flies. Without warning, a deluge of dung fell from just below Buster's tail and, fortunately, landed just ahead of his little sister. Taken completely by surprise, Anasta proceeded to walk right into it, falling face-first into the dung. Coming up sputtering from the steaming pile, she started to bawl and stamp her feet. Now she was not only muddy but covered with warm, smelly calf dung. Hisbil could only grin. *There is justice in the universe.*

"Oops—be careful," Buster said stopping and turning his head. "You should watch where you walk out here," he admonished. "We never really know when nature calls and dung falls," he said with a chuckle. Anasta did not see the humor in any of this.

"You wanted me to walk ahead of you 'cause you knew he would poop on me!" Anasta fussed.

Hisbil ignored her protestations as he wiped her face with her own muddy cloak and got her started again behind Buster who seemed totally unconcerned. Anasta didn't walk as close to the calf's heels this time and kept a close eye on his backside so as to avoid any other biological extrusions.

As they walked, Hisbil's mind drifted to Kassie and his pace quickened. *I've got to get back to help her.* "Can you move any faster?" he called up to Buster. "We've got to get back home."

Twenty—The Fence and the Forest

What would have taken the (relatively) small Seldith several long hours, took only a fraction of the time, thanks to the trail Buster made with his hooves. In no time, they were getting close to the fence that bordered the edge of the pasture. Buster's nonstop talking had slowly abated as they approached the post-and-wire fence. For some reason he was increasingly anxious about the barrier between the farmer's pasture and the adjoining forest. The fence had woven wire mesh along the bottom with a strand of twisted barbed wire near the top stretched between white knobs that looked a bit like white porcelain drawer pulls.

"This is as far as I dare take you…," said Buster in a somewhat timid voice. "I…I can't go any farther. I need to go back now. I hope you can find your way home. Yes, my mom's calling me. Bye!" Buster blurted, and in the blink of an eye, he had started a headlong, leaping gallop back toward the barn.

"I didn't hear his mom," Anasta said as she looked down the shallow hill at the calf racing away.

"Neither did I, but I bet he just wanted to get away from this fence," Hisbil said. Near the base of the fence, he saw a shape in the grass that distracted him for a moment. *Just what I need*, he murmured to himself. He walked over and found the remains of a uman's steel tool. *This will make a great sword.*

"It doesn't look that scary to me," Anasta said, staring up at the fence. "It's just wooden posts and a bit of wire. I can climb up over the top without any trouble at all," Anasta said as Hisbil retrieved and inspected his new prize. By the time Hisbil looked up, Anasta was already nearly at the top of the mesh and was about to climb over.

"Great stars, get down!" Hisbil quickly commanded in a harsh, but hushed voice.

"What for? I'm hungry and I want to go home. It was easy." she protested in her impatient voice as she continued to climb. Just then, a tall thistle on the other side of the fence swayed in the breeze—it was just tall enough to touch the top wire. With a bright flash and a sharp pop, the top foot or so of the weed was vaporized.

Anasta froze in terror. Her eyes grew large and filled with tears as her ears tucked back against her head and the fur across her back stood on end.

"Don't move!" Hisbil commanded. For once, Anasta obeyed. Her head was just below the top wire that had incinerated the blade of grass. "If you move, the fence will fry you like that weed!" he warned. Hisbil shared his sister's terror.

"W-w-what do I do now?" Anasta pleaded though her tears.

Ah, do what you're told to do the first time you're told to do it.

In a calm voice, he answered, "Just stay where you are, and let me think. Whatever you do, don't climb any higher. Can you climb down on your own?"

Anasta's knees trembled as she tried to shift her weight and climb down the mesh fence. She had not finished the first step before she realized that her long, dung-matted hair was tangled in the mesh. Anasta yelped as her hair stopped her descent. "I can't! I'm stuck!" she cried. She was not going anywhere—up or down.

She's going to get us both killed or worse.

At this point, Hisbil was out of ideas, but he knew that he needed to do something and quickly—they were too exposed out here in the open. As the seconds ticked by with his attention fixed on his fence-impaled sister, Hisbil didn't notice the shadow that flashed across the ground at his feet.

"You're going to *have* to climb back down," he called up to his sister, trying not to raise his voice. "Can you free your hair?"

"I can't!" she shrieked.

Contrary to her Seldith upbringing, Anasta began to wail louder as she clutched the top of the mesh, her feet dug in a few inches below, her whole body trembling from fear.

"Anasta…you need to stay calm and lower your voice. You're going to get us both killed, or worse." he said under his breath as he began to climb the fence.

"That's not the way to dooo it," a calm voice said from above. Hisbil looked up and saw that a rather large white owl had found a perch on the adjacent fencepost behind him. A cold panic ran though him as he instinctively dove for cover in the long grass at the base of the fence. Peeking out from cover Hisbil thought he recognized the bird as Bubou, an owl that his father had captured and converted not long ago.

"I said, that's not howwww to get her dowwwn," the owl hooted.

"Ah, Bubou, you *scared* me!" Hisbil replied breathlessly as he brushed off his clothes.

"So, how *do* we get her down? Are you an expert on these magical fences?" Hisbil queried. Anasta was still and silent for once—still trembling, but quiet.

"While I've seen small birds sit on the fence without anything happening, I've also chased a squirrel onto the fence, and he was attacked by the magic as he crossed the top."

"Did the fence kill the squirrel?" Hisbil asked but immediately regretted doing so as the words left his mouth.

"I don't knowwww, but he made a tasty dinner," Bubou seemed to smile with a twinkle in his eye.

Hisbil and Anasta looked at each other and Anasta renewed her quiet sobbing.

Hisbil returned his attention to the owl perched on the fencepost above him. He looked into the bird's great round yellow eyes and screwed up his courage. He needed to know where he and his trapped sister stood with this potential adversary. *Are we his next lunch?*

"You told us you knew how to get Anasta off the fence," Hisbil queried in a businesslike voice. He didn't want to show the owl that he was afraid.

"Ooooh, yes," Bubou said. "I can take her down, but it will not be easy."

Keeping his eyes on Bubou, Hisbil answered, "No, it won't be easy. Her hair is caught in the wire."

"Yes, I can see that. I'll have toooo cut her hair unless yooou can climb up there tooo do it. I don't think she can get it free by herself. She seems to be at a tender, succulent age…er, yoooung," Bubou said, correcting himself.

In the blink of an eye, Hisbil was back on the fence scrambling up beneath Anasta. "I'll free her," he said in reply. The sudden movement startled the owl, and Bubou flapped his wings as if he was going to take off. As Hisbil climbed, he realized that it was his own stubbornness that had put his sister in jeopardy and he should have climbed up immediately to cut her free before they were put into even more danger.

As Hisbil reached the top of the fence, he drew his blade and made quick work of Anasta's hair tether. Yes, it seems that, for the sake of speed, he cut off a bit more than necessary to free his sister. Once her hair was free, he helped his sister climb down—still keeping an eye on the owl perched above them.

"Sooo, you weren't in that much troooble after all," the owl said as the pair of Seldith caught their breath at the base of the fence. "Youuu should be more careful out here in the ooopen," he counseled as his head turned about his big, round eyes scanning the sky. "If I had not been beholden to your brother, Yenesem Anasta, you would have made a delicious breakfast."

Hisbil now realized that the large white owl was not really a threat; he was just trying to help. As Hisbil and his sister regained their feet and caught their breath, Hisbil thanked Bubou for his forbearance and wisdom.

"Sure, you're right. We should not have stood out here arguing in the open. There are lots of other creatures out here looking for an easy meal," Hisbil said for Anasta's benefit. "Let's get under cover."

Anasta, still shaken, got back to her feet straightening her clothes and running her fingers through what was left of her hair. She turned to Hisbil and said with a thin smile, "Thanks for getting me down..." Anasta gave her big brother a hug and put her head on his shoulder for a long moment. The then took a step back and punched him as hard as she could in the upper arm. "That's for the haircut."

Bubou's eyes were now fixed on what appeared to be a large eagle now flying a figure eight orbit high over the pasture. "You need toooo get into the forest...nowwww!" he said with considerable urgency.

Twenty-one—Weiger, the Uman, and the Mouse

*I*t was late afternoon when Weiger found himself cowering in a ditch after spotting a uman approaching on the footpath leading to the uman town. To a Seldith, all umans are a threat. As the uman passed, Weiger mourned his sorry state. *Here I lie in a ditch starving and besieged by umans. What I wouldn't give for a muddy puddle and a green Oregon grape berry right now.* Emperor had expelled him from Shutz Norte without any food or water or much of anything else besides a promise of riches beyond belief.

Peeking out from under his cover, Weiger could see the aging uman was dressed a bit strangely, wearing loose garments gathered at the waist with a rope belt. The uman walked right past his hiding place, turned, and walked a couple of steps back, pausing about twenty elf paces away. "Are you thirsty?" said the uman in a soft voice—almost a whisper but clearly audible. Weiger did not flinch. *There is no way he could have heard or seen me.*

"I won't harm you," the uman promised in that same soft, reassuring voice. Weiger did not move. The stranger looked right at him but made no attempt to move any closer. Weiger did not budge, but he *was* thirsty. *How did he know?*

Something came over Weiger as he lay there motionless. A voice told him, *You can trust him.* He considered the situation for a moment and kept an eye on the uman who sat cross-legged in the shade of a blue cedar at the side of the path.

Lifting his head, Weiger asked from beneath the leaves, "How is it that you speak my language?" He was ready to escape

Weiger and the Mouse Share the Stranger's Meal

into the dense undergrowth on the hillside above him if the uman made any move in his direction.

"I speak many tongues," the uman replied in the same gentle tone. "I heard you speaking as I passed. You're one of the ancient Seldith, are you not?"

"I was not speaking to anyone but myself," Weiger said.

"Yes, I know," he replied slowly and quite softly. "Don't be afraid. Nothing can harm you when you are with me and I am with you."

Weiger watched intently as the uman took out a gourd canteen and picked up a large maple leaf that he fashioned into a small Seldith-sized cup and fill it with water. He pushed it toward the wary Seldith's hiding place. The uman then produced a small scrap of what appeared to be newsprint, a chunk of brown bread, and a plum-sized piece of yellow cheese drawn from his cloth bag. He placed a small portion of these on the paper and, reaching over, laid this own meal next to the leaf cup filled with water.

"You are welcome to share what I have," the uman said as he motioned Weiger to share his food with his outstretched palm.

"I have no salt or sugar to pay you," Weiger said getting to his feet.

"Your company and trust is payment enough," said the uman who began to drink from his gourd canteen and eat the same food he had offered the Seldith. "This is a lonely path, and I know you would offer me the same if I were in need."

I'm not so sure of that... "What do you want of me?" Weiger replied. "Who are you? Where do you come from?"

"These are all good questions, Sem Weiger. The answers you don't already know in your heart will be made known to you in time," the uman said as he continued to eat his meal.

"How is it that you know my name?" Weiger demanded. "And by what name do they call you?"

"I have been given many names, but my parents called me *Eashoa*," the uman answered. "You can call me whatever you like. As to your name, is it not the name your mother and father gave you? Is it not the name the village elders wrote in *The Books of Truth* when you were born?"

"How do you know about *The Books of Truth*?" Weiger asked as he cautiously inched toward the food and water. "Umans are not allowed to see its pages." Weiger was more confused and concerned than ever. *Is this a powerful shaman that will…?*

"Have you read them?" asked Eashoa.

"Not nearly all of them…," Weiger exaggerated, "but we were taught passages in school." He realized that this uman knew quite a bit about the Seldith. Weiger had encountered a few umans in his travels, but this one was very different.

Still warily watching the uman, Weiger dipped his hand in the cool water and drew it tentatively to his lips. *It's just water,* he realized and began to drink and eat the cheese and bread ravenously—shoving a portion into his shirt.

"Do you live by its laws?" the man asked as he put the rest of his food away in his shoulder bag.

Weiger thought for a moment as he tried to swallow a bit more than he could chew. "I can't say that many do. There are so many laws and rules and "truths" (he fingered quotes in the air as he spoke) that no one should say they know and understand all that *The Books* dictate—but some of the elders do—or at least they say they do. They say that The Truth is revealed to them by the stars themselves—they speak to them."

"I understand," said Eashoa. He now had a sad look on his face.

"So many of the truths in *The Books* have been contradicted and discredited by new discoveries—new truths we have found since *The Books* were first inscribed in clay and transcribed to the ancient scrolls ages ago." Weiger said. He took the opportunity to refill his canteen from the leaf cup. After doing so, the cup seemed to be as full as it was before he drank his fill. There was also a generous portion of the simple food remaining.

"And some of the 'laws' don't make sense today, not with the way the world works and what we have learned." Weiger felt compelled to thank the uman for his generosity, but he was not sure how to do so. Finally, he simply said, "Thanks."

Eashoa nodded his head, saying, "You're most welcome, Sem Weiger. You have a good soul. I know you would do unto others as you would have them do unto you." Then he asked, "Do you plan to return to the village of your parents?"

As he spoke, a mouse darted in from the underbrush and grabbed a bit of bread that had fallen from the uman's tunic. It scurried away just as quickly, looking back to see if it was being pursued. Eashoa gave little notice but laid a larger bit of cheese and more bread down on the ground where the mouse could easily reach it.

"Both of you should feel free to fill your canteens and take whatever food remains with you. While the journey ahead is not long, you'll both need your strength for the challenges you will soon face."

"I cannot return to Stone Valley," Weiger said. "…as you probably well know. Do you see this mark?" said Weiger as he lifted the brim of his hat. "I was branded before they banished me—forced to leave those I loved and respected, and those that once respected me."

"What mark?" said Eashoa, now leaning slightly toward Weiger to get a closer look.

For some reason, Weiger had lost all fear of this uman. If he had wanted to catch him, he would have done so. Weiger looked down into the water's reflection but did not see the brand on his forehead. He spanked away the unkempt fur and rubbed away the dirt that blotched his face, but still he saw no scar—no sign of the wound made by the branding iron. As he looked up, the uman was gone. Only the leaf filled with water, a bit of cheese, and a few large morsels of bread remained on the paper.

The mouse returned to the roadside and again began to cautiously look for morsels of bread and cheese before Weiger realized what had happened to the uman: he was there one moment and gone the next.

He must have been a wizard—perhaps from the dark castle. As Weiger wondered if he had somehow been poisoned or enchanted by the food and drink, the mouse found another bit of cheese on the ground where Eashoa had left it. The leaf cup remained filled with water.

The mouse continued to bustle around, scouring the ground for any remaining bread crumbs or cheese, and found more of each scattered near the side of the road. He paused for a moment and sat on his haunches nibbling at another choice piece of cheese. Looking up, the mouse looked at Weiger and said in a squeaky but remarkably clear voice, "Did you know that man? Was he a friend of yours?"

Weiger looked up from his rucksack with a startled look on his face. He quickly looked around for someone else nearby. He was pretty sure he had heard someone speak. *There must have been something in the cheese or that water,* he thought.

"I haven't seen him on this road before, but I've heard of him," the mouse continued.

Weiger did not know what to think. To this point in his relatively short life, he had not heard a mouse speak—but stranger things had happened. "No, I didn't know him," Weiger answered. "But I feel that I do now."

The mouse continued to scurry around looking for additional morsels. After finding a few more, he ran off into the brush only to return a few moments later with a cloth sack slung over his shoulder which he began to stuff with collected bits of bread and cheese. Before long it was full, and the mouse realized that there was a limit to what he could carry away but no end to the number of bits of bread and cheese that seem to multiply as they were gathered. "Well," he said as he hefted the overstuffed sack onto his back. "That's about all I can carry. I'll leave the rest to the birds."

"Birds?" Looking skyward with some alarm. "Ah, excuse me," Weiger began, as the mouse seemed about ready to go about his own business. "How is it that you can speak…that I can understand you? Have you been awakened?"

"That's a good question," said the mouse as he turned back toward Weiger with a bit of a smile on his face. "I'm afraid it was a mistake," the mouse continued. "You see, I've always been able to speak like this."

"How is that possible?" said the Seldith. "I have never read about a speaking mouse in *The Books of Truth.*"

"While I've never heard of your truth books, surely you know that humans can speak," said the mouse with a wry grin on his face.

"Of course," said Weiger. "But how is it that *you* can speak?"

"I have not always been a rodent," the mouse said as he walked closer to Weiger, still carrying the sack over his shoulder. "Perhaps I should tell you how I got stuck in this mouse suit," he said, looking over his shoulder. "But not here, there are too many cold, black eyes and sharp talons out here. Would you like join me in my humble digs? It's nearby. Perhaps you could help me carry this sack."

Weiger did not know what to think but agreed that they were easy prey chatting by the side of the road—and Eashoa was no longer there to protect them. "Sure. Let's at least get off the road." He said as he put his own shoulder under the sack.

"Great, just great. My place is just up there," the mouse said pointing up the hill. It's been such a long time since I've spoken with anyone," said the mouse cheerfully as he started to climb up the hill. He was not at all sure if he wanted to follow the mouse into any dark "digs"—not wanting to relive the miserable sleepless night he had recently endured cowering in a rat hole. As Weiger found his way up the steepening trail, he kept his eyes on the mouse with one wary eye and on his next handhold with the other.

Looking up, Weiger suddenly found himself standing at the footsteps of the mouse's front porch. For some reason, he had not seen the house at all as they climbed the steep hill. The mouse's neat little home was tucked into the hillside and surrounded on all sides by a thick patch of elderberry bushes. It was more like a miniature uman home—hardly a hole in the ground as he had expected. While Weiger had to duck down a bit to enter, there was more than enough room for him inside, as the room had a high ceiling and was brightly furnished with colorful woven carpets and a few pieces of handcrafted furniture. In one corner, a sizeable stone-and-metal stove warmed the room with a crackling fire. A teapot sat perched on top gently blowing steam into the room. Everything was fastidiously arranged and appointed—quite uncharacteristic of a rodent.

The mouse placed his sack on a good-sized rectangular table in the middle of the room and began to disgorge its treasure of bread and cheese. Opening a tall cabinet, he took out a wooden breadbox which he began to fill with the large shards of bread.

Weiger settled into an overstuffed chair and found that he fit quite comfortably. "This is a very nice place," Weiger offered. "Aren't you afraid of marauders?"

The mouse turned briefly from his work and smiled again. "That's not a problem in this house." But he did not explain further. "Would you care for some tea?" he offered.

Weiger was beginning to relax with the mouse, but the number of questions he wanted to ask kept piling up in his mind.

He still had not been told how the mouse came to be as he is—a mouse. "Sure. I would love a cup of tea. But I would also like to know a bit more about you."

The mouse closed the cupboard and walked over to a rack of cups neatly hanging on hooks under the shelf over the stove. "I expect you'll want a bit larger cup," he said, "...and a few answers." The mouse said as he made tea. "I'm sorry, I've forgotten my manners. My name is Douglas, Douglas Stewart," the mouse said as he crossed the room with the large Seldith-size mug and his paw outstretched.

Weiger took the mug and shook Douglas' paw. "My name is Weiger of the Seldith community of...."

"It's nice to meet you," Douglas said while he crossed the room to make his own cup. Weiger continued to marvel at the furnishings and conveniences as Douglas placed the teapot back on the stove and began his story.

"Some time ago, I was a man, a human and a husband—not a mouse—although my wife, Ristina, disagreed from time to time on that point, we loved each other and were totally devoted. We lived quietly in the nearby town working as a carpenter building cabinetry and doing odd jobs. A few years ago, I was asked to help remodel the castle on the hill west of town—the one that sits just above us. The original owners had disappeared and the town officials had taken over the castle and grounds to pay back taxes."

"Years? What are 'years'," Weiger asked.

"A year? Your folk don't know years? How do you measure the passage of time?"

"By the seasons, the moon and stars and the activity of the wildlife. How is it that you mice measure time?"

"Well then, let me explain." It took Douglas almost fifteen minutes and a calendar get Weiger to understand the English, the 'uman' terms for measuring the passage of time. He thought it interesting and a bit puzzling that the Seldith had no dependency on mechanical clocks of any kind. While Weiger seemed to be a quick learner, he still insisted that measuring time by the moon and the length of days made more sense. Douglas had to agree, and eventually continued his story.

"The castle was to undergo general repairs and restoration so it could be sold. The project would take several months so the town hired cabinetmakers, plumbers, and stone masons to work on the restoration. The foreman, Mr. Heintzelman, told me that one of the built-in cabinets had large doors that were hopelessly stuck, and no amount of effort could get them open. I was asked to gain access to the cabinet by any means necessary without damaging it, and repair the doors.

"The room where I was to work was just off the entrance foyer. Its furniture was covered with sheets and pushed back against one side of the room to permit repairs to the flooring. The south-facing window in this room was unusually large—made up of a dozen framed panes.

"A tall bookcase stood against the far wall. The other walls, save one, were mostly bare, exposing faded wallpaper. Built into the inside wall was a large, ornately carved wooden cabinet—the piece they wanted me to repair. It was made of dark walnut, about four feet wide and standing over seven feet tall. I could see why they wanted it preserved; it was beautifully adorned with breathtakingly intricate carvings. It did not take an expert to know the cabinet and carving were made by a skilled craftsman, an artist far more accomplished than I had ever seen before or ever hoped to be. The carvings themselves were also very unusual—and not symmetric."

"Symmetric?" Weiger asked. What do you mean? He had been transfixed by the story and had been drinking his tea with some excitement.

"It means…," Douglas continued as he walked across the room to refill Weiger's mug, "that typical wood carvings are usually the same on both sides of a piece. Each side mirrors the other—top to bottom and left to right. However, on close inspection, the carvings on the cabinet seemed more like an inscription rather than ornate decoration. When viewed up close, they just looked like complex, but random carvings. Standing farther back, you could see that the carvings were blocks containing ornate symbols; the likes of which I had never seen.

"I also observed that on the opposite side of the room, there was another tall piece of furniture of similar design—a beautifully carved sideboard topped with a large, oblong mirror— every bit as tall as the large cabinet. As I inspected and admired the piece, I noticed that it had been moved. I could tell, because there were four indentations in the floor that matched the sideboard's pointed legs. For some reason, I felt compelled to move the sideboard back to its original position."

"Did it help?" Weiger asked.

"No, not really," Douglas said. "It was early morning at this time, and the sun began to shine more brightly through the dirty windows. I wondered if there were any other pieces of this caliber in the room, so I went around removing sheets from the other furniture. I uncovered a wall of books—a virtual cornucopia of knowledge, art and literature that ranged from ancient to contemporary. I knew that I wanted to spend more time here, as I could barely afford my own books.

"As I explored the marvels of this room, I also uncovered a large, dark walnut desk whose appearance matched that of the cabinet and mirrored sideboard. This beautifully carved piece had several locked drawers, but no keyholes. I surmised the drawer pulls might simply be decorative, as they did not yield to my tugs. Inlaid into its top were a number of polished metal emblems set into wooden blocks under a thick plate of glass. I had no recollection of ever having seen the symbols before—except on the cabinet on the other side of the room.

After dusting the desk's glass top, I found the symbol blocks were still quite shiny, so they might have been polished gold or a treated brass. I circled around to the drawer side of the desk to study the symbols more carefully. The sun was at my back, and my shadow obscured the desktop. When I stepped to one side to get a better look, the sun reflected off of the desk and seemed to illuminate the whole room. The emblem symbols imbedded in the desk reflected into the sideboard mirror, which in turn illuminated portions of the ornate cabinet on the opposite wall. I knew that I would need as much light as possible to work on the cabinet in this otherwise dark room.

"As I moved again behind the desk, I heard a distinctive 'click' as if a latch had been turned. I looked up expecting to see that someone had entered the room or had tried the latch on the door—but this was not the case."

"Where did the click come from?" Weiger asked.

"I was not sure, but it sounded like it came from within the cabinet. I decided to inspect the cabinet again more closely," Douglas continued.

"Was the cabinet still locked?" Weiger queried eagerly—he was getting more interested in the mystery.

"Yes, if there were any doors, they were still locked. I did discover that many of the same symbols appeared on both the desk and the cabinet, but in a different order. And there were these strange holes. Precisely drilled and all the same size—but in no discernible pattern.

"As I backed slowly across the room to examine the cabinet from a longer distance, I heard another click. It was definitely coming from the cabinet."

Weiger interrupted, "Was there something in the floor that was creaking or tipping the cabinet?"

"I considered that too—you would have made a good detective," Douglas said.

"At this point, the foreman returned and wanted a progress report. I said it might take some time to figure out.

"Mr. Heintzelman was pretty laid back. He told me to keep at it, but told me it would be more than a month before they would be ready to show the remodeled castle, so I had plenty of time to work. It was not long after that before I was able to figure out how to get the cabinet open."

"You did? How?" Weiger's excitement returned as he sat on the edge of his chair and gulped his tea. "Not with an axe, I hope."

"No, thankfully, I didn't have to resort to force, but I might be better off today if I had," the mouse said as his gaze dropped to the floor. I asked around in town about the previous owners and discovered a few interesting facts.

Apparently, they both disappeared in the last week of September—around the 23rd. At least that's when they were missed."

"Why is that special?" Weiger said.

"It's the autumnal equinox, when the length of night and day are…"

"Equal. Yes, that's a festival day for us." Weiger said suddenly.

"Yes, but I did not make that connection as quickly. It was not until Mr. Heintzelman came to me and said he and the other workers were going to take off a few days for our own End of Summer Festival. That was when I realized that the date the Lensmachers had disappeared was exactly one year ago."

"Lensmachers?" Weiger said.

"The previous owners. Lord and Lady Lensmacher."

"Interesting, but why…"

"Just hold on, you'll love this. I arrived at the castle in the predawn hours on the morning of the 23rd, on the equinox, and quickly got to work in the cabinet room. I drew back the drapes and washed the window behind the desk inside and out so I would have as much light as possible to work by once the sun came up.

"While I waited, I began to explore the bookshelf and found a small red-leather bound box on an upper shelf that looked interesting. Once I pulled it down, I discovered that it contained several tiny books—all bound in red and less than an inch high. Along with the books, I also found a set of handwritten notes. I decided to take these back to my home in the village with me to study, so I tucked the tiny box of books into my coat pocket.

"I spent the rest of the time reading through some of the other books on the shelf using my lamp. Lensmacher had a strange collection of books on alchemy, magic and sorcery from all over the world. Around eight in the morning, the sun began to shine through the windows behind the desk."

"Eight in the morning?" Weiger asked.

"Don't you understand measured time either?"

"Of course, but we measure time by the sun, the moon and the stars."

"Humans use mechanical 'clocks' that break the day up into twenty-four hours, each with sixty minutes. Eight in the morning would be a short time after dawn—when the sun rises at this latitude."

"That seems awfully contrived and very complicated. We have not needed clocks… but go on with your story," Weiger said, scratching his head.

"All right," Douglas said. "As before, the light reflected off the desk and onto the sideboard mirror and on to the cabinet. It seemed that some, but not all, of the symbols reflected light onto matching symbols on the cabinet."

WILLIAM R. VAUGHN

"Of course. Why didn't I think of that!" Weiger exclaimed.

"It might have been easier, but the blocks holding the symbols were not in the same order or arrangement as those on the cabinet."

"Did the cabinet open or click or anything?" Weiger asked—more excited than ever.

"Yes, it did click several times and then stopped. I rushed over to the cabinet expecting to see a knob exposed or a way to get it open. Still nothing."

"Another dead end," Weiger said dejectedly.

"At first, I thought so too. I also knew that something was different. The drawer pulls of the desk could now move—at least a bit. When I pulled on the center drawer, a latch clicked, and I could that see the blocks could also be moved. I looked at the cabinet and searched for the darkened symbols, and tried to find a match for it on the desk. I was right."

"It was not in the light?" Weiger offered.

"Correct again," Douglas said. "I had to somehow rearrange the blocks under the glass until the symbols left in the dark on the cabinet were getting the right reflection from the desk—from the correct symbol. I also wanted to be sure that the symbols already illuminated were reflections of the same symbols on the desk. They weren't, and the sun was still crossing the sky. I only had a couple of minutes to make any changes and get the right combination."

"Impossible," Weiger said.

"Yes, but then I accidentally caught my pocket on one of the now-exposed drawer pulls on the desk. When the knob was pulled, the blocks seemed to come to life. It sounded like they were being manipulated from a mechanism deep within the desk. Now I realized that it wasn't a desk at all—it was some kind of elaborate control panel—sort of a mechanical key."

"What?"

"Yes, it seemed so. Within moments, I was able to change the blocks through a dozen combinations by manipulating the drawer pulls. Each time they were changed, the cabinet across the room clicked and the desk whirred."

"Didn't you just want to run?"

"Yes, at first, but I didn't have time. All at once, the cabinet started to click madly and somehow transform itself. I was sure I had found the right combination."

"You did it!" Weiger exclaimed and nearly dumped over his mug, splashing tea as he jumped to his feet in excitement.

"With a low rumble, the cabinet retreated back into the wall and then the floor beneath it descended—exposing a stairway into the darkness under the castle. I was pretty startled, and I'll have to admit being quite scared."

"I can imagine!" Weiger said, blotting up the spilt tea with a rag Douglas had given him. "I would be too. Did you go down the stairs?"

"No. I didn't get a chance. Before I could cross the room and look down the stairway, a dark-hooded figure stormed up the stairs."

"My stars! Who was it? One of the other workers?" Weiger asked.

"Of course—that's what I expected, but I don't think so. He simply shouted, "It's about time!" in a booming voice. I didn't know what to answer; but before I could utter a sensible word, he forcibly ushered me out into the center of the great ballroom, raised his hand, and shouted something—a bright flash was the last thing I saw as a human."

Twenty-two—Anasta Is Captured

*A*nasta and her brother had still not made it past the wire fence that separated them from the farmer's pasture and the relative safety of the nearby forest. Bubou was still perched nervously on the wooden fencepost keeping watch—his head rotating from side to side without moving his body. Anasta had never, never been this close to an owl and it terrified her but at the same time she admired her brother for his courage—he was speaking to it like they were school chums.

"Yooou had best be getting ooout of sight," Bubou again cautioned in a dialect unique to converted owls. "I saw an eagle circling above. I expect he's spotted you already."

Anasta knew he was right—in any case, she want to get home—and fast. She impatiently watched Hisbil collect the shard of steel he had found in the grass and stuff it into his rucksack but never took her eyes off the owl which she perceived as an immediate threat.

"Come on, Anasta. We need to get to the forest," he said as he put on his pack.

Looking up at the fence that had just held her captive, Anasta's stomach turned. "We're not going up that fence again are we?" she protested.

"No, you're right, I don't think we should," Hisbil answered. "Let's see if we can find a way under or around the mesh. Bubou, can you see any paths that lead up to and under the fence—perhaps one used by other creatures who have gone before us?"

Still standing by the base of the fence, Anasta watched as Bubou flew off without a word and headed west down the fence line. He flew a hundred paces and then turned back. As he passed overhead, he called down, "Nothing down that way…." An equal distance along the fence to the east, Bubou dropped his left wing, turned suddenly, and swooped down as if to snatch up a stray rodent caught in the open. As Bubou was now hidden by the tall pasture grass, Anasta could not tell if the owl had been distracted by his hunger or some other treasure. "Where did he go?" she queried. "Is he going to leave us here unprotected?"

"Just be still for a moment and listen," Hisbil said softly. "We don't want to attract any more attention to ourselves—not any more than we already have. It might be better if he does not come back. I don't know for sure if we can trust him. He should be off working and not flying around in the forest on his own."

Without warning, the owl reappeared with its feathery legs extended forward—tipped with his long, curved talons. Anasta was deftly snatched and carried aloft. When she finally opened her eyes, she was suspended about thirty feet over the forest floor as the owl continued to fly higher into the forest canopy. She closed her eyes again and after a few long minutes the owl made a somewhat graceful landing on a large outstretched bough of a large big-leaf Maple; setting Anasta down on the branch in front of a large tree-hole.

"Wait here and dooo not moove!" cautioned Bubou in a voice as commanding as an owl could muster. He immediately flew off, leaving the frightened yenesem alone on the branch a dizzying distance above the forest floor.

Perhaps it was the prospect of being lost so far away from home, or the terrifying encounter with the cats, or the ordeal of being entangled in the deadly magical fence, or being snatched up like a wild owl's prey and deposited on a branch that made her realize that she and her brother were now in terrible danger. But she did not cry and resisted the urge to scream. Something inside her had changed.

Why did he leave me up here? Anasta asked herself not really wanting to know the answer. *I'm probably his chick's next meal. Well, I'm not going without a fight.*

Looking around Anasta discovered a branch about her own height and as big as her wrist broken off by the storm and hanging by a splinter. She broke it off and quickly began to sharpen the end as best she could. Anasta then explored the musty tree-hole which was large enough for a family of owls. The floor of the tree-hole was littered with bones and strange oval shapes left behind by the former resident. On closer inspection she found these to be the remains of the unfortunate creatures that an owl had eaten and regurgitated—owl pellets.

Ewww. These could be... me.

Inside, she found a good hiding place in a dark corner and covered herself with her cloak, now torn by the owl's talons. She lay there quietly and began to pray about her and her brother's fate. She longed for her warm bed, friends and everything to be the way it had been at home.

Listen to your brother, a calm voice said. It was an older female's voice, but not her mother's. Hisbil *can keep you both safe if you listen to him and do what he says.* It sounded like Casandra, Kassie's mom. The next sound she heard was the sound of wind on wings. She pulled the hood up on her cloak as she saw a large bird, twice the size of Bubou land on the branch. She closed her eyes and continued to pray. *It's come for me.*

Twenty-three—Over the Fence

*S*tanding at the base of the farmer's magic fence, Hisbil resisted the temptation to scream out as the owl disappeared into the forest. *That traitor! What a fool I was to trust him. It's my own fault. I should have...* He realized that he alone had been careless. He should have fetched his sister off the fence before the owl, and who knows what else, had witnessed them struggling on the wire. His mind raced as he struggled to come up with a plan to get back by Anasta's side where he could try even harder to protect her. But something stopped him. Gollsaer's voice echoed in his mind: *Think twice, and act only after you have a good plan and have another, in case the first plan doesn't work.*

Hisbil paused for a moment as he formulated a plan and then another. He dropped his rucksack, pulled out the piece of steel, and started using it to dig frantically under the fence.

Shoot. The farmer must have figured animals would try to dig out, the fencing is buried well below ground. This is going to take forever.

Sticking the metal shard back into his rucksack, he strapped it on his back and began to implement "plan B". He started at once to scale the fence as quickly as he could.

I've got to get over the fence without touching that magic wire. If I'm careful, I can squeeze through.

When he had climbed all but a few inches from the top of the mesh, Hisbil tucked his head down and tried to make himself as thin as he could—shifting his weight over the top and to the other side of the mesh while staying under the top wire. *Just a bit more and I'll be…*

Unfortunately, the metal scrap sticking out of his rucksack shifted again and wedged itself against the mesh.

Stuck! Maybe if I shift a bit to the right…

Before he realized it, the other end of the metal contacted the top wire. The last thing Hisbil heard was a deafening bang.

❧❧❧

Hisbil began to regain consciousness on the forest floor with a large bird standing over him—his yellow eyes blinking—staring down intently at the tiny Seldith. His talons were clutching a smoldering canvas rucksack.

An owl!

Hisbil tried to flee, but the pain reached out like a thousand hot needles, showering through his back and right shoulder. His left hip and leg were not much better, but he had little feeling on his left side, which spared him additional pain.

"Are yoooou all right?" Bubou said quietly. "I thought you were …"

"Bubou? What…what did you do with Anasta," Hisbil demanded, fighting off a dizzying haze, again trying in vain to get to his feet.

"She is safe. I left her high in the fooorest nearby," the owl said, still speaking calmly, trying to get Hisbil to understand. "If she does what she is tooold, she will be there waiting for you," the owl replied and tried to continue. "You tooooched the enchanted fence and fell to the ground. I saw the flash as I was returning for you." Bubou had not finished speaking when Hisbil interrupted.

"Why! Why did you take her?" Hisbil was frightened and angry. His voice made that clear. "What makes you think she's going to do as she's told? She hasn't listened to anyone for quite some time—especially not since her father…"

"I tried to save youuuur rucksack," Bubou said almost apologetically. "The piece of metal seems to have touched the enchanted wire—it took most of the force of the spell," Bubou continued, still a bit remorseful. "I'm sorry, but I had to take youuuur sister over the fence withouuuut telling her. She would never have let me carry her ooover—and I don't know that you would have let me."

Still trying to regain his senses, Hisbil realized that he was in no position to be yelling at an owl large enough to gobble him up—especially one that might have done him and his sister a generous service. Hisbil again tried to stand. "I don't think I can walk—or at least not far. Can you bring Anasta here so she can help me?"

"I don't think so…," said the owl. "She was very frightened and still wooon't trust me. I can carry yooou to her."

"I… I'm not sure I'm up for…that," Hisbil said with a tremor in his voice.

"Ontwaker, let me take youuuu to youuur sister. She is not far away."

Without another word of warning, the large owl gingerly picked up the Seldith while at a hover and carried him high up over the forest. A dark cloud crossed in front of Hisbil's eyes as he drifted off to unconsciousness. The backpack with his wand and all of its treasures was left behind.

Twenty-four—The Search

*B*ubou circled high over the forest canopy trying to retrace the route he took to the old maple tree where he left Anasta but his right wing had begun to ache which made it more difficult to fly and concentrate. Unfortunately for everyone, daylight navigation was not one of Bubou's strongest skills. Actually, one of the reasons he was not working was his lack of navigation prowess.

At least there aren't any little old ladies with pointed umbrellas to poke me.

He recalled trying to deliver a small package on a street where the human houses all looked pretty much the same. An old woman made things worse when she fought off his attempt to drop a package on her doorstep. Reporting back to the owl dispatch center, he had been instructed to return to fledgling school where he was charged with passing the navigation course again. Sadly, he had gotten lost on the way and his "Pardon me, sir, could you direct me to the School of Basic Owl Navigation?" did nothing but frighten an unsuspecting human. He had also forgotten that he was not supposed to talk to humans— ever.

So where is that tree? It has to be around here somewhere.

Hisbil began to stir and moan in his talons.

"It wooon't be much longer," the owl said softly.

There! There it is. I knew I could find it.

The owl circled the large tree and landed on the outstretched branch laying Hisbil down as gently as he could.

"Anasta!" he hooted. But he heard nothing.

Bubou stuck his head inside the hollowed-out opening in the tree but was startled to see nothing but a pair of tiny red eyes looking back at him. An ugly brown tree rat cowered against the back of the tree cave holding a frozen pose as it tried to look invisible. The rat did not have long to wait before he found out if this strategy worked—the next thing he saw (albeit briefly) was the inside of the owl's throat.

She's not here? Where could she have gone?

Bubou looked back at the still unconscious Hisbil. Yes, he was breathing.

Perhaps it's better that he's not awake.

And then he saw it.

This isn't a big-leaf maple, it's an oak!

"We're in the wrong tree!" he cried.

Bubou picked up Hisbil and dove off the branch and soared up to restart his search for the correct tree.

Maple, maple, big-leaf maple. To the south… or was it to the south-east?

The owl tried to hold his charge gently as his anxiety level increased as each minute passed.

Find a landmark and work out your destination in relation…

He tried to recall his navigation training which had been very hard for him. He never did understand human maps very well—just a bunch of squiggly lines. And the words that seemed to flip around on him didn't help.

There's another oak… and a cottonwood… and a… a maple. Yes, that's a big-leaf maple!

Bubou landed on an outstretched branch that like the first maple tree he had found had a large hole in the trunk. When he set Hisbil down he stirred and cried out.

This isn't good. I really need to get them both back home. In any case, I can't take much more of this.

"Anasta!" he called, sticking his head inside the tree-hole. Again, there was no answer.

This is the tree. I know it. I can see marks where I landed last time. She must have climbed down. Impossible, it's too high.

"Anasta come out!" he called as loudly as he dared. Still there was no response.

Hisbil began to stir again as a soft rain began to fall.

It's getting cold. I need to get him under cover.

The owl picked up Hisbil and hovered to the tree-hole and managed to lay him in a corner out of the wind. Hisbil did not stir—he did not appear to be breathing.

Twenty-five—Anasta is Found

"*G*et off of me!" Anasta said as she sprang up from her hiding place pushing her brother's body aside. At once, she was glad to see him but quickly became alarmed to see he was not kidding with her but unconscious.

"What have you done to him?" she shouted, taking a step forward and thrusting the sharpened stick at the owl.

In a flash, the owl snapped the stick in two with his bill and grabbed the remaining piece she held in her hand with his talons. Anasta fell back, and before she could make another move, the owl carefully placed his foot over Hisbil's now limp body to protect it.

"Please! Calm dooown. I can do yooou no harm. I have sworn to protect my ontwaker and those he protects," the owl said in a firm, calming voice. "Yooou are only threatening everyone's safety," he continued. "These are dangerous wooooods, and surely we have been heard by those whooo live and hunt here. I don't have the strength to carry both of you at once if trouble comes."

"Who is this 'ontwaker' you're sworn to protect?" Anasta demanded, albeit in a quieter voice.

"He who lies dying at my feet," Bubou said solemnly. "Your brother you call Hisbil."

"*Why* is he your ontwaker?" she asked. "And what have you done to him? Is this what you call protection? He's hurt! We need to get him back home where my mother can heal him…"

"This is not the time or place to discuss hooow I came to be as I am or why yooour brother is my ontwaker." Yes, we must get youuur brother back to youuur people where his wouuunds can be mended. I can't carry youuu or your brother far, as I toooo have been injured." The owl held up his wing to reveal a now festering wound.

"What took you so long? Did you get lost?"

"I'm sooory," Bubou answered gently. "Yes, I had trouble finding this tree again. I got turned around," he admitted sheepishly.

"A gigantic flying beast tried to eat me after you left me. It just flew away a minute ago!" Anasta said, moving over to kneel by her brother. "I had to hide in the tree-hole."

We can't stay here much longer—I'm in no shape to fight off another bird.

"Can you help your brother?" he asked. "We must find anooother place to rest and hide—perhaps all night."

Left alone in the tree-hole, Anasta had been given some time to think, and she had realized that it was up to her to help keep them *both* alive—to do her part.

"My mother is a healer. If we can get him home, she can make him well and strong again. It's her calling. If you rest a bit can't you find the strength to take us home?" she urged as she enveloped her brother's still unconscious body in her arms. She could tell he was barely breathing as she listened to his chest. As she cuddled him in her arms, her own body began to tingle.

"I don't know where yooou live," the owl said. "Could you find yooour home if I flew over the village?" Bubou queried. For the first time, the owl's voice began to quaver as he realized the deadly seriousness of their situation.

"I really don't know. We were carried off by a cat running this way and that in the night....I've never really been away from home before—not this far out." Anasta's voice trailed off as she realized that she and her brother were hopelessly lost. She began to quietly sob, her tears falling on Hisbil's face as she held his head in her lap. The owl stood over the two of them feeling helpless shielding them from the building wind and rain.

Twenty-six—The Eighth Sacred Volume

*W*eiger sat dumbfounded. The mouse! *He's a uman!* This shed a whole new light on the situation. Douglas still had his back to him, but Weiger could tell that the mouse had been shaken at the re-telling of his encounter with the hooded figure he had released from the dungeons below the castle.

"Well Weiger, how is it that you're out here on your own and in broad daylight?" Douglas finally asked as he dried dishes and put away the tea things.

The Seldith could see that the mouse didn't really want to continue talking about the castle or what had transfigured him, but he also knew that there might be something he could do to help the mouse. On the other hand, he didn't know if he should share any more information about himself or his own quest for the missing Sacred Seven—especially not to a uman—even if he was now a mouse. Weiger had any number of secrets that he would rather not share.

Getting up to peer out the large front window that provided a territorial view of the valley, Weiger asked, "You said that you were safe in this house. Wouldn't a passing beast or bird be able to pluck your tail off the front porch?"

Douglas smiled and wiped his tiny black eyes with the back of his paw. Turning back to Weiger, he replied, "The house is invisible. It's that simple."

Weiger was incredulous. He also smiled and, with a laughing tone, said, "Right. Invisible. So what did I see when I walked up?" He suspected the mouse had been putting yellow mushroom spores in his tea.

"You saw the house, of course; but if you walk past the front steps, you'll discover that the home disappears into the foliage. It can't be seen from above or below by human or beast—not unless they just stumble upon it."

"Is this your invention?" Weiger asked, turning to Douglas with a look of disbelief.

"No—as I said, I'm a simple carpenter but a quick study. Remember the tiny books I found?"

"Ah, yes. The books were hidden in a red leather-bound box made to look like a larger book."

"Right," said Douglas, walking toward his own bookcase.

"I have one here," Douglas said as he slid the top shelf his bookcase to one side. Behind it, he revealed a small cache of books bound in blood-red leather. He pulled one out and began to cross the room to show it to Weiger.

Weiger's demeanor changed as soon as he saw the shelved books. "Where did...how?" he stammered. "Those can't be! They *must* be *The Sacred Seven Books of Truth*! They are just as the elders described them!" *And just as Emperor had described them.*

"Really? You've seen them before?" Douglas answered as he opened the book on the table in front of Weiger. The pages were beautifully scripted in a flowing, ornamental calligraphy and illuminated with delicate hand-painted pictures depicting epic events along with detailed diagrams, maps, and architectural drawings. The books themselves were bound in fine leather, now aged to a deep blood red with the page edges overlaid with gold. The covers and spine were engraved stating the era that they included and the symbols of the millennia dating back to the earliest recordings of Seldith truths. Weiger was convinced that these books were most certainly the long-lost excerpts from the ancient books originally made of clay tablets, which were transcribed to archive these records long before the tablets crumbled back to dust.

Once Weiger realized what he was inspecting, he dropped to his knees and fell back on his heels, bowing his head in reverence. He folded his hands and laid them in his lap—the mouse dared not disturb him.

Weiger eventually rose and closed the book with gentle veneration as if its pages were made of delicate crystal that would break or be violated if mishandled.

"I...I've heard about these volumes but always assumed that they were a myth. No one has seen them in... in many hundreds of lifetimes." Weiger then realized that Emperor was right. *The Sacred Seven were* nearby—they were here in this room. His mind began to reel as he contemplated the endless wealth and power that stood on the shelf above him.

"What makes you think these are *The Sacred Seven Books of Truth?*" Douglas asked.

"Every Seldith—even exiles—knows of *The Sacred Seven*. I knew almost at once these were not just diaries of *The Books of Truth* that we see and read every day but were far more important—these are *sacred* texts. These books bear the selfsame red bindings and what I think are the ancient markings of volumes lost to the Seldith many generations ago. While the elders only whisper about their contents, everyone is schooled on their existence."

"So you don't really know what these books are supposed to contain?" Douglas asked.

"The elders never really said, but there were plenty of rumors. Consider that *The Books of Truth* are actually scores of diaries written since the dawn of time. You could think of them as a catalog of experiences to pass from generation to generation. The Seldith do not trust verbal history as umans do. Because of this, each book is inscribed:

'This Book of Truth counsels reader and leader alike. Read, understand, and learn lest you repeat the evil and folly recorded in these pages.'

The Books have become an encyclopedia of sorts with "truths" and knowledge discovered and recorded over the millennia.

As the story goes, at one time, there was an especially *sacred* set of books excised from the whole. These special books were written to document and discuss the truths that should *not* be told, truths that must be forever hidden for the common good. They described the ancient confusion spell and many other powerful spells including the awakening spell. These sacred volumes tell how the Seldith came to this world and how we were to leave it—and when. It's rumored that they spoke of spells to change coal into diamonds, lead into gold and spells that would make the weak strong and the strong unbelievably powerful. It was agreed (or so they say) that if these truths were generally known, the population of Seldith, umans, and animals would be put in dire jeopardy—our society and theirs would collapse from the forces of greed, avarice and lust. Because of the secrets they contain, *The Sacred Seven* have untold value to uman and Seldith, beast and bird alike."

"And this mouse?" Douglas said solemnly.

"And especially mice," Weiger said.

"Can you read the text?" Douglas queried sheepishly. "I have tried but have been unable to translate more than a few pages using the notes I found with the books. I certainly hope I have not violated their sanctity by reading them."

"I shouldn't think so," Weiger said, looking up at Douglas. "How many volumes did you find? As I said that there are seven volumes. Did you find them all?"

"No, there are eight in all," Douglas said as he brought another volume down from the shelf and stacked it on the table with the others.

Weiger watched in horror as Douglas plopped the volumes on the messy kitchen table. "By the stars, be careful," he urged. "Please, please—let me. There are protocols and traditions that dictate how *The Books of Truth* are to be handled." His hand touched the mouse's paw as he reached out for another book to dust it with a damp dishtowel.

"Let me," Weiger said as he carefully cleaned the table and then took down each volume one-by-one and reverently placed them on the table.

As Weiger laid down the eighth volume, Douglas said, "Right, as I thought, there are eight books. Something does not add up. Are you sure there are only supposed to be seven?"

"Of course," said Douglas as he set the book down reverently.

"Yes, seven. There are supposed to be only seven. It's been drilled into us from childhood," Weiger said and recited the rhyme Seldith were told in school.

'Bloodred Truth sevenfold. Volumes more sacred than purest gold. Stolen from the crypt by umen upright who search in darkness for Truths that enlight.'

"So they were taken by men—human men?" Douglas asked, watching Weiger begin to gingerly dust the books as one would clean a delicate glass ornament.

"Yes, many centuries ago. But I don't know the details," Weiger said. Not really listening to the mouse, he took a deep breath and pulled a chair up to the table, his eyes transfixed on the sacred volumes. Like magnets drawing a compass needle, the deep red volumes drew Weiger's undivided attention to the bindings adorned with the symbols and signs of the ancients. At the same time, his mind was fogged with conflict. *If I can read these… if I can unlock their secrets, all my troubles…the power…the wealth…the revenge.*

He closed his eyes and covered his face with his hands. These sacred books are not mine. Not mine to return to the *Seldith* and not mine to auction to the highest bidder—not yet.

"Didn't you say the books were in your pocket?" Weiger asked looking up. "How did they get here—here on your bookshelf?"

"Ah, that's another long story," Douglas said, returning from the back room of the house with a rather large bundle.

"I've got the time," said Weiger, still somewhat mesmerized by the mere presence of these books. He continued to arrange the sacred volumes on the table—occasionally opening them to see what secrets they defended within their covers. Like Douglas, Weiger found that he could not read most of the words or understand more than a few of the elaborate drawings or ornate symbols.

"Do you recall that I had figured out how to open the cabinet, and a hooded figure stormed up the stairs?" Douglas began.

"Yes, go on," Weiger said with his eyes focused on the volumes as he carefully turned their pages.

"Well, after the hooded man took me into the ballroom and I saw the light, I found myself on the floor buried in my clothes. I had been transformed to a mouse in the blink of an eye. I expect the hooded figure…"

Weiger interrupted, "A dark wizard. He was undoubtedly a dark wizard."

Douglas looked up and nodded his head. "Yes, I expect you're right. I was a mouse but I could speak and think like a man. I also realized that I could not stay there in the wizard's castle, so I began to claw and chew my way out. As I worked my way through the rough fabric, I found myself in my own trousers pocket. Here I found the eight books I had taken from the red box on the bookshelf—now larger but still small enough to handle quite easily.

"With some considerable effort, I managed to hide the books within the walls of the room—thanks to a convenient mouse hole. After that, I had no choice but to flee the castle and try to find safety elsewhere.

"I desperately wanted to return to my wife and family. Before long I realized that this was a hopeless quest. My wife would simply set my own cats on me before I had a chance to tell her who I was. I decided to stay near the castle and try to find some way to reverse this transfiguration.

"In the following days, which led to weeks, I retrieved the books from the inner wall and tried to read them. Unfortunately, I could not decipher the strange symbols or alphabet (if it was one)—except for one section near the front of the first volume. Here I easily deciphered several important spells and potions—I used these to hide my presence and ultimately to fashion this little cottage."

"Weiger?" the mouse asked.

But Weiger was focused on the books, still arranging the thick volumes one-by-one so the symbols and signs on their covers lined up. He ended up with a seven-sided figure that left a hole in the middle. Weiger held the eighth book using only his fingertips—it was very different from the others as the symbols did not match those of the other volumes. Yes, it was a bit larger and thicker than the others, but there was something else about it that was unusual and out of place. To make matters worse, the pages seemed to change each time they were turned.

Pausing from his concentration, Weiger took a moment to assimilate what Douglas had said. "So you were able to read the books?"

"Yes at least a bit, and that's how I was able to make my home invisible but nothing past the first chapter. So my friend, can you read the rest of the books?" Douglas asked again hopefully. "They might hold the secret to transform me back to a human. It might take me forever to translate, and…." Douglas' voice dropped off.

"And what?" Weiger asked.

"And mice don't live very long. I've been like this for about a year, and I don't expect I'll live for many more months. I don't have the time to translate enough to figure out how to change back to a human."

"I see," said Weiger. He stared down at the books laid out on the table. Not knowing what else to do, Weiger carefully laid the eighth book into the center and turned to speak to the mouse.

"Sure…I can read the books," he lied. "We are born with this gift. It's not hard, as the books are quite easy to understand if you know the ancient forms of the Seldith written language."

"That's easy for you and your kind to say," Douglas lamented. "For those outside your race, the books are impossible to decipher." Weiger was amazed and puzzled that Douglas had been able to make any sense at all out of *The Books*. The mouse couldn't be lying if he had been able to extract spells as he had boasted and the cottage was indeed shielded from view using some kind of spell or invisible fabric like his own cloak.

Weiger got up from the table and walked back to the window where he silently watched the afternoon sun descend through the treetops to the west. A shaft of yellow sunlight played over the books now arranged on the kitchen table. Weiger wished his home in the village had windows like this—the panoramic view was spectacular. He then remembered that he didn't have a home at all in the village or anywhere else, not even Shutz Norte—especially if he did not return with *The Books*.

Douglas crossed the room began to prepare a meal. As he did, they both felt a subtle shudder through the floor.

"What was that?" Weiger asked, moving over to the window.

The low, uneven vibration continued as Douglas paused, holding a bowl he was using to mix biscuit dough. "It's probably an animal or someone walking nearby," Douglas said. "Let's hope they don't step on the cottage. I haven't figured out how to protect it from a size-eleven boot," he said with a thin smile.

As he turned, he noticed a leg of the table rattling on the wooden floor. And then he looked at *The Books*. Slowly, at first, but with increasing speed, they began to tremble, rise, and rotate. Within a few moments, they transformed themselves into an undulating nine-sided shape.

"I think we found out why there are eight volumes," said Douglas, putting distance between himself and the table. Weiger turned back to the table and was amazed to see the enneahedron slowly stop spinning, hover a moment, and gently settle back on the table. The shape then became translucent, revealing a softly glowing sphere slowly spinning inside. Weiger said nothing—he was again transfixed by the transmogrified books.

A gentle voice seemed to come from the shape: "Who awakens *The Truth* and what is your bidding?"

Twenty-seven—The Healer Awakens

Anasta's knees folded as if a great weight had been laid across her shoulders. She crumpled to the mossy floor of the tree-hole, and she continued to weep. "I've killed my own brother and I'll never see my mother again!"

Bubou could only look down with dismay at the pitiful creatures collapsed at his feet. Hisbil lay motionless on floor of the tree-hole where Anasta had cradled him in her arms; he was still breathing, but just barely.

"Why did you bring us up here, Bubou? You need to take us *home!*" Anasta shouted in frustration through her tears. *If only the owl just left us alone!* Anasta could only watch as her brother slowly succumbed to the elements and his injuries.

"Anasta! I need you to help me," the owl chided. "I cannot carry you or your brother any farther," the owl chided. "You really must help me…help you, help you both. This hollooow belongs to some ooother flying beast that I don't have the strength or skill toooo fight. Together we must dooo *something;* but until yooour brother is stronger, we won't be able to mooove him again."

To make matters worse, as afternoon faded to evening, the misty rain began to intensify and was pushed into their faces by a quickening breeze. The tree's outstretched branches swayed as they caught the wind like the sails of a great ship on a rough sea. As Bubou fidgeted nervously, Anasta continued to rock on her knees, hiding her face in her arms; but she had stopped weeping.

I...I have to help him. He's the only one that can get us home.

Crawling back into the tree-hole, she knelt beside Hisbil and grabbed him by his coat and pulled him back into her embrace.

Bubou did what he could to shield them from the elements with his wings. "Can you help him?" the owl asked softly.

Anasta simply said, "I'll try." Gingerly taking her brother into her arms as one would handle a beloved doll, Anasta opened her cloak and tunic and mimicked her mother's caring embrace—holding Hisbil's body against the fur on her bare chest. She could scarcely feel the warmth of his limp body against hers; he was deathly cold and wet. *It's too late.*

Clutching him even tighter, she pulled away his tunic and shirt so the soft fur of his chest touched hers. At first, nothing happened, and nothing happened for some time. Anasta wondered if she was *really* gifted with her mother's healing embrace. *If mother could have given me a few lessons.* She tried to concentrate—to give her warmth to her only brother.

As Bubou watched, Hisbil seemed to be breathing more easily. Anasta could feel it too. *Perhaps the enchantment is working...* It was not long after that when Anasta began to feel her warmth returned by her brother's fur pressed against her own. Then she felt it: a small tingling sensation at first that grew to discomfort and then pain—stark, searing pain that spread throughout her body. Stifling a scream, she felt that she could not let go of her now-stirring brother, no matter what.

It didn't make much difference, as Anasta did not have the skill to break away—something that only an experienced healer could do and would do only to spare her own life. If anything, Anasta's arms embraced her brother even more tightly. The burning pain gradually moved to her legs and shoulder to reflect the wounds and injuries inflicted upon her brother. It did not subside as Hisbil showed more signs of life. Gradually, the warmth, strength, and life force drained from Anasta's body into Hisbil's. In time, Anasta's arms fell limp, and she collapsed under her brother's weight.

Twenty-eight—Kassie's Cage

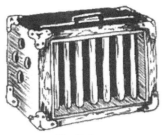

There she was at last—in a cage on the table. Hisbil caught just a glimpse of her flaxen hair and then just the side of her face as Kassie paced back and forth behind the wall of bars that made up one wall of the cage.

Managing to climb hand-over-hand up a window curtain, Hisbil finally reached the tabletop. From there, he could survey the entire room—including the mouse hole in the baseboard where he had managed to get into the room and the old bloodhound basking in the sunshine. Thankfully, the dog seemed to be oblivious to the world, his ears and legs twitching as he chased rabbits in his dreams.

Hisbil was careful not to make a sound as he crept across the desk, around the giant quill pen and past a large glass ashtray with the smoldering remains of a fat cigar that sent ripples of acrid smoke streaming toward the room's high ceiling. *The uman has not been gone long.* On the other side of a large green desk blotter, Hisbil could get a better look at Kassie's prison. It was a sturdy box about six paces on a side and about three paces tall. It seem to be made of black varnished wood and assembled with ornate brass corners and fittings. *Perhaps this uman catches and imprisons creatures for his amusement.* The cage seemed to be specially made for Seldith-sized creatures.

When Hisbil looked up above the cage, his worst fears were realized. The shelves on the nearby wall were lined with clear jars of all shapes and sizes containing liquid and the preserved remains of the uman's collection of creatures; organized and labeled like canned produce. In among the preserved grasshoppers, toads, and snails were several bottles that contained the remains of what appeared to be Seldith and faeries—their lifeless eyes still open, staring out into the room watching him. Hisbil looked away to keep from screaming out in terror.

Sweet stars he's going to dissect her! Hisbil whispered to himself as he continued across the desk and over to the cage. As if he had heard him, the dog abruptly stopped snoring. Hisbil was too close to the back of the desk to see if he was prowling around.

He's going to hear me for sure. As he tried to crawl up on the ashtray to check the dog's whereabouts, Hisbil slipped on the slick glass and fell, landing on the pen which immediately started rolling toward the edge of the table. Scrambling to race after it, Hisbil was too late; he held his breath waiting for it to hit the floor. As luck would have it, the pen hit the carpet under the table.

I've got to get her out of here and fast.

Hisbil crept around to the front of the cage. Kassie didn't see him at first, but when she retraced her steps their eyes met. When she first saw Hisbil, her face erupted with joy, and she rushed over to the bars—her arms reaching out for him.

"How did you find me?" she cried softly. Their bodies met as they embraced through the bars. Her head pressed against the bars and his shoulder as she wept and pulled him closer. Again, the smell of jasmine in her hair awakened the love he had longed for.

"I've…I've been so afraid." Looking up, she whispered through her tears, "He cuts open creatures and…"

"Yes, I know. I won't let that happen to you...I'm going to get you out of here," he said firmly with as much confidence as he could muster.

Looking around while Kassie clutched him even tighter, he tried to get a better look at the cage. It seemed there was no door or lock, just a panel in front that held the bars. It would be impossibly heavy for someone his size to lift. There might even be a latch and lock on top, but there was no way to tell.

"We'll have to work out a plan, some way to get you through these bars."

"Who is 'we'?" she asked. He could feel her warmth through his cloak. Hisbil had never held her closer but felt so far apart.

"A friend. He's come to help. I expect we'll need him."

"Hisbil?" she cried.

Suddenly, the cage and the table, and then the room seemed to dissolve, and Kassie with it. All he could hear was her screams, just as on the day she was captured.

"Hisbil don't leave me...Hisbil...don't leave me..."

"Hisbil! Hisbil! You're going to bring every beast in the forest down on us," Bubou said as he stood over him. Hisbil awoke and found himself in the darkened tree-hole, impossibly high above the forest floor. He was shivering and still longing to hold Kassie once more. He groped into his breast pocket to make sure her scarf was still there. It was.

Twenty-nine—Hisbil Awakens

*C*oming to his senses, Hisbil discovered he was lying next to his sister. She had very little color in her face—her cold, limp arms were now draped across his back and nearly as lifeless as the shorn cornstalks in the farmer's field. His pain had all but disappeared, but the memory of his dream about Kassie remained as though he had just held her in his arms through the bars. The burns across his back and shoulder were healed but he could still feel a deep scar—perhaps to remind him of this trip to the sheer cliff of death.

"Anasta!" he called to her, but she did not answer. Her eyes were partially open but stared blankly into the growing darkness. Like her brother before her, Anasta was drifting off toward the black pit of unconsciousness and death. Hisbil put his ear to her chest and for the longest time could not detect her heart beating—but it was, albeit weakly. He fastened her blouse and covered her as best he could in her shredded cloak, finally draping his own cloak over her.

"She's too young—she should not have tried to heal me!" Hisbil cried as he held his now limp sister's body in his arms. "Bubou, we need to get some hot food into her! Where are we?" Hisbil was almost himself again—as if he had never been hurt at all. "Is there any food left? Can we make a fire here? Where's the rucksack!" he barked.

Bubou was taken aback by these demands and by the sudden recovery of his ontwaker. He looked confused and a bit worried. "Is your sister going tooo recover? I had nooo idea what she was doooing. Yes, a fire will certainly be seen, but it can alsooo frighten away anything trying to reclaim this tree-cave."

"Okay, okay...we're all going to need fire and food, and *soon*." Hisbil knew that when his mother took on another's illness, she would only recover if she got enough of the right things to eat. Before attempting a healing, his mother always prepared a broth of mushrooms, wild carrots, and herbs to help both healed and healer recover.

"She should not have tried to heal me. No one believed she was ready—she did not have the maturity, and she was terribly foolish to try," Hisbil said.

"Or terribly brave," Bubou offered.

Hisbil looked into Bubou's eyes and saw the wisdom—he was right. Anasta's act was one of uncharacteristic self-sacrifice and bravery. "So, where's the rucksack?" Hisbil asked as he looked around the tree-cave, quite expecting it to be laid aside nearby. He continued his search out on the tree branch only to discover he was very high up on the tree. *Golly, we're high!* "How did we get up here?" he asked.

"I carried you both—one at a time from the fence. Your rucksack...it's not here...my wing is injured. I could barely carry you both up here one at a time. It's still back by the fence," Bubou answered, but in a voice that did not exude confidence. "I...I'm sure it can be found."

Hisbil realized that the flint and (more importantly) his wand were in the rucksack. *And the spell!*

"That's what I'm afraid of—someone will find it before we do," Hisbil replied, his voice showing more stress. He had just traded places with his sister as he realized how desperate their situation had become. They were a long way from home, and without a lot of luck, they were not going to get back there anytime soon—if ever.

She's not going to make it through the night without food and warmth.

"We need to get the rucksack," Hisbil said solemnly after a brief silence. He had worked out a plan, but it meant that he would have to trust the owl to do his bidding once again.

"Yes," Bubou said. "I'll bring it here—if I can find where it's hidden. It will be easier toooo navigate in the dark."

"No, you *must* find it Bubou. Our lives depend on it!" Hisbil countered.

Before Hisbil blinked, Bubou dove off the tree and disappeared into the foggy rain. He was gone, and Hisbil had been left alone with his sister high in a tree from which they could not possibly escape. Thankfully, Hisbil did not know that Bubou had considerable difficulty finding this tree the last time he tried. He also didn't hear or see the large bird circling the old tree.

Thirty—The Owl Meets the Pussycat

*B*ubou knew what he had to do. As he dove off the tree, the rain pelted his wings and face, making it harder to see and even harder to fly. *I must find my way back to the hiding place, But no!"* He suddenly dipped his wing to turn and flew in the opposite direction—back toward the big maple tree where he had left Hisbil and his sister. Trying to remember what he learned in navigation school, he looked at the tree from above and all of the landmarks around it. *The meadow to the south...the hilltop to the west, the grove of poplar trees to the east, and the farmer's field some way off to the north. Yes, I can find this tree again.* He turned again toward the farm, as he knew the rucksack was not far from the enchanted fence. *It has been there only a short time,* he reasoned. *No one will have bothered it.*

Because his improved night vision, and the fact that the rain had dwindled to a light mist, the owl was soon able to find the farmer's enchanted fence and where the Seldith had tried to cross. Landing on the same fencepost, he saw something moving in the dark at the tree line. *Dinner.*

Every muscle tensed as instinct and experience-honed hunting skill took over. In an instant, the owl had taken a bead on some animal in the deep shadows. Taking back to the air as quietly as possible, the owl flew at a tangent to gain altitude so it could attack the prey at full speed—multiplying the impact of his talons.

As Bubou began his attack dive, the moon broke out of the clouds briefly flooding the tree line in a soft light. He kept his bright yellow eyes fixed on the target as he gained speed. As he extended his talons and began his flare, Bubou was briefly startled by a reflection from the animal's neck. At the last instant, the animal darted to safety, and Bubou's talons closed on the space where it had just stood.

Missed.

Bubou rolled out of his dive and turned back toward his quarry, but the animal was nowhere to be seen. Bubou circled for a few minutes, but the animal had been able to escape its fate. Remembering that he had an important mission, Bubou returned to the enchanted fence and began looking for the rucksack. It was not there.

That was close. That owl almost had me. I'll need to be more careful Mink said to herself. The awakened cat also had a mission: She knew that if she did not guard her ontwaker's possessions, she would be dishonored—it was something she simply had to do. To her dismay she could see the bird picking around in the brush and leaves at the base of the fence, where it soon uncovered Hisbil's rucksack.

None of that weeee'll have, Mink said to herself. About the time the owl had pulled the rucksack out with his beak, Mink lept from the fencepost and tumbled the owl to the ground, trying to get a death grip on the owl's throat.

After a brief scuffle, the owl broke free for a moment and tried to get some air between himself and the cat. "Get away that easilyyyy, youuuu can't," Mink said as she launched herself several feet in the air to bring down the owl with her own long, outstretched claws.

"Wait!" the owl cried out as the cat pulled him to the ground and tried to get the upper hand (or paw). Mink was surprised to hear the owl speak almost as surprised as the owl was to hear the cat speak.

A bit curious (as cats can be), Mink loosened her grip on the owl long enough for him to escape. The owl landed a few paces away, too winded to fly again.

"Who are youuuu? What are you doing with my ontwaker's things? And how can you speak?" they said almost in unison in their own dialects. At once, they realized that they shared the same ontwaker—they were, in a sense, comrades and not adversaries.

"My name is Bubooou. This is *my* ontwaker's rucksack. I hid it here for him not long ago. And why do you think it belongs to *your* ontwaker?" Bubou said with some irritation in his voice.

"Following my ontwaker's trail I waaas, through the pasture and heeeere it ended. Come back for his rucksack before long, heee should." Mink replied.

"And Ontwaker Hisbil calls you…?" Bubou asked.

"Mink, call me they do."

After the pair answered as few of each other's questions (and each had quite a few) as the other felt prudent, they both realized that their shared ontwaker was marooned with his gravely ill sister and needed their help. In his usual impulsive fashion and in an attempt to complete his urgent mission, Bubou picked up the rucksack in his talons and started to fly off—back toward his ontwaker.

"Wait," said Mink in an insistent voice. "*I* should carryyyy the rucksack, I think. After all, found it first, I did."

"Hardly," retorted Bubou as he landed again. "Do youuuu know where the ontwaker is hidden? I will take him the rucksack, and you can follow along as you wish. Or perhaps youuuu expect me to carry youuuu?" Bubou said with a sly tone in his voice.

Mink knew that there was no way the owl could carry her off in his talons without shredding her flesh. "Ah, no. You can't pick me up without tearing me apart," the cat replied.

"I need tooo return tooo my ontwaker. He is in danger, so I can't wait any looonger," Bubou said as he began to take off again.

"Our ontwaker would neeeeed this piece of rock from his rucksack, perhaps?" Mink said mischievously as the owl was nearly airborne. Her paw covered what looked to be a gray rock about the size of the Seldith's fist.

Again, the owl landed, but far closer to Mink this time. He might need to deal with this cat once and for all to get back the flint she had tucked under her forepaw. While the owl knew he could dispatch the cat quite easily, he could not in good conscious harm an awakened brother or sister—especially one awakened by Hisbil their common ontwaker.

"Lead meee to our ontwaker, you must," Mink insisted. "Just fly low enough for meeee to keeeep you in sight, you must. Get back to him, weeee must—so stop arguing. Carry the rucksack, I shall, to make sure you do not try to lose meee." Mink dropped the flint stone into the rucksack and picked it up in her teeth.

Surprised by this clever move, Bubou had even less time to argue. He ran a few steps and barely pushed himself into the air.

Remembering the map he had drawn in his mind, the owl looked for his memorized landmarks and found them one by one. The meadow to the south…the hilltop to the west, the grove of poplar trees to the east, and the farmer's field some way off to the north. Although he had to turn back many times to help the cat catch up, before long, he found what he (more or less) believed was the right tree.

"I think this is it!" he called down to Mink who was bounding through the undergrowth trying her best to follow.

Mink, now standing at the base of the tree with the rucksack, looked up at the owl resting on a branch ninety feet in the air.

"Are you *sure?*" Mink asked, still trying to catch her breath.

"Yes…yes, they are up here waiting. Are you going to bring it up or…," Bubou said impatiently.

While it took the housecat a few minutes, she was soon standing (and breathing hard) on the outstretched branch in front of a tree-hole. The pack was still dangling from her mouth.

"Ontwaker?" she asked.

Thirty-one—The Blood-Tempered Sword

*T*he night grew darker as the misty rain squall blew through. Their old tree began to sway; the boughs complaining with creaks and groans. Only partially hidden by the darkness, the clouds continued to race across the sky as if being chased by far off demons.

Hisbil remembered that Bubou said that he had been keeping watch, looking out for the previous owner of the tree cave. *What if it returns? My sword, where's my sword!*

It didn't take but a moment to discover that his old blade and scabbard had been hopelessly entangled in his clothing. He took care to free it and draw the short sword from its scabbard. Yes, it was still intact—the gray iron blade was fairly sharp but still badly cracked near the hilt. That gave Hisbil a modicum of comfort, as he knew that he would at least have a fighting chance to protect himself and his sister from a marauder—if it wasn't too large. After a limbering swipe or two at an imaginary squirrel, he returned the sword to its scabbard and refastened the belt so he could draw it more easily if the need were to arise. *It will have to do.*

A thousand thoughts swirling through his head, Hisbil's mind drifted back to Kassie and then his own warm bed and cozy room. As he started to fall asleep, he realized that it was up to him to stand guard—*Stay awake! Think of something else,* he said almost aloud. Hisbil sat back down on the damp tree-cave floor and again cradled his sister in his arms. *She seems so helpless. Like Kassie.*

Anasta let out a soft moan. Hisbil put his hand on her neck and found that she was not as cold as before—she was a bit better.

We're going to need some firewood.

Feeling around inside the ink-dark tree-hole, Hisbil found a number of relatively dry twigs and sticks, along with what felt like nest-building materials and a number of oval chunks of…

Owl pellets. This is an owl's nest!

He gathered these as best he could and began to stack them out of the rain.

Without warning, the tree-hole's entrance was blocked by a great bird as it landed on the branch flapping its wings to gain a footing on the slippery branch. Hisbil knew at once it was not Bubou; this bird was dark and larger—considerably larger.

It's an eagle! A big adult.

So far, it kept its back to them so it had not seen Hisbil, and Anasta were still covered in their camouflage cloaks. Only her leg was exposed a few paces from the bird's long, razor-sharp talons.

Holy stars. Now what? Perhaps it's just resting and will fly off on its own…

Hisbil dared not move to cover Anasta's leg. On the upside, the bird was shielding them from the cold wind—he could feel the warmth of the eagle's body right through its feathers. Hisbil quietly drew his sword but knew that he would not likely be able to do much with it against so large a bird.

If only I had my wand, he thought as his mind raced through his options. *I've got to get the bird to leave long enough for Bubou to return and get us down from the tree. A lot of good that will do—Bubou would be no match for this monster. It's just resting… I hope it's just resting. It doesn't like the rain any better than we do.*

In its talons, Hisbil could see that the bird carried most of a salmon carcass.

It's been fishing. That's a King salmon. There must be a river nearby. Thought of the fish made Hisbil's mouth water. The eagle leaned over and began to rend the fish—tearing off chunks to eat. It didn't seem to be eating very much of the fish—just shredding it into smaller pieces.

Great. All I have to do is get this giant bird to fly off and leave us the fish. Right. Like that's gonna happen.

Suddenly, the eagle looked up.

It sees something. Or has it heard my heartbeat? It seems loud enough for the umans in the next valley to hear. No, it's spotted something in the sky.

The eagle craned its head to watch the approaching bird intently. It's another eagle! That's all we need—two eagles fighting on the same roost with my deathly ill sister a step away. I wish it would just go away! He then realized that it was more likely to be Bubou returning with his father's rucksack.

It's Bubou. I have to do something now! Maybe if I just jab it and yell it will fly off.

With the eagle's attention fixed on its circling adversary, Hisbil mustered up all of his courage and moved quietly behind the bird—strategically positioning himself between the bird and his sister. In one motion, he rammed his iron blade into the eagle's back at the base of its tail and shouted the first thing that came to mind, "*Valde Aquila Exsisto Mei!*"

Hisbil was blinded with a brilliant flash of light and a deafening sound that began at the hilt of his short sword and quickly engulfed the eagle in an immense ball of green light. The light quickly walked back up the hilt of the sword and halfway up his arm. Somehow, he had cast a spell—but what had it done?

The eagle seemed paralyzed, even after Hisbil extracted the tip of the sword which had barely broke the bird's skin. The eagle slowly turned its head around, but could do nothing but stare into Hisbil's eyes.

As the green glow faded, the eagle wilted, its eyes closed, and it staggered, eventually losing its balance. It toppled off the branch into the misty darkness below. Hisbil could not tell if it regained the ability to fly before hitting the ground—it simply disappeared without another sound.

I've killed it! I've killed a sacred eagle...I just...I only want it to fly away.

Hisbil looked down at his sword now tipped with the blood of this venerated and beautiful creature. The blade's crack had been healed, and it was still glowing. The spell had transformed

The Blood-Tempered Sword

it to polished metal as bright as any he had ever seen. As the glow slowly diminished, the sword dropped from his grasp and they were plunged into darkness again. What Hisbil could not read the inscriptions seared into the blade and hilt:

Fiat Voltas Tua

Or on the obverse:

Vicis Vita ob Virtus

Or the symbols on the end of the hilt:

中国制造

Still stunned, Hisbil was oblivious to the sound of wings that grew nearer with each beat of his heart or the pain that radiated from the ring of symbols darkening around his wrist.

Hisbil knew that his soul had been forever scarred. The Seldith dropped to his knees sobbing uncontrollably as Bubou landed on the branch outside the tree-cave.

"Ontwaker?"

Thirty-two—The Priestess of Truth

*D*ouglas and Weiger both backed away from the glowing *Books of Truth* now resting quietly on the wooden table where Weiger had arranged them.

"Did...did you hear a voice?" said Weiger with considerable trepidation.

"Voice? Ah, no," Douglas squeaked nervously.

"The...the books seem to be speaking."

"Speaking? What are they saying?" Douglas asked as he got behind Weiger who was still cautiously backing away from the glowing form as if it were about to explode. If Douglas had learned anything as a mouse it was that he was a *mouse*—almost anything was a threat.

"They want to know who I am..." Weiger had stopped retreating.

"Tell them who you are! I don't think you should make them mad...," Douglas said, his voice breaking again into a squeak. "And you had better not leave me here..."

While Douglas was speaking, the shimmering light repeated, "Who awakens *the Truth*, and what is your bidding?" but the mouse still didn't hear anything.

"Be quiet," Weiger hissed. "It's talking again. I'm not going anywhere—not without those books," Weiger said with some authority.

"Sorry, go ahead and see what it wants," the mouse said as calmly as he could.

Weiger walked a few steps closer to the form and said in a voice clear enough to be understood, "I am honorable Sem Weiger, son of Hisripley and Hergwen, and I dwell in the Seldith village of Stone Valley."

"No, you aren't," said the undulating shape in clear, measured tones, the glow flickering with each word. As if a thick cloud had crossed over the sun, the room darkened. Dimly at first, but increasing in clarity, a translucent figure, about as tall as the books, materialized out of the light. "While your name is Weiger, you were once *exiled* from the village of Stone Valley. You currently have meager lodgings in the Shutz Norte refuge. Shall I continue?" the figure said flatly.

Weiger hung his head and said almost under his voice, "No."

"I say again and for the third and last time, who awakens *The Truth* and what is your bidding?" the voice said in a soft but firm tone.

"I am Weiger, exile of Stone Valley. We wish only to gain enlightenment and wisdom from *The Truth*," Weiger replied.

"Very well," said the figure as she seemed to step off the enneahedron and grow to full height in front of the table. She changed from a flickering image and appeared as a beautiful living nesem standing before Weiger. "What do you want of me?" she asked in the same soft, measured tone, but in a more familiar voice.

Weiger took another step back as the nesem materialized before him. At once she looked very, very familiar. She was dressed in a long, flowing gown of gossamer fabric that seemed to blow gently in an unfelt breeze. He had seen this gown before—it was ceremonial garb worn only by the ancient nesem elders of *The Truth*. And, yes, she did look like and sound like the only nesem he had ever loved: Herangelica, the nesem who had been kidnapped the night of the great storm. The one that he had been searching for every waking hour since. And after all this time, the one he had almost given up on.

While Weiger stood staring into the eyes of the apparition, Douglas began to anxiously probe him for answers. "What do they say? Are they angry? Are we in danger? Should we…."

Weiger turned to him with a terrible glare. "Please," he said "…Please, relax. Let me handle this."

"Are we in danger?" Weiger asked the figure in a tone he would have used with his lost love. As the figure began to answer, Douglas blurted, "You're asking me!?"

Weiger turned again and pointed to the chair across the room. "Sit down and *please* be quiet," he said firmly under his breath. Weiger's glare followed him to the chair.

"No, you are in no danger from me," the figure replied. "I can do you no harm, but the knowledge I might impart can sorely injure you or countless others if wielded unwisely," the figure said in her calm voice.

These… these are truly the Sacred Seven. I…can have anything I would ever want…

Weiger's mind was again overwhelmed with fantastic images of riches and power and revenge. The yearning eyes of his lost love now standing before him refocused his thoughts.

"Are you the ghost of Herangelica?" he asked hoping the answer would not confirm his fears.

"No, I appear as the person whom you most trust to convey the truth."

Douglas could only watch as Weiger talked quietly to the softly undulating lights. Weiger figured that the mouse would certainly believe that he had either gone mad or really *was* talking to the glowing shape on the table.

"I am Veritas, Priestess of Truth. Those who hear and see me may address me simply as 'Veritas.'"

"Can others see and hear you?" Weiger knew it would simplify things if Douglas could see this beautiful apparition, hopefully about to answer all of their questions.

"Others can see and hear me if you so desire, but the laws of the Seldith prohibit sharing the *Sacred Truth* with those who would abuse it. You must choose between personal loyalty and loyalty to the Seldith laws," Veritas said.

Weiger was well aware that many would say he had already broken the Seldith laws, the brand that once scarred his forehead would have provided silent testimony to that. Anyone knowing the *real* truth would doubtless know of his failings. He recognized that he was far from perfect.

But why does Veritas trust me? Does she see what the stranger saw? Douglas trusts me and he has risked everything to get the books. We would have never been able to unlock their secrets without his sacrifice.

"I have decided," Weiger said solemnly. "I would like to share your knowledge and wisdom with Douglas Stewart—the uman-made mouse here in this room."

"So be it," Veritas replied.

Douglas fell over backwards in his chair when the Priestess of Truth suddenly appeared to him standing in front of the enneahedron.

"So you...you aren't crazy," he said, regaining his composure and getting to his feet to take in the beauty of the angelic creature now made visible to him.

"Douglas Stewart, may I introduce the sacred Priestess of Truth," Weiger said. "She tells me she can be called 'Veritas,'" Weiger said with some fanfare and a low bow—showing as much respect to the priestess as possible.

"I...I am honored to have you in my humble home," Douglas said, still taking in her beauty. "Ristina?" he said.

"Who's Ristina?" Weiger said.

"My wife. Is this my wife? Has something happened to her? Is this her ghost?" His questions grew more and more frantic.

Douglas took a step forward toward Veritas who held out her hand, palm out, to deter Douglas from coming closer.

"Ristina?"

"It's not your wife." Weiger said softly. "Veritas appears as someone you trust."

Douglas stopped, but his eyes, now clouded with tears, stayed fixed on the deep blue eyes he had known and loved most of his adult life. "What do you know of my wife and family?" he asked.

Douglas could almost feel Veritas staring into his soul as she replied. "I know what truths have been recorded in these sacred texts and those diaries of *The Books of Truth* maintained and guarded in each Temple of Truth. I am aware of whatever is written in *The Books* wherever it is recorded," Veritas said in a voice both soothing and comforting. It was like a mother consoling her young son frightened by summer thunder. "Douglas, I know little of your wife and family as they live outside the Seldith world."

"Why do you appear to me as Herangelica, a nesem in my village?" Weiger interrupted. Before she could answer, Douglas said, "She's my wife!" still fighting the temptation to take her in his embrace.

Veritas closed her eyes said, "I appear as the one who carries your love inside her—the one person you would trust to tell you the pure Truth."

There was a long silence as Weiger and Douglas both recalled memories of their own lost loves.

"How is it you became trapped in *The Sacred Seven*? Are you their prisoner?" Weiger asked.

"I am but a vision—a life-like manifestation. I have no life or soul as do umans, the Seldith, or other soul-bearing creatures that roam this world. I merely act as a gateway and arbiter of the Truth. If *The Books* are inscribed with words that are not true, it is my task to expunge them. The volumes of *The Sacred Books of Truth* contain information far too grave to permit access by those who would acquire their secrets and misuse their power. I act as a gatekeeper and pathway, a guarded portal to *The Truth* recorded and encrypted on the pages here in these sacred volumes and the pages dutifully recorded in all Seldith diaries. When I am queried, I only relate the truth—regardless of what is recorded.

"Understand that *The Sacred Seven* are protected so that those who would acquire their secrets to do evil or act against the common benefit would be thwarted. And the most guarded secrets of the seven cannot be unlocked without the eighth—and an unselfish soul."

"But I was able to read some of the pages," said Douglas. "That's how I discovered the secret of the camouflage cloaking spell for this very cottage."

"Of course," said Veritas. "Might I ask *you* a question?"

"Yes, feel free," Douglas replied, feeling more comfortable talking to Veritas.

"Was your intent to do harm with the cloaking spell or any of the spells you were able to decipher from the volumes you read? Was your intent to pass *The Sacred Seven* into the hands of those who would abuse or misuse the Truth?" Veritas queried, but before Douglas could answer, she added, "Remember that I can record only that which is true. If you try to deceive or tell me half-truths, your soul will betray you and I will know."

Weiger and Douglas were surprised at this new revelation. They would have to think carefully about what they asked and said in the presence of Veritas. They both held secrets that they did not wish to share with anyone (even each other), much less get recorded in perpetuity.

"I truly believe my intent was to return to my life as an honest human carpenter and husband—nothing more. I kept the books and guarded them as best I could to protect my own future. Frankly, I had not thought about keeping them from others, but now that I know how important and dangerous they are, I plan to redouble my efforts to protect them from getting into the wrong hands. I do so pledge."

Weiger could tell that Douglas gave his pledge with the utmost sincerity. He also felt that Douglas might have to prevent Weiger from gaining access to *The Sacred Seven.*

"It is because of your intent to do no harm that you were permitted to decipher these basic spells—those that would shield you and *The Sacred Seven Books of Truth* from harm or from being reacquired by the dark wizards and their evil minions. If *The Sacred Seven* were to be removed, the spells you cast to protect yourself and this cottage would quickly dissipate."

Veritas' new revelation put Douglas back into his chair as his knees suddenly became quite mushy.

Weiger was also concerned about his ability to get *The Sacred Seven* out of the cottage—especially if it meant putting Douglas' and his own life in danger. He had no idea if Veritas knew of his conversation with Emperor. If she did, she probably wouldn't have appeared before him now.

"Do you know how we can reverse the spell cast on my mouse friend, Douglas?" Weiger asked, "…the spell that transformed him from a man to a mouse?"

After hesitating a moment, Veritas said "Written in these pages—it is foretold that a Seldith hero will conquer the curse. I know that only you, Weiger, could have asked that question. Only a selfless act can reverse an act of malice as deep as that which converted Douglas the human to Douglas the mouse."

Weiger smiled and realized that he must be the Seldith hero foretold in the prophecy.

"Has such a retransformation ever been recorded?" Douglas asked.

Veritas closed her eyes for a moment, and the enneahedron began to glow more brightly. Veritas' eyes reopened and she answered, "Yes, on several occasions: once, ages ago in a distant land."

"But since it's written, how I can be returned to…," Douglas began. Weiger held up his hand to stifle the mouse's question.

"Let me," he said and re-asked the question, knowing that Veritas would not answer the mouse, as the answer would only benefit Douglas. "Can my friend Douglas be returned to his human form?"

"Yes, as I said: The path to the retransformation is recorded," Veritas responded. "But the secret of retransformation must be only be revealed to a Seldith hero hitherto untarnished by evil lest he use it unwisely."

"Well, I didn't really expect it would be easy," said Douglas somewhat dejectedly as he turned away from Veritas and crossed over to the window.

Then this 'hero' isn't me. Weiger said to himself.

At this, the light surrounding Veritas began to flicker.

Thirty-three—Reunion and Feast

*H*igh above the rain-soaked forest canopy, the clouds had been shredded behind the storm to let moonlight cast flickering shadows over the miserable, wet souls now inhabiting the tree-hole. Bubou's landing on the outstretched (but slippery) branch in front of the tree cave was not his best.

"'Any landing you survive is a good landing' my mom used to say," Bubou said, rearranging his feathers and making sure he had a good grip on the branch.

Mink crawled up but had to use every inch of her claws to gain a claw-hold on the slimy branch that stuck out a few inches below the tree cave. Her fur was a matted mess, and she was scared and mad—mad as a wet cat.

Bubou called out again, "Ontwaker? Are you there?" There was no answer. *I've found the wrong tree again!* Searching just inside the tree-hole, Bubou was very relieved to find his ontwaker in a daze. Hisbil was still on his knees, and his chin on his chest. A bright steel sword lay at his side. He was sobbing to himself and somehow looked different—older perhaps?

Hisbil looked up into Bubou's eyes and cried: "I didn't mean to kill it. I...I just wanted to scare it off."

Bubou looked puzzled. "Kill what? Did the bird cooome back?" he asked.

Hisbil replied, "It was an eagle—a great, beautiful bald eagle. I...I jabbed it with my sword to get it to fly away."

"That probably should not have killed it...," Bubou said. "What makes you think it's dead?"

"It collapsed and fell! It was the spell—I know it. I shouted the first thing that came to mind, and it must have put a spell on the creature. I think I killed it," Hisbil answered between sobs. "I didn't think I could cast a spell without the wand."

"When did this happen? Perhaps it's still alive and we can help it," Bubou offered.

"Just before you arrived—I think," said Hisbil, slowly regaining his feet. He picked up his sword and wiped off the blood with his cloak—the blood spread into the fabric like ink dropped into clear water. Returning it to the scabbard, he said, "Bubou, can you see if the corpse is still there? I would like to make sure it's buried properly...I would not want anything to carry its carcass or feathers off; each are sacred to the Seldith."

"Of course," said Bubou, and with his characteristic obedience, he dove off the branch and disappeared again into the night.

ৠৠৠ

About this time, Mink, trying to find yet another quiet place to get warm, brushed by Hisbil and nearly stepped on his sister curled up under her camouflage cloak. "Mink? What are *you* doing here?" Hisbil said.

"Passing by, I was, and decided to hitch a ride with an owl, I did," she said somewhat playfully, now that she had her second wind and was out of the rain.

"Right. You got Bubou to show you where we were hiding. But how did you manage that feat?" Hisbil asked.

"Well, eeeeasy it was not. A bite or two about his neck to convince him it took," Mink meowed drowsily as she curled up around Hisbil's sleeping sister. Anasta seemed to appreciate the new source of warmth—even though the cat was still a bit damp. Mink wrapped her tail around Anasta to block the cool breeze and continued to lick the rain out of her own fur.

"How did you and Bubou meet?" Hisbil pressed.

"Sniffing around the near the fence, I was, near where your trail disappeared. Your rucksack I found. After a brief wrestling match, convinced the owl oaf to bring me to you I did. And here I am."

"Bubou. His name is Bubou. So, where is the rucksack?" Hisbil asked.

"Oh, out on the branch it is. There it should still be…Fetch it, shall I?" Mink replied eagerly.

Mink had almost gotten up from her warm spot, but before she could, Hisbil had already walked out and fetched the rucksack from the branch. "I need to make a fire to prepare some food for Anasta and get us all warm again," Hisbil announced.

"A fire?" Mink said. Hisbil could hear some trepidation in her voice. "Fire, bad it is. Hurt by my human's fireplace I was. Jumped out and burned me it did, just to be nasty. Very rude."

"It will be all right. I don't have enough wood to make it very big," Hisbil said as he gathered together the twigs found earlier once he had the flint in hand he was able to make a small fire in no-time.

Mink seemed transfixed in fear and amazement. Before long they could all feel the meager warmth fill the tree cave and work its way through their fur.

"Now to cook some of this fish," Hisbil said.

"Fish? Did you say fish?" Mink said with a great deal of excitement. She was on her feet in a flash, flipping her tail. Anasta was left behind no-doubt wondering what had happened to her warm cat-fur pillow. Mink made her way over to the partially devoured salmon left behind by the eagle.

"Eat as much as you want, there's plenty for all," Hisbil said.

"What's that?" Anasta asked groggily. She sat up and put her hands out to the fire.

Hisbil knelt next to her. She seemed stronger, her color seemed better, but it was hard to tell in the dim firelight. She also didn't wince when he put his arm around her. "How are you feeling?" he asked.

"What happened?" she asked. "How are *you* feeling? And what happened to your arm?"

In the flickering firelight, Hisbil looked at his forearm. It was now circled with two dark rings of symbols, very much like the rings he had seen on Alred's arm. He pushed down his cloak not wanting his sister or the owl to start asking any more questions that he couldn't answer. Alred *has some explaining to do when we get home… if we get home.*

"It's nothing. I'm fine," he said. "I'm fine, thanks to you. You used the healing. Of course, mother is going to throttle you when you get home just after she kisses you for saving my life. The elders won't be happy either—you broke the rules…you didn't have the training…," Hisbil began. But, at once, he realized that she was too weak for admonishment, and he was too grateful for her unusual selfless act of kindness—an act that nearly cost her life and apparently saved his. "But thanks. Bubou said I was pretty badly hurt; I might have gone over the edge—and dragged you with me."

"I'm hungry and thirsty, and you didn't tell me where that smell is coming from," Anasta said with a more familiar attitude and smiling weakly.

"It's fish cooking," Hisbil said.

"How did you get it?" Anasta asked.

Hisbil turned back to the fire to turn the skewered chunk of fish. "I think you'll like it."

"I doubt it. Don't you have any mushroom stew or carrot salad?" Anasta said with a twang of whine in her voice, half in earnest. She was quickly becoming her old self again.

"This is what we have to eat. If you want it that's fine, if not, you'll go hungry. Mother and I have told you this a thousand times," Hisbil said in his big-brother voice, but this time, it seemed a bit deeper.

The sound of heavy wings immediately turned Hisbil's attention to the opening of the tree cave as he drew his sword.

Thirty-four—The Eagle Has Vanished

"I looked everywhere," Bubou said as he landed on the branch outside the tree cave where Hisbil, Anasta, and Mink were warming themselves and the fish over the fire. I saw no sign of an eagle or anything else for that matter. "Are you sure you didn't imagine it?" Bubou asked.

"Did I imagine the fish we're eating?" Hisbil said, pointing to the remains of the salmon.

"Fish! I didn't notice. Do you mind if I have some?" Bubou asked. "I guess he was able to fly away after all...," the owl said as Hisbil nodded approval. Bubou bent over and grabbed a healthy chunk of salmon. In doing so, he pulled a piece out from under Mink's paw.

"Watch it, feather face!" Mink said with a low growl. Her ears laid back on her head as she watched Bubou gobbling down the chunk of fish.

Bubou was startled at first. In the dim light, he had not seen the coal-black cat eating quietly. "Sorry...I'm sure there is enough foooor all—even fooor prissy fur-balls," Bubou bantered playfully.

"Listen, you two...I have my wand back, and I'm not afraid to use it," Hisbil said half kidding. "Don't make me turn you into squirrels."

"Do that youuu...yoooou wouldn't, would you?" said Mink. Bubou just stood there with a frightened look on his face—his big yellow eyes blinking nervously.

"If you don't treat each other with respect, I will make you wish you had. You need to act like you deserve the gift of speech and consideration." Hisbil realized at this point that simply being able to understand someone else's tongue does not make two dissimilar beings soul-mates overnight.

Mink looked down and apologized to Bubou, "I was rude. I hate rude creatures. I apologize." She looked up at Bubou, searching for forgiveness.

Bubou said contritely, "I'm sorry as well. There is nothing to forgive. Enjoy the salmon—there is enough for a stampeding herd of cats." With that, the tension was broken, and both began to eat once more. This was the beginning of a strong, lasting friendship between the owl and the pussycat. But that's another story.

"Could you really transform them into squirrels?" Anasta whispered. She had seen her brother awaken the cat so it could speak and understand the Common language, but she really had no idea of the depth or breadth of his magical powers.

"Of course," Hisbil said playfully with a grin and a somewhat serious tone. Frankly, after the incident with the eagle, Hisbil was not sure of what he was capable of doing or undoing. He knew the words to only a few spells and had little experience using them. He had no idea where the words he used on the eagle came from—it was almost like he was born with them stuck in his mind for just such an occasion.

"Bubou said he could not find an eagle? What eagle?" Anasta asked.

"An eagle landed here carrying the salmon. I jabbed it with my sword to get it to fly away and it fell out of the tree. I really believed I killed it," Hisbil answered quietly.

"You killed an eagle? Isn't that a banishment crime?" Anasta said with alarm.

"Yes. Yes, it is. But I don't think it's dead. Bubou could not find the bird's body on the ground," Hisbil said.

"Bubou, did you check the branches on the tree as you went down? Could the eagle have gotten hung up on a branch?" Hisbil asked.

"Yes, I checked. I did see sooome broooken and bent branches as if something had fallen throoough, but nothing but a few feathers were on the groooound. They could have been left there quite some time ago. There was noooo sign of a bird, living or dead," the owl said, shaking his head.

Without a word, Bubou stepped off the branch again and flew off. Perhaps, he wanted to look for the eagle again. But he was back in a few minutes with his talons full of wild mushrooms, carrots, and leafy herbs, which he placed at Anasta's feet. Somehow, he knew that she needed these things to fully recover from her healing magic. "Thanks for healing my ontwaker. Perhaps these are the ingredients you need to heal yourself," he said quietly to Anasta.

Anasta could only blush. She looked up at the great owl and stared into his eyes to say "thank you." She reached out compassionately and patted him on the wing, and as she did, a soft glow came over Bubou's wing—just around the wound he had acquired the previous day. Suddenly, an ugly red welt appeared on Anasta's forearm, but just as quickly, it disappeared. "You're welcome," she said sweetly. "You brought me back my brother." Bubou stretched out his wing to discover his pain was nearly gone.

Using some of the maple leaves to wrap treasures brought by Bubou, Anasta was able to make a tasty (albeit a bit overseasoned) pie that she cooked over the coals of the dwindling fire. She still had a bit to learn about cooking, but Hisbil had learned that eating your own concoctions is a great way to learn what *not* to do. Still, the pie was edible, and the Seldith ate more than enough to get them through the night.

During the night, Mink and Bubou, who were naturally nocturnal with excellent night vision, stood guard while the Seldith slept curled up at Mink's side—her tail wrapped around them. Talking quietly, the two guardians quietly entertained each other with whispered tales of their exploits and conquests in life and love. They spoke of friends and enemies, likes and dislikes, and their favorite sunsets. It did not take long to discover they had a lot in common—despite their differences. They agreed it was interesting how a common tongue and common purpose could bring dissimilar beings together.

Thirty-five—Time to Return Home

In the morning, the sun kissed Hisbil on the cheek but he was already awake making plans in his head. "We need to get Home." Hisbil announced as Anasta rubbed the sleep from her eyes. After a short discussion, the Seldith were taken to the ground one-by-one with Bubou's assistance. Mink was able to make her way down the tree after a brief rest stop and a few doubtful moments where she took a wrong turn in the middle branches.

"We need to retrace our steps so we can get back to our village," Hisbil began. "That is, unless you know where it is, Bubou. Do you?"

"What was that? I was not paying attention…," Bubou said. He had been studying the ground where the leaves had been compressed—as if something heavy had lain there and made a depression in the layer upon layer of leaves.

"Look! There are a few drops of blood here," Mink said. "By the smell, I would say some sort of bird…" The hair on her back and tail stood on end with excitement. "…and it went off in that direction." Mink darted off into the underbrush as if being shooed out of the kitchen by the farmer's wife. A minute later, she returned breathing hard. "The trail leads over to the south a bit to a small clearing and then ends. I think it flew off—or was carried off," she said.

"Well, there is no way to trail an eagle on the wing," Hisbil said. "If the poor animal can fly, then the wound and fall must not have hurt it too badly. In any case, we need to keep moving. We have a long way to go and only a rough idea of how to get there." Hisbil didn't want to think about what might have happened if the eagle had survived the fall but been eaten by predators.

"Bubou," Hisbil said, trying to get his attention, "in which direction should we travel?"

After a thoughtful pause, Bubou said, "I think we had better go back to the fence and work back from there. I know where the farm is." Shifting onto his other foot, "I think," he continued under his breath.

"I'm sure you'll be able to help us find our way back," Hisbil said trying to bolster the owl's confidence. However, in his typical fashion, Bubou simply took off without saying where he was going or why.

"Now where is he going?" asked Mink.

"I have no idea," answered Hisbil. "I guess we need to move toward that hill so we can get our bearings. We should be able to see where we are from that clearing near the top. Mink, Are you up for climbing another tree to scout around?"

"Sounds like a plan…but I'm not that good at finding my way from above. I use my nose and whiskers to feel my way around on the ground," said Mink.

"Anasta, let's go. Didn't you want to get home?" said Hisbil, calling back to his sister. Anasta was on one knee picking up something. "Look!" she said as if she was in her own private world. "See what I found!" She got up and carried over several downy eagle feathers—a couple of which were spattered with blood.

"Bless the stars! Put those down! Those are venerated and should *never* be touched!" Hisbil admonished his sister as she walked over holding out the feathers. "Haven't you listened to any of your *Books of Truth* lessons?"

"Why? I want to *keep* them. They're pretty," she complained.

"No, not a one. Drop them now, and let's go," Hisbil said firmly as he turned and started to lead the small troupe up toward the hill. Anasta quickly turned her back on Hisbil and tucked the downy feathers into the lining of her coat and ran to catch up with the others.

"Wait!" came a cry from above. "You're going the wrong way!" It was Bubou. He had climbed up high enough to see where they needed to go. "Keep the rising sun on yoooour right. That will lead yooou back north to the farm and the fence."

Not having a better plan, Hisbil took the owl's advice and started to move in the opposite direction toward the fence.

"The fence?" Anasta exclaimed. She was using that voice again. "I don't want to go that way. I *won't* go that way!" she said as she stomped her foot defiantly in the mud—the puddle splashed up, and the spatter made her face even dirtier. "I'm going another way—that way!" she said, wiping her face with a dirty sleeve and pointing off in the opposite direction. "Anyway, that owl could not find his way out of a closet if the door was open. He got lost last night trying to bring you back to that awful tree." Anasta started marching off away from the group—back toward the "awful" tree.

Hisbil knew better than to try to convince his little sister of anything when she started acting like this. He signaled Mink to keep an eye on her. She nodded and circled back.

Mink could easily follow Hisbil's trail by scent once Anasta changed her mind. Mink was also capable of carrying (or dragging) her to safety if the need should arise.

Hisbil was right. Anasta went her own way for about two minutes before deciding that she did not want to be left alone in the forest. A loud tree frog and a strange noise in the brush (which Mink supplied) finally convinced her—she turned around at once and headed back toward the others—or at least she thought she had. Mink was nearby but out of sight, and when it was clear that Anasta had strayed off the trail the others had taken, Mink met up with her.

"My collar, have you seen it?" Mink asked Anasta almost casually as she strode out of the undergrowth.

"It's around your neck, you silly cat," Anasta said as she tugged at Mink's collar. She was glad to see the big cat, as she was not really sure which way the others had gone. She also had not noticed that a large white owl was circling back from time to time keeping an eye on both of them.

"Oh, yes. Thanks, looking there first, I keep forgetting," Mink said sheepishly.

After a few minutes, Mink and Anasta rejoined her brother who was heading almost straight north—thanks to occasional course corrections offered by their airborne spotter circling above.

Hisbil did not really acknowledge the fact that Anasta had caught up—and he didn't mention the fence again. He too was nervous about another encounter with the mysterious power of its top wire.

Thirty-six—Veritas Vanishes

The news that Douglas' fate was in the hands of an unknown Seldith hero further crushed the mouse's spirits. He crossed the room and curled up in a ball on his bed, tucking his long tail under his head. Weiger did not know what to say to console him.

"Weiger?" Veritas said quietly.

"Yes, do you have another question?" Weiger answered.

"I must rest," she said with a pained look on her face. "Do you know the secret to regenerate my strength? My keybook and volumes have been hidden in darkness for so long, I must witness the light…." Veritas did not get to finish the sentence. The image faded and collapsed back into the enneahedron, which re-morphed into an inanimate stack of books with a pop. She was gone.

"Veritas?" Weiger said to the stack of books, not understanding why she had disappeared and finding it even harder to believe that she was gone.

Douglas looked up and said, "She's gone? What did you do to her?" He got off the bed and walked over to the table. "We still need her help!" He looked to Weiger with panic and anger flashing in his tiny black eyes.

"Nothing! I did nothing to her! She said something about being tired—needing rest and light—and then she just collapsed into the books," Weiger answered defensively.

"Then *you'll* have to decipher the texts yourself to find a way to get me converted back to my human form," Douglas said firmly.

Weiger remembered how he had boasted about being able to easily decipher the texts, while not being able to read them at all. If he had learned anything during his relatively short exile, it was how to lie in order to survive. And each time he did, it got him in deeper trouble.

"I can't," Weiger said, looking Douglas in the eye. "I can't read the texts at all—not even as much as you can. I'm sorry, but I can't."

"Can't or *won't*?" said Douglas angrily. "You just want *The Sacred Seven* for *yourself.* You want to take them back to your village to be the hero or worse—or take them off and sell them to some dark wizard!" Douglas stepped between the books and Weiger as he backed away from the table.

"No, no, I *really* can't read *The Sacred Seven*. They are protected to prevent just anyone from reading them. I expect that because I'm an exile, Veritas does not see me as worthy. I never could read these books—just the diaries in my village. I don't know how you could read even a single page. I'm really sorry, I…"

"Why should I believe you?" Douglas said.

"I don't know," said Weiger as he turned back toward the window. The afternoon had slipped away to night, which brought a sky peppered with stars that blinked through the wispy clouds drifting high above. Not a single light could be seen in the valley below where a light fog was forming.

"Douglas, *The Sacred Seven* are *yours*," Weiger began after a long pause. "You rescued them from the dark wizard at great personal risk and sacrifice. I expect you need them far more than I do. I assure you that I won't do anything to get them away from you." He turned and looked into Douglas' eyes again. "I only ask that you let me have them when you find they are of no further use."

Douglas pondered for a moment and, in a softer tone, said, "Okay, I do need your help—I know I do, and I think that's why the human on the road brought us together." He crossed the room and held out his paw to Weiger. Weiger reciprocated, and as they shook, Douglas said, "I'll hold you to your word," looking Weiger in the eye.

"So, now what? How do we get me changed back to a human—I'm getting really tired of this silly tail…," Douglas said, pushing his tail away, which seemed to have a life of its own.

"Well, what do we know now that we did not know before?" Weiger asked.

"If we are to believe Veritas, we know that if *The Sacred Seven* leave here, the cloaking spell will dissolve," Douglas said.

"And that it's possible to be retransformed."

"It must be," Douglas said. "I need to go back to the castle and find out what I can about what goes on up there."

Weiger did not hesitate to add with a smile, "And I'll tag along to pull your tail out of the trap the wizard is bound to have set for you."

Thirty-seven—The Best Laid Plans of Mice...

*W*eiger and Douglas spent much of the night making their plans and drinking strong tea while huddled together at the large table. *The Sacred Seven Books of Truth*, had been replaced in the compartment behind Douglas' bookcase. They decided to hide the eighth "key" volume in plain sight— stacked with an assortment of other notes and papers near the kitchen window. All of the sacred books would have to be kept here in the cottage until they could figure out how to reinvigorate Veritas. Since she had brought them both good news and bad, neither one of them felt any immediate need to ask more questions. They knew what needed to be done but few ideas how to accomplish it.

When the need for sleep muddled their minds and dampened their enthusiasm, both mouse and homeless exile drifted toward their own beds—Weiger found an overstuffed chair covered with maps, diagrams, and sundry collectibles. He unceremoniously cleaned it off with a great shove and tried to get comfortable for the night. It was not long before he ended up on the floor covered in a luxurious hand-crocheted afghan.

Perhaps it was the tea, but Weiger had considerable trouble finding a way to stop thinking about how meaningless his life had been up to this point. It seemed that everyone in the village had a job and was constantly busy contributing to the community. Weiger had made his own business by getting the Owl Wrangler to awaken a couple of crows that he hired out to those who needed the thrill of a flight or a quick trip to a distant village. But much of his time was spent in idle times with friends at one pub or another or chasing eligible females. He didn't speak of his time as a Protector or his experience with a sword or how many others he had to kill to protect what his leaders had called 'freedom'. It wasn't until recently that he had met Herangelica and his life had only begun to take on new meaning. And now his former life and Angie were gone—perhaps forever.

After his exile, Weiger never stopped looking for Herangelica or worrying about his crows and the friends that he had left behind. Soon he realized that perhaps the Council didn't want him around for other reasons. His 'trial' had come about a day or two after he had flown over the wizard's castle scouting for clues about Angie's kidnapping. Perhaps someone was worried about what he might have seen.

About this time, Douglas brought Weiger's unsettling dreams to an abrupt end. "Ristina, it's me! It's me, Douglas!" he shouted as his legs pumped frantically.

Weiger got up and touched his shoulder. The mouse startled awake—still half dreaming. "Ristina...she was trying to stomp on me!" Douglas said.

"It was just a dream...just a dream," Weiger said calmly, trying to comfort him. "Try to think of something else—we both need to get some rest if we're going to be alert tomorrow."

Douglas nodded, "I'm sorry," and drifted back to sleep—or pretended to. Weiger curled back into his afghan, but spent most of the night staring at the moon as it crossed the horizon above the clouds and disappeared behind the brightening hills.

In the morning, they both had another hot cup of tea and ate a couple of the biscuits Douglas had made the previous day. "So the plan:" Weiger began. "It's decided that we get back into the castle and figure out what or who else was transformed."

"Yea, Squeaky, but more importantly, *how* it was done."

"It won't be easy."

"Is anything worth doing, easy? Anyway, I don't have much time left. It's now or..." Douglas offered.

They had no idea how very little time they had left.

Thirty-eight--Home is Southwest

*B*efore the mid-morning sun had reached very high in the sky, Hisbil and his companions had returned to the dreaded fence—the source of so many of their problems. None of them really wanted to deal with it again, so they paused at the tree line well back from the mesh obstacle. Sitting under the tree, Hisbil got on his knees and pushed away the leaves, exposing a flat surface of dirt—polishing it smooth with the side of his hand. Drawing in the dirt with a stick, he tried to figure out where they had come from, where they were, and how they had arrived there. He had seen his father do this from time to time when they were hunting together. Down the hill to the north beyond the pasture he could see the barn and the fence; and off in the distance he could see a gate—something that was previously obscured by the tall pasture grass.

While he was not sure where Mink had taken them on their mad dash or where the owl had taken them by air, he now reckoned that they were somewhere northeast of Stone Valley—at least two day's walk and possibly quite longer. Mink concurred but admitted she had been turned around as well.

We've been walking in the wrong direction—again. Hisbil lamented.

Hisbil didn't share this revelation with the others—he was not *that* sure of their location, at least in regard to the distances they needed to travel to get back home, and he didn't want to trigger more consternation and dissent from Anasta. Their best course would probably be to follow the fence back to the gate and see if they could get Mink to remember the route she had taken to get to the farm. *Perhaps she...*

"We've rested long enough," Hisbil announced. "I think Stone Valley is off in that direction to the southwest," he said, pointing with his arm. "But I think it makes more sense to follow the route Mink used to get us here. It's quite a long way by foot, so perhaps we can get Mink to carry us. Mink, are you rested enough?" he said as he obliterated the map with a brush of his foot.

"Ready I am, Ontwaker."

"Okay, let's see if we can go north to the uman road and follow it back southwest until I can pick up a landmark that I recognize," Hisbil said as he pulled himself up on Mink's back.

"Will we be home by dinnertime?" Anasta asked as Hisbil pulled her up behind him.

"Yes, we're all hungry—and, yes, we should be home for a late dinner."

"Bubou, don't you need to get back to work?" Hisbil asked as Mink started off toward the gate in the fence.

"It's oookay. I don't need tooo get back right away," he said but without a lot of conviction. "I have a few days oooff," he continued as he flew ahead landing on a cedar branch ahead of the cat.

As they travelled toward the gate, they walked as close to the treeline as possible. No one really knew what made the fence so dangerous, and nobody wanted to find out.

Scanning the sky for predators, a sense of dread came over Hisbil. Every snap in the underbrush, every wind-blown tree branch seemed like the sign of another beast ready to strike. *Should we wait until dark to travel?* Hisbil wondered. *What would my father do?* Hearing another bird's shrill call in the distance, he listened intently for movement focusing his attention on the underbrush. Bubou flew ahead from branch to branch acting as a scout, but he was focused on the ground watching for predators.

Despite their vigilance, they all failed to notice the outstretched wings of a large raptor hovering nearly motionless behind them on the hill's warm updraft.

Riding comfortably on Mink, the Seldith were making good progress toward the gate and the road that lead back home. Like a bolt of lightning on a cloudless day, Hisbil suddenly found himself snatched and taken aloft in the talons of a large bird that had appeared out of nowhere.

Thirty-nine—Snatched by Talons

*H*isbil regained his senses as the cold rush of air pummeled his face. He looked down, and he realized that his worst nightmare was coming true—he was being carried off by a giant bird of prey—another bald eagle. For some reason, the bird's talons had only speared his clothes and the rucksack but still tore a painful gouge across his back. Squirming a bit, Hisbil realized that his arms were also pinned—there was little he could do. *We should have been more watchful.* His mind raced ahead to the horrible conclusion of their flight, when the eagle would share him with its hungry chicks.

"Hisbil…," a voice to his right said weakly. "Hisbil, are you there?" It was Anasta—the bird had snatched her too.

"Yes, yes, I'm here. Just hold still—I'll think of something."

"It's going to eat us, isn't it?" She began to weep and struggled against the powerful talons.

But then the eagle spoke to them. "No. You are in no danger—as long as you hold still."

"Who are you? Where are you taking us? Let us go!" Hisbil demanded and began to squirm again, trying to get his hands and arms free. It suddenly occurred to Hisbil that the eagle was *speaking*—it had been awakened! Someone had awakened this eagle and it had now turned on the Seldith. It didn't make sense.

"I wouldn't move around, Hisbil. I don't want to accidentally drop you or your sister," the eagle admonished.

"How...how do you know us?" Hisbil shouted against the wind. He had managed to get one arm free and reached down for his blade.

"Leave it be. You're going to need that blade before too much longer. Remember, you cannot harm that which bears you aloft lest it thrust your soul against the rocks."

Hisbil knew at once that those were his father's words, but it did not seem to be his voice—not really—but he recognized the advice he had given on many occasions. It was good advice. It was not long before the eagle circled a stone castle at the top of a cliff overlooking a sleepy human town to the southeast.

"Hold on, Anasta," Hisbil shouted as they spun down in a dizzying spiral. She did not answer, nor could he hear her weeping. The eagle turned and hovered into the stiff wind near a large bramble that formed a thorny border to the hillside that sloped off further to the west. At this point, Hisbil was unceremoniously dropped onto the center of the lawn. His sister tumbled down beside him like a rag doll. She did not move. The eagle landed next to them on the grass.

"Is she hurt?" the eagle said, standing over Hisbil and his sister.

"I can't tell," Hisbil said angrily, leaning over his sister who lay lifeless on the soggy lawn that had cushioned their fall. "How can you expect her to be all right after being dragged away in your talons? She's probably scared to death." Anasta still did not move as the wind raked the top of the hill, snapping their cloaks away from their bodies.

"Anasta, are you okay?" Hisbil said as he leaned down to his sister. She nodded and he helped her to her feet. She looked up at the eagle without saying a word. Her eyes told Hisbil that she was too frightened to speak. "Come over here out of the wind," Hisbil said, putting his arm around her shoulders.

Hisbil looked up at the eagle. "She's all right, no thanks to you. You nearly killed us."

"It couldn't be helped, Hisbil," the eagle said kindly. He seemed very relieved. "Both of you, come closer, out of the wind." The eagle spread his wings and wrapped them around the pair who stood shivering at his feet. Hisbil's arm crossed his body with his hand on the hilt of his sword. He didn't notice that it had begun to glow once again.

"How... how do you know our names?" Anasta finally said still shivering from the cold and fear —barely able to get the words out.

"I just do. I know all there is to know about you," the eagle said. "I've been watching you since before you left Stone Valley on the back of that cat. That was really a remarkable feat. Your father is very proud of you."

"What do you know about father?" Anasta said in a some-what braver voice.

"He and I are very close," the eagle answered.

"So what became of him? Is he alive? Tell me!" Hisbil de-manded.

"All in time... young sem, all in time..."

"Why then, why did you bring us here?"

"Hisbil, I led you and Kassie to your father's cloak, sword and his wand. I wanted you to bring the wand here."

Hisbil at once patted his cloak and felt the wand's stiff shaft safely tucked into its folds.

"Why? Why would you be watching us? And how did you know where to find our father's... where our father..." Hisbil asked. "Did you kill him? Did you snatch our father from that meadow and ...?"

"No, I didn't hurt your father. He is safe—still in danger, but alive. How is your mother?"

"Our mother is in tatters. And what's it to *you*?"

"Because I love her and miss her desperately," the eagle said softly, his words carried off by the wind.

Hisbil's mind suddenly swirled with a million disjoint thoughts and uncertainties as he tried to make sense of what he was being told.

"How could you…who *are* you? Hisbil said, looking into the eagle's eyes that somehow looked very familiar but they were still the eyes of a dangerous bird of prey.

"Hisbil, Anasta, I love you both. I raised you both; I know it's hard to believe but I'm your father," the eagle said, looking down on the two shivering creatures at his feet.

It took a moment for this new revelation to sink in. Perhaps, it was the lack of food and water or the wounds he had received over the last two days, but Hisbil's mind continued to spin. He could feel his knees going soft.

"How…father, we thought you were *dead*. What happened to you?" Hisbil asked when his mind cleared.

Anasta clung more tightly to Hisbil at this new revelation but seemed too frightened to speak.

"The night I went hunting, I was snatched out of the meadow by an owl controlled by Lord Lensmacher. It brought me here to his castle."

"But why? What would he want with you?" Hisbil interrupted.

"All in time. Just rest here by my feet and try to stay warm as I explain what I can. We don't have a lot of time. The wizard expected my return some time ago."

Anasta looked up into the eagle's eyes and took another step closer into the warm shelter of his wings. Hisbil did not follow her. She must have seen something that Hisbil didn't—he was still not convinced this eagle was his father.

"Lord Lensmacher is really the reincarnated wizard, Tovenaar, at least he imagines that he is. He said that he's the direct descendant of the ancient wizard that put the confusion curse on the world—the curse that prevents umans, Seldith and animals from understanding one another."

"Is he really?" Hisbil asked.

"Wait, he wants the awakening spell!" Hisbil exclaimed. "Is that why you brought us here?" Hisbil asked.

"Partly, but let me finish. You're right. It seems Tovenaar desperately wants *our* secret. It seems that he wants to perform these awakenings himself."

"Why? Weren't we sending him enough owls?"

"It was not owls that he wants. He wants to convert wolves, foxes, and other wild creatures to create an army of voracious creatures that would understand and do his bidding. He realized that all of the animals we converted were beholden to the Seldith and worked only for the Owl Master because their ontwaker asked them to do so," the eagle explained.

"How did you end up here?"

"I was captured the first night of my hunt. Tovenaar's owl had been watching me and knew where I would be hunting. He snatched me up and brought me to his castle. At first, *Lord* Lensmacher apologized for having kidnapped me, but his attitude changed dramatically when I told him that I would not, I could not betray our secret. He then demanded that I give him my wand, but I could not do that either. It seems that I had dropped it when the owl grabbed me. This made Lensmacher furious, and he transformed me into an eagle. He said he would not change me back until I brought him the wand."

"The wand? This wand?" Hisbil said as he pulled out the wand from the inner lining of his tunic and stepped back away from the eagle, pointing the wand at the great bird's head.

"Yes, I'm afraid so."

"So you've done his bidding after all. You've delivered the wand and your bastard son to this evil lord to be tortured and killed, or worse!" Hisbil exploded.

"What are you saying?" Anasta said, looking up at her brother. "This is your father, my father—*our* father."

"He's *your* father Anasta, but not *mine*. He has brought us *both* here to die at the hands of an evil wizard!" Hisbil cried as he tried to think of a way to use his wand to strike back at the eagle. At that, the wand began to shake and feel warm in his hand.

"I've already been enchanted, Hisbil," the eagle said. "Put your wand away. There will come a time when you'll need it. Son, I did not betray you for the wand—but we need it. I could not think of another way to defeat Tovenaar and his maniacal schemes. This is a serious dilemma, one that threatens the entire village and every being that lives in it—including your mother and probably all Seldith everywhere. Whatever happens, you must *not* let him or anyone else get the wand. If there is a chance Tovenaar might get the wand, you must destroy it, even though it might mean our own destruction."

"Then take us back home and away from this place," Hisbil demanded.

"I cannot. You still don't understand that you and your sister would not be any safer at home in the village—not for long. Tovenaar plans to destroy Stone Valley and the entire Seldith population. We must stop him *now*; he has already gathered his army of goats and wolves. He plans to awaken them all and compel them to attack. He as even recruited senior ministers of the Council of Truth.

"How can they get by the briar wall?"

"Strangely enough, he plans to decimate the blackberry thorn wall with a tribe of goats, level the village, and loose the wolves to kill all those who survive the onslaught."

Hisbil's stomach hardened as Gollsaer continued to lay out Tovenaar's plans.

"You must understand: we *must* break Tovenaar's grip on the Seldith, at least long enough to get them to move to a safer place. I have been spending quite a bit of my days searching for another quiet corner for them, but the number of umans and their buildings, roads, and farms has grown considerably since he let us move into Stone Valley."

"You know as well as I that they don't want to move," Hisbil said sternly. "Fox says that the rumors of how Lord Lensmacher plans to deforest the land are not true. The new Council ministers won't listen to anything that disagrees with their version of '*truth.*'

"I know, I know. I'd been talking to Alred as well. And, Hisbil, I *am* your father in all ways but one. I have loved and apprenticed you as my own son; I have no other."

"Then why have you put me—and Anasta—in so much danger?"

"Son, we live in a dangerous world. You're old enough to take on the responsibilities and risks of your herditas or one that you choose and do your duty for the Seldith. Anasta is no safer in the village than she is here by your side, where you can protect her and she can help you. This challenge will be your *and* your sister's initiation into adulthood, and part of your challenge will be to protect your sister and help her help you."

"Hisbil, I could carry you, your sister, and your mother away to a distant forest, away from all of these dangers, but we could not survive for long on our own—and as an eagle, I would not be much comfort to you or your mother. As Seldith, we all depend on one another. Without the help of the community of Seldith, we too would be swallowed by the next threat."

Hisbil did not know what to say. He took a step toward the warmth under his father's wing. Anasta looked at him with the same eyes. He was still her brother.

Forty—Hisbil's Challenge

*H*isbil understood how Lord Lensmacher could be a serious threat if only half of what the eagle told them was true, but he was still mystified as to how he could possibly help.

"What is this *challenge?*" Hisbil asked the eagle towering above them. "What can *we* do against a wizard?"

"Hisbil, I brought you here to help someone special, someone you both can help," the eagle responded. "It's important, critically important."

"Before we help anyone, we need to get under cover and out of this wind before we're seen—preferably before we freeze to death," Hisbil said firmly.

"Yes, of course, but you both need to do as I say—exactly as I say—and no one can overhear us in this wind."

"Why should we trust you?" Hisbil said with a pointed dagger of doubt in his voice.

"You *must*. You have no choice if you love your mother and care about your sister and the others in the village—and if you care about Kassie."

"Kassie? You've seen Kassie? Is she here?"

"Yes, she's here, and she's in terrible danger."

Hisbil looked down at his feet and thought for a long moment. "What do I need to do?" he said solemnly.

"Just below us on the hillside is a small cottage in the brambles. It's hidden by a spell like the magic in the Seldith cloak;

you won't see it until you're upon it. Just follow the mouse trail that begins just past that small tree. Once you find it, you'll need to help the creature that lives there to get you into the castle."

"And do what? Give the wand to Tovenaar?" Hisbil asked. His father seemed dead set on getting him into the castle, along with his wand.

"No, of course not," the eagle said, shaking his head, "...but you'll understand what to do once you talk to the mouse."

"A mouse? You want us to help a mouse?"

"Yes, especially the mouse. I've been watching him. He's the key to recovering *The Sacred Seven*."

"The Sacred Seven? What do some old books have to do with this?"

"All Tovenaar wants are the secrets locked away in The Sacred Seven. If he gets his hands on those we're lost."

A sharp pain twisted Hisbil's forehead into a tight knot. "Why does Anasta have to go? This is way too dangerous for her. You need to take her back home or at least to safety before she gets hurt," Hisbil demanded.

"Yes, you're right. It's unfortunate that I had to bring her along, but who else would help protect her? And I expect you will need her skills again before the day is over."

"Her skills as a healer?" Hisbil said. "She's not ready, not nearly ready. She nearly died last night impaling herself on my burns."

"Nevertheless, we'll all need her."

"Can't I...I just want to go home," Anasta said, her softening eyes meeting the large round eyes of the eagle. He stared down at this creature as if Anasta was his own chick snuggling against him for warmth.

"Anasta, it's important for you to be strong and brave and help your brother however you can."

Looking up at the eagle, Hisbil could see that he was suddenly distracted. He had felt or heard something Hisbil had not.

"Step back…I have to go now, but I'll be watching over you—as I always have. Be careful, protect the wand, and one more thing: Be wary of the exile."

But before Hisbil or Anasta could say a word, the eagle flapped his wings and was last seen flying low across the grassy lawn away from the castle where he ultimately disappeared above the trees. He didn't hear Anasta's cry for him not to leave her there. They were both left on the lawn in each other's arms even though he still had a dozen unanswered questions.

Hisbil surveyed the area to find that the eagle had dropped them onto the castle's ornate gardens. Beneath the bay window just above them was a large brass sundial that formed the centerpiece of an elaborate bed of petunias, tulips, and other flowering plants that filled his eyes with early spring color. The flowers and shrubs provided a cornucopia of aromas that mixed in the wind and was almost too much to take in all at once. It was the most beautiful thing Hisbil had ever seen.

"What are we supposed to do now?" Anasta asked, looking up to her brother.

"I'm not sure, but we need to get to…" Hisbil winced as he turned. He had been reminded of the deep scratch along his back.

"What's wrong? Are you hurt?" Anasta said as Hisbil reached around to his back—his hand returned stained with his own blood.

"I think the eagle's talon got me when we were snatched."

"Take off your rucksack so I can see the wound. Perhaps I…"

"No. We are too exposed here out in the open. We need to get under some cover. Look, over there—let's get under that rhody."

The pair scampered beneath the stiff branches of a nearby rhododendron bush. Hisbil let Anasta help him take off his rucksack, *amiculum obscurum* cloak and tunic. She found that his cloak, tunic, shirt and back had been sliced by halfway across his back.

"Just look," Hisbil said. "Don't try to heal it." While Anasta examined his wound, he took a closer look at the band of symbols on his wrist. They were like none he had ever seen—except on the wrist and forearm of his mentor, Alred. He folded his arm over his chest to keep Anasta from seeing the bands.

"I just want to clean the wound. Mom can heal it when we get home." She found the canteen of water in the rucksack. It had enough water to gently cleanse the wound with the edge of her tunic. For some reason, as she dabbed the cut, it began to close on its own, leaving a jagged scar.

"That's the best I…ow," Anasta began before she too winced in pain.

"You didn't," Hisbil said.

"I…ow…I didn't mean to… It, ow, just happened."

"Let me see." Hisbil said, turning around to find his sister fighting off the pain of a new wound on her own back. He tried to pull up her shirt to check out her newest wound.

"I don't think so…," she said, modestly pulling down her shirttail. "It's already passing. I'll feel better in a few minutes. Remind me not to touch you again when you're hurt."

Hisbil dressed as he watched the pain leave his sister's face. He was thankful that she did not ask about the bands. He rechecked the rucksack and made sure his wand was tucked into his tunic where he could easily get at it if needed. He also noticed that the hidden pouch was undisturbed.

I guess I need to find the mouse. Perhaps it will know what this is all about. But how am I supposed to talk to a mouse?

"Hisbil?" Anasta asked. "I've seen you a million times. Your skin and fur somehow look and feel…older."

"It's just your imagination. I'm just filthy dirty," Hisbil said as he looked at the back of his hand.

It does look more like my father's—at least before it became a talon.

"Let's go find that mouse," Hisbil said as he picked up the rucksack.

Forty-one—Hisbil Meets a Mouse

"Wait. Do you hear that?" Anasta said as she stopped to listen.

"Yes. Get back under the bush; something's coming." Hisbil could hear the sound of heavy wings that drove them deeper under the rhododendron bush. Judging from the sounds, a large bird had made a rather clumsy landing on the lawn.

"Just stay here. I'll see what's going on." Hisbil drew his sword and made his way to the edge of the bush where he had a better view of the garden. "Anasta! It's Bubou."

"I see you found us!" Hisbil said happily as he walked up to the owl who was trying to get to his feet and arrange his wings back in place. Hisbil was glad to have another ally in case they got into any more trouble. "Not a very good landing though." At first, Hisbil had not noticed the blood dripping from an open wound on the owl's neck.

"That...that blasted cat clawed and nearly...killed me," Bubou said as he fell over exhausted and nearly spent from loss of blood.

"Mink did this?" Anasta said as she rushed out from under the rhododendron. "She wouldn't."

"No...Mink saved me," the owl gasped just before his eyes fluttered and closed.

Hisbil stopped Anasta before she was able to touch the owl, now collapsed on the grass.

"Don't touch him. You're too weak to heal him," Hisbil warned.

"I can't just let him die. He's not that far gone. I...I'll let go if he's hurt too badly," Anasta said, looking up at her brother.

"I...I don't know. I think we...," Hisbil responded.

"Well, I do." Anasta broke free and reached down to embrace the owl, first stroking his neck. She winced, and Hisbil could see a blood stain grow as it soaked through to Anasta's cloak from a deep wound opening low on her own neck. Her hands were now red with the owl's blood, but the owl's wound was closing.

Hisbil reached down and put his arm under Anasta and gently pulled her away.

"No...I'm... not done. He's not well."

"But that's as much as you can bear. It will have to do for now."

"Dogs...," Bubou said. "Big dogs..."

"Dogs? Did you see dogs? Could they be wolves?" Hisbil asked as he helped Anasta sit on the cool grass to rest.

"He has dozens of big dogs. Yes, they could have been wolves...and goats loaded in a wagon. I flew over them when I followed the eagle. Why has he brought you here to the Owl Master's castle? Why would he need all of those animals?"

"I...I don't know. But he wants my wand and the awakening spell as well."

"Perhaps I can help?" said a squeaky voice from a small gray mouse suddenly appearing out of the forest. He was carrying a canvas bag on his shoulder and armed with what appeared to be a lady's hatpin in his belt.

Hisbil wheeled around, his sword now pointed at the round-bellied rodent standing on its hind legs. "Did you say something?" Hisbil asked.

"Why, yes. I might be able to answer some of your questions," the mouse said quite clearly but in a distinctively squeaky voice. "As to the wolves, he wants to somehow enslave them."

Hisbil stood there, quite stunned at what he had been told—and by a mouse—just as his father had said.

"Why are you talking to a mouse?" Anasta said, still a bit woozy. Hisbil knew at once that she had made a good point. Small mice were sometimes kept as village pets or beasts of burden or used to control insects and pests, but Hisbil had never heard of a talking mouse before.

"I...don't know, but the eagle said we...," Hisbil said to his sister. Turning to the mouse, "Do you have somewhere that we can rest in safety for a while? Perhaps some food...and I have many other questions."

"Of course," said the mouse. "I think I can accommodate you."

"What are *you* doing here?" another quiet but vaguely familiar voice erupted from behind Hisbil. He whirled again and swung his blade around in a single motion. Hisbil's eyes met those of a tall Seldith wearing a wide-brimmed hat and scarf that covered much of his face.

"I could ask you the same question," Hisbil asked, keeping his eyes fixed on the stranger's eyes ready for any further sign of hostility. Hisbil knew that he could kill only if there were no other way to escape, but there was nothing in *The Books of Truth* that enjoined him from crippling or disarming this adversary—if that's what he was.

"Put your sword away, champ," the stranger said, raising his hands in mock surrender. "Aren't you from Stone Valley?"

Hisbil thought for a moment before answering and realized that the sem standing before him hiding his face looked very familiar. The tip of his sword dipped to point at the stranger's midsection. "Hisbil, son of ...," he began.

"Of course, you're Rachele's and Gollsaer's son."

"You're from Stone Valley, right?" Hisbil said.

"Isn't your father the Owl Wrangler? But that can't be his sword—I know, because my sister, the swordsmith made it. Weiger took the end of the sword in his fingers and examined it. "That looks like a fine blade, like none I've ever seen. And I thought you were only about seventeen—you look like you're at least twenty-five."

From where Anasta was standing she was able to get a better look at the stranger's face. "I recognize him," Anasta whispered, tugging at Hisbil's arm, "he's an *exile*," with a tone one would use to defame a vile criminal or a faerie. "We must not talk to him—or even *look* at him."

"Are you an exile?" Hisbil said.

"Excuse me? Can we continue these pleasantries in a somewhat safer place?" said the mouse, scanning the sky.

"Squeaky is right," the stranger said. "We need to move to cover where everyone's questions can be answered." He turned and quietly moved deeper into the shrubbery. Without another word, the mouse followed.

The eagle had told him to help a mouse. This must be the one—and to beware of the exile…

"What about Bubou?" Anasta asked as she slowly regained her feet; her legs were still a bit wobbly.

"What *about* Bubou? He seems to have gone."

"Not exactly," said Bubou who had managed to hide himself under the large rhododendron bush. "I think I need to rest for a while…"

"Perhaps, that's best," Hisbil said. "Are you going to be okay if we leave you here? I need to…well, I need to help this mouse."

"Yes, yes, of course. I'll just rest here until I get my strength back. I'll be fine. And, Anasta?" Bubou queried.

"Yes?" Anasta said.

"Thank you. Your healing touch is really a miracle."

*I wonder what we've gotten into this time...*Hisbil mused.

Quickly crossing the garden by darting from shrub to bush to tree, it was not long before they met again in the security of the dry patch of earth behind the hedge.

"Who are you? Are you really an exile?" Hisbil drilled the stranger abruptly as they approached.

"Is that really important?" Weiger answered curtly, keeping his face in the shadows.

"It is to me," Anasta said, looking away so as not to pollute her eyes with the visage of an exile.

"You didn't answer the question," Hisbil responded with more tension in his voice.

Weiger stepped out into the light, pulled off his hat, and swept back the long, dark fur from his forehead. "Do you see the brand of an exile? And what are *you* doing here, scamp?" Weiger said.

Hisbil kept his eyes fixed on the exile whom he now recognized as Weiger, owner of Crow Air. "An eagle brought us here," he said, staring into Weiger's face.

He has no mark of the exile. Is he the exile the eagle warned us about?

"An eagle? Squeaky, do you have any eagle friends?" Weiger quipped.

"No, I'm afraid I don't...perhaps you can understand why. Incidentally, Hisbil, my name is Douglas Stewart, and please pardon the rudeness of my Seldith companion whose name is..."

"Weiger, yes, I know the *Sem* Weiger branded and exiled from Stone Valley for high crimes against *The Truth.*"

The mouse extended his paw to Hisbil who took his paw in a handshake and then the mouse bowed and kissed the back of Anasta's hand. She simply smiled and blushed.

"Yea, sure. I was raised with the kind and caring folks that now run Stone Valley," Weiger said sarcastically. "I... left some time ago. What makes you think *you* can help us, scamp?" Weiger sneered as he donned his hat.

"I don't know, since I have no idea why you're here or what you intend to do," Hisbil said. "The only reason we're here is that I was told by an eagle to find a mouse that needed help."

"Perhaps he knows how to awaken Veritas," Douglas said to Weiger behind his paw.

"Could be. Did you see that sword?" Weiger turned back to Hisbil who was sheathing his gleaming sword. "We came up here to the castle to try to find the spell that can change my mouse friend back to a uman. It's as simple as that."

"A uman? Why would I want to create another uman monster? Are you nuts?"

"It's a long story. If you don't want to help then just get lost."

"Don't be so harsh," Douglas said. "Perhaps if you told him that we plan to confront Tovenaar."

"Tovenaar? You two plan to go up against a uman wizard? Good luck with that." Hisbil was again uncertain what the eagle, his 'father' had gotten them into. But he somehow knew Kassie was nearby. Someone kept whispering in his ear—unless he was losing his mind and imagining things.

"What makes *you* think that the secret is here in Lord Lensmacher's castle?" Hisbil asked echoing the same sarcastic tone Weiger had used.

"*The Sacred Seven Books of Truth*...they spoke to us," Douglas said.

"Where did *you* get *The Sacred Seven Books of Truth*? And they *spoke* to you?" Hisbil said with a great deal of skepticism in his voice. *This is getting harder to believe with every breath.* "Right. *The Sacred Seven Books of Truth* spoke to a mouse, a mouse once a *uman.* I find this impossibly hard to believe. How can books speak?" *How stupid or crazy or gullible do they think I am?*

"Our story is not any nuttier than the tale you spun about being laid here by an eagle," Weiger said.

"Why do you expect me to believe that the secrets of *The Sacred Seven* would be revealed to an outsider or to an *exile* for that matter?" Hisbil retorted.

"I don't have the time or inclination to explain it to the likes of you, scamp," Weiger said gruffly. "Can you help or not? If not, then get out of our way—we have a tough job to do." Weiger pushed by Hisbil's sword and disappeared into the bushes near the castle's outer wall.

"Hisbil, Weiger is telling the truth," Douglas pleaded. "I found *The Sacred Seven Books of Truth* in the castle. When we placed the eighth book among them, a vision calling herself 'Veritas' appeared who spoke to us. It's all true. She said that the secret of retransformation could only be revealed to a pure Seldith hero—we assumed the secret is somewhere in the castle. Perhaps, *you* are the hero Veritas spoke of."

"I'm no hero, and I've never heard of any *Veritas*," Hisbil said and paused while he collected his thoughts. *Gollsaer brought us here for a purpose—but this?*

"So where *are* these sacred books now?" Hisbil began. "And why isn't Weiger returning these sacred books to their *rightful* owners—the Seldith elders? Is he also doing the bidding of the dark wizard or the exiled terrorists?" Hisbil demanded.

Weiger had overheard their conversation and charged out of the bushes toward Hisbil who lifted his sword, but Weiger simply pushed it to one side. "*The Sacred Seven* are safe, scamp. I have pledged to help Douglas because he risked his life to rescue them. I can only depend on his generosity if and when he's converted back to a uman. If he chooses to return them to the Seldith, it will be *his* decision, and his alone." Weiger now stood toe to toe with Hisbil. "So keep your sword in its scabbard until you plan to use it against Tovenaar." Weiger turned back to the wall, and Douglas followed.

Forty-two—Veritas' Counsel

*H*isbil followed the pair behind the bushes to the castle wall where Douglas was chipping away at the mortar between the walls enormous stones. I need to see *The Sacred Seven*," Hisbil said flatly and firmly. "If you want our help, I need to see books for *myself*. If not, we're returning to Stone Valley," he announced. Douglas and Weiger continued to chip at the mortar around a mouse-size opening in the castle's outer wall. Anasta moved back behind Hisbil as he stood his ground. "I don't want to risk our lives on a fool's errand."

There was no response from Douglas or Weiger, not at first. A moment later, after an animated exchange that Hisbil could only partially hear, the pair turned. "You're right. You should see the books. Perhaps, you can get them to reveal the secret of retransformation," Douglas said.

"There is no time like the present," Hisbil agreed.

"Of course, they are not far from here. We can go now and return once you're satisfied we're telling the truth," said Douglas, marching past Hisbil and Anasta. "Come with me."

Weiger followed a moment later and, without comment, trailed the mouse around the edge of the lawn and into the brambles. He threw a burning glare back at Hisbil as he passed.

Hisbil turned to Anasta and took her hand.

"Let's go. I don't want to lose them."

"I'll stay here, with Bubou," Anasta said, pulling back and digging in her heels. "Just come back for me when…"

"Come on, we need to stay together," Hisbil urged.

Anasta begrudgingly complied like a cat on a leash. Even dragging his sister-anchor, it did not take long to catch up with Douglas and Weiger, as they had waited just inside the bramble.

"I had a little sister like that once. I fed her to the guppies in the pond," Weiger said with a grin on his face as Hisbil and Anasta passed.

Anasta managed to come to life long enough to kick Weiger in the shin. Hisbil quickly encouraged her to move on with a shove that got her out of range of Weiger's retaliating foot. She ran on ahead to walk with Douglas. "Behave," Hisbil chided. "*Both* of you!" Weiger seemed to ignore him and limped along a few paces back but with a sly grin on his face that matched Hisbil's.

After ducking and turning this way and that, they suddenly came up to Douglas' front porch. Anasta had already climbed the stairs and was swinging on the lounge chair suspended from the overhanging porch roof by a couple of braided cords.

"Come in, come in and get a cool drink. Perhaps, you would like some food as…"

"Yes, I'm starved," Anasta said as she bolted through the door, nearly knocking the mouse over.

"She's quite a handful…," Douglas began.

"Yes. She can be a challenge," Hisbil agreed, "…but she has her healing graces," Hisbil continued as he followed Douglas into his home. The room was cozy—smelling of oregano and cheese. He took off his rucksack and laid it by the door.

"But you haven't found a finishing school that would teach her some manners," Weiger quipped.

"Dropout, I'm afraid," Hisbil said with a grin. "We all have our burdens."

"You *must* be the mythical hero Veritas was talking about," Douglas said.

"Hero? Hardly," Hisbil replied as he crossed the room while he studied the handmade tools and cabinetry. He had not seen anything this elaborate in any of the Seldith homes—not even those in the southside neighborhood.

"You *must* be a hero to put up with her for more than a few hours," Weiger said. "How long have you been away from home, and what brought you way out here away from Stone Valley?"

"It's a long story," Hisbil began. "Perhaps, another time; right now, we both could use some food and water."

"Of course, yes, let me see what we have to offer," Douglas said as he started pulling down packages of wrapped food from the pantry and drawing water for the teapot. "Weiger, can you stoke the fire?"

"Huh? Oh, sure," Weiger replied as he walked over and started twiddling the damper on the stovepipe. "Why don't you give us the short version of your epic, champ?"

"The name is *Hisbil*," Hisbil said as he found the overstuffed chair and sat comfortably for the first time in almost two days.

"Ah, sure, Hisbil. What possessed you to take this untamed yenesem into the wild?"

"I had to rescue her from the cat," Hisbil said, knowing full well that Weiger's curiosity would not be satisfied.

"A cat? You were running from a cat?"

"Yes, and riding another. We rode it about twenty leagues from Stone Valley, Hisbil nearly got fried on a magic fence, we spent the night nearly freezing to death in a tree-hole, got fed salmon by an eagle and another one brought us here," Anasta said.

"Right. You're a bigger liar than I am," Weiger said in obvious disgust.

"So where are *The Sacred Seven*? Where are the books you said were here?" Hisbil asked Douglas, ignoring Weiger's growing confusion. Hisbil did not get up from his chair, but he noticed that Anasta's head was bobbing as she was about to fall asleep on Douglas' bed at the end of the room—apparently exhausted from healing. He also noticed the blood stain on her cloak where her new wounds had seeped through her clothes. So had Douglas.

"Is she going to be all right?" Douglas asked.

"She'll be fine if we can get some food and drink into her. Do you have any mushrooms or carrots?"

"Why, yes, of course. I have a few left over tucked away somewhere. I'll make a broth for her."

"Don't give her anything that would poison the fish," Weiger quipped.

Hisbil gave him another glare. He realized that Weiger was kidding again just to act tough.

Douglas kept puttering at one end of the room, putting on a pot of water to which he added several ingredients, most of which Hisbil recognized and some of which he didn't.

Weiger continued his inquisition. "So you look pretty torn up. How did you get that burn scar on your neck and your cloak shredded like that?"

"Like she said, I was burned by the enchanted fence. An owl friend of mine tore my cloak when he flew me to the tree, and an eagle..."

"Right. I can see I'm never going to get the straight story out of you."

"The books?" Hisbil asked.

"Oh. They're in a compartment hidden behind the bookcase," Douglas said, walking over to the bookshelf above his bed where Anasta was now sleeping. He pulled his crocheted afghan over her and carefully took down *The Sacred Seven*. Placing them on the table, he returned to the kitchen window sill for the eighth volume. It was still warm from basking the mid-morning sunlight.

"I don't know that they will be able to reveal anything," Weiger said. "Veritas said something about being 'tired'."

"Let me be the judge of that," Hisbil said.

Douglas reverently placed *The Sacred Seven* in the seven-sided shape and placed the eighth sacred volume in the center as they were when Veritas was last seen. "Perhaps the magic was used up by our questions."

Hisbil was awestruck. Like Weiger, he had learned of *The Sacred Seven* in school. But he, like many of the other youngsters, thought they were one of the litany of made-up legends the elders used to make themselves seem more important and to hold on to their authority. He could not take his eyes off of them. "You asked the books questions? Why didn't you just read them?" Hisbil asked. These books looked similar to the diaries he had seen in the Temple of Truth, but far more adorned. Following Weiger's example, he felt compelled to drop to his knees and bow his head to show respect.

"We both tried but were unable to decipher much of anything." Douglas said softly. "They're written in a strange language of pictures and symbols. I don't think they are books as we know them but some sort of enchanted fount of knowledge," Douglas said, stepping away from the books that were still lying on the table.

Hisbil got to his feet and reached out to open the first volume when they began to glow and form the enneahedron as they had when Douglas and Weiger had first arranged them.

Hisbil's reaction was much like Weiger's: he took a big step backwards and fell over a hassock. Regaining his feet, the shape began to speak as before.

"Who awakens the Truth, and what is your bidding?"

Weiger answered, "I am Weiger, exile of Stone Valley."

So he is an exile. Hisbil thought. He realized that he was expected to answer.

"I am Hisbil son of… Seldith of Stone Valley. We wish only to gain enlightenment and wisdom from the Truth." Hisbil said.

"Very well," the voice from the shape said. At that, the figure reappeared as the beautiful nesem image of Veritas as it stepped off the enneahedron, growing to full height in front of Hisbil. "What is your bidding?" she asked in the same soft, measured tone but in a more familiar voice.

Hisbil saw Veritas as well, but as Kassie. "Kassie? Where…what are you doing here?" he cried and moved to embrace her. His arms folded through the figure being projected from the shape as one would embrace a shadow but he could smell the sweet aroma of jasmine in her hair.

"I am but a vision of the one you trust most in this world," Veritas said.

"But Kassie. Where is Kassie? Do you know where she is?"

"Kassandra was taken by the uman who calls himself Tovenaar. That occurred two days ago. She is imprisoned nearby in the castle just to the north. I am not sure of her fate. She may indeed be lost to us."

The memory of Kassie and how she was captured flooded his mind with sweet and painful memories. He turned away from the image of Veritas standing before him. *She is here, here in the castle.*

His spine straightened and steeled his determination to free her from her cage and the clutches of this uman—wizard or not.

"Ask her about the retransformation spell, champ," Weiger said. "She can't be very strong. She might retreat back into the books if we don't hurry."

"Is this the pure Seldith hero you told us about?" Weiger asked impatiently. "You know, the one that can hear the secret of retransformation?"

Veritas' eyes closed briefly, and she nodded. "Yes. Hisbil is the one. He bears the first ring of Krista."

"What?" Hisbil said. "What is the ring of Krista? I wear no ring." He held up his hands as proof.

"The ring of symbols that circles your right arm—it is the first ring of Krista. It marks the bearer of the sword of Krista and records each deed of selfless valor. The sword of Krista is tempered in the blood of the venerated eagle."

"So, it means you're the only one that can ask the question," Weiger said. "You're the *marvelous* hero—the pure Seldith that can hear how to work the retransformation spell."

"What *retransformation* spell are you talking about?" Hisbil asked, not taking his eyes off Veritas.

Douglas came over to Hisbil and took his hand. "It's for me. It's so I can revert back to my human form and return to my wife and family."

Hisbil pulled away and walked toward the door, turning his back on Douglas and Veritas. A moment later, he turned around with hatred and frustration in his eyes. "How is this going to help me defeat Tovenaar? How is this going to save Kassie or my village? Why should I help a *uman*? All you monsters have ever done to us is destroy our villages, trample us underfoot, cut down our forests, and carry us off as toys for your children. It was one of your kind that stole my Kassie. Why should I help a mouse who wants to be a uman?"

Douglas fixed his tiny black eyes on Hisbil's. "Yes, humans can be and are all too often ignorant, selfish, greedy, and cruel beyond belief. We're cruel to each other, to the animals that live and serve around us, and the world we all share. It is human ignorance and greed that have brought the earth to its knees and the world to the sad, primitive state that it's in today—all in a few generations. I have no excuse for humans. At this point in my life, I would not blame you for not wanting to help me. As I see it, you and the Seldith can use all of the help you can find wherever you can find it—even if that help comes from a human. I can only pledge with all my heart and soul to help you and your people whenever and however I possibly can. But I can only do that if I'm retransformed into a father, husband, and, yes, a human—a human who has seen your world as you see it…a human who understands what it means to be very small and vulnerable and subject to the elements and the beasts that roam the world."

"The eagle…father said you were to help the mouse," Anasta whispered. She had been awakened by the arguments and apparition. "I think you should help him," she said softly.

"So do I," said Weiger. "He's promised to return *The Sacred Seven* to me once we've transformed him back to uman form."

"To you?" Hisbil said skeptically.

"I would be willing to give *you* the books, Hisbil. It seems they are meant to be given to you," Douglas said. "You are the pristine hero of whom Veritas spoke."

"And go back on your word?" Weiger said angrily.

"Yes, I'm sorry. But Veritas does not seem to trust you. She must know something that you have not shared with me."

"Father said to beware of the exile," Anasta added loud enough for all to hear.

Weiger gave her another stare but said nothing. In a moment, he turned to *The Sacred Seven* and addressed Veritas.

"Veritas, why was I exiled? I mean, *really*, why was I branded and expelled from the village?"

Veritas' eyes closed, and she fell silent for a moment before she spoke. "Because corrupt Council ministers were bribed by a sem called Emperor," she began. "It seems that Emperor had learned of the discovery of *The Sacred Seven Books of Truth* and wanted them for his own purposes—perhaps to give to the wizard Tovenaar, perhaps to keep for himself. Members of the council also wanted to squelch any word of Tovenaar's plans— plans you might have discovered by flying over the castle."

"Well, now you know. I was made a scapegoat, as I suspected. They just made up a bunch of bogus charges, branded me, and tossed me to the wolves…probably, to hide their own dealings with Tovenaar and Emperor."

"Did Emperor send you to the castle to find *The Sacred Seven*?" Douglas asked.

Weiger paused a moment but answered, "Yes. He offered me immeasurable wealth—more salt than you can fit in this room." He paused. "But I met someone, the uman on the road, and he took away my exile's brand, giving me another chance to redeem myself and return to Stone Valley—the place where I grew up, the village where people hate me and love me and respect me, and where I wanted to marry and raise my own family. But I can't return there without *The Sacred Seven* and not without defeating Tovenaar."

Hisbil did not know what to think. He collapsed into the overstuffed chair again, and the vision of Kassie moved and appeared to stand next to him. A moment later, she bent over and whispered in his ear. Hisbil listened intently, and the color returned to his face. He turned to whisper something back to her, and she answered, but no one else could hear her say a word.

After a few moments, Hisbil said, "I know what to do, and I think I know how to do it," as he rose to his feet. "Thank you, Kassie, er, Veritas. You have been very helpful. We won't need you for a while, so I suggest you save your strength."

At this, Veritas smiled and retreated into the undulating shape which reverted back to a set of books with a sharp pop. Hisbil rose and reverently took the middle volume and replaced it on the kitchen windowsill. He reverently stowed the rest of the volumes one by one in the hidden compartment behind the bookcase.

"Douglas, weren't you making us something to eat? We're going to need it if we're going to get into that castle and transform you into a uman again," Hisbil said, sweeping his eyes to the others where they stood in the middle of the room dumbfounded and well relieved.

For the next half hour or so, Douglas prepared food for the newcomers and encouraged them to rest while he retold the story of how he had become a mouse. Hisbil seemed especially inquisitive about the process of transformation, but Douglas did not remember much, just that it had involved a bright flash of light that came from the wizard's hand.

The mouse did not fail to notice Weiger, who could not seem to take his eyes off the eighth book sitting on the windowsill soaking up the sunlight.

He really wants those books.

Forty-three—The Crystal Ballroom

"We need to get started," Hisbil announced somewhat abruptly shortly after they had eaten and Anasta had recovered.

"Okay, let's get packed up and get back up the hill." Douglas said. He was glad to be heading out. *Perhaps these elves can help me.*

Hisbil picked up his rucksack and ushered Anasta ahead of him as he went outside and began to work his way up the path toward the castle. Douglas followed close behind. Half-way up the hill they paused and waited for Weiger who followed a twenty paces behind.

"Forgot my hat…," he said sheepishly as he caught up with the others adjusting his backpack.

As Hisbil reached the top of the hill and the inner gardens, Anasta had already run ahead to check on Bubou. She returned with news of the owl.

"He's asleep. I didn't want to awaken him," she said.

"Anasta, how many times have we talked about not running ahead? You simply *must* stay close. If you want to go somewhere, you need to tell me, and we can talk about it," Hisbil rebuked.

"But…I wanted…"

"I understand. But you need to learn that when *you* get into trouble, you put everyone in danger. Try to think of others."

"But Bubou…I was thinking of Bubou."

"I understand, but…"

Great. A little kid that's out of control. "Are you two coming?" Douglas asked with some urgency. He had been standing a few feet away listening to the same speech he had given his own daughter some years ago.

"Yes, we're coming," Hisbil responded. Anasta took one more look in Bubou's direction and reluctantly followed her brother across the lawn. After a bit of scurrying as they crossed the gardens, Douglas and his houseguests again found themselves concealed under the shrubbery at the base of the castle's outer wall.

Douglas tried to help everyone understand what they were up against. "Listen, this hole leads through the outer stone wall and into a space behind the inner wooden wall. Once we're inside, the slightest noise is carried into the rest of the castle. We also have to watch out for the beasties that roam the castle day and night. Understand?"

Everyone nodded.

"Beasties?" Anasta asked Hisbil. He just shrugged his shoulders.

"You don't want to know," Douglas said to Anasta. He really didn't want to frighten anyone. Perhaps Tovenaar's beasties were asleep.

"Let's go," Douglas said as he motioned that they should follow him through the tiny hole.

"Ah, you need to make that hole a bit bigger than mouse-sized if you expect us to get through. Perhaps this will help," Hisbil said as he handed Weiger the piece of steel he had found near the fence.

"You're full of surprises champ", Weiger quipped as he used the metal shard like a pick-head to help Douglas widen the hole.

Douglas pulled himself through the hole with ease, and with considerable effort, the somewhat larger Seldith and their packs were also able to join him.

Once inside the wall, they caught their breath with the cool stone wall to their backs and an inner wooden wall ahead. The smell generated by decades of rat droppings and filth was nearly overpowering. He pinched his nose but it did not a bit of good to quench the acrid odor.

"It *stinks* in here," Anasta said aloud.

"Shhhhh!" the others hissed in unison.

Douglas pushed a stone into the hole which shrouded them in inky darkness and cut off the fresh air. "We don't need to encourage any more visitors," he said as he started moving toward a light in the wall some six feet away.

Their eyes slowly adjusted to the dark passage, lit only by a point of bright light at the far end and a thousand tiny speckles shining through the tiny flaws in the plaster and paneling.

"This way," Douglas whispered, barely audibly. Anasta was moving quite slowly as she inched her way through the detritus that littered the floor. Hisbil hung back behind her to further encourage her forward progress.

Douglas could hear Anasta and Hisbil whispering but it could not be helped. He realized that they must be pretty scared.

"I...I'm not so sure about this," Anasta whispered.

"Neither am I, but we don't have a choice. It's no worse than Aunt Herruth's perfume," Hisbil quipped, squeezing her hand in reassurance. Anasta didn't laugh.

Weiger caught up with Douglas and tugged at his arm.

"Whiskers!" he whispered a bit too loud, "What's the hold up? We need to get out of this stench! Are you sure we need these elflings?"

"They're coming," Douglas whispered as he looked back at the younger Seldith, and Hisbil echoed, "We're coming. We've had a long day," in a near whisper.

Douglas reached out and grabbed Weiger's arm. "Wait—did you hear that?" he squeaked.

"I can only hear the brat and her brother tromping through the rat poop," Weiger whispered quietly.

"There it is again," Douglas motioned for Hisbil to freeze. He and Anasta had already stopped moving. They had heard it too and had seen the shadow of a creature in the dots of light shining through the pinhole flaws.

It's a beastie. He's heard something. Douglas said to himself.

Douglas put his paw to his lips to encourage everyone to remain silent while they listened to the animal sniffing at the wall.

"He's heard us." Douglas mouthed.

He'll alert Lensmacher for sure.

They spent what seemed like an eternity listening to the creature pacing up and down the room on the other side of the wall, while they could only breathe in the stench—the smell that hopefully disguised their own scent from whatever beast was on the other side of the wall.

I think he's gone. And we can't take much more of this.

Douglas hoped the beast had given up and led the others to the end of the passage inside the wall. He had no problem finding the opening in the inner wall where the space between the walls was blocked by a vertical beam. He unlatched and gingerly opened a hinged panel that artfully concealed the mouse hole from the room. He poked his head out of the opening.

A cold shiver ran through Douglas's spine as he peered out into the room where he had been transformed. It always seemed to have the same effect on him. His tail began to spin clockwise as he studied the great room.

Let's do this.

"Weiger, stay here and wait for the others. I'll be back when it's safe to go on."

Douglas crawled through the mouse hole and into the enormous room and closed the panel behind him. He spent the next few minutes reconnoitering as he had always done when exploring the castle or foraging for food or supplies.

The beastie's gone. He tried to convince himself.

When he reopened the panel covering the mouse-hole, the Seldith were more than ready to move out of the darkness and stench.

"The beastie seems to be gone," Douglas whispered, "but he or one of his cousins could come back anytime, so we need to move quickly and quietly, as we'll be exposed until we can reach the large armoire at the far end of the room." He pointed off to the right. "There's a hiding place behind it."

Weiger and Hisbil nodded. "We'll need to leave the packs here, as we can't risk making the mouse hole any larger—not with those beasties out here. It will be a tight squeeze as it is, but I think you can make it," Douglas said.

"Are you sure?" Weiger said. "I'd like to keep my…"

"No, there's no time and we probably won't need them inside." Douglas admonished.

Nodding their heads in agreement, Hisbil and Weiger dropped their rucksacks. Douglas covered them with a piece of loose lath to hide them from prying eyes. "Out of sight, out of mind, I always say," Douglas quipped. "We can come back for them later."

"If there is a later…" Anasta lamented.

When they were all through, Douglas carefully latched the hinged panel that concealed their escape route.

"That way," Douglas directed as he pointed toward the far end of the ballroom.

Douglas and his Seldith allies immediately began to run along the baseboard toward a pair of immense armoires that stood like a great wooden escarpment framing the doorway to the entry-way.

"What is this place?" Anasta whispered to Douglas as her head twisted this way and that to take in the magnificent room.

"It's the Lord's grand ballroom," Douglas whispered. "That's the study over there, just past the foyer—where I found the cabinet and desk." Douglas could tell that the Seldith had never seen anything like this and were quite overcome by the size and opulence of the room.

"Anasta, stay close to the baseboard and keep moving," Douglas warned. Weiger and Hisbil found themselves hiding behind a large overstuffed chair breathing hard. Like country-folk visiting the big city, they were dazzled by the immense room lit with a magnificent crystal chandelier that gave off a flickering, icy-blue glow. Around them they were amazed at the giant-size ornate chairs, tapestries, and beautiful antique furniture. "He must be a King or something," Hisbil suggested in a whisper.

"Or something…" Weiger replied with a smirk.

Suddenly the silence was broken by melodious chimes.

"What's *that*?" Anasta said.

"It's just the clock," Douglas assured her.

"A clock?"

Douglas remembered that the Seldith did not have any need for clocks so he understood her confusion. "It's a mechanical device humans use to keep track of time."

"Why?" Anasta said.

"Just keep moving," Hisbil said.

Above the doorway to the foyer on a decorative shelf, the ornate clock reported the time with flowery chimes; the hands and bells announcing it was quarter-past ten.

On the wall on the opposite end of the room, the portrait of a majestic woman held a place of honor above the wide fireplace, crowning a beautifully carved mantle. The portrait was evidently painted in this room, as the same mantel was prominently featured behind her. Centered on the mantel in the portrait was a beautiful but abstract piece of art made from eccentrically cut glass and crystal.

"What is *that*?" Anasta asked, pointing up to the portrait. "The uman woman seems to be watching us."

"I expect it's a portrait of his wife, Lady Lensmacher," Douglas whispered.

"It's just a painted drawing of the lady, like the picture of Councilman Neychen hanging in our classroom," Hisbil offered.

"Yea, that one's eyes follow me too…," Anasta said as she wandered spellbound out into the vast room.

Douglas had progressed about halfway along the baseboard toward the armoires when the clouds parted enough to admit the sun through the bank of ornate windows that looked out over the gardens. The wall of glass extended to the ceiling and curved inward at the top to form over a third of the ballroom's roof, which was easily twenty feet high. The wall and roof of glass was made up of hundreds of cut glass panes set in unusual geometric shapes; no two alike arranged in seemingly random patterns. Freed from the shackles of the clouds, sunlight broke through and the room exploded with light—the prismatic glass cascaded a dancing waterfall of color across the walls and ceiling.

A beam of the dancing light reflected off the mirror on the north wall and played into the corner where Douglas was waiting for the others to catch up. For a moment, he was dazzled, but he quickly recovered when Weiger stepped in front of the shaft of light. Douglas had seen the magic of the dancing light before, but the feeling he experienced was different this time. It made his whole body quiver.

"Are you all there, Squeaky? We need to get out of the open," Weiger whispered with some concern.

"It's clear how his family got its name—Lensmacher is a master artisan with crystals, lenses, and light," Douglas said sleepily as if he was just awakened from a dream.

"Douglas?" Hisbil said touching his shoulder.

Regaining his senses, Douglas responded, "Yes, okay, we need keep moving. There's a hiding place big enough for everyone behind the armoire on the right."

"Armwa?" Weiger said. "What's that?"

"The big cabinet down there on the far wall, the one on the right. Just stay next to the baseboard and follow me," Douglas said, scampering on all fours toward the armoire.

Turning to check on his sister, Hisbil realized that Anasta was transfixed, frozen like a tiny statue standing near the middle of the room where she had strayed. She just stood there hypnotized by the dazzling world of umans and their magical lights. "Anasta," Hisbil hissed a bit too loudly. Douglas and Weiger turned back to Hisbil, and together they motioned him to be quiet.

"She's not moving. It's as if she can't hear me," Hisbil whispered as he made a dash across the ballroom toward his stupefied sister. For a moment, he too was stunned by the light but was able to shield his eyes and toss Anasta over his shoulder. He quickly carried her back to the baseboard where Douglas and Weiger were impatiently waiting for them.

Relieved that Hisbil had been able to rescue his sister, Douglas just waggled his head. *I knew she was going to be trouble.*

"I thought she would be trouble too," Weiger said grinning. "It doesn't take a mind-reader to know what you were thinking."

"Anasta, wake up!" Hisbil demanded in a frantic whisper as he stood her up against the wall and tried to shake her back to her senses. Finally, he slapped her face. At that, the color returned to her face, and she began to blink.

"You slapped me," she said groggily. Hisbil grabbed her hand mid-slap and held it by her side until she had calmed down. "We need to go, and *now*. You need to stay out of trouble and don't look at the lights."

"The lights, they were so…pretty…," Anasta said, still in somewhat of a daze as Hisbil got her moving in the right direction.

"Come on!" urged Douglas as he encouraged them to continue moving quickly along the baseboard.

Following Douglas' lead, Weiger, Hisbil, and Anasta finally reached the foot of the large armoire—they were all out of breath. Fortunately, the elaborate floor molding left a narrow gap behind the cabinet—just large enough for the Seldith and the mouse to hide and rest.

"We'll be safe here for now. The beasties can't get to us and we can't be seen," Douglas assured the others. After resting for a few moments, the Seldith followed the mouse out to the edge of the light shining in from the foyer.

"I've seen this room before," Hisbil said softly. "In my nightmares…"

Forty-four—Tovenaar's Beastie

"*Wait* here!" Douglas commanded in a whisper, and without another word, he ventured out across the foyer and into the study where he had deciphered the mystery of the locked cabinet.

Ah, something isn't right...

Some primal instinct told Douglas to freeze. It was a feeling he had experienced many times since becoming a mouse, and he had quickly learned to heed the warning. He slowly turned to see a nose poking out from the shadows on the opposite wall of the foyer. He turned and dashed into the study not wanting to lead the beastie back toward the Seldith. Hearing no pursuit, he quickly explored the room and quickly made his way back across the foyer and into the ballroom.

Returning to the Seldith a bit out of breath, he whispered, "It's open. The cabinet is pulled back, and the door to the laboratory is open. I think I could see a light down there," he puffed.

"Is...is *he* down there?" Weiger asked.

"Is Tovenaar down there? I didn't risk it. He might very well be...but there is a problem."

"A problem?" Anasta whined with a fear-strained voice. Hisbil pulled her to him, wrapping his arms around her from behind.

"The beastie—one of Tovenaar's ferrets—he's posted under a chair in the foyer. I don't know how he missed seeing me unless he was daydreaming again. I've caught him napping on several occasions. He's not very bright and not much of a sentry."

"So, how do you plan to get around this 'beastie'?" Weiger said tugging at his sling and palming a small stone from his pocket.

"I guess we could lure it away or feed it something." Douglas thought out loud.

"Like what?" Hisbil's tone suggested his dislike of the suggestion.

"Like your bratty sister...," Weiger offered teasingly.

Hisbil tightened his restraint on Anasta who tried to lash out with her feet again.

"I do hope you're kidding," Hisbil said with a smile. Weiger's expression did not change from his taunting leer.

"We need to split up. One of us needs to lure the toothy fur ball into another room so the rest can get down into the laboratory," Weiger announced with conviction.

"Are you volunteering?" Hisbil asked.

"Yea. *You* go," Anasta said. "Maybe we'll get lucky, and it will chomp off your..." Hisbil stifled her again, and she looked up at her brother with a devilish glare.

Douglas could tell that their situation was deteriorating and realized that they didn't have a lot of other choices; but before he could make a sound, Weiger had stepped out into the doorway.

"I'll lead him off down the corridor to the left," Weiger said firmly. "Douglas, you know what to look for in the study. Hisbil, you need to get out that sword and protect him. And Anasta...you can just stay out of the way."

Douglas and the others just stood there frozen.

"Squeaky, what's wrong with you? Don't worry about me. You just get the spell so we can...," Weiger ordered.

Over Weiger's shoulder Douglas only saw the salivating toothy grin of a small brown ferret creeping toward them. "Weiger, behind you…" Douglas said as he pointed.

In a single motion, Hisbil flipped the hood of his cloak over his head and forcefully pushed Anasta back into safety behind the armoire. For once, she did not protest; she seemed too frightened to scream.

As Douglas watched, Hisbil seemed to evaporate into the woodwork as he reached for something inside his cloak.

When the ferret started bounding across the foyer, Douglas and Weiger both turned and fled for their lives for the relative safety of the armoire.

Hisbil stood his ground and dodged just as the leaping beast passed over his head. At that instant, as Douglas raced toward the armoire with Weiger close behind, the chandelier high over his head was illuminated with a blinding pulse of sea-green light A resounding *bang* echoed off the walls, knocking him and Weiger to the hardwood floor.

Scrambling to regain their footing on the polished wood floor, Douglas and Weiger were barely able to stay out of the ferret's reach before realizing that the beast was encased in a shimmering green ball of light anchored to the floor by a glowing tether of that ended where Hisbil stood. While the light slowly faded, it left the startled animal dazed, but still constrained. As hard as it tried, snapping and growling, the furious ferret was unable to escape its green, glowing cage. To everyone's relief, in a few moments it became dramatically more docile.

How…how did he do that? Douglas asked himself after he had regained his feet and his heart rate returned to near normal. "How did he do that?" he asked Weiger who was hiding behind the wide leg of a wooden chair still holding his loaded sling.

By the time Douglas and Weiger had crossed the room, the ferret was lying at Hisbil's feet like a kitten in front of a warm stove. Hisbil reached out to gently stroke the ferret and began to talk softly to it as one would speak to a street waif who had lost its parents.

Douglas then realized that Hisbil had turned a deadly foe into a docile ally. *Yes, it was a good thing for Hisbil to come along. He might prove very useful,* Douglas said to himself almost loud enough for others to hear.

"He *awakened* it," Anasta piped up excitedly as she emerged from behind the armoire.

"Awakened? He awakened it?" Douglas asked.

"Yes, it's what our father did. He was the Owl Wrangler. It means the animal can talk and behave itself. The ferret thinks Hisbil is his new master."

"Well, unless I'm mistaken, that's not an owl lying there talking to your brother," Weiger said as he rejoined the others in the center of the ballroom.

"No, silly, that's a bellua of some kind. Owls have feathers and can fly."

"Of course, pest."

"Perhaps you had better go back and hide behind the armoire over there—out of the way," Douglas chided. Anasta chose to ignore the advice and boldly walked up to the ferret. Douglas could only shake his head in disapproval. *If she were my daughter, I would turn her over my knee.* This reminded him again of why he was putting himself and these Seldith in danger—so he could rejoin his own daughter...*and no, I would not spank her— much.*

"Hisbil, that was... amazing. Are you hurt?" Douglas asked as he approached the young warrior still keeping a respectful distance.

"Yes...yes, I guess so."

"Hisbil, we need to get out of here...Hisbil?" Douglas said. "That spell or whatever it was made enough noise to wake the dead."

"Yes, we.... So you can work your father's spell." Weiger joined in as he made his way back across the ballroom. "So you're an Owl Wrangler after all..."

Still holding his wand, Hisbil came to his senses. "Yes, okay, let's get back behind the armoire and regroup. Anasta? Get away from that beast. It's not..."

"Not *what*, Ontwaker?" the ferret said as it rose to its feet and followed Hisbil toward the armoire with Anasta at its shoulder.

"Oh great, another talking beast," Weiger quipped as he too retreated a few steps. "Are you planning to ride this critter back to Stone Valley?"

"His name is *Fret*. He also tells me that he has a least one brother roaming around the castle," Hisbil said. "Fret, what else can you tell us about the uman that lives in this place?"

As Hisbil continued to interrogate the ferret, one of Douglas' most potent adversaries, the fur on Douglas' back began standing straight up, and his tail began to whip around like a willow branch caught in a windstorm. There was something about the ferret's toothy grin and swarthy speech that still made him want to run for his life.

"I think we had better keep a close eye on this newcomer," Douglas whispered to Weiger, not taking his eyes off the ferret whose own shifty eyes seemed to be sizing him up. "I don't trust him. He might be putting on an act."

"I have the same feeling. I don't know much about Hisbil and how his magic works, but I wonder how much experience he's had with this *awakening* spell."

Douglas overheard Fret tell Hisbil, "Lord is...unkind. He tell me kill filthy rodents I see. I eat nasty mouse if you want..."

Hisbil answered unequivocally, "No, no…you aren't to eat or harm any mice or my friends. Just tell me what you can about the uman and what goes on in this house."

"Lady kind to me and all kin. She bring nice things we eat. Lord not like us."

"What happened to Lady? Is she here about somewhere?" Hisbil asked.

"No Lady long time. Lord angry. Lord down caves day and night."

"What does he do there?" Douglas asked.

Fret snapped his attention to Douglas and took a step toward him with a strange look in his eye and a hungry grin on his face. "Are you sure I not kill…?" Douglas took another step back and pulled out his stickpin foil with a swish. He pointed it at the ferret's nose. "No, no, you should not do anything to my friends," Hisbil admonished. "They are under my protection, and you should guard them as you would your own friends. Where is Lord now?"

"He down caves. He search and work, search and work, and make stinky brews. He put creatures in bottles."

"We might be in luck. He would have been up here by now if he had heard the sound of the awakening," Hisbil said.

Hisbil is right. Douglas thought. *We would have been discovered long ago if there was anyone nearby. The castle might be deserted, or we're walking into a trap. Tovenaar might be expecting us, and this stupid fawning ferret is just part of his plan.*

"I don't like it," Douglas whispered to Weiger, his tail still twirling nervously. "This feels like a ruse."

"It could be, Whiskers, but we knew that coming in. I think we need to get this done and get out of here. In any case, I don't want to hang around that smelly ferret for any longer than I have to."

"Can I have him?" Anasta asked nicely as she reached up and scratched behind Fret's ears, the ferret obligingly lowering its head without taking his eyes off of Douglas.

"No," Hisbil said firmly. "Now go over there behind the armoire and stay hidden. We are still in a lot of danger here."

Anasta put on her ugliest frown and slowly retreated to a place on the floor in the shadows behind the armoire where she sat and pouted.

"Fret says Tovenaar is somewhere down below in the caves, but I need to get him into this room somehow," Hisbil said.

"Up here?" Douglas asked. "Why?"

"Yes, here. I think this room is what Veritas described as the crystal ballroom; it must be. If I can get him up here, perhaps my awakening spell can make him placid enough to reveal the retransformation spell."

"Crystal ballroom?" Douglas queried.

"Yes, Veritas told me to find…," Hisbil began but stopped mid-sentence. "Well, all I know is that this room is important."

"That makes sense," Douglas said. "Tovenaar is a skilled glass artisan; it was lenses like the ones in the windows in here that opened the hidden chamber. Maybe if you told us what else Veritas told you…"

"I can tell you she told me that only Tovenaar knows the secret to the transformation spell and something else I don't really understand fully."

"What was that—can you tell us?" Weiger asked.

Hisbil didn't answer right away but then said, "She also said to 'Reflect evil in the crystal ballroom so that all might be freed'. I'm not sure what that means, but I have a pretty good idea."

Somehow Weiger and I must lure Tovenaar out of his caves and get him back here into the crystal ballroom where Hisbil would perform his own magic.

"Let's go, Weiger," Douglas said. "We need to find Tovenaar and get him up here into this room somehow. Hisbil, let's hope you and that wand of yours can do him in," Douglas said as he headed for the foyer.

"It had better work," Weiger said, "...or there won't be any of us around to tell the story to the Council—not that they are going to believe any of this."

"Yes, your wand had better work," Douglas added over his shoulder.

"I thought you said you couldn't use the wand but once a day?" Anasta whispered to her brother as he joined her behind the armoire.

"I did," Hisbil said softly. "Stay here. I'm going to look for Kassie."

Forty-five—Setting the Trap

*D*ouglas paused at the top of the steep stairway that descended into the bowels of the castle as the clock struck half-past ten. The laboratory and castle's catacombs lay somewhere at the bottom of these stairs. He had been down into the laboratory on a few occasions, and each expedition had terrified him more than the last. He realized that it would not take much for Tovenaar to end his life as a mouse and a uman. Another shiver ran down his spine as he peered down into the pit of inky darkness. He also didn't like to think about what he had seen in the laboratory where Tovenaar practiced his sorcery and dissections.

"Aren't we going down there, Whiskers?" Weiger asked impatiently, motioning to the opening that led down into the laboratory.

"Wait a moment. I might have a better way." Douglas took a step back and motioned to Weiger to follow him as he scurried behind the desk.

"Are you afraid to go down there again? I'm not…," Weiger said fearlessly peering down into the inky darkness. When Weiger caught up with Douglas, he was looking up at what looked like drawer pulls on the window side of the large black wooden desk.

Douglas tried to reach up to the lowest drawer pull on the desk but was unable to reach it, even after jumping up. He continued to search for a way to get to the controls.

"What do you have in mind?" Weiger asked.

"Tovenaar's fear of enclosed places," Douglas said. "The last time I saw him, I brought him out of his caves by opening the passageway to the dungeons. He was completely irrational as if he were terribly afraid of being trapped down there forever. If we can close the doorway and reopen it a while later, he might be more inclined to evacuate his lair for fear of being trapped again."

"The only way of knowing is to try it. The problem is, I'm a lot smaller than I was when I last operated the controls, but I hope the entrance will close by moving just one of the levers and reopen by moving it back once we're ready. Help me look for a way to get up to the controls."

"Can't you just climb up there whiskers?"

"Well, I could if I was really a mouse. But I have a human's fear of heights so I don't do a lot of climbing," Douglas admitted somewhat sheepishly.

"So we'll figure something out that doesn't involve falling..."

Weiger joined the mouse as he studied the desk for a way to gain access to the drawer pulls. "Didn't you say you operated these controls on the fall equinox? What makes you think it will work now?"

"I'm *not* sure," Douglas said as he sat back on his rump to think. "But perhaps the desk can be set to any date or time. I'm hoping that as long as there is daylight, it will work. If we can close it, then at least we have him trapped in his own laboratory until we can come up with a better plan. Without Lady Lensmacher or anyone else up here to work the controls, there isn't anyone who would know how to free him, or even know they should try."

"Is there some other way to manipulate the controls?" Weiger asked as he looked around for something useful to get up on the desk.

"A length of rope might help. I don't need to get to the top of the desk—that's just the indicator symbols and reflectors. But if we could figure out how to pull on *that* knob, the big one on the end, I think it might do the job. I expect it's the linchpin," Douglas said as he pointed.

"Let me see what I can find. You look over that way, and I'll look over near the stairway," Weiger said, pointing to the far side of the room. "…and I'll keep an ear out for Tovenaar or one of his other toothy friends."

Forty-six—Descent into the Lab

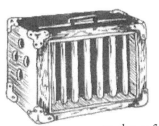

I need to help! Anasta said to herself. More and more, she felt like she was simply a burden to Hisbil and the others. She desperately wanted to help get them all to the safety of their home and hearth. Looking around from behind the armoire, she discovered that the ferret was no longer watching her.

I wonder where he's gone? I'll bet he's up to mischief.

Following the sounds of whispering voices, it was not long before she had found her way across the foyer and into the study. To the left, she spotted Weiger peering down a dark stairway, so she crept up behind him.

"Yeah, he's down there somewhere—or something is, I can see a flicker of light." Weiger said quietly to himself as he continued to listen intently.

"Who's down there?" said Anasta.

Weiger was nearly scared out of his wits. He reached for his sling, spun around, and knocked Anasta to the floor with a sweeping kick before he realized who she was. "What are you doing here, pest! Shouldn't you be back behind the armoire?" he whispered in an angry voice.

"You didn't have to knock me down, you big oaf!" Anasta said as she stood up, impulsively pushing Weiger with both hands.

Weiger flailed his arms and took a step back to regain his balance only to find he was falling into the stairwell. He hit the second step and tumbled down into the darkness like a sack of laundry being dumped down a chute.

"Weiger, are you all right?" Anasta whispered as she leaned into the stairwell. It was too dark to see any sign of him at the bottom. "Weiger?"

I've done it again, Anasta lamented. *This time, I've killed someone.*

Anasta stood on the top step and tried to figure out how to get down the stairway to help her latest victim. On each side of the stairs, she found a sloping surface about as wide as her backside, which seemed a perfect fit.

I'll just slide down like the mud slick at home.

Anasta sat down on the molding and began to inch down into the darkness with her boots slowing her descent. Everything went as planned, right up to the point where a patch of slimy moss covered the board. Try as she would, she could not keep from sliding faster and faster. In a few moments, she found herself at the bottom of the stairs. Fortunately, the only part of her that got hurt was her backside that took the force of the fall.

Oh great! She stood and rubbed away the pain. Once her eyes got used to the dark, she found Weiger lying at the bottom of the stairs in a disheveled heap. He had not been so fortunate so she dared not touch him until figuring out how badly he had been hurt. "At least he's breathing," she said to the darkness.

"No thanks to you, pest," Weiger whispered. "I think I've broken my...arm."

"No, I don't think it's broken, but your shoulder is out of place." Anasta could see that his arm was pointing in a strange direction.

"Did you hear that?" Weiger said as he sat up despite the pain.

They both listened intently for a moment and heard another sound from deep within the bowels of the castle. It was coming from a dark tunnel about fifty paces away.

"Someone's coming," Weiger said in a loud whisper. "We need to get out of sight, and fast. Can you help me up?"

Feeling sorry for Weiger, Anasta put her arm around Weiger's back to steady him as he tried to get to his feet. Within a few seconds, she was feeling his pain; her shoulder began to swell, and her own legs and ribs ached from a dozen new bruises. A moment later she had fainted.

❧❧❧

Thanks, but you shouldn't have done that. Weiger scooped up Anasta and carried her into a dark corner as gently as he would carry his own child. They hid under the stairs where they could wait for what was coming up the tunnel. They didn't have to wait long.

Forty-seven—Trapping Tovenaar

*D*ouglas hunted all over the room and under the window but didn't find anything useful. Finally, he looked up and spotted a sash cord for the curtains that might work as well as anything, but it was far too high to reach.

When he backed out from behind the curtain, Douglas felt hot breath on his neck. He whirled around to find Fret grinning at him from ear-to-ear, his beady eyes flashing with mischief.

"Why nasty rodent in Lord room? This no rodent place," Fret snarled.

Douglas froze and put his hand on the ball at the end of his stickpin foil tucked under his belt. Moving slowly backward into the curtain, he slowly withdrew it and raised it toward the ferret's nose.

"Lord say no nasty rodent in Lord room," the ferret insisted.

"Yes, of course, Fret. We were looking for some rope to…to tie up the little Seldith, Anasta. Yes, she has been getting into trouble, and we wanted to tie her up to keep her out of the way."

"Ana nice. No tie. No hurt. Ontwaker protect Ana," Fret said with growing excitement in his voice. A dribble of slobber from his snarling grin fell to the floor at his feet.

"Okay, okay. We won't want to hurt Anasta. We'll find some nice way to keep her safe. You…can go back to your ontwaker to make sure he is safe."

"No rodent in Lord room," Fret menaced again as he took another measured step toward Douglas. The tip of the stickpin rose about as much as the fur on Douglas' back while he tried to catch his nervously swishing tail with his free hand.

"Fret!" Hisbil said in a commanding voice as he came around the corner of the desk. "What are you doing here? You need to go back into the ballroom and watch Anasta."

"No rodent in Lord room," he repeated with a whine in his voice.

"Now, Fret, it will be all right," Hisbil said calmly as he walked up to the ferret and tugged on his ear to fix his eyes on his own. At this, the ferret turned and started for the door to the foyer, haltingly looking over his shoulder at the terrified mouse. Fortunately, Hisbil still seemed to have quite a bit of control over this newly awakened beast.

"No rodent in Lord room," the ferret said again as he passed into the foyer.

"Ah, thanks," Douglas said with a trembling voice as he tried to put away the stickpin without stabbing himself. "I...I wasn't sure if he was going to..."

"Neither was I," Hisbil said. "He's been acting strangely ever since his awakening.

"Where were you?" Douglas asked.

"Looking for Kassie. I think she must be upstairs some-where—if I can believe my dreams."

"There are several rooms upstairs that he uses for..."

"And there is something else..."

"You've never done this before?" Douglas asked solemnly.

"Actually, just once before, and that worked out much better. But that's not...not the problem. I don't think I can per-form another conversion until at least this time tomorrow."

"What?" Douglas said with panic in his voice. "What were you planning to do when we got Tovenaar to chase us into the ballroom—assuming he doesn't first blast us to bits with his wizardry? When were you planning to tell us?"

Hisbil looked at his feet and, with his voice beginning to break, answered, "I... I don't know. I just knew that I had to act quickly to protect Anasta and you. I did what had to be done."

"Hisbil, I'm just as scared as you are, but I saw you out there in the ballroom when that ferret jumped us. You found the guts to stand there and cast your spell and had the chutzpah to stop that beast from eating me just now. I know you can do it. We just have to make sure Tovenaar does not escape his laboratory before tomorrow at this time."

"How can you do that?" Hisbil asked with a fleck of hope in his voice.

"I think we can seal off the entrance and reopen it tomorrow once you've rested and the spell can be repeated."

"Then by all means, we need to do so. What can I do to help?"

"I think we need the drawstring for the curtains to pull one of the controls on the desk. That should close the door to the laboratory and trap Tovenaar until we're ready for him."

"I'll climb up there and cut it free," Hisbil offered as he looked up the towering column of brocade cloth.

"Okay, if you think you can do it, be my guest."

Hisbil immediately started to scale the curtain and was soon about half-way up. With a free hand he pulled his sword and as he cut the cord, the weapon began to glow brightly, brighter than ever before. It flooded the room with a blue-green light, and as it reflected off the glass top of the desk, the gears and levers inside began to grind, click, and whirr.

"Stop, Hisbil, stop! Put your sword away—it's activated the mechanism!" Douglas shouted. But it was too late. As the cords fell to the floor, the enormous cabinet slid forward, sealing the entrance to the laboratory with a thunderous crunch.

"Now we've done it," Douglas said solemnly.

"I...I'm sorry. I had no idea it would do that. It has glowed before for some reason, but I don't know why...."

"Well, I guess having him sealed in there forever is better than having him roam around up here causing trouble," Douglas offered.

"I guess so. But I'm sorry we didn't get his retransformation spell before we entombed him," Hisbil said as he climbed down the curtain.

"It was just an accident; a twist of fate. There's nothing to be sorry about. Let's go round up your sister and Weiger and get out of here."

"Weiger? Where is he?" Hisbil asked, gathering up the sash cord and beginning to coil it into a loop he could wear over his shoulder.

"Wait! Where *is* Weiger? Did you see him when you came into the room?

"Uh, no. Where did he go?" Hisbil asked.

"He went to look for rope. He should have been back by now. We need to find him; help me look." Douglas immediately ran around to the other side of the desk and began to search.

"Could he have gone down into the laboratory?" Hisbil asked.

"Let's hope not; why would he? Anyway, we need to go find Anasta and make sure that the ferret has not started chewing on her for lunch."

"Douglas? What is that on the floor by the cabinet?"

Douglas stooped over and found Weiger's sling wedged under the cabinet. "It's his sling all right. I guess we know where he is. He's probably down there with Tovenaar," he said dejectedly.

"Anasta," They said in unison.

After darting across the hall to the ballroom, Douglas and Hisbil immediately began searching for Anasta. She was nowhere to be found—but Fret was there lying contentedly on the floor licking his chops near the armoire as if he had just finished off a fine meal.

"Where is she?" Hisbil demanded. "Where is Anasta?"

The ferret got to his feet lethargically and, keeping his eyes on Douglas, answered, "She follow into Lord cave."

"Followed who? Followed Weiger, the other Seldith?" Douglas queried sternly.

"Ana go down Lord cave," Fret snarled.

"We need to get the passageway open again," Hisbil said emphatically. "Anasta's trapped in there with the wizard. There is no telling what Tovenaar will do to her…"

"*If* he finds her," Douglas said. "And it looks like Weiger's in there too. There are a lot of hiding places down there. They might even find a way out that Tovenaar can't use."

"But…"

"But you need to wait until tomorrow before your awakening spell can work again. If they can hold out until tomorrow, we can try to open the passageway then. If we open it now, we'll be defenseless."

"Yes, but I…"

"No, I would not want to be trapped in there either. I know you feel that we have to *do* something," Douglas counseled.

"Anasta is down there…" Hisbil nearly knocked Douglas down as he raced across the foyer and into the study. Douglas found him on his knees staring up at the knobs on the desk.

The clock above the doorway struck ten forty-five before Douglas could get Hisbil back to the relative safety of the space behind the armoire where Fret's siblings and cousins could not reach them.

"Is there any food?" Hisbil said at last, his mind clearing.

"Yes, I'll be back in a little while. The pantry is just through that door in the next room." Douglas made a beeline for the kitchen as if he owned the place.

"Just stay here with me Fret," Hisbil commanded as the ferret got up to follow Douglas. Fret's eyes tracked the mouse cross the room. He produced an audible sigh as Douglas squirted under the kitchen door with ease.

Just after the clock struck eleven, Hisbil lay in the inky shadows behind the armoire—the last echoes of the chimes fading into the cold silence of the ballroom. *I've done it again,* he lamented. He felt that once more he had failed to protect his sister and the village. He could only imagine the state she must be in, hopelessly trapped in the darkest regions of the castle beneath these oaken floors with no food, water, light—or hope. *If she lives through this day....*

Forty-eight—Bargaining for his Life

"It's a uman. It must be *Tovenaar*. I wonder if he heard us talking," Weiger said. Anasta didn't answer. Moments later, the uman entered the laboratory and reached up to the fixture at the center of the room. He twisted a lever, and the crystal began to glow; it quickly illuminated the room with what seemed like reflected sunlight.

Weiger pulled the still-unconscious Anasta farther into the now-brightening shadows, covered her with her cloak, and watched as the wizard went to his desk and began to study a large book, gingerly turning the pages as if fearing they would break. From time to time, he would make notes with a quill pen and mumble to himself—issues about refraction and something he called 'angstroms.'

And then their world changed. Above them on the wall, a large metal mechanism made a snapping sound like a large, dry stick breaking. The wizard looked up immediately, sprang from his desk, and lunged for the mechanism's control panel but was unable to get it open before the stairs began to flatten and rise into the ceiling. In a moment, the opening to the room above was sealed off with a great, grinding crunch. What had been Weiger's and Anasta's hiding place was now completely in the open.

Tovenaar just stood there looking up at the stairway for a moment before cursing and shifting his focus to the metal box on the stone wall next to the stairway. He returned to his desk and rummaged through the drawers muttering unintelligibly about worthless mechanisms. He slammed one drawer shut and yanked opened another. "If Fret has jumped on that desk again, I'll turn him back into a flea," he fumed, cursing once more as he dug through the wide drawers along the back wall. "And it won't be for just an hour this time," he said as he found a long-bladed screwdriver.

Walking back to the metal box on the wall, the wizard tripped and happened to look down. At his feet, he caught a glimpse of Weiger trying to drag Anasta deeper into the shadows.

"Well, well! What do we have here?" the uman bellowed.

Weiger froze and tried to pull Anasta's cloak up over his head, which had slipped off as he carried Anasta, but it was too late. He pushed Anasta into the darkness and her cloak blended into the surroundings.

Weiger immediately found himself in Tovenaar's meaty grip as he took him across the laboratory. Reaching for a drawstring, the wizard pulled back a curtain to reveal a bookcase covered with barred boxes and canning jars. Nearly all of the jars were glass tombs filled with a clear liquid containing all kinds of creatures suspended in mid-life—their wretched naked bodies often in parts, their dead eyes staring out in perpetual terror. His stomach tried to turn itself inside out. He fought back the urge to vomit.

Tovenaar reached up and pulled down a cage, which he opened with one hand and up-ended. When Weiger stopped falling and tumbling, he found himself lying in inside the sturdy wooden cage with the door barred.

"That should hold you until I get the stairway open…," Tovenaar said as he held up the cage to admire his new captive. "I think you're the third or fourth Seldith captive in as many days—I've lost count. What are *you* doing down here in my lab?"

Weiger had been cornered a few times by one predator or another, but never by a uman and never caged. He had to think fast to get himself out of this fix or he too would be just another dissected specimen in a jar.

"I came to find you," Weiger said boldly as he surveyed the inside of the cage, casually measuring the strength of the bars and seams.

"Oh, really! Well, that you've accomplished. What business could a disheveled Seldith have with me? Did the Council send you?"

"No, but I do have something you want. Emperor sent me."

"Emperor? You mean the gangly sun worshiper who lives on the beach down by the river?"

"Hardly. Emperor hates the light, and he's fastidious to a fault and kinda pudgy," Weiger replied.

"Yes, now that I recall, he is a bit chunky. One cannot be too careful. So, what is it that they call you, and what is it that you have that *I* want?"

"They call me Weiger, and first, I want out of this cage. It's affecting my ability to remember what it was that I was supposed to give you."

"Weiger? Ah, yes, the exile. Some have spoken of you. Freedom? All in due time. Let's hear what it is that you have to trade—for your freedom and your *life.*"

"Well, if I recall correctly, they are small, red and...," Weiger answered as he quietly tested and measured the distance between the bars with his shoulder.

"*The Sacred Seven Books of Truth*—you have my *sacred books?*" Tovenaar interrupted. "So Emperor was lying; I knew he was. If you look up at my little specimen collection, you'll see several of his toadies. Each of them told me that Emperor didn't have *The Sacred Seven.* I guess he did after all."

"No, they were telling the truth," Weiger said solemnly. The wizard turned the cage so that Weiger could see the tortured remains of a pair of disfigured Seldith floating in large jars on the shelf. One of them was the thick chump that had roughed him up in the bar at Shutz Norte—or what was left of him. He could not recognize the other—Weiger doubted if his mother could either.

Weiger again pushed back the urge to heave and stiffened his courage. "Emperor knows where they are but couldn't get *The Sacred Seven* without help. That's where I came in," He was not sure how much of this story had already gotten back to Tovenaar, so he had to fold at least some threads of truth into the fabric of the story he was spoon-feeding him.

"And now *you* have them? How convenient," Tovenaar said, his voice softening.

"Ah, I only know where they are. But I can have them back here before you know it, sooner with a bit of help—but I can't fetch them from here."

"Show me. Show me where they are," Tovenaar demanded as he pulled the row of bars out of the top of the cage and reached in to get Weiger. Again, Weiger again found himself in the grip of the uman wizard a dizzying height off the unforgiving stone floor.

"Oh, I would, I really would, but what's to keep you from pickling me in one of those jars once I give them to you?" Weiger said, trying to push the wizard's fingers apart so as not to be crushed.

"You have my word. My word as a gentleman," Tovenaar said sweetly as he put him down on a tall table still stained with the blood of Tovenaar's previous specimens. Weiger could see there was no way down without a rope, and even then, it would be a perilous drop. Weiger's mind was running at breakneck speed to figure out his next move. *If Douglas was right, Tovenaar has not been able to decipher more than one or two simple spells from the few parts of the book that could be read—and perhaps not even those given his evil heart.*

"I'm not sure I can take that to the refuge stores to buy food and supplies."

"What was Emperor paying you?" Tovenaar asked as he leaned in to get a closer look at Weiger.

"Paying me?" Weiger asked.

"Don't patronize me! I know the arrangement between you and Emperor. What did he promise to pay you to get *The Sacred Seven*?"

"Salt. Fifty full measures of salt and a like amount of sugar."

"It was twenty-five measures of salt and sugar about a pound if I understand Seldith weights and measures. Don't lie to me, you conniving little elf. You've seen what happens to liars here in my laboratory," the wizard said, pounding the table with his fist to make the point. The table shook hard enough to throw Weiger off his feet.

"Right. Twenty-five. It was twenty-five measures of salt and sugar."

"Ha! It's a pittance—a mere pittance," Tovenaar laughed. "Just a moment. Let me show you something." Tovenaar turned and ducked into an adjoining cave. Weiger took the opportunity to explore every inch of the table. No, there was no way down...not unless... He spotted Anasta. She had come to; while a bit dazed was now hiding behind the leg of Tovenaar's desk. Weiger motioned for her to stay hidden and keep her hood up over her head. She did so, just as the wizard came back into the laboratory.

"Here. You want salt? Here's a fifty pound block," Tovenaar said as he hoisted a large white block of salt onto the table, nearly knocking it over. "Taste it. It's 96% pure rock salt. I've got a half dozen blocks of it down here. I feed it to the cattle. To me, it's worth a pittance."

Weiger reached over and picked off a bit of salt to taste. It was pure or very nearly so. From Weiger's point of view, Tovenaar had a lot to offer, so he decided to play another card.

"So even if I bring *The Sacred Seven* to you, what makes you think you'll be able to read them? Have you had any luck so far?"

"No, but I will crack the language cipher in time," Tovenaar admitted.

"No, no, you won't. Because it's not a language—it's a spell."

"A spell?"

"Yes, and I have unlocked it. *The Sacred Seven* have revealed their secrets to me, and only me."

"To you? An exile?" Tovenaar said as he reached out for Weiger again. Weiger scurried away and dodged the wizard's half-hearted attempt to snatch him up again by hiding behind the salt block.

"Yes, I convinced the guardian of *The Sacred Seven* that I was unjustly exiled. It *spoke* to me and erased my exile brand. Look for yourself!" Weiger's heart sank. He had given the wizard far more information than he had wanted to.

"Spoke to you? They cannot be read?"

"No. They only speak to a *trusted* Seldith—only to me, because I rescued them from an evil mouse that had stolen them." Weiger knew he was venturing way out on thin ice as he skated farther and farther from the truth.

Tovenaar took the news hard. He turned away from the table and walked over to his desk where he collapsed into his chair, leaving Weiger stranded on the tall table in the middle of the lab. The uman put his head in his hands, apparently lost in thought.

After a moment, the uman sprang up and picked up the screwdriver. Using the blade, he turned a screw and opened the metal box at the base of the stairway. This exposed a now-dormant clockwork of gears and levers. Twisting a dial that appeared to have hands like a clock and pressing a lever, he snapped the mechanism back to life. In a moment, the stairway began to open and descend to the laboratory floor. Above, the cabinet moved back into the wall again exposing the entrance to the lab and dungeons.

"Do you think I would be fool enough to permit myself to be trapped in here again?" he said, standing at the base of the stairs. "Well, elf, I believe part of your story. You might be privy to the contents of *The Sacred Seven*, but so is the son of Gollsaer. Of all the Seldith, he is far more likely to have the trust of the book's spell. If I'm not mistaken, it is he you have brought to me, along with his wand and spells. I'll tend to you later."

Tovenaar charged up the stairs with Weiger stranded on the table and Anasta hidden under the stairs. He had left them alone with his maniacal collection of specimens—their lifeless eyes and gaping mouths shouting perpetual screams foretold all of their impending fate.

Forty-nine—The Crystal Dagger

*A*nd then Hisbil caught a fleeting whiff of jasmine. Before his mind could lead him to Kassie, he heard a single click—like a pebble dropped on a rock at the edge of a stream. As he listened even more intently, he felt a vibration accompanied by the now-familiar metal-on-metal whirring sound from the study; as when the cabinet had sealed off the opening to the lab. It ended as abruptly as it had begun but was closely followed by a heavy, rhythmic sound that Hisbil had also heard before, the day Kassie had been taken. But this was faster. If this was a uman, it was moving quickly and coming his way. Hisbil pushed himself farther into the shadows behind the armoire and pulled up his cloak.

Fret was resting on his tummy on the ballroom floor, his eyes glued to the kitchen door, still waiting for Douglas to return. His head popped up the instant he heard it and at once, he was on his feet and bounding across the room for the foyer, his long claws skittering to get traction on the hardwood floor.

Hisbil dared not call out to the ferret for fear of giving away his hiding place. Instead, he cautiously peeked out to see a tall uman crossing the foyer in long strides. The man was dressed in long, black flowing robes that barely kept up with his stride. His stern face had a wild, angry look—his eyes darted from point to point like a wolverine whose cubs had been threatened.

Tovenaar! Hisbil's mind screamed, and every muscle in his body tensed as he retreated deeper into the shadows behind the armoire. *He's escaped!*

As the robed man came back toward the foyer, Hisbil could hear the quisling ferret pleading to regain Tovenaar's favor. "They trick Fret, Lord!" Fret squeaked. "I try stop! Seldi creature hurt Fret!"

Tovenaar Interrogates Fret

naar's lips like summer thunder. "So, you've been awakened?

There *is* a Seldith wizard around here somewhere—as I suspected, Weiger is not alone. Tell me, Fret where is it? Weren't you supposed to tell me if you saw an intruder come into my control room?"

"Yes, Lord. I try. Seldi *attack* Fret," said the ferret, pleading with its big round eyes. "Seldi pull my ear," he said, pawing his ear.

"Where is it? Tell me, or I'll make you curse the day you were born," Tovenaar threatened again as he began tossing furniture away from the walls on the far side of the ballroom.

Peering out from the shadows, Hisbil could see Tovenaar produce a small, cool-blue crystal dagger, about six inches long, and point it down at the cowering ferret at his feet.

"Tell me. *Now!*" Tovenaar commanded with a roar.

Hisbil quietly moved to the corner of the armoire so he could make a quick escape. *I hope he doesn't give me up,* Hisbil prayed just as the ferret began to speak.

"The Seldi creature, he…he is…," Fret stammered. Something was preventing him from betraying his ontwaker.

Hisbil realized that Tovenaar's limited patience was now exhausted. Pointing the shimmering dagger at the crystal chandelier overhead, he shouted "*Sigtransformus Fret ash puce a luce!*" In an instant, the dagger began to glow from hilt to tip, followed by a stream of sea-blue light that caromed off the chandelier and the mirrored walls refocusing on the ferret still cowering in the middle of the ballroom. With a sound like the crack of a whip, Fret was transformed. All that remained was a puff of acrid smoke that hovered over the floor and quickly slinked away like rats deserting a sinking ship. The wizard grinned from ear to ear, his eyes still flashing with fury.

Judging by the smell of singed fur, Hisbil assumed the ferret had been roasted alive, but no, Fret had simply been transformed, like Douglas. Where Fret had been standing on his back legs begging for his life, a tiny flea now stood. It remained motionless for a moment, but then hopped onto Tovenaar's long robe and then up to sit on his shoulder; perhaps it was still begging for forgiveness but its voice would be too tiny to hear from where Hisbil was hiding.

"He's where? Speak up, you miserable flea!" he screamed. "Behind the big cabinet? Let's see..."

Betrayed. Hisbil lamented as he quickly cataloged his options for escape. It didn't take long as there weren't many choices.

Tovenaar strode across the room and took a hefty lance from a wall display. With a great heave he pushed the armoire on the far side of the doorway a few inches away from the wall. Using the lance point, he swept the space between the cabinet and the wall. Finding nothing, the wizard shouted to the nearly invisible quisling, "So where *is* he?"

Before Tovenaar could hear the answer, Hisbil figured out that he would have to move, and fast. *Perhaps I can make it to the mouse hole.* Keeping his cloak pulled up, he ran down the baseboard behind the armoire. As Hisbil emerged from behind the armoire, his cloak snagged on an exposed nail. Turning to free it, Hisbil did not notice the giant boot—not until he ran into it.

The tiny seldith was now confronting the moment he had dreaded from his first step inside the wizard's lair.

"Hello," Tovenaar boomed. "Could it be Hisbil, the young Seldith my winged friend Gollsaer has long promised to deliver?"

Hisbil heart sank as he knew he'd been doubly betrayed—not only by the cowardly ferret, but by his own father. "How do you know me?" he demanded.

"So it *is* Hisbil," the wizard said. "Your father and I have spoken about you many times. I know all about you, your mother and your darling sister, Anasta."

"What have you done with her?" Hisbil shouted.

"Nothing. Nothing whatsoever. I expect that she's still safe at home with her mother. Now tell me, didn't you bring the wand? Your father said you would." Tovenaar's voice was still calm.

He doesn't know about Anasta!

"I'll bet you're worried about Kassie," Tovenaar said.

"Kassie? Where is she?"

"She's…safe enough for now. She's resting upstairs with one of my wife's pets guarding her. You can never tell with these beasts. Let me do this for you: I'll take you upstairs to visit her if you give me the wand."

Hisbil's heart jumped. *Kassie* is here. She's upstairs right here in the castle. A million thoughts went through his head. Yes, he could give *Tovenaar* the wand, but it would betray all *Seldith*—and what would stop the wizard from capturing and imprisoning all of us? And what of the village? If Gollsaer and Bubou were right about the wolves, he would use the wand to ravage the countryside, and his village would certainly be lost.

Oh father, what have you thrown me into?

"Why do you need the wand? Isn't your magic strong enough? I saw the spell you cast on Fret with your crystal dagger. It was very impressive."

"Yes, the crystal can be of use, but it has its…limitations," Tovenaar replied. At this, he patted the crystal dagger now tucked inside his robe.

Limitations? Hisbil wondered.

"Perhaps you need a spell to wield in the far reaches of your estate? Perhaps something to help set the wolves on my village?"

"Who told you that? It's a lie," Tovenaar said indignantly. "I would *never* use it to harm anyone—not even your pitiful village. Even that miserable ferret will be restored before long. If I wanted to destroy your squatters' camp, I would not need wolves…a half-dozen goats or a few felled trees would be quite sufficient."

Hisbil could tell that the constraints that held back Tovenaar's fury were about to snap; like a fraying rope holding a vicious dog at bay. Hisbil had already witnessed what had happened when it snapped. He also knew that Tovenaar was a skilled liar and manipulator—just as Alred had said. If he had found Anasta, he would have used her as a bargaining chip to get the wand just as he was using Kassie and his father.

"I want the wand," he demanded again. "Don't make me transform you into something…ugly and even easier to squash."

Hisbil realized that he was safe enough—until he gave up the wand. "You…you don't frighten me *Lord* Lensmacher," Hisbil said defiantly. *Much.*

"Don't you want to see your dear Kassie again? She calls out for you night after night. Just get the wand for me, and I'll take you up to her. I hear from the Council that you don't want to bear the wand's herditas and all of the grief and danger that goes with it."

Hisbil put his hand on the wand beneath his shimmering cloak. *But it hasn't been long enough.* The large clock in the foyer had chimed eleven some time ago; it had only been an hour at most since he had used the wand to awaken Fret. "*I have to try, he's probably going to get it anyway,*" he said to himself as he pulled the wand and pointed it at Tovenaar's face.

"Here it is, come and take it," he said with as much conviction as he could muster. His hand seemed steady at first, but as Tovenaar reached down, it began to shake more and more.

Just as Tovenaar's hand was about to reach the wand, Hisbil dove down toward Tovenaar's feet and reaching up, he jabbed the wand into his foot shouting, *"Derlumen ahsben wakkan,"* as fervently as he could. Nothing happened—except Tovenaar leapt back and laughed as he reached down and swept up Hisbil like a child grabs a darting kitten off the nursery floor.

Thrashing for all he was worth, Hisbil strained to free himself from Tovenaar's grip as the uman bent his bones and squashed the air out of his lungs.

"You foolish imp, don't you even know how to cast the spell? Well, I do, now that you've tried to use it on me." Tovenaar chuckled as he twisted the wand out of Hisbil's tiny clenched fist and just as quickly dropped him. Hisbil fell but landed in the soft folds of the wizard's robe. From there, he slid to the floor, clawing at the material to brake his descent. Scrambling to his feet, he ran across the ballroom and hid behind a rolling tea table parked against the north wall of the ballroom while Tovenaar admired his tiny new treasure.

Still quite pleased with himself, Tovenaar put his fingers to his lips and produced a shrill whistle. In a moment, the distinctive rhythmic claw-on-wood sound of a ferret came around the corner from the kitchen. Either Fret had been re-transformed, or the ferret had been telling the truth—there were more of his kind patrolling in the castle. Another one of them was now panting at Tovenaar's feet, looking plaintively up at his master while he performed a frenzied dance of sideways hops back and forth.

"Ah, that's a good fellow. Just stand still for a moment…," Tovenaar cooed while he held Hisbil's tiny wand between his forefinger and thumb as one would hold a sewing needle. As Hisbil watched, he pointed the wand at the fawning ferret.

"Stand *still*, you bouncing beastie!" Tovenaar bellowed. The ferret froze, now too frightened to move beyond its uncontrollable trembling. With a thundering voice, Tovenaar aimed the wand and said, "*Derlumen ahsben wakkan.*"

Hisbil knew he himself or even his father could not have said the spell any better. But nothing happened. No pop, no light—nothing.

The wizard looked at the tiny wand as if it were a clogged pipe, twirled it in his fingers, and repeated the spell several times, emphasizing the words a different way each time, all with the same result. Nothing happened. The ferret, still frozen to the floor, now cocked his head as if he was confused at his master's most recent bizarre behavior.

"You dare try to deceive me?" Tovenaar said angrily as he threw the wand like a dagger at the ferret that turned and fled the room in terror. "Get out here, Hisbil, and give me the *real* wand, or I will bring this room down upon you."

Hisbil froze against the wall under the table; he dared not move or make a sound. His heart sank as he watched Tovenaar reach down and retrieve the wand; it seemed he regretted his last eruption of rage and wanted to keep it after all.

"Show yourself, you miniscule miscreant!" Tovenaar commanded. Hisbil peeked out from behind the table as Tovenaar started working through the room again. But this time, he had drawn his crystal dagger and was waving it like a scythe that emitted a narrow beam of light that splintered the furniture as if it was made of balsa wood. The last broad sweep splintered the tea table over Hisbil, driving a great splinter into his upper leg and pinning him against the wall like a butterfly in a display case.

Hisbil's scream was lost in the crash of wood disintegrating all around him. While he tried to free himself from the debris, each attempt to move brought new jabs of searing pain. He realized that he was hopelessly trapped. While Tovenaar could probably not see him hidden by the debris and his cloak, he could not escape. *Father you have killed me.*

Tovenaar was busy upturning and fragmenting chairs and furniture closer to the kitchen when Hisbil realized that Douglas was at his side—apparently, the mouse had been hiding nearby and had also hidden under the tea table's debris. Like Tovenaar, Douglas could not tell that Hisbil was hiding close enough to hear him breathe. As Douglas got closer, Hisbil reached out and put his hand on his shoulder as he pulled the hood of his cloak off his head. Quite startled, Douglas whipped around to discover who was laying behind him. "My Lord you scared me," he said.

"I thought I would stick around for a while," Hisbil said with a wince.

"I guess we didn't exactly lock him in," Douglas said as he ducked the debris from a long buffet nearby crumbled to the floor with a crash. "Perhaps he escaped out another way?"

"No," Hisbil said, wincing in pain. "I heard the cabinet move back; he came up…he came up the stairway. I don't think he can see me under this cloak, but he can see *you*. You need to get out of here. He said Kassie is upstairs somewhere. Can you go find her and get her to safety?"

"I'm not going anywhere without my personal wizard. We'll work our way back over to the stairway, find your sister, and then figure out how to get Kassie and everyone else out of here. Just wait until he…"

"I don't think I can walk. I'm pinned and can't…can't really move…," Hisbil said, fighting off the pain.

"Pull off your cloak so I can take a look."

Hisbil gingerly pulled the cloak off his legs.

"That looks…pretty bad. I'll put on a tourniquet to stop the bleeding. Let's hope that human first-aid works on Seldith." Douglas tore off a piece of fabric that once decorated the top of the tea table and tied it around Hisbil's leg where it met his hip. He used a short piece of wood to tighten it until Hisbil winced again. It was still bleeding but not as much.

"Tight enough?"

"Pppplenty," Hisbil said. "Anasta and Kassie. You need to get them out of here. Promise me you'll get them to safety. Bubou can help you get them back to the village…"

"Sure, sure, we'll *all* get out of here, but we need another plan. Did you try your wand?" Douglas asked.

"Yes, I…I tried to use it; it didn't work, and now Tovenaar has it and knows the spell. It was too soon to use again, but he didn't know that." Douglas now had a firm grip on Hisbil's arm, trying to hold him up.

"Just hold on and think. How did Veritas tell you to defeat Tovenaar? Is there something that can help?" Douglas' whisper was strained but controlled.

Hisbil realized that he was lucky to have an ally, a friend as brave and loyal as Douglas—even if he was once a uman. While his mind was wracked with pain, fear, and worry, he took a deep breath and cleared his head as best he could to recall what Veritas had whispered in his ear: *Reflect evil…in the crystal ballroom so that all might be freed. Reflect…reflect. This room is full of glass and prisms and…*

"Mirrors…," Hisbil said. "Mirrors to reflect his spells."

"Yes, I think you're right. But what is it that the mirrors will reflect…?" Douglas' grip on Hisbil's arm grew tighter. Hisbil looked up through his cloak to see Tovenaar standing directly over them. Fortunately, Hisbil's exposed leg was behind Douglas.

"Well, well. What now? A talking mouse? My, that little Seldith has been busy. Perhaps, I underestimated his abilities," Tovenaar said in his condescending voice.

"My current state is *your* doing, *Lord* Lensmacher," Douglas said bravely, moving a bit to further hide Hisbil. "Don't you remember the day you escaped from the laboratory and transformed a carpenter into a mouse?"

Hisbil pulled his cloak back over his leg and head as Douglas spoke; he disappeared again into the jumble of shredded wood.

"Douglas, is that you? Is this the inept carpenter that released me from my self-made prison?"

"Yes, yes, it's me, and I still haven't been rewarded for your rescue. All I have to show for my efforts is this blasted tail," Douglas said, holding up his tail, which was swishing nervously.

"Ah, that I sincerely regret, my poor man...er, mouse. I would transform you back to your former shape, but I'm somewhat distracted at the moment...." Tovenaar stopped to scan the room again, listening intently. "Do you know where I can find the little Seldith?" Tovenaar's voice changed as he remembered why he was destroying his own ballroom.

"What's a sel duth?" Douglas asked. "I've just been helping myself to the fine selection of cheese you stock in your larder," he said, holding up a large piece that he had just liberated. "You have excellent gouda. Your cheddar is a bit off, but it seems to appease the rats; however, they have far less discriminating tastes..."

"Enough!" bellowed Tovenaar. "Do you want me to finish the job? Didn't you see how I turned that groveling ferret into a flea? Do you want to give him a playmate? Tell me where the Seldith is hiding, and *quickly*!"

"Now, let's not get excited. I'm sure we can find your sel duth or whatever it is, but don't you agree that if I were a human, it would be easier for me to help you search? And perhaps I could help you find your little red books as well."

Hisbil was no longer sure of Douglas' motives at this point and began to squirm. "What are you *doing?*" he whispered.

"My books? You have my sacred books of truth?" Tovenaar bellowed. "So Weiger was right. Are they are close by?" Tovenaar asked impatiently.

With this revelation, Hisbil's heart sank again. He and his village had been betrayed by yet another Seldith. *Someday, I'll learn to be less trusting.*

"*Your* books? Didn't you say they belonged to the Seldith?" Douglas queried.

"They're *mine*. I acquired them fifteen years ago and paid dearly for them. They're *mine*, and they always *will* be mine. What have you done with them?" Tovenaar's voice was sharpening to an edge that Hisbil had witnessed a few minutes ago, just before he transformed Fret.

"Be that as it may, I'm in no position to return them to you in my current state. If I was transformed back into a human, I would be happy to return to you what is rightfully yours."

"You can't," whispered Hisbil. "They aren't *his*, they belong..."

"Be quiet. He'll hear you." Douglas whispered.

"Intriguing. Well, actually, it's really quite easy to transform back into a human: all you need to do is stand under my crystal chandelier at noon." Tovenaar pointed up to the ornate crystal fixture that dominated the room. "When the midday sunlight hits it from my special skylight, the transformation is undone. While you might feel a bit under-dressed, you'll be no worse off for your ordeal as a mouse."

Douglas was speechless at first, but then he also did not trust Tovenaar who could deceive so easily. "So, what's the catch?"

"Ah, well, there is one *little* detail that I left off. I need to place my crystal dagger into a very special place; without that, all you'll experience at noon would be a short-lived life as a human—perhaps just a few minutes."

"So, where does one place the crystal?" Douglas asked casually.

Hisbil now thought he understood what Douglas was doing. After all, he and the others had come here to rescue Douglas from his life as a mouse. Tovenaar had been the only one who held the secret of retransformation. And now the mouse had it.

"Well, I can picture it in my mind. My late wife would tell you...If only little Kassie or her mother Casandra was here. I'm sure they could read my mind and tell you, but only *I* know where the crystal is to be placed. Now *you* need to tell me what you've done with my books. Where are they? My patience is at an end." Tovenaar punctuated his sentence by pulling out the crystal dagger and pointing it directly at Douglas; its tip began to glow menacingly.

"How fast can you draw that sword?" Douglas whispered to Hisbil.

"Fast enough...I think," Hisbil replied.

"Not now. If he starts to cast the spell on me, draw your sword. The glow might distract him long enough for me to..."

"Who are you whispering to? Don't tell me... Hisbil is standing right there next to you, isn't he? He's hidden behind that cloak of invisibility of his. Yes, how nice. I want that secret too," Tovenaar sneered. "Are you going to tell me, or not?"

As the wizard began to speak, Douglas shouted, "Now!"

Hisbil immediately pulled back his cloak and drew his sword. As he raised it as high as he could, the glowing blade exploded with light. He wished almost out loud that his sword could help them get out of this. At this the sword glowed brighter than ever.

Both Douglas and Tovenaar were instantly blinded by the pure white light, but Hisbil seemed unaffected. While the room was bathed in dazzling light, only he could see that each piece of glass in the room reflected and refracted the light in every direction. The rays danced around the room in a cascade of radiance that would have put the aurora borealis and the brightest stars to shame. The crystal dagger in Tovenaar's hand glowed most of all.

Tovenaar held his arm over his eyes as he waved his crystal dagger around the room as if he was slashing back at attacking vultures. The white-hot shafts of light tore through the walls on the far side of the room; the vermin hiding inside scrambled for cover.

Undeterred, Hisbil pointed his glowing sword at Tovenaar's face, and shouted the first spell that came to mind; "*Sigtransformus Tovenaar ash puce a luce!*"

The glow from Hisbil's sword stretched down his sword arm as the glow intensified to a white-hot blast of pure energy. Hisbil closed his eyes, but before he reopened them, Tovenaar's body had disappeared with a loud bang that rattled the windows and shook the dust off the rafters. Now empty, Tovenaar's robes collapsed in a heap.

Hisbil sword returned to its chrome-steel sheen as he sank it back into its leather scabbard, but the light in the room took some time to diminish. Eventually, the glow from the chandelier was restored to a cool blue, its dangling bits of cut glass flickered with dancing sparks of light. Drained of energy, Hisbil fell over onto Douglas, breaking off the shard of wood that had impaled him against the wall.

"What happened?" Douglas said, uncovering his eyes.

"He's…gone. At least, I *think* he's gone," Hisbil said, but he had no way of knowing if the wizard had been transformed or reduced to smoke.

"Gone? And he left his robes?" Douglas said with a grin. When he turned back to Hisbil, his smile disappeared as he surveyed the Seldith's wounds.

"That's quite a sword—a brilliant move if you don't mind the pun."

Increasingly woozy, Hisbil smiled weakly and whispered hoarsely to Douglas who had dropped to his knees to hold Hisbil's head. "Find the wand. He had it before I cast…"

"Yes, of course. Your wand isn't going anywhere; you just rest. I need to find your sister and Weiger and get you some help for that leg."

"Douglas, just find it. Please. I can't let it…," Hisbil insisted.

"Okay, okay. I'll look for it now," Douglas said. He immediately began searching through the heavy robes, poking about with his stickpin foil and pulling the thick fabric this way and that. It took some time but then he reported, "Lord Lensmacher was not really very well kempt. That's the second crawly critter I've seen in his robes in as many minutes," Douglas said as he held up his stickpin with a large flea impaled through its leg—still squirming. "And, *there*—I found your wand," he said, holding it up like a trophy.

"Thanks. That might very well…be *Tovenaar* on the end of your foil," Hisbil said, propping himself up on one elbow.

Douglas held up his stickpin foil and was about to dispatch the flea when Hisbil said, "Wait, before you kill that flea, try to see if it's Fret. I would hate to see an awakened creature destroyed."

"Huh? I heard him betray you to Tovenaar. He deserves to die," Douglas said as the flea seemed to be pleading for its life.

"Perhaps, but it's not our way. His miserable fate as a flea will be punishment enough."

"I found something else as well...Tovenaar's crystal dagger," Douglas said as he launched the flea across the room with a flick of his stickpin foil. It skittered to a stop against the far baseboard and immediately began to limp away.

Hisbil nodded as he looked at his right arm that was still burning. Another dark band of symbols had been added to the others.

Fifty—The Rescue

*D*ouglas appreciated the look of relief on Hisbil's face when his wand had been found. He also saw that Hisbil looked noticeably older—perhaps it was just the ordeal. But Douglas had now gained something far more important. He knew what needed to be done to become transformed back into a human. He looked up at the clock.

It was already twenty past eleven. If he wanted to be retransformed, he would have to figure out the riddle of the crystal dagger and be under the chandelier at the stroke of noon.

I've got to move fast.

"Can you walk?" Douglas said after he had given Hisbil his wand.

"Perhaps, but we can't stay here," Hisbil said as he shoved the wand into his cloak. "Another ferret might come back at any time. I need to go find Kassie and hunt up my sister and Weiger."

"Well, I need to stay here, at least for a while. If I want to get retransformed, I need to be in this room at noon—that's only forty minutes away." Douglas said, looking into Hisbil's eyes.

"You're right. We don't have much time," Hisbil agreed.

"There is always tomorrow," Douglas offered, but he was anxious to get the retransformation done. A lot can happen in a day—especially when there's a threat of ferrets and who-knows-what else on the loose.

"Let's get back to the study while the stairs are still exposed," said Hisbil. Douglas was only too glad to help him limp across the foyer to the control room and the stairway.

Before long, the pair managed to reach the top of the narrow stairway that led into the laboratory and the catacombs beyond. Peering into the darkness, Douglas considered calling out to Anasta and to Weiger, but he didn't.

Hisbil was not so wise. "Anasta!" he called. There was no answer.

Despite his wounds, and not wanting to wait any longer, Hisbil began making his way down the steep slope at the edge of the stairs—just as his sister had done. Hisbil felt as if he was being drawn into the mouth of a great dragon waiting to close its mouth and swallow him as it had devoured his sister.

Douglas stood at the top of the stairs and called down, "Be careful, that stairway can be …"

Hisbil broke his concentration for a moment to look back at Douglas, and as he did, he began to slide and tumble down the stairway.

"…slippery," Douglas said as he could only watch Hisbil tumble into the darkness. "Hisbil!" he called. He heard no answer. *It's a pit of no return.*

❧❧❧

Hisbil lay in a tangled jumble of arms, legs, sword, and cloak at the bottom of the stairs. It took a minute or two to regain his senses and to count his bones, which was getting easier all the time.

"I'm okay…sort of," Hisbil called up to Douglas as he assessed his latest bruises and pains.

"Did you find Anasta?" Douglas shouted from the top of the stairs.

"Not yet. I think you had better stay up there until I figure out where they are."

"I'm here, brother of mine! Am I glad to see *you*…," Anasta said as she hugged Hisbil before realizing he was hurt again.

"Yes, she's here!" Hisbil called up to Douglas.

"Ow… Hisbil. Why can't I ever get—ow!—close to you without… Ow, my leg. Oh, great—now I'm bleeding again," Anasta squawked as she collapsed to the stone floor unable to support weight on her now-injured leg.

"Sorry. I had a wooden table disintegrate on top of me. Here, I think you need this more than I do…" Hisbil said as he unwrapped the tourniquet and bandage from his leg and put it on his sister.

"It's nice to run into you again, champ," Weiger said from atop the lab table. "Why did you lock us down here with that monster?"

Hisbil was not sure he knew how to treat Weiger since he had betrayed them all. He chose to ignore him.

"We need to get you out of here, Anasta. We only have a few minutes before noon."

"Why? Is the wizard coming to get us?" she said.

"No, I don't think so. He won't be bothering us or anyone else any longer," Hisbil assured his sister who was now doing her best to heal from her new wounds. His leg was far better even though Anasta had only embraced him for a moment. He could tell that her skills were maturing even if she didn't realize it.

"Douglas! Douglas, are you up there?" Hisbil called up the stairway. He heard no reply.

"Hey, scamp!" Weiger yelled. "Hisbil? Can you get me down from here?"

"We'll figure out something," Anasta said, looking up to Weiger who was standing on the edge of the table.

"No, we won't," Hisbil declared quietly but firmly. "He betrayed us. He told Tovenaar all about *The Sacred Seven*. He can just stay up there as far as I'm concerned. From now on we treat him as the traitorous exile he is."

"No," Anasta said as she tried to put weight on her leg as it continued to heal. "Weiger just said what he needed to say to keep Tovenaar down here and keep us from being dissected and put in one of those," she said, pointing up to the specimen display case. "He lied to Tovenaar, but the wizard already knew about *The Sacred Seven*. Someone called "Emperor" had sent him. I think you need to give him a second chance."

Hisbil began to take in the monstrosity of the laboratory and the shelf of specimen jars. A moment later, he saw something he wished he hadn't. His heart sank and he immediately turned away. He hoped Anasta had not seen what he had on the ghastly wall of jars. While it was impossible to know for sure, one of the specimens in the fluid-filled jars looked like Casandra—her hair floating around a grotesquely distorted face that had died in agony. He turned to Anasta and scooped her up in his arms twisting her around so she could not see the specimen wall. "We need to get you out of here. We'll talk about him later..."

"I'm ready to get out of this smelly hole," Anasta said.

"What was that?" Hisbil said, turning toward a sound like the old clock he had seen in the foyer, ticking and whirring. "There's something running here; something mechanical," Hisbil said.

"Yes, I hear it too," Weiger agreed. "It's coming from that metal box over there next to the lever Tovenaar used to lower the stairway. He set something just before the stairs came down."

"Wasn't that lever in the middle a lot lower a moment ago?" Anasta said. The lever was now pointing nearly to the ceiling and inched a bit higher like the minute-hand of a clock approaching midnight.

"You need to get your kiesters out of here *now*!" Weiger said almost frantically. No one took any convincing.

"Douglas?" There was still no answer. "Douglas!" Hisbil called a bit louder. *He's gone. Something has happened to him. He warned me about the ferrets.*

"Hisbil?" Anasta whined. "We're going to be trapped in here with *those eyes*," she said tilting her head back at the specimen display.

"It's moving. I saw the lever move again," Hisbil said solemnly. It's going to reset and close the stairway again. We're going to be entombed in here if we can't find a way out.

"Well, stop flapping your gums, champ, and *think*!" Weiger urged from atop the table. "Whiskers is not going to help anyone now—those ferrets probably got him. Find something to get you up those stairs!"

"Hisbil catch this!" Douglas called down as he threw down the cord cut from the drapes. The cord was just long enough to reach all but the last step.

Laying his sister down, Hisbil immediately started to pull himself up to the first step. "Here, grab hold," he said as he knelt down and extended his hand to Anasta once he had reached the first step.

Anasta hesitated at first, but it only took a piercing glare from Hisbil to get her moving to the foot of the step where Hisbil was waiting to pull her up. As Hisbil reached down again for Anasta, a bell chimed from within the mechanism and the stairway began to shudder. Behind the walls, gears and clutches began to mesh.

"It must be starting—keep *moving*!" Douglas called down.

"Get your bratty sister up the stairs!" Weiger commanded gruffly from the tabletop.

"What about Weiger?" Anasta asked, looking up at Hisbil.

"Don't worry about me. I'll get out of here somehow," Weiger said confidently.

Hisbil was tired of waiting. He reached down and grabbed Anasta by the wrist. In a moment she was on the first step, and in another moment Hisbil had thrown Anasta over his shoulder and started pulling himself up the rope as he ascended the flat board at the edge of the stairway. Having reached the third of thirteen steps, the mechanism clicked again and cabinet above them suddenly began its rattling approach to seal off the opening above the Seldith. Hisbil's eyes fixed on the terror on Douglas' face as he stood above unable to help. Half-way up the staircase, Hisbil's muscles were burning and he stumbled. His grip on Anasta tightened as his knee buckled and he fell back nearly two steps—the rope sliding through his hands cutting away the flesh.

"Hisbil!" Anasta and Douglas screamed almost at once. The stairway's ascent was now gaining speed as it rose toward the approaching cabinet. "I'm o...okay," he stammered as he regained his feet and restarted the ascent with even more determination.

With only inches to spare, Hisbil was able to shove Anasta through the opening and managed get his foot clear just before the cabinet slammed forward to seal off the dungeons.

"Weiger? Where's Weiger?" Douglas asked with alarm.

"He stayed behind. We'll have to figure out how to deal with him later." As he spoke, the clock in the ballroom began to chime.

"Could it be noon already?" Hisbil said as he and Douglas began to run toward the ballroom. Anasta limped along, not far behind.

Fifty-one—Noon in the Crystal Ballroom

"*G*et under the chandelier!" Hisbil shouted as they crossed the foyer into the ball-room. Douglas arrived first and was already doing his best to shove debris away from the spot directly under the crystal fixture hung from the ceiling. Hisbil arrived a moment later helped clear what they could. As the last stroke of twelve noon resounded through the shattered ballroom, Hisbil and Douglas both stood under the chandelier. Douglas and Hisbil looked up not knowing what really to expect. And nothing happened. Douglas and Hisbil waited until the hands of the clock moved to one minute past noon. And still nothing happened.

"He lied—he lied to us!" Douglas cried as he fell to his knees in despair. "Tovenaar died with the secret!" Hisbil put his hand on the mouse's shoulder, but he was inconsolable. "I'll never see my family again!" Douglas wailed.

You should be thankful that you didn't kill that flea—he might still be useful. But perhaps the crystal dagger simply needs to be in the right place for *anything* to happen," Hisbil offered. Douglas looked up and clutched at this last glimmer of hope.

"Yes! Yes, that must be it. But where does the dagger go?" Douglas queried as he got up and started looking for the dagger.

"I don't know, but I think we have until tomorrow at this time to figure it out," Hisbil said in an attempt to assuage the mouse's distress.

Anasta had made her way to the floor-to-ceiling glass doors that led out to the gardens to check on Bubou. "Hisbil, I can see Bubou from here. He's still sitting under the rhododendron. Wait! There is a black cat down there. It must be Mink. Yes, it's Mink!"

Hisbil came over to the window and was surprised to see that Anasta was right. Mink was curled up around Bubou. "She must be trying to keep him warm and safe."

"I found the dagger!" Douglas exclaimed. It was right where I left it. Can you help me move it? Something tells me we're going to have to…"

"Get under the chandelier again, now!" Hisbil cried. "Now!"

Douglas stood there staring at Hisbil for a moment but then made a mad dash back across the room and stood under the crystal fixture, looking up for some sign of the magic that would transform him. And then, as if someone had opened a great shutter, the room was flooded with light. The mirrors positioned on the ceiling and walls reflected and refracted the light streaming in from the crystal ceiling onto the chandelier. The light swirled like a tornado's vortex over the spot on the floor where Douglas was standing.

The mouse screamed for a moment and disappeared in the light. In a blink, the light in the room returned to normal and Hisbil witnessed the results of the retransformation—a five foot ten naked uman standing in the middle of the room.

Douglas took a moment to regain his senses, and as he reached back to see if he still had a tail, he realized that he was standing there sans garments. "It…it worked! I'm transformed!" he cried. Tears ran down his face in joy as he gathered up the wizard's robes and began to put them on.

"Hisbil, how can I ever repay you?" Douglas asked with glee as he finished dressing.

"Douglas. I hate to shatter your joy, but this transformation will only last for a few minutes, if that," Hisbil counseled.

"How did you know that it was the right time? Is the clock wrong?" Douglas asked.

"Yeah, how did you know?" Anasta echoed.

"The sundial. Since the re-transformation spell is triggered by sunlight, it must happen at *solar* noon. As I was looking out in the gardens, I noticed the sundial said it was nearly noon."

"Yes, you're right. Solar noon is often several minutes ahead or behind mechanical clocks. So, I need to figure out where to place the crystal while I'm still large enough to position it so that it can unlock the rest of the retransformation spell tomorrow at this time."

Douglas picked up the crystal dagger as he stepped into the wizard's sandals. Hisbil found it somewhat unsettling to see Douglas as a uman. He had never helped a uman before or even considered doing so.

"There is something I want you to do for me," Hisbil said. "I want you to go upstairs and find Kassie. We have to get her out of that cage. I think she's in a room directly above us—one with a large window that faces out on the gardens. None of us are large enough to free her. It's something only a uman can do."

"Hisbil, I need to…I have to figure out where the dagger is placed," Douglas answered.

"Anasta and I will stay here and do what we can to figure it out. Please. Just do this for me…and her."

Douglas hesitated for a moment and then nodded.

"I at least owe you that. I'll find her," he said over his shoulder as he placed the crystal dagger on the fireplace mantle before striding out through the foyer and up the wide circular steps that led to the second floor.

Fifty-two—Kassie's Nightmares

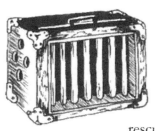

*K*assie passed the interminable days since her capture pacing in her cage, occasionally gazing out the large picture window in Tovenaar's upstairs office for any sign of rescue. Last night, she was sure Hisbil had come to save her. They embraced through the bars and he kissed away her tears. She could feel the warmth of his body against hers—it was all very real. But it *must* have been a dream, as he was gone almost as quickly as he had appeared.

Kassie had not slept since. While she wished that he would come to rescue her, in her heart she did not want him to. She knew that if Hisbil did try, he too would be captured by the uman, and while they might be together for a precious moment, they both would perish at the hands of this evil beast. So she did not reach out to him, her mother, or anyone—she resolved to accept her cruel fate alone.

The next morning she saw him again—was it another dream? Hisbil and his sister were being carried into the gardens by an eagle. *They had been captured as well.* She called and screamed his name and tried to get him to feel her presence to no avail. She collapsed in her cage in tears.

Hours later, Kassie heard strange mechanical noises and then the sounds of a terrible commotion downstairs. She saw lights shining out of the downstairs windows; flashes of colors even shown through the cracks in the floorboards, but it had stopped some time ago. Her mind swirled with images of shattered furniture and tortured creatures. It made very little sense and terrified her beyond endurance.

Her heart sank again when the robed uman crossed the room toward her cage. *Tovenaar has won. I'm finally going to join the tortured creatures in the specimen bottles that line the shelves.*

"Kassie? I'm Douglas, a friend of Hisbil." The robed uman whispered as softly as falling snow. "He's sent me here to free you." Kassie was sure she was hallucinating again.

In a moment, the uman had opened the cage and gingerly picked her up. Unlike Tovenaar, this uman barely whispered when he spoke and handled her like his own delicate child. All she could do was cry with the joy of disbelief.

"Hisbil is safe? He's here?" she cried.

"He is. Let's go find him," he said gently as he stepped over the sleeping dog spraddled across the carpet in the center of the room. Douglas closed the door as he left the room, trapping the dog.

As the uman was half-way down the wide staircase, the clock in the ballroom clicked and the uman disappeared. All that remained were his robes—emptied of the uman. Kassie screamed as she tumbled into the soft robes at the bottom of the stairs.

It's another nightmare…another nightmare! Hisbil…Hisbil come rescue me, come hold me again…

And he was there. She felt Hisbil's lovingly tender arms carrying her to safety.

Fifty-three—The Reunion

"Kassie, I'm here, I'm here. Just hold me and don't let go," Hisbil said, embracing Kassie in his arms as he had dreamed of doing nearly every moment since she had been kidnapped. He pushed his lips against hers and kissed her as they did in the forest just before she was taken. Kassie returned the kiss.

"Hisbil, don't leave me…don't…!" she cried as her arms pulled even tighter around him.

"It's all right. I'm here. You're safe."

"Is she going to be okay?" Anasta said as she looked over at Hisbil and Kassie as they embraced.

"I hope so." Hisbil said quietly. "She's had quite a tough time. Perhaps you can help."

"Do you want me to heal her?"

"Not just yet. Let's just try to get her to eat something. Douglas brought some food from the kitchen before Tovenaar found us. I think it's over there," Hisbil said, pointing to the wreckage of the tea table. "See what you can salvage."

"I'll help her," Douglas said a bit groggily.

"Douglas! I'm so glad to see you. Now I guess we know what happened to you," Hisbil said, when he realized that he had reverted to a mouse. "I'm sorry, but I'm so thankful that you rescued Kassie."

"You were right. She could not have taken much more up there. I'm glad we made the right choice," Douglas said as he helped Anasta pick through the debris looking for the food.

"This is pretty silly," Douglas said at last. "I can go get more from the kitchen. Anasta, why don't you come with me and help? I'll need someone to keep a lookout for Fret's kin if he's stopped running."

"Are you feeling better?" Hisbil asked Kassie, now that they were alone.

"Much. I think the reality is sinking in," Kassie said. The color had returned to her face and she had stopped crying. "How did you find me?"

"It's a long story. It's going to take until the next new moon to tell it all."

"Your face...and hands. What has happened to you? Hisbil... you look...*older*," Kassie said with concern.

"Do I? I'm not sure, but it might be the spells..."

"Spells? What have you been up to?"

"Later, we'll have plenty of time to ..."

"Then let's go home," Kassie interrupted. "You can tell me on the way."

"I wish we could, but we have more to do here. We need to help Douglas. After all, it was Douglas who rescued you. I would have had a lot of trouble getting upstairs and into that room—especially with that dog standing guard and I would have never gotten that cage opened."

"The dog? How did you know about the dog? Don't tell me...you came to me last night. I saw you, embraced you, kissed you—and...and you disappeared."

"Yes, I dreamed of you last night. It was very real..."

"*Mother*. It was my mother," Kassie said, getting to her feet. "I don't think she could see more than the cage and saw you trying to reach out to me in your dreams. She must have connected the dreams."

"Then she must know that I love you," Hisbil said, taking her hand and giving it a tender squeeze. He didn't know how he was going to be able to tell her about her mother's fate. He immediately began to think about something else.

"Yes. She and I have known how you felt for some time," she answered, reaching up to kiss him on the cheek when a strange look came over her face. "But what do we need to do to get out of here? Something here is out of place. You said something about a dagger?"

"Yes, a crystal dagger. It was Tovenaar's. It's used to enable the retransformation spell that's triggered by the noonday sun."

"And it 'goes' somewhere? Like the missing piece in a puzzle? That's my specialty!" Kassie said cheerfully as she started looking around the room. "This is a real mess. What came through here? A windstorm of saws?"

"Pretty much," Hisbil said.

"Is that the dagger up there on the mantelpiece? It looks out of place. It should be in that stand under the portrait."

"What? How do you know? Oh…I understand. It gives off some sort of psychic energy."

"Not really. I looked at the painting. The dagger is in the crystal stand in the picture. Anything else? Can we go now?" Kassie said brightly.

"I could just kiss you!" Hisbil said. "And Douglas will want to as well."

"I can certainly arrange for the former, but I'm not so sure I want to kiss any mice," Kassie said playfully as she joined Hisbil in another embrace and kiss.

"Ahem…are we interrupting anything?" Douglas said as he and Anasta came back from the kitchen, their arms loaded with food.

"We found it…," Hisbil said.

"*I* found it," Kassie corrected.

"Yes, Kassie found where the crystal dagger is supposed to go…or at least we think so. The answer was right in front of us all the time."

"Where? Where does it go?" Douglas asked as he looked around the room again.

"Look at the portrait," Kassie hinted.

"All I see is Lady Lensmacher…the fireplace, the fire, and…," Douglas began, "and the crystal artwork. It's not the same! It's missing the dagger. Brilliant! I could just kiss you!"

Kassie held up her hand and held off the mouse's lips but did let him give her a warm hug.

"You're welcome. Can we go home now?"

"Well, almost. All we need to do is figure out how to get up there and move the crystal back where it belongs," Hisbil said.

"Is that all…?" Kassie said with a bit less pep in her voice.

"Let's eat on it. I don't think very well on an empty stomach," Anasta said perkily.

"Neither do I!" said Weiger as he crawled out of the mouse hole on the opposite side of the room where Douglas, Hisbil, and Anasta had first entered.

"Weiger? Where did…how did you get out of the laboratory?" Anasta said.

"Well, after your escape, you left the rope on the stairs. When the stairway lifted up to the ceiling, the rope got tangled in the mechanism and ended up dangling over the table. I was able to grab it and swing over to the specimen shelf. I climbed down and just followed the smell of clean air to the outside—and here I am."

"Well, that makes things easier. We don't have to worry about you starving to death on that awful table," Anasta said as she went over and handed Weiger a slice of cheese.

"We need to talk," Hisbil said firmly.

"Once we get out of here," he said, turning to Douglas "I guess you didn't get up here by noon."

"Oh, we were here and I was retransformed, but it didn't last long—not more than a few minutes."

"We need to place that crystal dagger into the glass artwork on the other end of the mantelpiece before the spell will have any lasting effect," Hisbil said.

"And we can't try again until noon tomorrow, solar time," Douglas remarked. "So we have a little less than twenty-four hours to get it done."

"Less than that, I would say, a lot less than that." Weiger said. "There are a half dozen umans riding up here from the town. They should be here in less than a half hour."

"How do you know?" Douglas queried.

"Let's just say a little bird told me. Actually, it was a pretty big bird that scared me half to death. Apparently, he had been doing orbits around the castle and saw the umans coming up the town road. When I walked across the lawn, the bird swooped down and warned me."

"Bubou. Yes, he's a friend of ours," Anasta said. "Did you see Mink?"

"Mink? I'm not sure, but I did see a big black cat with a red collar and especially long claws. It was asleep, wrapped around one of the stone bird statues in the gardens. I didn't really want to wake it. I don't know how it missed me."

"That's Mink. She's another friend of ours, and she was cuddling Bubou the owl." Anasta said. "She saw you but probably figured you were a friend."

"So your friends include a large bald eagle and a black cat. Interesting."

"Eagle? Bubou is an owl. Don't you know the difference?"

"Sure I do, but this was an eagle that talked to me, not an owl."

"Oh, that must be my father," Anasta said as she took another bite of cheese.

Weiger just shook his head in disbelief. "You certainly have a lot of dangerous chums," Weiger said, still shaking his head.

"So we don't have time to wait. The umans from the village will want to speak to Tovenaar. We need to do something *now*!" Douglas asserted.

"I have an idea," Hisbil said.

Fifty-four—The Crystal Comes to Life

The odd quartet watched Hisbil as he positioned himself beneath a large mirror in the ceiling. He had a strange, determined look on his face.

"Douglas, get under the chandelier. I want to try something," Hisbil said, "if you don't mind being a part of the experiment."

"What do you have in mind, champ?" Weiger said with his usual flip tone.

"Yes, what are you thinking about?" Douglas asked almost at the same time with some uncertainty in his voice.

"What if the spell works with *other* sources of light?" Hisbil said. "Perhaps, there is nothing special about sunlight."

"Yes," said Douglas, "perhaps, it works because all of the mirrors are pointed to aim the sunlight properly. That's the way the controls in the desk worked…and it was triggered by the light from your sword."

"And what if it doesn't?" Weiger said. "What if it simply incinerates him?"

"It won't," Kassie said simply and calmly. "Go ahead and try. It's bound to work."

"I'm not so sure," said Weiger, shaking his head.

"I am," said Douglas solemnly. "I don't have much to lose."

"Your life? That's not worth anything?" Weiger said emphatically.

"As a mouse? Not really. An average mouse lives only for a few years and I've lived that long already—I can feel the end drawing near. No, as a human, I can try to return to my wife and daughter. I can also make something of what's left of my life. I can't do any of that as a mouse."

Douglas had already moved under the chandelier. "Go ahead. If something prevents us from getting back into this room or someone takes the dagger, I'll never get another chance. It's now or never."

Hisbil withdrew his sword with a flourish, but nothing happened. It did not glow as it did when he drew it on Tovenaar. The tip dropped as he realized it would not give them the light they needed to enable the spell. He dropped the sword to the floor.

Kassie walked over to Hisbil and picked up the sword. "Where did you get this?"

"You don't want to know," Hisbil answered.

Putting the sword back in Hisbil's hand, she took his other hand in hers. "You need to *want* it. You need to wish it. Didn't you read the inscription?"

"No, I saw the words but didn't understand them," he whispered.

"I think they say 'Your wish is my command' and something like 'Exchange strength for life.' Ask the sword what you want—just make a wish." She stood by him while he raised the sword again.

Hisbil closed his eyes and opened them with more determination, willing the sword to glow. With a bang that was loud enough to unsettle the pigeons on the castle roof, the sword began to glow and then produced a snow-white light in a focused beam. Again, all were blinded but Hisbil who aimed the shaft of light toward the ceiling and willed the light to bend so it reflected off the mirrors as if it was sunlight coming in through the skylight at solar noon. As before the light covered his arm and etched another dark band above the others.

Douglas looked up and was swallowed by the light from the chandelier. An instant later, he disappeared.

Hisbil dropped the tip of the sword and returned it to its scabbard and fell to his knees exhausted. He looked toward the center of the room. Douglas had been retransformed into a uman again but this time he was lying in a ball on the floor. He did not appear to be breathing.

Anasta was first to go to his side.

"No!" Hisbil shouted as Anasta touched Douglas and collapsed.

Hisbil and the others ran to her. Hisbil knelt down and picked her up. He held her to his breast, but she was not breathing. He looked up at the others in terror.

"Let me," said Kassie firmly, taking Anasta's limp body from Hisbil and stretching her out on the floor. Kassie opened her mouth, placed her own mouth over Anasta's, and blew breath into her. "Come back, Anasta. It's not your time. Come back, away from that cliff…," Kassie encouraged with authority. She pounded Anasta's breastbone with the side of her fist and blew another breath into her mouth, and another, and another; and Anasta finally twitched and opened her eyes.

"She's back," Kassie said as she kept Anasta lying down. "Just rest a few minutes."

"Thank God!" Douglas said as he blessed himself with the sign of the cross. He had recovered but was unable to regain his feet.

"Thank the stars," Hisbil said. He embraced his sister as if he had lost her forever but had her back once more. "Anasta, by now you know I love you; but by the stars, if you don't learn how and when to use your healing touch without killing yourself, you won't live out the day," Hisbil counseled.

"I…I just wanted to see if he was alive," Anasta said sheepishly.

"Douglas, I would do something about that crystal before you change back," Weiger said. "There's no telling how long the spell will last this time."

"Yes, you're right," Douglas said as he got up and went directly to the fireplace and picked up the crystal dagger. He positioned it into the abstract crystal artwork, trying to match the position shown in the portrait. It took several tries as everyone offered suggestions as to how it should be repositioned, but just as the dagger clicked into place, Douglas the human again became Douglas the mouse—tail and all.

"They're here," Kassie said. Looking out the gardens window, she could see several umans on horseback tying up their mounts in front of the castle.

"Douglas, I'm afraid we're going to have to do it again to make the retransformation permanent. Are you ready? We nearly killed you last time…Douglas?" Hisbil said.

Douglas did not move or speak. His eyes were closed but he was breathing, although just barely. He had not moved from the fireplace's stone hearth where he had been re-re-transformed.

Weiger was already at his side. "He's unconscious. The spell nearly killed him this time," he said, trying to revive him.

"Perhaps, I can help," Anasta said as she tried to get up. Both Kassie and Hisbil grabbed an arm and said almost in unison, "No, not this time." Hisbil just shook his head, and Kassie ran over to help him move Douglas back under the chandelier. About halfway back, Douglas came to. He shook his head. "I don't know if I can survive *that* again…"

"Do you still want to try?" Kassie asked gently.

"I think so. But as I said, I don't have much choice. But let's not leave the light on for as long," Douglas said.

"Kassie, can you come back and stand where you stood last time?" Hisbil said as he motioned for Kassie to join him on the other side of the ballroom. "It might have affected the spell." She walked quickly across the room to join Hisbil and took his hand. "And, Anasta, whatever happens, you cannot touch Douglas afterwards. I can't risk losing you."

Anasta nodded and took several steps back.

"Hisbil, however this comes out, I just want to thank you for your friendship and courage. I would have no hope if…"

Someone banged the great iron knocker on the castle door and then knocked again.

"Ready?" Hisbil said.

Douglas nodded, and Hisbil moved into position and raised his sword again. At his wish, the shaft of light illuminated the room and the chandelier as it had done before.

Another knock came from the door—louder and more insistent. "What's going on in there?" a human voice said from outside. Hisbil was distracted for a moment and let the light shine almost twice as long as before. When he put his sword down, he looked over to the center of the room. Douglas was standing there as he had been at solar noon. *It worked.* And another band had been added to Hisbil's arm, which now appeared even older.

Douglas looked around and, again, felt for his tail. It was gone. Another, even louder pounding came from the castle door. Douglas matter-of-factly walked into the foyer donning the wizard's robes and pulling up the hood so his face was shrouded in darkness. Weiger ran across the room to peek around the corner. Douglas went to the door and opened it to confront the men. Everyone when into hiding but watched the hands on the clock.

Fifty-five—Passing on the Estate

"Yes, what is the meaning of this insolent disturbance?" Douglas said abruptly to the men that had been pounding on his door.

"We saw dem lights and heard 'plosions, Your Lordship," said one of the men holding his hat, giving a slight bow as he spoke.

"Yeah, we saw da lights clear ina village. De're scaring ur youngens," said another meekly.

"And we're tired of dem wolves makin' all dat howling all night," protested another with more courage. "What do you plan to do wid dem?"

"What of it? You know I perform many experiments here. They hurt no one. In any case, I plan to relocate the wolves deep into the northern forests many hundreds of miles from here to... to repopulate the endangered packs. There is no need for concern."

"Well, try not to...," said the boldest of the men.

"Not do my experiments? I think not..." Douglas paused for a moment not sure how else to dispatch these townspeople—all of which he knew. Fortunately, they had not recognized his disguised voice. He heard the clock behind him tick off another minute.

And then it came to him—almost as if someone had planted the seed of a solution in his mind. "Perhaps you have nothing to worry about. I plan to relocate my experiments to the far reaches of the world so as not to be disturbed, so I will have no need of this castle and estate. I will... yes, I'll leave it in the hands of someone I trust from the village, so there won't be any further trouble."

The men seemed relieved and their worried frowns dissolved into smiles.

"But before you go, I want you to take a document to the office of deeds and records. Wait here and I'll fetch it," Douglas said. He closed the door and charged off as if he owned the place.

❧❧❧

When Douglas reached the base of the stairs, he motioned to Weiger and the others who had gathered behind the armoire to stay back and keep quiet. As Hisbil joined Weiger, he thought it was uncanny how Douglas was able to mimic the gruff speech and manner of the former owner—but then all umans sounded alike to the Seldith.

The men stood just outside where Hisbil could barely hear them muttering to each other. The clock ticked by several more minutes, but Douglas did not return from upstairs.

"What are we going to do?" Hisbil asked Kassie.

"Just be patient," she said calmly.

The clock ticked away another minute and then another. Suddenly Douglas returned to the foyer and opened the front door. The men were still standing there in the sun looking a bit impatient. Douglas produced an official-looking scroll, tied with a ribbon and sealed with red wax. It was hard to tell for sure, but it looked as if it bore Lord Lensmacher's signet. As Douglas handed it to one of the men, Hisbil could see that Douglas was indeed wearing a large gold ring that bore Lord Lensmacher's family crest.

"I'll thank you to have that recorded and posted immediately. I expect no further interruptions. Gentlemen, do I make myself perfectly clear?"

The umans seem dumfounded but agreed to take the document to the mayor. "He'll know what tu do, yr Lordship"

"Thank you gentlemen," Douglas said as he closed the great door and breathed a great sigh of relief.

As Douglas returned to the ballroom, Hisbil and the others came out of hiding. He realized that this mouse had certainly turned back into a human—arrogance and all. He looked up at the clock. It ticked again and struck the half hour. It had been more than fifteen minutes since Douglas' retransformation.

"What did you just do?" said Hisbil with a wry smile.

"Oh, nothing much. Lord Lensmacher just signed over the castle and the entire estate to a trust to be maintained by one Douglas Stewart and his family in perpetuity—that's me. It's to become a nature preserve. This is in recognition of Douglas' dedicated service in the employ of Lord Lensmacher. It explains where I've been, and it gives me and my family a comfortable living wage—small recompense for the time I spent as a mouse. More importantly, it leaves a protected sanctuary where the Seldith can live, work, and wrangle owls to their heart's content without fear of encroachment by the evils of men."

Hisbil did not know what to say. *Perhaps not all umans are beasts.* Kassie squeezed his hand. *No, they aren't,* Hisbil could hear Kassie say, but he did not see her lips move. He did say, "Thanks."

"Where did you get the ring?" Weiger asked.

"It was in his desk upstairs. It added a nice touch, don't you think?" Douglas observed.

"Classy," Weiger said with a grin.

"There is a lot to be done here to bring life back to normal. Of course, I want to return to my family as soon as I can. I also need to make arrangements to…"

"There is someone else at the door," Kassie said with a strange smile on her face.

"Get back…I'll get rid of them," Douglas said as he shooed the Seldith into hiding and headed for the castle door at the end of the foyer. He opened the door in his Lord Lensmacher persona apparently ready to abuse anyone who dared to bother him again, but there was no one there. He looked back at the Seldith who were still in the foyer watching.

"Look down," Hisbil said.

"Hi, Papa," came a small voice from a black cat standing just outside the door. "Can I come in?"

"Mink!" Douglas said as he scooped up the cat. "Mink, I have missed you so much!"

"Missed you too, I have," Mink said as she burrowed into his arms and began to purr loudly.

"How is it that you can speak?" Douglas said. "No, don't tell me—you were awakened."

"Ontwaker safe, he is?"

"I'm quite safe, Mink, thanks to your help and the help of my friends here," Hisbil said from behind Douglas.

"And Bubou?" Mink said.

"And Bubou," Hisbil said as he watched the owl fly through the doorway and take up a perch on the clock.

"Hisbil is your ontwaker? Does that mean you won't be coming home with me?" Douglas said, looking down at Hisbil.

"Hardly," Hisbil said. "Mink, as my last request, I would have you protect and serve Douglas the uman made mouse, made uman again. Serve him as you have served me."

"Do it joyfully, I will," Mink purred. "Need me again, you do? Call me, you shall."

"I'm glad to see you're safe, ontwaker Hisbil," Bubou said. "Is this the new Owl Master?"

"Perhaps. We can ask him," Hisbil replied.

"We can talk about it. Perhaps, you can stay here and tell me what the job entails Bubou?" Douglas said.

"I must see my ontwaker, Hisbil, home first. It's still a long way," Bubou said.

"I can fix that problem," Douglas said. "I saw a large covered basket in the kitchen that'll hold you all. I'll take you as close to the village as you like."

"Can we go home *now?*" Anasta said, pulling at Hisbil's cloak. "Mother must be frantic."

"Yes...yes, we can go home. We can all go home. But, first, we need to retrieve *The Sacred Seven* from Douglas' home," Hisbil said, thinking about what he had seen on the shelf in the laboratory.

"There is no need for that, champ," Weiger said.

Hisbil turned to Weiger with anger in his eyes. "And why not? What has happened to them?" he said sharply.

"Relax, I have them here," Weiger said as he produced his rucksack and pulled out one of the volumes.

"How...," Hisbil asked, keeping the stern look on his face. Had Weiger shown his true colors as a rogue and exile again? Kassie put her arm through Hisbil's. His mind cleared, and he suddenly wanted to give Weiger the benefit of the doubt.

"I put *The Books* in my pack before we left the house."

"You took the books?" Douglas said.

"Yes. I...I was not sure how our venture would come out. I just wanted them to be safe."

"I see," said Hisbil solemnly. "Douglas, these books are yours. You earned them, so I see it as your call to say to whom they should be given."

Douglas looked Hisbil in the eye and thought for a moment. "I want Weiger to have them, I made a deal with him, and I am a man of my word. I respect his sense of duty and respect for the books. I know he will do what's right, but that decision is up to him."

Weiger looked at his feet and seemed to be fighting off a tear. "Thank you for trusting me and living up to your word."

Hisbil was a bit concerned. "I…can't let," he began.

"And I want to return them to Stone Valley," Weiger said. "That is where they must be taken. We cannot let them fall into the hands of the likes of Emperor. I'll just have to learn to live on a bit less salt."

"Salt?" Douglas said.

"Yeah. A tiny bit of salt will feed a sem for a fortnight. You can trade it for almost anything."

"Now, that's a problem I *can* solve. You're welcome to the salt blocks in the lab. I heard you telling Hisbil about it. I'll get down there and…"

"And you need to free the souls of all of those entombed in specimen jars," Kassie said.

Hisbil looked into Kassie's eyes. *I want to get home to my mother,* her eyes said. She did not have to utter a word.

How do I tell Cassandra that Kassie's the one…, Hisbil began to think before he realized that Kassie could read his thoughts, *…going to be glad to see Kassie too.*

"Yes, of course. There are many things that must be done to atone for the evil that was committed within these walls," Douglas said with a solemn look on his face.

"Can we go *home* now?" Anasta said.

"Yes, we can go home *now,*" Hisbil answered as he walked out the great front door. For once he noticed the large bald eagle orbiting in the thermals high above the castle.

If anyone had looked up at the glass ceiling of the ballroom, they might have seen the face of a pudgy Sem who had been witness to everything that had happened after Hisbil and the others entered the castle. Not long after that, Emperor mounted Yeremy and flew south. He would arrive back in Stone Valley long before the heroes.

Fifty-six—The Heroes Return

 efore they all got started, Mink decided to return on her own to Douglas' home, as her tummy was complaining again. Hisbil bade her farewell and thanked the cat for all her help. Mink nearly knocked him down when she showed her affection by rubbing up against him. As he had said, Bubou wanted to tag along and keep watch from above until the Seldith were safely home. Hisbil nodded approval as the in his usual fashion, the owl took off without another word.

Douglas lifted the lid of the large picnic basket and gently helped each of the Seldith get inside and get comfortable on a folded gingham tablecloth that lined the inside. "So, where is this 'Stone Valley'? I know it's off to the south, but I'm not sure where," he asked.

"Okay, Squeaky… ah, *your Lordship*, perhaps I had better ride on your shoulder to guide you back," Weiger said, realizing that 'Squeaky' was no longer a good nickname.

"Well, yes, I guess that's best," Douglas replied as he offered his open hand laid on the ground. Weiger quickly climbed aboard and Douglas gently placed him on his shoulder. "You'll have to duck under my collar if someone comes," he warned.

"Sure, sure. Just head south and follow the road for a while until I get my bearings."

Douglas picked up the basket and carried the Seldith off to the south—just as he had promised. Weiger's experience as a crow pilot made it easy for him to guide Douglas along the road and then into the forest toward their home. It wasn't that long before the four exhausted and hungry Seldith approached the trail east of Stone Valley.

"Douglas, this is far enough." Weiger said at long last. "I don't think you should get much closer—you might scare the villagers."

"Okay, I'll set y'all down here. Are you sure you'll get home okay?" Douglas whispered softly as he knelt down on his knees to gently set the basket down on the forest trail.

"Yes, I'm quite sure. And thank you again!" Hisbil said as he lowered himself down from the basket to the trail.

After dropping into Hisbil's outstretched arms, Anasta ran over and hugged Douglas' little finger, which he had extended as one would a hand for a handshake. "Thanks! Thanks for taking us home. I hope you don't turn back into a mouse."

"I...I hope I don't either," Douglas said with a peculiar look on his face.

Kassie followed Anasta over the side of the basket, but stayed in Hisbil's arms a bit longer as he helped her down. She also thanked Douglas and strode over to hug his outstretched pinky as well.

Douglas helped Weiger to the ground when he took his turn briefly hugging the uman's finger. "I'll be back for that salt," he said with a broad grin.

"I'll be more than happy to deliver it anywhere you want. Come by my house...well, perhaps you should leave word at the castle where we can meet once you get situated."

"Yes, I'll leave a note on your desk in the study; just leave the window open," Weiger said as he turned down the trail toward the village. "And do something with that dog and those nasty ferrets!" he said over his shoulder.

"Yes, they need to find new homes. And Weiger, wait a second. Here is enough salt and sugar to grease the palms of the Council. Perhaps it can buy you back into their good graces," Douglas said as he handed Weiger two bags filled with white crystals.

"Ah… I don't know what to say," Weiger said as he tucked the hefty bags under his coat. "Thanks—you never know about politicians."

"Oh, no. I *do* know about politicians. But no, thank *you*. Thank you, all. If you ever need anything… *anything*, let me know," Douglas said warmly. "I'll do whatever I can to keep your village safe," Douglas promised as he slowly walked backwards toward town before he turned to let the Seldith go the rest of the way on their own.

The Seldith were spent, hungry and ready for their ordeal to be over. Hisbil could sense that Anasta was the most eager to get home. With each step that brought her closer, he could see her excitement put more spring in her steps, hear it in her voice, and in the glow on her face. *It will be nice to be home.* While Weiger was straggling farther and farther behind them, Kassie did not leave Hisbil's side.

"Are you coming?" Hisbil asked over his shoulder. When he saw that Weiger had not quickened his pace, Hisbil stopped and sat down on a branch with Kassie to wait. Weiger made his way toward them as if he was pulling a great weight behind him. As he approached, Hisbil asked, "Are you worried about the Council?"

Weiger's stony countenance told the real story. Hisbil understood. He was not ready to rejoin the settlement, and perhaps never would be.

"Let's go get this over with," Weiger muttered. At this, Hisbil and Kassie rose, and in silence they walked the last hundred paces to the portal in the thorn wall. Before Hisbil drew his sword, the briar maze parted without a word being spoken.

"Come on!" Anasta cried as she pushed past her brother into the maze.

"Wait a …," Hisbil said, but his sister had already run ahead into the thorns. Everyone waited and a few moments later, she reappeared, a bit worse for the wear and tear of charging into the thorny maze without knowing the path. She stood by as Hisbil impatiently picked thorns out of her hair and the ragged shards of her cloak.

"So lead us through, oh great thorn wall ontwaker, wizard" Anasta jived as she held on to Hisbil's sleeve.

Hisbil ignored her, fixing his gaze on Weiger who seemed more troubled than ever.

"Here, Hisbil. Take these relics," Weiger said abruptly, holding out the sack that Kassie had fashioned to carry *The Sacred Seven*. "I don't want any part of them. They've brought me nothing but grief."

"No," Hisbil answered quietly. "It was your courage and wile that helped us get them back into Seldith hands. Returning them to the Council can only help get you accepted back into the community, assuming that's what you want. You have earned that right."

"Weiger, what's the worst they can do? Banish you again?" Hisbil quipped. "You know I and my sword won't let that happen. Come on, we're all tired and hungry, and we all want to bathe and sleep in a warm, clean beds tonight. You'll at least get a home-cooked meal for your trouble—that I can promise." Hisbil stepped into the maze entrance. Kassie and Anasta followed close behind.

Hisbil led everyone through the maze, and once clear of the thorns, Anasta bolted off toward home; there was no stopping her. Kassie emerged and stood by his side and then reached for his hand.

Weiger did not emerge.

Did he turn back? Hisbil thought.

He's coming. He heard Kassie think.

A few moments later, he emerged, a bit scratched. "Took a right instead of a left," he said a bit sheepishly. At least, he had followed. Hisbil smiled and patted his shoulder as Kassie picked off a few long thorns. "Let's go to my place. My mom can heal those cuts in no time," Hisbil said.

"I want to go home too, Hisbil," Kassie said. "I'm worried about my mom."

"I…I understand," Hisbil said trying to keep his mind clear of what he had seen in the lab. "I'll see you this evening. Come and get me if you need anything…*anything.*"

"You do the same. I'll see you tonight," Kassie said as she leaned over and kissed Hisbil on the cheek before turning toward her own house. *She's in for more grief.* Hisbil thought to himself once she was out of sight.

Hisbil and Weiger slowly walked up the commons toward Hisbil's house. Word of their return had already spread like wildfire. When the villagers saw Weiger, some herded their children inside, slamming and bolting doors behind them. Others just turned their backs. A few others started to congregate at the west end of the common—only a few at first, but more every minute.

It wasn't long before several members of the Council joined this growing mob, their huddled heads nearly touching as they stood in a closed circle, no doubt discussing what to do. The village's political underlings milled around, circling the Council ministers like jackals waiting for their share of the kill. Someone deep in the crowd screwed up his courage and shouted, "Exile!"

at Weiger and shied a stone at him. This brought the idle conversation to a stop for a moment, but it soon renewed with a new fervor.

A reporter for the Fox shoved his way through the throng and called out. "What makes you think an exile has the right to contaminate these honest citizens with your lies?"

"I might ask you the same question." Weiger retorted.

"Just ignore them," Hisbil said as they pushed through the throng toward Hisbil's home. His mother was standing there waiting for him with a weak smile on her face. Hisbil could tell she had not slept a moment while they were gone. Anasta was at her side clutching her around the waist. The marks from Anasta's encounter with the thorns were now healing on his mother's face.

Rachele reached out one arm and put it around her son's neck and she pulled him to her—burying her face in his chest. "Thank you…you brought everyone home… I was so worried."

"I'm sorry mother. We had a few problems getting back…"

"Let's get inside, young sem," came a gruff, but stern, voice from behind. It was Alred, his hand on Hisbil's shoulder encouraging him through the door. "We need to talk before you confront the Council—you too, Weiger."

Alred ushered them into Hisbil's small house and turned to glare at the growing crowd. Shaking his head, he closed the door and dropped the long beam across the portal with a great thud. "Hisbil, the Council wants you to appear before them tomorrow morning," Alred said solemnly.

His scowl told Hisbil and the others that this was going to be every bit as serious as they had feared. "You're in big trouble."

"What do they think I've done?" Hisbil said. "We've saved the village from Tovenaar. We should be greeted as heroes."

"Well, *hero*," said Weiger, "you brought an exile in through the briar maze into the center of the village, for starters." He took a seat at the table and began helping himself to the warm biscuits and honey Rachele had just pulled from the oven.

"It's not just Weiger. It's all of you, and Kassie too. You are all to appear at first light tomorrow," Alred said. "They have heard of any number of serious violations including heresy and killing a sacred eagle. Not to mention killing our benefactor Lord Lensmacher."

"Who told them we attacked the eagle?" Anasta cried from her mother's side where she had been attached since she had come through the door. "We haven't spoken to anyone since we came home. How could they know anything about where we've been or what we've been doing? And anyway, we didn't find any sign of the eagle's body."

"So it's true. You did attack an eagle," said Alred. "That's very serious…"

"I jabbed an eagle with my sword to protect Anasta, but it was not hurt, or at least not badly."

"It just lost a few feathers, see?" Anasta said as she produced what was left of the eagle down she had been carrying with her through most of her ordeal.

"Sweet stars," Alred said as he collapsed into a chair at the table. "Then the rumors are true. If this comes out, you have condemned yourselves to branding, exile, or worse." His face turned to stone like the day his own wife was taken.

"Alred, it can't be that bad. Surely, the fact that the eagle was not killed and flew away is important," Hisbil said. "Can't you do anything? No one has heard what *really* happened out there. They might actually be heroes," Rachele pleaded.

No one had the heart to tell Rachele that her husband was the wounded eagle in question. They had talked about this on the trail back to Stone Valley as there was no easy way to break the news to Rachele that her husband was not coming back.

"I am a minister of the Council of Truth—of *Truth*. I can't look the other way when the truth is staring me in the face, even if Hisbil is…," Alred said.

"Don't. Don't say another word, Alred," Rachele interrupted, giving Alred a pained look.

Hisbil was at a loss. His world had turned upside down. He suddenly gained a new appreciation for the way Weiger had been acting. He now understood what it was like to be shunned—or he was about to. While the memories of the harrowing experiences he and the others had endured were still fresh in his mind, he thought back and did not see where he had any choice at any step of their journey. He and the others were all heroes. *I risked my life a dozen times to protect the Seldith, this village, and my family,* he thought.

"I need to tell the Council what happened, just as it happened," Hisbil said with his father's voice.

"And I will too," said Anasta.

Weiger looked up from the table and began to speak.

"Don't even offer, Weiger," Alred said, holding up his hand. "The Council will not want to hear a word you say. Quite the contrary, they won't even permit an exile to speak in anyone's defense—probably not even your own. Hisbil, given your association with Weiger, they are already inclined to disbelieve your story. As far as they are concerned, there is no fact that could overlook an attack on a sacred eagle, especially since all evidence we have tells us that the eagle has been killed."

"We *are* heroes—all of us. Mother, you would be proud of Anasta. She healed me and the others without concern for herself. And Weiger risked his life and livelihood to help us. He could have taken *The Sacred Seven* and sold them to the underworld at a great price. Anasta tells me he showed great courage when confronting Tovenaar," Hisbil asserted. "And Kassie, she faced the terrible ordeal by being captured and nearly joined the countless others in specimen jars in Tovenaar's laboratory. She helped all of us and helped bring Anasta back from the brink, but me most of all. Without her, I would have never found father's sword and learned how to…"

Hisbil paused a moment, and then he drew his sword. Alred was dumbfounded. "Where did you get that sword?" the old wizard asked.

But Hisbil only closed his eyes and his lips mouthed a few unheard words. When he reopened them, he was standing alone on Tovenaar's castle parapet with his sword still held high over his head, shining its light into the evening sky.

"Father. You need to return here," he said firmly, and he closed his eyes again. When they reopened a moment later, a large bald eagle was circling the parapet.

"Hisbil? Is it you who called me? I expected it to be Tovenaar," the eagle said. "My son, how…"

"I'm not sure. But since I used Tovenaar's own spell to transform him into a flea, I've felt a new…strength, a new way of seeing how our world is put together. I don't know where it comes from or if I really am any different. Kassie and Veritas helped me understand that the sword can enlighten in more ways than one."

"Then you've learned your true herditas?" the eagle said softly.

"Have I?" Hisbil said. "Have I been a wizard all along? I didn't think someone could learn a herditas only inherit it through the blood of his parents."

"Not usually learned, but I did," the eagle said. "But you're right. You inherited your herditas from your father."

"My father?" Hisbil said, looking up into the eagle's eyes. "It's Alred, isn't it?"

The eagle nodded. "Yes. How long have you known?"

"I suspected some time ago, but mother never said a word. Alred treated me, well, differently, and he almost revealed the truth a few minutes ago," Hisbil said.

"Father, do you know why I called you here?" Hisbil said.

"Father?" the eagle said.

"You are the only father I have ever known, you *are* my father in all ways but one."

"Why *did* you bring me here?" the eagle said.

"You were the eagle that brought us the fish aren't you?"

The eagle nodded. "You were cold and hungry. I did what I could to protect and feed you."

"I'm sorry I jabbed you. I just meant…"

"To scare me off, yes, I know. That took a lot of courage."

"We are accused of killing you. Anasta has some of your bloody feathers which makes it look like we're guilty. The accusation…it could mean exile for both of us and Kassie as well."

"Yes, I know. I have been spending quite a bit of time over the village."

"I also wanted to talk to you about Tovenaar. What was the *real* reason you sent me into the castle with the wand? Didn't you know he would probably get it away from me? I could, we both could have been killed…"

"Yes, son. You could both have been killed, but that's the risk we all had to take. I can't tell you how hard it was to send you into the castle with little else than a stick and a spell you've never used. I also knew that if we did not stop Tovenaar, our entire clan and perhaps all Seldith clans could have been wiped out. Fathers have been reluctantly sending their sons and daughters in harm's way since the dawn of time. They went out to fight battles that they could no longer fight themselves, but nevertheless had to be won regardless of the cost."

"But Anasta? Why…"

"I saw that she could already use her mother's healing her-ditas. I expect she helped you more than once. I was completely committed to doing all I could to protect the clan—even to the point of sacrificing myself and my family…and that's the *truth*," the eagle said, looking down at his beloved son.

"You were there the whole time?" Hisbil said.

"The whole time."

"Why didn't you…," Hisbil started to ask.

"Because you hadn't learned your true herditas; it took some doing, but you finally were able to find it and turn it into a powerful force for good, one that Tovenaar did not count on. No one knew, so the secret could not pass to his ears. If you knew your real herditas, Kassie might have known as well and revealed it to save you, herself, or her mother."

The sky had turned golden in the west as the long day was passing into night. Hisbil needed to ask one last favor of Gollsaer. Once he had done so, he raised the sword again and closed his eyes. Once again, he was standing in his own home as if he had never left.

"Hisbil? Are you all right?" Rachele said.

"Yes…yes, of course," Hisbil responded as he put the sword on the table for Alred to examine. "I understand that you had a sword like this in your youth."

Alred smiled. "Yes, I did. But not exactly; mine was fired by the blood of an eagle. It gave me…"

"Powers? A new strength and understanding of the world?" Hisbil asked.

"Yes, but those seemed to evaporate, about the time you turned ten."

Hisbil put his hand on the old sem's where Alred could see the dark bands that circled his arm. "Sometime we need to talk about our bands…I have a lot to learn."

"Yes. I've been waiting for you to come to me for a long, long time, but I don't think we have the time now. I think we need to figure a way to convince the Council of your innocence with the truth in a way that they can't repudiate."

"I have a plan, father. Weiger, will you excuse us for a while?" Hisbil said. He was not sure Weiger would help carry out what he had in mind. But he knew that he needed Alred.

"Not on your life, hero!" Weiger retorted. "I have a big stake in this. Any plans you make had better include me. That mob outside wants to dip me in boiling tar and drag me out of the village on a pole—after branding me again. If you have some planning to do, I need to be a part of it."

"Sure… you're right," Hisbil said, realizing his mistake.

৵৵৵

Hisbil, Alred, and Weiger spent much of the night talking about strategies and the day ahead of them.

Several hours before dawn, Alred left by way of the escape tunnel so as not to be seen by the angry mob incited by the Fox reported and a few members of the Council that circulated through the crowd making up lies and new accusations.

That night, the Fox ran a salacious story full of lies and half-truths that was hard for Hisbil to believe and his mother to read. It was mixed with just enough truth it would be hard to defend and easy to believe. To make matters worse, it included pictures of Hisbil and Weiger standing triumphantly over a slain eagle.

Hisbil and Anasta tried to get a few hours of sleep in their own beds. He wanted to stay awake until Kassie came—she never did. *She's learned about her mother.*

Weiger found a warm place by the stove as he also tried to sleep. Only Anasta got any rest. She had been fed a double portion of the mushroom and carrot healer's broth and tucked into bed early. They all had a lot to think about. The Council session would be their last and only chance to plead their case and tell The Truth. By dawn, the villagers were already laying wood for fires to reheat the branding irons and boil tar.

Fifty-seven—Douglas' Reunion

There was a certain spring in Douglas' step as he made his way back toward his home on the south side of the little town nestled at the base of the castle. Along the way he practiced and polished what he would say when he saw his family again after his long ordeal. He was not sure that his beloved Ristina would take him back, but with each step he hoped and prayed that she would. But why should she? He had disappeared without a single word, and it had been at more than a year since their last embrace. Douglas accepted that she had been forced to start her life over, survive, and take care of their daughter on her own in desperate times. She had to endure countless nights of not knowing if he would ever return.

"Douglas? Douglas, we thought you were dead," Dave Heintzelman, his old boss said, thrusting his hand out. "Where have you been? You kind of disappeared on us."

"I've been away... ah, working for Tov...for Lord Lensmacher. Overseas... he sent me overseas."

"That's great but we... you should have gotten word back to Ristina. After you disappeared we... we waited. We...we were engaged to be married—at least until yesterday. She suddenly broke it off."

"I need to get home Dave. I'll explain it all later." Douglas said pushing past Dave and heading toward his house.

"Sure, sure. I understand."

While it saddened him, he realized that Ristina was right to find security in the sheltering arms of another. Mr. Heintzelman was a good man who probably felt an obligation to them both. Douglas' mind was swamped with waves of uncertainty but strengthened by his steadfast love. He would have to at least try to win her back.

His doubts had slowed his pace considerably by the time he reached the small row house on a narrow side street near the edge of town. Sitting near the kitchen door was a pair of black cats waiting there to greet him.

"Welcome home, Pop…or '*Master*' say I should?" Mink meowed gleefully. Ink just meowed incessantly and walked between Douglas' legs, purring. "*At least* they're *glad to see me.*

"'Pop' will do…but let's keep your awakening to ourselves for a while. I think the surprise of seeing me might be quite enough excitement for your mistress."

"Oh, agree I do. Inside she is. Dinner she's making."

"Perhaps that's best," Douglas said as he hesitatingly opened the door. Ristina was standing over the stove with her back to him stirring what smelled like one of his favorites: beef stew. Apparently, she had not heard him come in, so he quietly closed the door and walked a few steps closer to her. She was still as beautiful as she appeared in his dreams night after night—but thankfully he was not scurrying around on the floor dodging her broom. The golden afternoon sunlight spilling through the kitchen window flowed and danced through her hair just as he had imagined it would.

"Ristina?" he said softly.

Ristina stopped stirring for a moment but did not turn around. What Douglas didn't see was the tear that trickled down her cheek. She began stirring again.

"It's about time you got home, dear. Dinner is almost ready. Vicky, your daddy is home," she said sweetly.

It was as if he had never left. Over the next few minutes, filled with hugs and kisses all around, honey biscuits, and his favorite stew, Douglas never got to use his well-practiced speech. He learned that Ristina had broken off her engagement with Mr. Heintzelman after a visit from a kind stranger who had come by two days before. It was then that she realized that she could love only Douglas and knew that she just needed to have faith that he would return—and he did.

Douglas also had a special present for Vicky—a beautiful dollhouse that looked remarkably like the house Douglas had built. "For me?" she said gleefully.

Eventually, Ristina asked about Lord Lensmacher and his spells, especially about the spells that transformed him to a mouse and back to a man. "Will it last?" she asked.

"I hope so. It has so far. I don't have a lot of experience with this sort of thing, but Hisbil seemed to think it would. I do have this burning desire for more cheese though…," he quipped with a twinkle in his eye. Ristina was not particularly amused for some reason but pushed over the plate of cheddar slices.

Unusually tasty… Douglas thought.

෴෴෴

They spent the rest of the evening and much of that night trying to make up for the time they had been apart. In the morning, well past dawn, Ristina quietly got up to make a big breakfast and serve it to her husband in bed. When she returned to the room, his covers were pulled back and all she saw was a small brown mouse on his pillow where she had left Douglas sleeping contentedly.

"Douglas!" she screamed, dropping the tray with a crash.

"What is it?" Douglas shouted as he charged into the room from the shower ready to fight an intruder in his birthday suit.

"I...I thought you had...turned back...back into a mouse!" she cried with relief rushing into his wet arms.

It didn't really surprise Ristina when Douglas refused to dispatch the mouse, which quickly ran into his hand after Douglas squeaked a few times.

"I think we'll just let him off with a warning," Douglas said as he gingerly dropped the trembling creature beside the bushes outside the back door. "I asked him to stay outside." Douglas turned to Mink who had been sleeping on the end of the bed but now was showing considerable interest in the consternation. "Kindly see that the mice and rats do not come in again, if you please," Douglas asked as if the cat understood him. Mink winked and nodded. Ristina had long been used to her husband talking to the cats as if they understood, so she thought nothing of this exchange.

But Ristina's revelations were not over. A few days later, as Mink returned from a long day terrorizing the neighborhood birds and rodents (which she no longer brought home clinging to life), the cat made a slip and asked her mistress for dinner, "Tonight the canned salmon, if you please."

After Ristina's startled scream that again brought Douglas running, there was another lengthy conversation about the Seldith, awakening spells, talking cats and many other things he had experienced during his time as a mouse.

"Is there more that I should know about your adventures?" Ristina asked.

"All in good time, my love, all in good time," Douglas said, smiling and putting his arm around her. "What do you think about living in a castle?"

Fifty-eight—The Trial and the Truth

*H*isbil left home through the escape tunnel long before the horizon in the east had revealed even a hint that dawn was approaching. This gave him one last time to think and enjoy the forests around Stone Valley that he loved so much. He remembered that Alred had warned him that the Council might have him exiled and sent across the mountains into the great desert wilderness. He looked up and listened for the morning birds and heard the usual chorus of voices thanking their Creator for another day. This was to be another blessed rainy day. He actually liked, no, loved these cool, misty days as the air was clean and pure and he always thought he could hear the evergreens thanking the skies for its bounty.

Sitting down on a fallen log, he stared up at the sky as the rain began to gently tap him on the shoulders. He slowly pulled his sword. *With a wish, I can be anywhere. But* Kassie *is here. My life is here, my family is here.* The edge of the sun touched the wisp of dark clouds to the southeast as dawn drew near. He got up and began a slow walk back toward the village.

Hisbil passed through the village along familiar paths he could traverse blindfolded. Strangely enough, there were already a number of people rustling about at this early hour, far more than usual. He detoured around a noisy klatch winding up their courage outside the tavern, and eventually arrived at the base of the tall stone-faced cliff that formed the western boundary and protection for the village.

"Up there!" the hooded guard growled after he recognized Hisbil.

Hisbil nodded his head and began the long climb up the rocky path that ended in a set of steps carved into the sheer rock face. It took him some time to work his way up the slippery steps to the thick oak door tucked into a small alcove.

Hisbil stood alone in the rain with his back to the door. Hung on ornate, rusted hinges, this portal was the first sentinel, the only outside entrance into the Chamber of Truth and the formal meeting place of the Council of Truth. The villagers, elders and Council members would have entered from the public entrance below. While there was another one-way exit, taken only by those condemned to exile, this stairway cut into the rock was the path traditionally taken by the accused.

Hisbil looked back down the narrow, winding stairway to see if anyone else was coming. While rainwater cascaded down the stairs like a miniature waterfall, Anasta, Weiger, and Kassie were nowhere to be seen. *They should have been here by now,* he said to himself, trying to judge the time by the height of the sun. It was hopeless—the sun was trying to peek over the horizon but was obscured by a thick layer of clouds that tried to make the morning seem dismal and depressing.

Let's get this over with.

Hisbil finally gave up waiting and pulled the thick iron ring at the edge of the door. The door's hinges protested with a low growl as the wooden sentinel gradually gave in to his efforts. Taking one last look over his shoulder, Hisbil stepped out of the rain and into the unlit vestibule. As he pulled the door closed behind him, his nose wrinkled at the damp mustiness that seasoned the air with the aroma of thick moss tinged with the pungent odor of the flying creatures that populated the darkest corners of these stone corridors and caverns. While waiting for his eyes to get accustomed to the darkness, a bat almost his size fluttered by his face, nearly knocking him down.

"There must be another way out," Hisbil said, his words echoing back to him as he waved his arms to warn any more of these flying vermin of his presence.

"Yes, there is, hero." The voice came from someone ahead in the darkness. "Haven't you seen the bats stream out from the top of the hill at dusk?"

"Weiger?" Hisbil said as he pushed his back against the door and started to pull his sword. As it left the scabbard, it gave off a cool green glow and illuminated the vestibule just inside the door.

"Who did you expect?" Weiger said, stepping closer. "I got the same invitation you did."

"What took you so long?" Anasta's voice came from somewhere farther ahead. "We've been here for ages. Did you expect us to wait out there in the rain on those slimy steps?"

Hisbil put his sword away, and the chamber was plunged again into darkness. He really preferred it that way. He didn't want anyone to see the fear on his face.

The smell of jasmine and hands as warm as fresh biscuits moved in close to Hisbil. "We wouldn't let you go in there alone." He could feel Kassie's breath on his cheek as she put her hand in his. Hisbil relaxed the vise-like grip on his sword. *Kassie.* "Thanks for coming," he said almost in a whisper.

Your fate is mine, Kassie thought back as she snuggled trembling against Hisbil. Being able to hear her thoughts was nice and disturbing at the same time.

Down the long tunnel carved over the millennias by water chiseling through the limestone, Hisbil could just make out the flickering yellow light of a lantern reflected in the rivulets running down the sides of the stone walls. The light swayed with the gaited rhythm of someone slowly walking toward them, pausing every ten steps or so to light a torches impaled in rings high on the wall. Gradually the snaking stone corridor that led to the inner sentinel of the Chamber of Truth was illuminated. Their path was clear.

"Dis way—you'll all need to come dis way," a passionless voice said while still some distance away. "Dey're waiting for you."

Turning slightly, Hisbil could barely see Kassie's eyes looking up at him in the torchlight. She put her arm around his neck and pulled him down so their lips touched. Her lips still tasted sweeter than any berry he had ever picked, but they trembled a bit as her lips gently brushed his. Hisbil's mind cleared as he felt Kassie bolstering his courage.

For luck, he heard her think. As their lips parted, he could taste the salt of her tears.

"Don't be afraid; we'll get out of this somehow," Hisbil said.

"I...I hope so," she said, taking his arm in hers.

I couldn't do this without you, he thought. Kassie turned her face to him and smiled.

They all moved down the shadow-strewn corridor toward the great door two dozen paces ahead. He arched his hand out to find the wall but found the ceiling—far too close. The cold, wet stone sapped his warmth and resolve, sending a rattling shiver though him. Kassie clutched his hand a bit tighter as they felt their way down the tunnel together, soon moving in single file. Hisbil heard Weiger's and Anasta's footsteps behind them as they trailed along behind without saying a word—except for the complaint as Anasta stepped in something unsavory.

The narrow tunnel opened up into a much larger vestibule blocked by the second sentinel—another great oaken door that stood twice Hisbil's height. It was festooned with heavy iron fixtures designed to prevent anyone or anything uninvited from gaining entrance to the Council chambers.

Hisbil raised the large iron ring and dropped it on the door. The sound, like distant thunder, echoed through the tunnels. A heartbeat later, another bat flew out of the corridor to the right. Following close behind, a flood of screeching creatures streamed out of an opening above as if they thought the cave was about to collapse. In a heartbeat, the vestibule was full of panicky bats fleeing the caves.

"Get down," Hisbil shouted over the din of bat calls and thrashing leather wings, but before they could move or he could pull his sword, they were gone, save a few stragglers.

Kassie was now glued to Hisbil's chest, holding on for dear life. "Did I tell you I have a thing about bats?" she confessed.

"I'm no better. I guess I need to awaken one…," Hisbil began.

"Please don't!" said Anasta and Kassie in a single voice.

At this, the great door began to creak on its hinges and open inward with the help of two sturdy sems robed as ceremonial Seldith warriors.

On the far side of the chamber, another narrow, chimney-like passage led out to the left where another bat made its escape up and out of the cave.

"That must be another way to the surface," Anasta remarked.

"It's the path of the exile," Weiger said solemnly. If you're exiled, it's the only way to get out of the mountain. At the top, there is a long, slippery slide that leads to the base of the hill. I had to climb out that chimney once before. I don't relish doing it again."

"Youse go stand in da dock," the taller guard commanded.

"All of youse!" the second one said with a bit more authority.

"But only Weiger and I have been summoned!" Hisbil protested.

"All of youse!" the guard repeated.

Hisbil had only heard rumors and fanciful stories of the Council Chambers, but had no idea of what it looked like inside—yesems and yenesems were not permitted to attend. Hisbil could not see the cavern ceiling, but the way their own footsteps echoed, it must be quite high. A long, high bench had been built on a rocky shelf above the cave floor. It provided seats for a dozen ministers. The gallery, built on the slope in front of the minsters, was lined with backless wooden benches like in his classroom. Only about a dozen scattered villagers attended as witnesses to the proceedings, including Professor Nadeel who sat close to the front. She was wearing disdaining look number seven—one of her finest.

Everyone's eyes were on Hisbil and his "co-heretics." Hisbil recognized many of them from the mob that had formed outside his house. The Fox news reporter and his artist sat next to Nadeel and Neychen's wife Hersarah busily manufacturing the news. The artist was finishing a salacious drawing of Kassie as a deranged witch.

Hisbil and the others were led to a raised platform with a waist-high rail set up in front of the ministers' bench. As they climbed the steps, the villagers began to murmur and point.

The old torch lighter lit several to illuminate the cavernous room. "The sergeant will be ready in a minute. Just stay put fuh now. I don't know dat dey want all of youse up der," he said quietly.

A portly sem, dressed in formal but somewhat natty attire, apparently the sergeant at arms, appeared at the door and boomed: "Hear ye, hear ye. All rise. The Stone Valley Council of Truth is now in session. Be forewarned that any disruption of these proceedings is punishable by exile or fine. The Most Honorable Sem Herodotus presiding."

As the Council ministers filed in, Hisbil recognized Alred and another two Council ministers who he had met at Alred's house during his afternoon talks. It was comforting to see that at least someone he respected was going to stand in judgment. The Council ministers, dressed in formal attire, took seats on the left part of the bench leaving two seats on the far end and the center seat vacant. Five more Council ministers closely followed them, sitting on the right, again leaving the center chair empty. Hisbil also recognized the three newest members of the Council Neychen, Dubjay, and Vecarlro who had been elected some time ago before the trouble started.

Some time passed before the presiding minister came in and took his seat, slowly walking across the platform. No one made a sound—no one save a small bat that seemed to have been separated from the rest. It fluttered around squeaking like it has lost its mama but eventually found its way out through the vent at the top of the cave.

As Herodotus, the presiding minister, took his seat in the center, the sergeant of arms told everyone to be seated. The gallery took their seats and restarted their low murmur as the Council ministers began to look through the indictment papers laid out before them on the bench. Herodotus looked down on Hisbil and the others with a deep scowl that rivaled Professor Nadeel's finest attempt to appear foreboding. "Hisbil, son of Gollsaer, and Weiger, exile of Stone Valley, you are accused of heresy and crimes against the laws of The Truth. How do you plead?"

"I must protest, your Honor," Alred said, rising to his feet from the seat next to Herodotus. "The accused are brought here without counsel. It is clearly stated…"

"Yes, I'll have to sustain your objection," Herodotus said, raising his hand to stifle Alred and the grumblings from the right. "And where are the other Council ministers?" Herodotus asked.

"They have been delayed. Given that the indictments were delivered to the defendants less than twelve hours ago, they have had some difficulty returning here from important business to the south."

"I see," growled Herodotus. "And who sent them out on this 'important' business?"

"I would petition the honorable Council for a postponement and representation by competent counsel," Alred said, still standing.

"I object!" Minister Neychen, just to the right of Herodotus, exploded as he sprang to his feet as if he had been sitting on a spring. "The Council and the village as a whole cannot endure the defiling presence of a convicted exile or his eagle-killing accomplices one more moment. He will only corrupt our youth just as he has corrupted these in the dock. I insist..."

"Sit down. Everyone, just...sit...down," Herodotus intoned. "This is not a witch hunt, and I will not let it degrade into one." Alred and then Neychen slowly sat down.

"So far, the only information we have about what has occurred over the last two days is rumor and speculation—and much of that from dubious sources. And sit down, Neychen, you'll get your chance to question the accused once we hear Hisbil's story," Herodotus said as he saw Neychen rising to interrupt again.

"So, Hisbil. Can you tell the Council what happened?"

"Yes, Your Honor, but I'm not sure you or anyone on the Council would believe me," Hisbil said. He looked over to Anasta who had begun to tremble and quietly weep. "Your Honor, might I ask that my sister, Anasta, and Kassie—who are not accused of anything—be permitted to sit in the gallery until they are called?"

"Yes...yes, of course. They should not be standing up there with the accused at all."

"Your honor?" Kassie asked. "Might I stand here with Hisbil? I can vouch for his honesty and devotion to The Truth."

"I want to stay with my brother too," Anasta said bravely. "He has risked his life many times over the last few days to rescue me, mostly from myself. It's the least I can do to help him."

"If that's where you wish to stand, it makes no difference to this court...unless there are objections?" Herodotus said as he looked left and right at the other members sitting on the bench with heads bent together whispering to one another. "Seeing none, you are welcome to stand by the accused. Now, Hisbil, you were going to tell us what happened in your own words."

"Your honor, with your permission, might I have someone *else* recount the story? I would like to call on someone that you and the entire Council have sworn to trust, someone who *must* speak The Truth."

"Who is this person?" Herodotus said, his eyebrows rising.

"Veritas," said Hisbil flatly.

"Blasphemy!" Neychen said, jumping to his feet again. "How dare you use the name of the Oracle of *The Sacred Seven Books of Truth*? Veritas has not spoken to the Seldith for centuries. He could not possibly be called upon. Your honor, do we have to be blasphemed by this liar, this anarchist, this terrorist?"

Herodotus put up his hand again and glared at Neychen. "While this does seem quite irregular, if Hisbil can produce the Oracle Veritas, I will not go on record as opposing hearing *The Truth*. Well, Hisbil, can you produce Veritas here in this chamber?"

"I can, Your Honor, if you would provide a small table, and a moment to prepare."

"Granted. Bailiff, bring forward the evidence table," Herodotus commanded. "Where would you like it placed?"

"There in front of the bench, if that's all right, Your Honor. And please, do not ask any more questions until we are ready." Hisbil and Kassie pulled out a cloth bag from Weiger's rucksack and walked up to the evidence table. Hiding what they were doing as much as they could from the Council, they reverently took out each book. As they did, the gallery began to whisper and then talk louder and louder until there was quite a din.

"I will have order!" Herodotus demanded. "Any further outbursts, and I will clear the gallery. Professor, you should know better," Herodotus said firmly as he banged his gavel on the bench and glared at Professor Nadeel who had been fomenting the disturbance. "Proceed, Hisbil."

"Thank you, Your Honor," Hisbil replied, stepping back from the table. "Members of the Council, Sem Weiger has rescued *The Sacred Seven Books of Truth* from the outcast known as Emperor at great risk to his life. It is through his courage and moral commitment to the Seldith that I can present Veritas, Oracle of *The Sacred Seven Books of Truth*." At this, Hisbil placed the final book in the center of the seven-sided heptagon as they had done in Douglas' parlor. But nothing happened.

This had better work or we're cooked.

It will be all right. Just stay focused. Hisbil could hear Kassie think.

Hisbil looked up and reverently recited the Oracle's creed from the placard above the Council bench. "Bloodred Truth sevenfold—truth more sacred than purest gold. Taken from the crypt by men upright who search in darkness for what can enlight." As he finished, the image of Veritas emerged from the eighth volume and stood before the Council. The room fell as silent as the falling of the last autumn leaf.

"Who awakens *The Truth*, and what is your bidding?" the figure said quietly. To most people in the room, but not all, Veritas appeared as a trusted friend, parent, sibling, or spouse. All seemed spellbound. In another moment, many were all on their knees or sitting with their heads bowed—as was the Council, except for the three: Neychen and two other members on the right side of the bench, Dubjay and Vecarlro.

"Fraud. I see nothing and hear nothing," Neychen said, again standing to protest. "Why are you kneeling?"

"Nor do we," Dubjay said. "What is this? Sorcery?"

"No," said a minister on the right sitting next to Vecarlro, "This is *not* Veritas. I see my brother standing before me—my closest confidant."

"No, it is *not* your brother," another minister said, "It is my own mother long since passed." And on and on it went around the bench until Hisbil raised his hand and addressed Herodotus.

"Your Honor. As you may know, Veritas appears to each person as someone whom they trust implicitly to tell *only* The Truth. To me, she appears as Kassie, the person on this earth I trust the most." Kassie looked at Hisbil and squeezed his hand. "The fact that each person on the Council sees her as a different person is testament to her…her…"

"Veracity," Alred interrupted. "It means this cannot be any other than Veritas whose very name means truth."

"Who awakens *The Truth*, and what is your bidding?" Veritas repeated patiently.

"It is I, Hisbil, son of Alred and Gollsaer. The Council of Truth and I have a number of questions for you," Hisbil said, looking straight at Alred who did not flinch, but again the tongues in the gallery began to wag until Herodotus raised his hand again.

"Yes, Hisbil, hero of Stone Valley and conqueror of Tovenaar, what is your bidding?" This brought another round of whispers that swept the gallery and the Council.

"Can you tell the Council what transpired since the cat we call 'Mink' appeared in the village commons two nights ago?" Hisbil asked.

"This is a very broad question, Hisbil. It would take far too long to relate and I only have a few minutes of energy remaining. Should I instead tell just *your* story?"

"Please confine your account to my actions and the actions of those I met on my journey. I would like the Council to know the truth. Did I, or any of my party, commit a heretical act, speak blasphemy, or otherwise break the dictates of *The Books of Truth*? Leave out no detail that would indict me or my party."

"As you wish." Veritas began. "Two nights ago, Hisbil…"

And Veritas told Hisbil's story, the whole story, to the Council and the gallery. She told of how Hisbil repeatedly risked his life to protect the village and rescue his sister on many occasions. And of how Weiger had been unjustly accused by corrupt Council ministers, exiled, and his brand healed by the uman stranger Eashoa. She told of how Douglas, the uman-made-mouse, had found *The Sacred Seven* and kept them safe and returned them to the Seldith, and how Hisbil had helped retransform him back into a uman. She told of Anasta who gave of herself willingly to heal others, and how she unlawfully but innocently collected the downy feathers of an eagle from the forest. She told of Kassie's kidnapping and how she endured unspeakable torture at Tovenaar's hand. She told of everyone's countless acts of bravery and courage, wit, and wile that ultimately defeated Lord Lensmacher who was, in fact, the evil wizard Tovenaar. And, finally, she told of the unfinished story of Hisbil's father. And how he was kidnapped, tortured, and forced into servitude by Tovenaar, and that he, to this day, flies above this chamber as a sacred eagle watching over his son and daughter and the Seldith clan.

When Veritas had completed the story, the room was silent again. The gallery had ceased their chatter and kept their eyes on the image of Veritas still standing before them. But a moment later, her image wavered as she retreated into the eighth volume.

"Where…what happened to her?" Herodotus, the presiding minister said.

"She can only speak for a few minutes at a time. She's probably resting," Hisbil replied. "Would you have me answer another question?"

"I would," said Neychen abruptly. "I'll play along with your little game, Hisbil. Since I did not hear what others said they could, can *you* answer this one question for me?"

"If I can," said Hisbil.

"Did you kill an eagle?"

"No," Hisbil said flatly.

"But I understand that you stabbed the eagle with that fancy sword of yours, and your sister has bloody eagle feathers. Is that not correct?"

"Yes, yes, that is true," Hisbil said reluctantly but firmly.

"And didn't you say that your sword was 'tempered' in blood, the blood from this stabbed eagle?"

"Yes, that's also true, but the eagle…"

"The eagle was stabbed with your sword, and you were able to get its feathers from its carcass, but it didn't die. Is that your testimony?"

"Yes…I mean, no. No, the eagle did *not* die," Hisbil said firmly, even though he was shaking.

"How do you plan to prove this?"

Hisbil looked down for several moments before being bantered again and again to prove that he had not killed the eagle.

When he looked up, he took out his sword, raised it, and closed his eyes. When he opened them again, the ministers, the gallery, and the guards were all standing in the village common. At first, there was considerable confusion, fear, and consternation, but Herodotus raised his hand, and everyone stopped talking.

Hisbil's sword was still raised and now pointing at the sky, which had cleared over the valley. He waited without saying a word as the rest of the village came out of their homes and shops to gather in the commons.

"I wanted you all to witness that I am telling the truth. The only way I could do so is to show you the eagle." At this, Hisbil lowered his sword, and a large bald eagle landed among them, causing many to flee in terror and others to prostrate themselves on the ground.

"Don't be afraid," Hisbil said calmly. "This is Gollsaer, the sem and Owl Wrangler who raised me as his son. He was enchanted by Tovenaar and enslaved as an eagle. As you can see he is quite alive."

"How are we to know this is not just an eagle that you have bewitched and awakened with your spells?" Dubjay said, mockingly.

"Ask him, if you don't believe me!"

Dubjay did not get a chance to speak.

"I am Gollsaer," the eagle said. "As my son said, you popinjay. I have spent these weeks watching over my family as I tried to free myself from Tovenaar's grasp. I also found that at least three of you ministers were helping Tovenaar work his evil upon this valley as he tried to gain our magic and decipher *The Sacred Seven Books of Truth*. I was forced to put my only son and daughter in harm's way to finish the fight that I could not win alone. Because Hisbil's herditas is that of a master wizard, he alone had the power to overcome Tovenaar. And that he has done. Do you want to see the wound where he stabbed me?"

Dubjay fell silent and took a step back into the crowd but found a wall of indignant arms to stop him. Before long, Neychen, Dubjay, and Vecarlro all found themselves in the middle of the commons facing the eagle and fearing for their lives.

Hisbil raised his sword again and closed his eyes. The crowd gasped and held their breath. When he opened them again, a shaft of light shone from the sword tip that seemed to reflect off the treetop canopy and shower the eagle with a brilliant light. When the eagle disappeared, Hisbil lowered his sword. The light faded and the crowd opened their eyes; before them stood Gollsaer, who was quickly robed by Alred standing at the ready. Hisbil scabbarded his sword and turned to embrace his fathers. Another dark ring of ornate symbols had been added to his arm.

As they embraced, the remaining Council ministers huddled together a short distance away and before long emerged with their verdict. No one knows if it was a genuine respect or fear of this young sem who had become a powerful wizard or Veritas' account of the harrowing journey and defeat of Tovenaar that had won them over, but they found Hisbil and the others to be heroes and to be accorded the best the village could offer.

"As for Neychen and his cronies, we will convene on that matter tomorrow morning," Herodotus pronounced. "Officers, take them away and make sure they don't leave before their hearing." At that, the uniformed guards took Neychen, Dubjay and Vecarlro into custody. They seemed relieved to be rescued from the mob which was already disrobing them for their dip in the awaiting tar.

Fifty-nine—Homecoming

A while later, as Hisbil began to grow weary of the handshakes, backslaps and fawning, the newly minted hero felt Kassie pulling him away from the jubilant adulation. He had been entangled in a crowd of school friends and new admirers who wanted him to magically do their homework or make them wealthy—or both. "They're *all* my friends now," Hisbil said. "I couldn't get most of them to say four words to me after my father disappeared."

"Don't worry about them," Kassie said, putting her arm in Hisbil's as she guided him through the throng. "They'll get over the novelty and learn to ignore you again."

"Oh great. I hope *you* don't start ignoring me," Hisbil said coyly as he was stopped to be patted on the back by an old sem and his wife celebrating with a large mug of blackberry wine.

"Not likely. I need you to come home with me."

"I *think* I can fit that into my busy social calendar," Hisbil said glibly.

"That's very generous of you Sem Wizard, but my mother wants to talk to us." A smile had returned to Kassie's face as she skipped ahead.

"Your mother?" Hisbil said incredulously as he ran to catch up.

Casandra was standing on the porch when they strolled up now hand-in-hand. "I am so glad to see you're safe and well—

a bit thinner and a bit older, but none the worse for your ordeal." She was wearing the tearful, happy smile of a mother at her only daughter's wedding.

Motioning for Kassie to go inside, Cassandra put her arm around Hisbil and would not let him go as she held him near. Hisbil's mind reeled with each moment of the embrace and the powerful smell of the honeysuckle in her hair. It was then that he realized that she was reading his mind, reviewing the story of their ordeal. He pushed her away before the story flashing by in his mind had reached the castle.

"I'm afraid, I can't let you see some of the story," Hisbil said as he cleared his mind. "And you don't want to see how Kassie was caged. I would not inflict that on anyone—especially not you. And there are some images that...we just can't share."

"You saw my sister...there in the laboratory," said Casandra quietly. "She was lost not long after we came to Stone Valley. Thank you for not sharing that image," she whispered.

"But what happened to you? The last time I saw you, you were flying off on a crow," Hisbil asked.

"Yes, I had some difficulty with Yeremy. He seemed to be loyal to Lord Lensmacher, and while he tried to protect me at first by trying to go to River Landing, he delivered me right to Lensmacher's desk despite my attempts to control him.

I saw Kassie locked in that terrible cage and realized that I did not have a chance to free her—not without help. It took a bit of 'persuasion' to get Lord Lensmacher to release me, but he did in time. I was also able to encourage Yeremy to take me back here, but by then you and your sister had left the village. I sent you a dream to help guide you to the castle and another to help Kassie know we were coming to rescue her. I hope these helped."

"They did...yes, they did," Hisbil said as Kassie joined him at his side.

Kassie tugged at Hisbil's arm as Casandra nodded her head and said, "I...was worried, worried about you *both*. Perhaps, you're right. There are some things that I need not see. What I can see is how you two are devoted to each other. Hisbil, I've been talking to Rachele, and we think you two should..."

"Take it slow?" Hisbil said, blushing a bit around the ears.

"Mother, we're not doing anything you and father didn't do at our age," Kassie scolded.

"That's what I'm afraid of," Casandra said as she shooed Hisbil and her daughter into the house. Waiting for them inside were Rachele, Anasta, Weiger, and Hisbil's fathers—both of them: Gollsaer and Alred. As the three crossed the threshold, Hisbil knew he was home and loved as much as anyone could be, and that he had found his place in the world.

"Hisbil?" Alred said, to get his attention away from Kassie.

"What is it?"

"You need to take the diary of your story to the Grand Council of Arbiters at the Summit of Truth—to get *The Truth* recorded in the *Great Book of Truth*. I've already begun recording it. You and Veritas need to help me transcribe the story in as much detail as possible."

"Can it wait until tomorrow?" Hisbil asked.

"Yes. It can wait until tomorrow, my son." Alred said.

Gollsaer smiled as he pulled Hisbil aside and gave him a hug. In the embrace, he asked "Son, what did you do with the sealed envelope in my backpack?"

"Envelope?" Hisbil responded.

The Series Continues

*N*ow that Hisbil and his teenage cohorts have exposed the traitorous members of the Council of Truth, they find their troubles have just begun. *Guardians of the Sacred Seven* continues their story and *The Seldith Chronicles* series.

Driven by a raw lust for power and greed, it's clear that the ousted council members and their minions will do *anything* including silencing the entire village to regain control. Hisbil is snared in their wicked plot until he discovers that his magical powers are virtually without limit—but at a terrible price, that nearly costs him and everyone else their lives.

Pleases click like on the series' Facebook page http://facebook/owlwrangler for details on its progress, or post comments. You can also post comments on http://williamvaughn.blogspot.com.
Now that you're finished with The Owl Wrangler, please take a moment to post a review on Amazon, Goodreads or just pass the book along to a friend.

Thanks

The Cast

$\mathcal{T}$he Seldith Chronicles cast is made up of Seldith, the tiny forest elves no taller than a mushroom and the giant 'umans'. Of course, the cast would not be complete without the house-cats, an owl, an eagle, and a couple of crows; all of whom play important roles in the story.

Cast members in order of appearance:

The Owl Wrangler:

The first book of *The Seldith Chronicles* introduced:

Gollsaer	The clan's only owl wrangler and Hisbil's father. A former carpenter, he spends most days out hunting for owls to awaken or recovering from his wounds.
Hisbil	A 'yesem' (a young male seldith). A teenager whose life is about to get complicated when his father disappears.
Anasta	A 'yenesem' (a young female seldith) and Hisbil's little sister who's learning to heal with a touch.
Professor Nadeel	A middle-aged and stern one-room classroom teacher with a PhD in evil looks.
Kassie	Hisbil's girlfriend (at least that's what she thinks). She takes after her mother Cassandra who's a talented clairvoyant. She learning to read other's thoughts and push 'suggestions' into their minds.

Alred	A senior member of the Council of Truth and Hisbil's natural father. He's also an aging wizard that's retired from his craft due to failing health.
Rachele	Hisbil and Anasta's mother and Gollsaer's wife. She's the clan's empathic healer, a skill she's reluctant to pass down to her daughter. She's also a good friend of Alred.
Hissamuel	Rachele's first husband and the former owl wrangler. He left on a hunting expedition and never returned.
Casandra	A widowed 'Southsider' whose full-time job includes watching after her daughter Kassie and helping the villagers find the lost.
Yimminy and Yeremy	A pair of hungry crows awakened to carry wealthy sems on 'business' trips.
Dubjay	President of the Council of Truth and a pawn of Vecarlro and Neychen.
Mink	A black domestic housecat who Hisbil awakens so it can speak.
Ink	Mink's sister. She's just an ever-hungry housecat looking for her next meal.
Hersarah	Neychen's wife and head gossip monger in the village.
Sally Jo	A mute Holstein cow awakened by Gollsaer.
Buster	Sally Jo's a frisky and extremely talkative calf.
Bubou	A large barn-owl awakened by Gollsaer but who flunked navigation school.
Lord Lensmacher AKA the wizard Tovenaar	A human ('uman') that traded sanctuary to the Seldith clan in exchange for a number of 'favors' regarding owls and magic spells. Lensmacher is convinced he's a reincarnated wizard who wreaked havoc over 5,000 years ago.
Neychen	Senior member of the Council of Truth and purveyor of secrets to the exiles and Tovenaar.
Vecarlro	Another member of the Council of Truth and Neychen's closest friend.
Weiger	Formerly the owner and operator of Crow Air, but exiled to live apart from the Stone Valley Seldith clan.

Emperor	Nefarious villain and exile who controls the exile encampment at Shutz Norte.
Larry	The bartender in the hotel bar at Shutz Norte. One of Emperor's 'physical' assets.
Eashoa	A mysterious human that turns Weiger's life around and then disappears.
Douglas	A human carpenter and family man turned into a mouse by Tovenaar.
David Heintzelman	Douglas' foreman.
Veritas	The gatekeeper of the Sacred Seven Books of Truth.
Fret	One of Tovenaar's guard ferrets with a distinct hatred for the Seldith and other 'rodents.'
Herodotus	Chairman and presiding Minister of the Council of Truth.
Ristina	Douglas' wife who's deathly afraid of mice.
Vicky	Douglas' daughter and owner of Mink and Ink.

The Lexicon

$\mathcal{T}$erms used by the Seldith that might confuse uman readers.

Amiculum obscurum	A magical cloak that morphs its color and texture to whatever surrounds the wearer.
Herditas	An inherited skill, often magical, like healing, wizardry, or fire-master, or simple, like carpenter, weaver, cook, or swordsmith. Ordinarily, a herditas passes from parents to offspring through birth, but rarely adopted without a parental lineage. Training in the herditas begins around age seven or even earlier and upon completion, the youngster is considered an adult, sem or yesem.
Protector	A soldier or police officer.
Seldith	One of a race of nomadic forest elves about as tall as a mushroom.
Sem	A form of address for an adult male Seldith. Equivalent to 'sir.'
Nesem	A form of address for an adult female Seldith. Equivalent to 'ma'am.'
Yesem	A young seldith male before reaching adulthood. Equivalent to 'boy,' or 'sonny'.
Yenesem	A young Seldith female before reaching adulthood. Also known as a 'yene.' Equivalent to 'girl.'
Yene	An abbreviation for 'yenesem'.
Uman	The Seldith term for humans.

William Vaughn

Made in the USA
Charleston, SC
07 February 2015